I0298782

9 40165661

Also by Pippa Wright

Lizzy Harrison Loses Control
Unsuitable Men
The Foster Husband

Pippa Wright

the Gospel according to Drew Barrymore

PAN BOOKS

First published 2015 by Pan Books
an imprint of Pan Macmillan, a division of Macmillan Publishers Limited
Pan Macmillan, 20 New Wharf Road, London N1 9RR
Basingstoke and Oxford
Associated companies throughout the world
www.panmacmillan.com

ISBN 978-1-4472-3836-2

The film credits on pp. 406–407 constitute
an extension of this copyright page.

1 3 5 7 9 8 6 4 2

A CIP catalogue record for this book is available from the British Library.

Typeset by Ellipsis Digital Limited, Glasgow
Printed and bound by CPI Group (UK) Ltd, Croydon, CR0 4YY

To the Sisters.
You know who you are.

Acknowledgements

I had a lot of fun researching this book and trawling through my memories of growing up in the eighties and nineties. But I had even more fun trawling through the memories of others who were generous enough to let me do so. Thank you to Rebecca Folland, Emily Brooks, Julia Nicholls, Jo Roberts-Miller, Jenny Geras, Zoe Gilbert, Valentina Rice, Alexis Venn, Sophie O'Neill, Suzie Dooré, Cath Lovesey and Samantha Mattocks for sharing stories of teenage shame, poor outfit choices, romantic disappointments and associations with Princess Diana's astrologer.

Thank you to Emma Rice of Hattingley Valley Wines for giving me a full vineyard tour, explaining the winemaking process, and making an excellent sparkling rosé which I have sampled quite a lot (for research purposes).

Enormous thanks to my editor, Caroline Hogg, for her endless patience when this book took twice as long to be written as it should have done, for not blanching at the first two drafts she had to read, and for advice, lunches and encouragement throughout.

Grateful thanks to dogsitters Jo Paton Htay, Kate Morgan and Rory Gallard for taking the dog out on my last frantic weekend of writing.

And thank you, of course, to Drew Blyth Barrymore for the idea in the first place.

1

October 2013

If I asked about your best friend, who would you think of? Straight away, first name that comes into your head. Did you say your husband? Or maybe your boyfriend? Not allowed, start again. By my definition a best friend should have known you long enough to see you through at least one failed relationship, snot in your hair, smoking an inhuman number of cigarettes, eating nothing. A best friend shouldn't be that romantic relationship, failed or not. Did you name a relative – your mum or sister, perhaps? Sorry, not permitted either. Those are the people who have to be there, no matter what; they are bound to you by blood. A best friend is different. A best friend is someone who doesn't have to be there, but chooses to be, through everything. Someone like Laura.

Right up until the point when she chose to be somewhere else.

Her mother calls me at six in the morning. I've already been up for an hour, trying to get Linus to take a bottle, and I leap on the shrilling mobile phone before it disturbs him. Even so his eyes fly wide with surprise at the interruption, before sliding closed again, pale blue eyelids flickering with a delicate pulse that shows he's not yet safely asleep.

'When did you last hear from Laura?'

Margie's interrogations always begin like this. No introduction, no greeting, and certainly no apology for calling at dawn. I always think she must have had the conversation running in her head for so long before she picks up the phone that she forgets I'm starting from the beginning.

'Hi, Margie,' I say. 'What's wrong?'

There is always something wrong.

'When did you hear from her last?' she demands, as if I haven't spoken. 'This week?'

I have to think. Ever since Linus was born, my timeline runs not in days of the week, but from feed to feed, nappy to nappy. I have measured out my time in Calpol spoons.

'I don't know, we're in touch all the time. I'm not sure I can remember. We FaceTimed last week, maybe?'

'Do you remember what she said?' she asks. 'I need to know exactly what she said.'

My husband appears in the doorway, T-shirt riding up above his faded pyjama bottoms. He makes a face at the phone in my hand, pointing to an imaginary watch on his wrist. I mouth Margie's name and he swirls his index finger near his temple – *crazy* – and shuffles down the corridor into the kitchen.

'I can't remember *exactly*,' I say. The rumble of the electric kettle starts up in the next room, and I hope that means I'll get a coffee soon. 'We didn't talk for long – Linus kicked off and I had to go.'

'Yes, Linus, of course,' she says, briskly, as if she has only just recalled his existence and is not pleased to be reminded of it.

'What is this about? What's going on?'

'Do you have *any* idea where she is?' demands Margie, and beneath her snappish tone there is a tremor of panic at which, I am sorry to say, I roll my unseen eyes.

'Margie?' I say, stroking the back of the baby's head where the fine blond hair has worn away into an odd little patch of monkish baldness. 'Is this like when she went to Calistoga Springs that time? You know how cross she was when you called the police. I'm sure she'll be back soon, there's no need to worry.'

'Calistoga Springs was a simple misunderstanding,' she says, her consonants hissing with annoyance. 'Although that very nice policewoman quite agreed with me that a mother has every right to expect regular contact from her only child when she is thousands of miles away from home.'

'Yes,' I agree, keeping my voice low and calm. 'But

Laura promised to call you more often, so you've got to hold up your end, and not panic every time she goes away for a few days without telling you.'

Cold War Margie, Laura used to call her mother when we were teenagers. Whatever worst-case scenario you could conjure, Margie was always one step ahead of you, lining the walls with tinfoil, preparing for disaster. Half an hour late? You are surely dead in a car crash. Not phoned for a while? Kidnapped.

'It's not just a few days,' she insists.

'It's harvest time,' I say. My soothing tone is partly for her benefit, but also partly for the baby's as he stirs next to me. Linus uncurls a little, his tiny fingers flexing before they fall back into sleepy fists. 'You know that. You can't expect her to be in touch when it's the vineyard's busiest time of the year.'

'Well, that is my point exactly,' says the voice on the end of the phone, rising higher. 'It *is* harvest, and Laura's boss has called me as her next of kin to ask if I know why she hasn't turned up to work since Thursday.'

Linus lets out a little squawk as I sit upright, leaving him marooned on an island of cushions.

'Since Thursday? But that's – it's – '

'It's Tuesday,' snaps Margie, correctly divining from my hesitation that I don't really have much of an idea what day of the week it is right now.

Thursday to Tuesday – that could conceivably be a long weekend away somewhere, couldn't it?

'Are you sure she didn't go away?'

I hear Margie sniff down the phone. 'As if she'd tell *me* anything like that. I hoped she might have told you.'

'No,' I say. 'No, she didn't.'

'Anyway, she didn't book the time off work,' says Margie. 'You know she'd never just not turn up.'

'Do they think she might have had an accident or something?'

'They've checked the hospitals,' says Margie. The tremor in her voice threatens to turn into a wail. 'There's not a sign of her. Her car's gone too. Why would she have gone like that, Esther? She would have told you if something was wrong, wouldn't she? You're her best friend.'

Until this very moment, I thought so too. I'd have said, of course Laura is my best friend, of course I'd know. I would have said we didn't need to live in the same country to be close, we didn't need to speak every day to understand what was going on with each other. But what if Laura has disappeared, truly disappeared, and I know nothing? Can I call myself her best friend then?

The baby's face reddens and crumples as he registers, still with his eyes closed, that I've moved away. I pick him up quickly and feel him sink back into drowsy heaviness on my chest.

'What did her boss say?' I ask, holding the phone between my ear and shoulder so that the room tilts sideways. 'Did he notice anything? Was she acting oddly?'

'No,' says Margie. 'Stanley said she was just the same as usual. Tired, but not more than anyone else at work. He couldn't think of any reason for her to have gone like this.'

Work is everything to Laura, she always jokes that it's the most committed relationship she's ever had. For her to just not turn up is bizarre, especially in the frenzy of harvest season. I can feel my raised heartbeat fluttering anxiously against Linus's cheek; Margie's paranoia is infectious.

'I thought you'd know,' she says, and her voice cracks at last. 'I really thought you'd know, Esther.'

I let her cry and I say comforting things that I'm not sure I believe – Laura will be fine, you'll probably hear from her tomorrow – and when Margie has calmed herself we agree that I will try to contact Laura myself before we leap to any dramatic conclusions. Sometimes there are things it's easier to tell a friend than your mother, I say. There will be a reason for this, everything will be okay.

When she hangs up at last, I scroll through the emails on my phone to see exactly when I last heard from Laura. As my thumb slides further down the screen, and still further, my guilt grows – I said to Margie that we were in touch all the time, but when I find Laura's last email I see it is from nearly a week ago and, worse, unanswered.

It was a weird message, I remember it now; that was

why I hadn't replied straight away. I never seem to have time any more for the sort of freewheeling 'how is life with you?' correspondence. I only answer the direct questions: Are you free on Tuesday? Shall I pick up milk on the way home? Is Linus sleeping better? No, yes, no.

Laura's email was just a silly little thing, kind of meaningless, I thought. Not in need of an urgent reply.

Hi Est, she'd written.

> *Sorry you had to go just now, hope my shrieking godson is okay, I wish I could see him in person. I wish I could see you too. Could do with your wise words on many things, but in the absence of a four-hour rant over a bottle of Pinot Noir, I'm keeping on keeping on. And channelling Drew Barrymore, as ever – you know it makes sense. The Gospel, right?*
>
> *Love you the most.*
>
> *L*

I should have answered. I thought it was just a moment of feeling blue far from home. But now that I am looking at her email not as a message but as a clue to where she might be now, I wonder if it means something more. It's an invitation, isn't it? An invitation to ask why she needs my advice. And I didn't reply.

Even worse, I remember sighing when I read it. Thinking, for once, Laura, will you just come out and say what you need instead of dropping hints like a trail of breadcrumbs that I'm meant to follow?

As for Drew Barrymore, well, that means something and nothing – it means a silly joke between young girls, it's shorthand for friendship and growing up and making decisions without knowing they might change your life. But it's not a map, it doesn't tell me anything about where Laura might have gone. It only reminds me of where she's been.

E.T., 1982[1]

[Mary hits E.T. with the refrigerator door without noticing him.]

GERTIE: *Here he is.*

MARY: *[absently] Here's who?*

GERTIE: *The man from the moon. But I think you've killed him already.*

2

Esther's mummy told her she must be especially kind to Laura when she arrived for lunch, because she would probably be feeling a bit scared and shy. Laura was an only child, she said, with no brothers or sisters to play with, and she had to leave all her friends and all her toys behind when her daddy was posted back to England from America.

Esther remembered when she got King Alfred, her guinea pig – how she had to be so, so quiet and careful not to scare him. The best thing was to sit really still on the floor and let King Alfred come to you when he was ready, not chase him all over the playroom, even if it seemed like he was enjoying it. She expected it would be like that with Laura. Guinea pigs were from America as well, but not the same part, said her mummy.

So Esther and her little sister arranged the best of their toys in welcome: they flanked the blonde head of the almost-new Girl's World with Esther's favourite

Sindy dolls, and in front of them Sophie positioned the stuffed owl with real feathers that usually sat on the playroom mantelpiece, too old and precious to be played with every day.

But when Laura arrived she wasn't shy at all, or scared. While the grown-ups said hello to each other, she took off her coat and folded it over her arm. Then she looked at them from under her straight dark fringe and said 'Hi' in a loud American voice. Sophie hid behind their mummy's legs, but Esther said 'Hi' back and gave a small wave.

Laura was taller than Esther, even though she was two months younger, and she had a lot of freckles on her nose. Her hair was cut short, in a bob like Milly-Molly-Mandy's, and over her shoulder she carried an actual handbag with a picture of Snoopy on it. When she tucked her hair behind her ears, Esther was dazzled to see that she had had them pierced.

'Are those real?' asked Esther, unable to help herself from pointing at the sparkling studs.

Laura's hand reached up, pinching an earring between her fingertips like she had forgotten it was there.

'Yeah,' she said, glancing at her mother. She didn't seem to think having your ears pierced was a big deal at all. 'My dad let me have them done before we came back.'

'No,' said Esther's mummy immediately. 'Before you ask. Not until you're ten. And don't point.'

'Oh, I quite agree,' said Laura's mummy. Laura's mummy didn't look like Laura one bit, and she didn't have an American voice either. She had very yellow hair, all curly and long, and glasses with big round frames.

'I didn't want her to have it done at all – the risk of infection, for one thing, and I can't help worrying they might get ripped from her ears in the playground. You know what children are like. But Edward took her off and had it done as a surprise.'

'What can I say?' said Laura's daddy, ruffling his daughter's hair, black and straight like his own. He grinned at the girls. 'I expect you two know how to wrap your dad around your finger too.'

Esther saw Laura's mummy shush him, nudging at him with her shoe. He rubbed at his eyebrows and Esther saw that he was embarrassed.

Even Laura rolled her eyes and said, 'Daa-aad.'

'Sorry, you two,' he said, crouching down to Esther and Sophie's level as if they were babies instead of seven and five. 'You must miss him. I'm sure he misses you too.'

Esther just shook her head. She stared at his shoes and didn't say anything. The skin under her eyes seemed to go hot and tight, and her throat went all narrow. The best way not to miss Daddy too much was not to talk about him, or even think of him. Whenever she felt sad, she just thought about something else, like school or Brownies.

'He is on a *ship*,' said Sophie, poking her head out from behind her mother's legs. 'And it's really far away, right in the middle of the sea.'

Sophie was too little to understand – she kept asking when he was coming back. That just made it worse, not just for Esther, but for her mummy.

'I expect he'll be sailing back to you very soon,' said Laura's daddy, giving Sophie a clumsy pat on the shoulder before he stood up again. 'Sorry, Caro, how are you holding up?'

'It's fine,' said Caroline, brightly, showing all of her teeth in a smile that went from side to side instead of up at the corners like a real one. Esther would have liked to hold her mother's hand, but Mummy did not agree with feeling sorry for yourself, especially not in front of other people, so Esther put her hands in the pockets of her dress instead, and squeezed her thumbs tight inside her fingers till they hurt.

'Now, girls,' Esther's mother said, in the children's-television-presenter voice she used when talking to them in front of other grown-ups. 'Why don't you take Laura and show her the playroom? I'll call you when it's time for lunch.'

Sophie ran ahead down the corridor, excited to show Laura the display of toys she'd helped to arrange. Esther was slower, waiting for Laura to follow, and so she heard what Laura's mummy said to her own, even though Margie had lowered her voice to a murmur.

'The news from the Falklands is so terrible, Caro. Those poor men on the *Coventry*; you must be worried sick.'

Esther wasn't allowed to watch the news, not even *John Craven's Newsround.* But boys talked in the playground about Harrier jump jets and Argies, and some of the bigger girls had started a campaign to ban corned beef at lunchtime, because corned beef came from Argentina and England was at war with Argentina. Esther knew her daddy was at the war, but it was never ever talked about at home.

Her mummy scowled, and waved her hands at the two of them, shooing them down the hallway and out of earshot. 'Go on,' she said. 'What are you waiting for?'

Esther led Laura to the playroom without any of the excitement she had felt when setting up the toys just a few hours ago. She could only think of what Margie had said. What did happen to those poor men? Why should Mummy be worried sick?

She only remembered the toys when she saw Sophie waiting there already next to them, excitedly hopping from one foot to the other. But Laura walked straight past without even noticing, and instead sat down on one of the high-backed wooden chairs by the window, crossing her legs like a grown-up. She looked bored but also a little expectant, like someone who was waiting for a train.

'Do you want to play with our owl?' offered Sophie,

picking it up to show her in case Laura had missed it by mistake.

'Is that real?' asked Laura, shrinking backwards.

'Yes, it's stuffed,' said Sophie, with pride. 'Our granny had it when she was little, from Scotland, and then our mummy, and now it's ours. But you can play with it if you like.'

'Gross,' said Laura. 'No.'

'No, *thank you*,' said Sophie crossly. She took the owl into a corner of the playroom and stroked its moulting feathers in case it had been hurt by Laura's rudeness.

Esther knew it was her turn to say something. She was the eldest and that meant she was the hostess. She was in charge. But she felt nervous, confused by the talk of her father. And this confident Laura was not at all the shy guinea pig she had been expecting.

Everything she had planned to offer as entertainment – the Sindys, her newest colouring-in books – seemed suddenly babyish and silly to someone who had pierced ears and a handbag.

Laura picked at the Snoopy picture on her handbag. Part of his tail was coming off when you looked closely, but that didn't stop Esther admiring it. Her only bag was an orange drawstring one for her swimming costume and towel at school, with her name written on it in black marker pen. It wasn't nearly as nice.

'Do you like Snoopy?' Esther asked, sidling alongside Laura and taking the chair next to her.

'I guess,' shrugged Laura.

'I do,' said Esther.

She hoped she might be invited to hold the bag or maybe even carry it for a while. Just around the playroom, not outside or anything. It was the sort of thing one friend might do for another. But Laura said nothing, just looked around the room from object to object like she was going to play that game where you had to close your eyes and name everything you could remember.

Looking at the playroom through Laura's eyes, Esther felt like a spell had been lifted from her own. Instead of seeing the toy hospital she and Sophie had made under the table, she saw just a pile of dirty old dolls with missing arms or legs. The bandages were embarrassingly exposed as bits of loo roll, and the Princess Castle was nothing more than cardboard boxes that they'd drawn on with felt-tips. If you didn't know it was meant to be ivy, the snaking green vines looked like scribbles that a toddler might have done.

Laura slid off her chair and wandered to the toy display at last, circling it slowly.

Over in the corner by the fireplace, Sophie was pretending to have a conversation with the owl. She tilted him towards her so that his beak reached her ear, and then she laughed loudly, but all the while she watched Laura, and so did Esther.

'Is this – I don't get it, is it like a Barbie?' asked Laura, holding up one of the Sindys.

Sophie stared at Esther and then back at Laura. It didn't sound like Laura was as impressed with the best toys as she should have been.

'It's a Sindy,' said Esther. She joined Laura in front of the Girl's World and picked up the other doll. 'That one's Patricia and that one's Pauline. They're sisters.'

'Like us,' said Sophie. 'We're sisters. I'm five.' Esther remembered that Laura didn't have any sisters. Perhaps it was rude of them to have mentioned it.

'I've got a Disco Barbie,' said Laura, returning Patricia to her place next to the Girl's World as if she had no further use for her. 'She's got a skirt that comes off so she's just in a leotard. For dancing.'

'Oh,' said Esther.

'*And* I've got a Ken,' said Laura. She hitched her handbag up on her shoulder, and started rummaging inside it.

'What's a Ken?'

Laura looked up for a moment and rolled her eyes. 'He's Barbie's *boyfriend*.'

'Oh,' said Esther again. Patricia and Pauline didn't have boyfriends. She didn't know they were meant to.

'You can play with them if you like,' said Laura. 'When the packing crates arrive, I mean. I don't have them yet.'

Esther barely had time to absorb this unexpected offer of friendship before another was made.

'Want some?'

'Is that *chewing gum?*'

'Bubble gum.' Laura already had a piece of it in her mouth, and now she offered the packet to Esther.

'We're not allowed chewing gum,' said Sophie, from the corner. For no reason that Esther could tell, she was wrapping the rejected owl in a sheet from the dressing up basket so that just his face showed.

'Yes, we are,' Esther said quickly, taking a piece. 'Sophie doesn't know what she's talking about. And anyway, this is *bubble* gum.'

When she took the gum out of its paper wrapping she saw that it came in a squashy pink doll's pillow that dented when you squeezed it with your fingers. It smelled like shampoo or bubble bath, not like food at all.

When she chewed it, her mouth went all watery and she had to swallow a lot. Laura didn't seem to have this problem; she blew a bubble that was nearly as big as her face, and when it popped, she just grinned and put all the popped gum back in her mouth again. Esther tried to copy her, but nothing much happened except for a few embarrassing farting noises.

She pushed the gum to the side of her mouth, so she could ask Laura a question. 'Is this from America?'

Laura nodded. 'It's Hubba Bubba.'

'Hubba Bubba,' Esther repeated, like she was learning a foreign language.

'It sounds funny when you say it.'

'It sounds funny when *you* say it,' said Esther, feeling braver now. 'You talk like someone in a film.'

Laura smiled. 'Like someone famous?' she asked, hopefully.

Esther nodded, not so much because it was true, but because she could tell Laura hoped it was true, and she wanted Laura to like her.

'Mummy says chewing gum stays in your tummy for seven years,' said Sophie, appearing next to them with her eyes fixed on the forbidden packet. 'She said it sticks your insides together.'

'We're not going to *swallow* it,' said Laura. She looked over Sophie's shoulder to where the swaddled owl lay abandoned, its clawed feet poking out from the white sheet. 'Hey, is that E.T. over there?'

'What?' said Sophie, crossly, spinning round to look behind her.

Esther started laughing. The owl did look exactly like E.T., in the bit where he was in the bike basket at the end. The sheet had made a hood around his face, so that you could hardly see his shiny eyes or his yellow beak. It really could have been E.T. inside.

'Why is it funny?' Sophie demanded, stamping her foot.

'Didn't she see the movie?' asked Laura.

'She wasn't allowed,' said Esther. 'She's too little. *I* went with Annabel and Louise, for my birthday.'

'I didn't even want to go,' said Sophie. 'The cinema is stupid.'

'I know!' said Esther, struck by a thought of sudden brilliance. 'Let's play E.T.! The owl can be E.T. and I'll be–'

'No, he can't,' said Sophie. 'He doesn't want to. He thinks it's stupid.'

'I think *you're* stupid,' said Esther.

Sophie's face went bright red and Esther worried that she might be about to cry, but instead she spun on her heel and marched out of the playroom.

'I'm telling Mummy,' she called over her shoulder.

'You're so lucky not to have a sister,' Esther said, but Laura wasn't listening. She had gone over to the dressing-up basket, and was considering it as if seeing it for the first time. There was a funny scratching noise as she walked around it. It sounded like King Alfred trying to get out of his cage, and as Laura passed her, Esther saw that she was running her fingernail across the wicker weave of the basket all the way from one end to the other.

'This could be the spaceship,' said Laura, thoughtfully, when her walk had taken her all the way to the playroom wall. 'If we took everything out of it.'

Esther ran over to join her, already breathless at the idea of an actual spacecraft in the playroom.

'And we could shine a torch through here,' she said, pointing at the hole in the basket where one of the handles used to be, back when the dressing-up basket was used for picnics. 'For space lights. My mummy has a torch in the cupboard under the stairs.'

She started lifting armfuls of dressing-up clothes out of the hamper and onto the floor so there was room for the two of them to get inside.

'Cool,' said Laura, setting aside her Snoopy handbag to help clear the spaceship for takeoff. 'And you can be Elliott and I can be his sister, the little girl.'

Esther stopped to look at her in surprise. Laura was her guest, and she knew that a guest was allowed all sorts of special treats that she was not – the best toys without fighting for them, orange squash instead of plain water, pudding even if she hadn't finished her main meal. But *everyone* in E.T. was a boy – there was only one girl, and playing E.T. had been her own idea. She should get to be the girl, even if Laura was the guest.

'Gertie,' she said. 'Her name is Gertie.'

Laura hadn't even known that. It wouldn't be fair if she got to be the girl when she didn't know her name.

'Yeah, that's it,' said Laura, as if the name wasn't important. 'I'll be Gertie.'

'Why don't *you* be Elliott,' Esther said, piling the dressing-up clothes high next to the hamper and trying not to look like she really minded. 'You are the guest so you should have the main part, and Elliott is the main part in E.T.'

Laura dropped the clothes she was holding onto the

floor, not on the pile they'd been making but just next to her feet.

'No,' she said, meeting Esther's eyes with an expression that said she wasn't fooled. 'It's okay. You can be Elliott. It was your idea. The little girl's cute. I'll be her.'

'Your hair is too dark,' Esther blurted. She couldn't stop herself. 'It's black and Gertie's hair isn't black.'

Laura's mouth opened in surprise at this direct attack, and her eyes narrowed. 'Your hair isn't the same colour as hers either, yours is just brown.'

Before Esther could answer Laura said, meanly, '*Elliott's* hair is brown.'

Esther was not used to arguments like this. Arguments she didn't win easily. When she and Sophie fought it was brief and physical, and quickly stopped by their mummy. If there was something clever to be said, she was the one who said it.

'Anyway, hair doesn't even matter if we're *pretending*,' Laura said, suddenly changing tack. 'I should get to be Gertie because I'm from America, and she's from America too.'

That wasn't fair. Esther couldn't help where she was from.

'You're not really from America,' she said, remembering. 'My mummy says you were born in the same hospital as me.'

'So?' said Laura, to which there was no answer. 'You don't talk like Gertie. I do, I talk just like her.'

'You talk just like *Elliott*, too,' said Esther, feeling desperate.

Laura put her hands on her hips and stared in a scary sort of way. It was worse than if she had said something, this being quiet and looking angry. Behind her, on the floor, Esther could see the owl. There could be no E.T. without E.T.; no game without the owl. She realized her advantage and swooped down to grab the sheet-wrapped bundle.

'I've got E.T.,' she said. 'He's mine.'

'It's not E.T., it's just a dumb owl,' said Laura.

'It *is* E.T., and so I get to be Gertie, because I have E.T., so there.'

'You have to share,' said Laura, and lunged for the owl. She missed him, but grabbed the sheet instead and pulled with enough strength to make Esther stagger for balance.

When they had stopped pulling, Esther still had the owl and Laura had the sheet. She threw it to the ground, and advanced on Esther with fury on her face.

'I. Am. Gertie,' said Laura, through clenched teeth. 'Give me the owl. I am Gertie!'

Esther backed away, but had barely taken two steps when she felt the dressing-up basket blocking her retreat. Laura, seeing her trapped, made another grab for the owl. This time she got hold of his head, and Esther had to dig her hands right into the owl's feathered chest to hold on. The owl's claws had got stuck on her jumper, as if it didn't want to go with Laura either, as if it had taken her side.

Esther braced herself against the dressing-up basket and pulled as hard as she could. At last, with a satisfying pop, she felt Laura's resistance give. She nearly fell over backwards into the basket but righted herself just in time, careful not to release her hold – it would be terrible to drop the owl now she had won. But when she looked at Laura in triumph, she could not quite understand what she saw.

Laura's eyes were wide, her mouth open, and she looked down at her hands in horror. How could it be? Esther had the owl, she could feel him in her arms, his stuffed chest against her own. But his shiny plastic eyes stared at her from Laura's hands.

'You pulled his head off!' she said.

'No, you did,' said Laura, but she did not look sure of herself at all. She looked like she would like to throw the head as far away from her as possible.

Esther felt all the disappointments of the day bubble up inside her at once. The talk of her far-away daddy. This new friend who wasn't a friend at all. The game they hadn't even started playing before it went wrong. Her face started to go all hot and she felt the tears she'd held back before rise up again, this time, unstoppably. Laura looked even more horrified at Esther's tears than she had at the owl's head.

'Here, you can have it,' she said, holding out the head towards Esther.

'It's ruined,' said Esther. She could feel her chin tremble so that the words came out sounding wobbly. 'My mummy's going to be so cross with me.'

She wiped at her nose with her sleeve. The owl in her arms was heavy with guilt. When Laura tried to take it from her again she didn't resist.

'Look,' said Laura. She sat down on the floor and stood the headless owl upright in between her outstretched legs, his curled claws almost hidden under the feathers on his tummy. 'Look, we can put his head back on and you won't even know.'

Esther didn't want to look, but Laura pulled at her skirt and said, 'Gimme your gum.'

Esther saw that there was already a wad of pink chewing gum stuck on the owl's bristling horsehair neck, right in the middle of stuffing. It must have been Laura's. Esther wanted to tell her to stop it, she was making it worse, but she couldn't think of another way for the head to be stuck on without telling Mummy. So, since there was no other choice, she pulled the sticky gum out of her own mouth and squashed it obediently on top of Laura's.

Laura balanced the head on top, and moved it from one side to the other, trying to get it straight. She got it a bit wrong, so the beak wasn't properly in the middle like before. Esther crouched down next to her and pulled the head so the beak lined up with the paler bit on the owl's chest. It looked nearly right. If you didn't know to look for the missing feathers around the neck, or the wiry stuffing hairs sticking out where they hadn't before, you might not even notice that anything was different.

'But,' she said, 'but as soon as you pick it up, its head will fall off again.'

'So don't pick it up,' said Laura, getting to her feet and studying her handiwork. 'If you don't pick it up you can't even tell. It looks just the same.'

'My mummy will be able to tell,' Esther said. 'My mummy always notices everything.'

Laura sighed. 'You saw E.T.?'

Esther frowned. Was Laura going to start again about being Gertie? She didn't care about being Gertie any more.

'You remember how E.T. was in the house and the mom didn't even see him? When he was right there by the refrigerator?'

'Yes.'

'Adults don't notice stuff. They think they do but they don't. If she doesn't know the owl's broken, she won't even look at it.'

Esther thought about this. It was true that her mother had a way of not noticing some things – for instance, if Sophie got a bigger piece of cake than she did, Mummy would say they'd had just the same amount. Or if they argued in the car, Mummy would say she didn't care who started it, even if it was really obviously Sophie who did. Perhaps they could hide it. At least for long enough to be able to say they'd had nothing to do with it.

'The owl's normally up there,' Esther said, pointing at the mantelpiece, too high for them to reach by themselves. 'She might not be able to tell if she doesn't see it close up.'

'Okay,' said Laura. She went to the window and took the chair she had been sitting on when they first came into the playroom. She dragged it across the carpet with both hands, and stood it carefully so that all four legs were on the fireplace tiles for balance. Then she climbed up onto the chair and held her hands out.

'Come over here, E.T.,' she said. 'Time to get back in the spaceship and fly away home.'

Esther picked up the owl, with one steadying hand on his bubble-gummed head, and carried him to Laura. Between the two of them, they lifted him high up onto the mantelpiece, and pushed him back against the chimney breast so he wouldn't fall off. His head moved a little from the lifting, so when his head was set back in just the right place, with Esther's approval, Laura pressed down on it quite hard, to make sure it would stay there.

Esther helped Laura climb down from the chair, and they both stood under the mantelpiece looking up. The owl stared its plastic stare over their heads, as if it was looking at something far beyond them, and wondering how it had come to this, from the forests of Scotland, to a head stuck on with Hubba Bubba. It looked exactly the same, but Esther felt sick with the knowledge that it was not.

'What if she finds out?'

'She won't.'

'But what if she *does*?'

Laura turned to face her, hands on hips. 'Esther, no-one saw it happen but you and me. I'm not gonna tell, are you?'

Esther gulped. Of course she wouldn't tell, but what if she was discovered – could she lie then?

'We'll take it to our *graves*,' said Laura. 'Cross my heart and hope to die.' She made a swishy and dramatic hand movement over her chest, from one shoulder to the other.

Esther saw that she was expected to do the same, so she mumbled the words and moved her hand quickly and hoped she had done it right. Keeping secrets was a thing that friends did, so she would do it. And shortly afterwards Esther's mummy came to get them for lunch, and though they kicked each other guiltily under the table a few times, they knew they'd got away with it.

Esther didn't quite take it to her grave, though.

She took it to the age of twelve, when her mother knocked the owl off the mantelpiece while dusting and discovered not just the severed head, but the incriminating wads of bubble gum that said this decapitation was no accident.

Esther admitted it all; everything except Laura's involvement. She'd crossed her heart, after all. She'd never tell.

3

October 2013

Now it's Laura's turn to ignore me. I've sent her four emails, two a day since Margie told me she was missing, and nothing. No answer to my phone messages either. Five days away from work isn't much, really, says my husband. But it is. It's a week. A week is a long time; it's a possibly-dead-in-a-ditch time.

Of course Margie called the police in Napa. I knew she would, and I was secretly glad she cracked before I did. That way I could be reassured without being accused of overreacting myself. But they said there was nothing they could do. Laura is an adult, and she is entitled to go away without telling anyone. If that is what she's done.

Margie even got Laura's boss to agree to go to her apartment and look around for clues, like in a detective novel. He said it all seemed fine. Normal. How would he know what is normal? asked Margie, when she called to tell me that, against her dire predictions, he had failed to discover an incriminating bloodstain on the floor, or a bullet hole in the plasterboard. He doesn't know Laura like we do, she said, he wouldn't understand what is normal for her and what isn't. He wouldn't even know what to look for.

The longer Laura is missing, the more certain Margie is about everything. *You* would know what to look for, she says. *I* would know, she insists. *A Mother Knows*. I'm not sure I believe it; there must be plenty of things she has missed as a mother and I as a friend, but I can't bring myself to contradict her. I look at Linus, who has been alive for just nine months, and about whom I know everything there is to know, and I wonder how it would feel if one day he was gone. They say the passionate intensity of a mother's love for her baby diminishes in time – you learn to let go a little, you let them leave you. I can't imagine it yet. I know it would entirely destroy me to lose him, and that is what gives me sympathy for Margie even at her worst.

And her worst arrived pretty soon.

'Just leave it,' said my husband, when he saw Margie's mobile number flash up on my phone. It was one of those rare nights when Linus was asleep, we had managed to eat dinner together and now – a miracle – it looked like we might be able to get through an episode of *Breaking Bad* without interruption.

A call from the mobile was weird. Laura bought her

mum a mobile a few years ago, paid the bill even, and gave me the number. But I don't think Margie had ever called me on it. She always rang from home, from her kitchen, alone apart from whichever three-legged hedgehog or half-blind fox cub was currently expiring its last breaths next to the radiator. She always hopes she can make them better; she rarely does.

It was too bizarre that she should call me on it now, with Laura gone. I had to answer. But it wasn't Margie, it was a man's voice, hard to hear through all the accompanying noise. It sounded like he was somewhere very busy and very loud. There was a tannoy announcement in the background as he introduced himself, so all I heard was a perky ding-dong sound, like a doorbell, and then the words 'at Gatwick Airport'.

Then he said, 'Am I speaking to Esther Conley?' So I knew at least that Margie must be okay, she must have given him her phone and told him to call me – she never remembers my married name. I think even when I am an old lady she will still think of me as a teenager, eating toast in her kitchen with Laura. I said yes – why correct him? – and asked him what was happening.

It was even harder to hear his reply when the volume was turned up next to me, in a heavy-handed hint that I should get off the phone. I got up instead, and took the call in the hallway. Margie had been stopped at the airport, said the man, trying to board a plane to San Francisco with a passport that was twelve years out of date. She had broken down when she was turned away, and refused to say where she lived in case they tried to send her back. *She says*, the man said on the end of the phone, *that it's a matter of life and death. Is it?*

Up until that point, my sympathy had been a passive thing. I was the voice at the end of the telephone, I was the helpful best friend. But I hadn't done anything. I'd let Margie carry the burden of fear and worry, and I'd just sat back and hoped everything would resolve itself while I made reassuring comments from the sidelines.

But here was Laura's mother – who hadn't left Hampshire for a decade, who barely ventured out of her village, who couldn't drive a car or use the internet or remember to renew a passport she never used – desperate enough to fly to America to find her daughter.

I drove to get her straight away, of course; it was only a few hours at that time of night. I brought her back to ours and put her to bed, and afterwards my husband and I had a fierce marital argument entirely conducted in don't-wake-the-baby whispers. As heated as it got, the fight was hushed enough that underneath it all, like a radio playing in the background, we could both hear the quiet sobbing of Margie in the spare room.

I think that's what made him relent. I know it's what pushed me over the edge. And that is how I find myself on a flight to San Francisco, on my own, in search of Laura.

Even as I'm boarding the plane I keep thinking I've forgotten something: my arms feel empty, and the bag on my shoulder is disconcertingly light. Cleared of its usual cargo of bottles, nappies and rice cakes, it feels like it belongs to someone else. I *feel* like I'm someone else. I assumed that without Linus I'd revert to my pre-baby self, snapping back like a released elastic band: liberated to read a magazine on the plane, watch a film, eat a meal undisturbed. But it's not like that.

There was a joke in my NCT class that when they give the just-born baby to you in its blue hospital blanket they also hand over a giant package of guilt. 'Oh, no thank you,' you say, smiling the naïve smile of the first-time mother. 'No guilt for me. Just the baby, please.' But the nurse shakes her head: it's a buy-one-get-one-free that you can't get out of. Since Linus was born I have felt intense, overwhelming guilt over the smallest things: the too-scratchy wool of his buggy blanket against his soft cheek, the strong coffee I shouldn't have drunk before breastfeeding. And over bigger stuff too, that goes without saying. But none of it is anything compared to the guilt I feel as the plane takes off. It overwhelms me suddenly, like nausea, lifting me from my seat, and I scrabble so frantically at the seatbelt that an air hostess has to come over and tell me to calm down.

Three days, I tell myself, as she continues to give me the evils from her own seat across the aisle. That was the compromise. I promised Margie three days and two nights for Laura, and I promised myself that Linus would barely have time to miss me. I didn't think properly about how much I'd miss him.

As soon as we're up in the air I release myself from the seat and go to the bathroom. I sit on the closed toilet and splash cold water on my face. It doesn't help that I keep thinking of those stories you read about people who go on holiday leaving their children at home for a week with nothing but two frozen pizzas and a bottle of Fanta. Surely it can't be counted as abandonment if you've left the baby with your mother and your husband, an Ocado delivery arriving mere hours after you've left? Tell me I am not a terrible person.

It doesn't matter; I feel like one. I wouldn't do this for anyone but Laura. After all, she's done it for me.

Because, of course, underneath the guilt that I feel over Linus, is another, older layer that I feel for her. It's buried deep underneath a thousand new maternal guilts, but it's still there, laid down over so many years that it's as much a part of me as the colour of my hair or the shape of my nose. You're responsible for your best friend, even if you're grown-up, especially if she's got no-one else.

I should have known Laura wouldn't ask outright for help. She's only done that once, when she had no other choice. No, with Laura you have to look for what she isn't saying – for the casual and seemingly innocent comment that means she's foundering, on her own, thousands of miles away. I should have known that mention of Drew Barrymore was a red flag. But Linus's needs have been so immediate and overwhelming to me that I have failed to notice Laura's until it is too late. She always thought she could rely on me, and I've let her down.

There is a sudden hammering on the bathroom door and I realize I've been in here far too long. I pat my face dry with a paper towel, and flush the loo so that my visit seems legitimate. When I emerge there is a line of people waiting and with my eyes downcast I murmur apologies as I squeeze past on the way back to my seat. If I see a single angry face I think I might lose it; the only thing that would be worse would be a sympathetic one. I've hardly sat down when the air hostess comes over to check if everything is okay. The words are kind but her expression isn't. There's a hard line between her eyebrows that lets me know she's clocked me as trouble. The person most likely to lose it on her watch.

I want to laugh in her face when I think it could have been Margie sat here instead. Then she'd know trouble. But instead I agree that a glass of water would help, thank you, and let her think she's doing something useful to calm me down. The man next to me, businesslike in his grey suit, glances over and offers a nervous smile that says, 'Please don't be insane'. I return with a tight-lipped acknowledgement that isn't a smile, not really, just an agreement to be British about this and politely ignore each other all the way to California.

I want to tell him that I am the sensible one, I always have been. I'm not the one who needs looking after. Other people lose it, I pick up the pieces. Aren't I here doing it all over again?

Only this time I'm not sure where any of the pieces are.

1990: LITTLE GIRL LOST: A CHILD STAR'S DESCENT INTO ADDICTION – AND OUT AGAIN, BY DREW BARRYMORE WITH TODD GOLD[2]

'I had my first drink at age nine, began smoking marijuana at ten, and at twelve took up cocaine.'
Drew Barrymore

4

Esther didn't take the bus home on Thursday afternoons. After school she had her oboe lesson with Miss Coombe and after that she went to Laura's house until her mum could pick her up. Laura was supposed to be home from ballet by half past four to let Esther in. She was supposed to be home by half past four *anyway*, since the class finished at four and it didn't even take that long to walk back from town.

But today, as she had for the last three Thursdays, Esther sat on the front step, still waiting at five o'clock. The Thomases' house was close to a busy road, not hidden behind a long drive like Esther's own. Anyone passing could see her sitting there by herself, and though she was prepared this time, had brought a book from the library just in case, it was too dark to read it. Instead she felt like a dog waiting for its owner, alert to every approaching footstep, in case it might be Laura at last.

A couple of older people smiled sympathetically as

they glanced up the driveway to where she sat, all too visibly; one woman with a baby in a pushchair stopped to ask if she was okay, and Esther, embarrassed, mumbled into her hair that she was fine, thanks. Some girls her own age, but in the green blazers of the High School on the other side of town, scurried past giggling, though that could have been at something else and not at her.

If she had been smaller like Laura, she felt, a slighter, more ethereal presence in the autumnal gloom, she might not have caught the eye so easily. In the fading light passers-by might have mistaken her for a willowy sapling, or a delicate garden sculpture.

But instead she was obvious to everyone. Obviously alone and obviously herself, even in the near-dark. When she saw a group of boys approaching in the same Portsdown blazer as her own, Esther ducked her head down and prayed not to be seen, but it was too late.

'Hey, Fester – Fat Fester! Why you sitting there?'

'You stuck outside? Too fat to fit through the door, Fester?'

Darren Brentwood had started it all, in the second year. Some of the bigger boys were teasing him at the back of the biology lab, near where she was sitting. 'Are you bent then, Bentwood? Are you a bender?' Esther had flushed with shame for Darren, and guilt at not doing anything to stop them. She wondered if she should tell the teacher, but Mr McDonald was at the blackboard, oblivious to everything but the safety warnings for the use of the Bunsen burner that he was writing there in chalk.

She'd been at primary school with Darren, and he had come to her birthday parties since they were six. She sent him a fleeting look of sympathy, to let him know he was not alone, and in return, Darren spotted her weakness and sneered. 'Yeah? Least I'm not Fat Fester,' he said, loud enough for everyone to hear.

Mr McDonald had turned around. 'That's enough,' he said, but it was too late.

It wasn't like she was truly fat, not *Guinness Book of World Records* fat. But she was bigger than the other girls, just fat enough for the name to stick.

'Hey, Fatty Boom Boom. Wanna chip?'

She didn't even know these boys: they were younger than her, maybe twelve or thirteen, but they knew her. The tallest of them waved a paper-wrapped packet at her above his head, as if she might leap for it like a dog.

'Course she does, you've seen the size of her. She fucking lives on chips, I bet. Come on, Fester, come and get a chip.'

Esther tried to ignore them, but it was hard to pretend she couldn't hear from just a few feet away. The gate to the back of the house was locked, she'd already tried it. The only way out was past the boys, and there were three of them against one of her. There was nothing to do but turn her face away, looking stoically into the distance like a soon-to-be martyred saint ignoring the taunts of the heathen hordes. Rise above it, her mother said: don't lower yourself to their level. But she wouldn't have had to rise above anything if Laura was here when she was supposed to be.

There was a breath of air by her ear, like a gasp, and then a thud as something soft hit the side of her head. The missile glanced off and landed in the pea shingle of the Thomases' drive. Esther rubbed at her hair out of surprise rather than pain, and her fingers came away greasy and smelling of vinegar. Before she could look at the ground to confirm that she'd been hit by a chip, another one caught her on the shoulder, splitting open, and then another thumped against her chest.

She scrambled to her feet, holding out her library book against the rain of chips, but as soon as the boys saw she wasn't a sitting target any more they whooped and ran away. Their laughter echoed down the streets, growing fainter until Esther was left alone in silence again.

She brushed down the front of her jumper where little flecks of potato had settled like snow. It didn't work. Instead of falling off, the potato just smeared right into the knitted wool. There wouldn't be time to wash her uniform before school tomorrow. It would smell of deep fat fryers and humiliation until the weekend, and so would she.

Esther sat back down and tucked her arms around her

knees. It was getting cold. There were lights on in the houses across the street, people moving around inside, the blue flicker of a television. It was nearly time for *Neighbours*.

When Laura came marching up the drive – finally! – you wouldn't have even known she was a schoolgirl like Esther. You might have thought she was from the sixth form college or even from university. Every day, as soon as she walked out of the school gates, she replaced the top half of her school uniform with a baggy black jumper and a long black coat, like the one Judd Nelson wore in *The Breakfast Club*, and her pleated grey school skirt was rolled up short so it looked almost fashionable. Her big dark eyes were even bigger now she'd ringed them in eyeliner, and as she approached, Esther could smell the unmistakable scent of betrayal, of time misspent with cooler people: cigarettes.

'Shit, Est, sorry,' said Laura. She was panting as if she'd been walking very fast, or maybe even running. 'Didn't realize it was so late, have you been waiting ages?'

'Since half past four,' said Esther, pointedly, but Laura didn't seem to notice. She skipped lightly up the steps and went to open the door.

'Ugh, God, what's that?' she said, lifting her foot to look at the bottom of her loafer. 'Chips? And you didn't save any for me? You selfish cow.'

She scraped her shoe on the concrete edge of the doorstep to clean it.

'I saved a whole load for you on the gravel,' said Esther, standing up. 'Help yourself.'

Laura just laughed and let herself in. Esther picked up her school bag and then her music bag, and hooked the plastic Sainsbury's bag that had her lunchbox in it over one hand. With her free hand she lifted the oboe case and then, fully laden, she stepped heavily over the threshold of the house she knew as well as her own.

Maybe she knew this house even better, since she was an observer here, a visitor rather than a native, ever alert to the differences. Her parents' house was old-fashioned; with its fireplaces and flowery fabrics, it might have belonged to someone's grandparents. Her parents still listened to scratchy records on a turntable, and ate meals that had been cooked in an oven instead of a microwave. But the Thomases' house was like stepping inside an episode of *Tomorrow's World*: there was always something new to admire. If it wasn't a home computer, or a VHS recorder to replace the old Betamax one, then it was satellite television, or a remote control that operated, of all things, the sitting room curtains. Laura's dad even had a phone in his car.

Laura had gone ahead to the kitchen, so Esther let her bags slide from her arms onto the floor and then hung her blazer over the banister. When she checked her jumper in the light of the hallway the stains from the chips were faint, only a slight darkening of the fabric from the grease and little bit of white potatoness that she hoped would rub off when it dried. Once, she might have told Laura what had happened – if Laura had been back on time, straight from ballet. Though if she'd been back on time, it wouldn't have happened at all. But Esther felt enough of a loser without admitting that while Laura had been smoking cigarettes somewhere, she had been being pelted with chips by pre-pubescent boys.

In the kitchen Laura already had the toaster on, and she started laying out the plates so they'd be ready to eat in front of *Neighbours* like they always did. She stood on tiptoe to reach for the Marmite in the cupboard above the microwave, and as she lifted it off the shelf, Esther saw that she had new friendship bracelets on her wrist. Not the ones they'd made for each other in the summer holidays, from her mum's embroidery thread, but different ones that looked like they'd been bought from a shop.

'So how come you were late?' asked Esther. She was very casual, taking the Marmite jar from Laura's hand and unscrewing the lid as if it was all the same to her.

'Told you,' said Laura, pushing the cutlery drawer shut with her hip. 'Just didn't realize the time. I said I was sorry.'

She moved unselfconsciously around the kitchen, opening the fridge, reaching for the popping-up toast. She wasn't constantly checking to make sure her school jumper hadn't ridden up, or to see if the zip on her skirt had opened to reveal inches of unrestrained flesh. More than Laura's flat stomach or her ballet-toned thighs, Esther envied this, the lack of awareness of the many awful ways in which your body might betray you to ridicule.

'Wait,' said Esther, as Laura put a square packet of butter on the counter, still in its foil wrapper. 'Haven't you got any low-fat spread?'

'Not much point in sticking to low-fat spread if you've already eaten a load of chips, is there?' Laura laughed, and Esther winced. It was bad enough to be accused of greediness when you had eaten chips, but truly unfair when you hadn't.

'Anyway, it's Margie's latest thing. Kind of ironic, but Margie's decided margarine gives you cancer.'

'Cancer?'

'I knoooooow. Well, the Berlin Wall came down, so Cold War Margie had to find another enemy, didn't she?'

'Flora? She's gone from communist superpowers to sunflower spread?'

'Exactly. You know what she's like.'

'You'd think she'd be more worried about other things that give you cancer,' said Esther, leaving a careful pause. 'Like cigarettes.'

Laura wrinkled her nose and didn't take the bait. 'Yeah, maybe.'

When the toast was ready, they went into the sitting

room. Laura took her usual place in the big black leather chair with the padded footrest that flipped up, and Esther hers on the sofa, balancing her plate on the arm and pulling her feet up beside her. Laura pointed a series of remotes, like a conductor, until the television sprang into life and the floor-length curtains hummed electronically closed across the bay window.

Neighbours wasn't the same since Kylie and Jason left, but that didn't put them off watching. Sometimes, if Esther was off school for some reason, she'd watch the episode at lunchtime and the same one again in the evening. There was something reassuring about the closed world of *Neighbours*, where everyone lived in the same cul-de-sac and no-one ever ventured further than Lassiter's lake. In Ramsay Street, Esther felt, someone would have come to her defence when those boys started throwing chips. Helen Daniels would have bustled out of her house and demanded to know what was happening. Someone would have noticed Laura smoking and made a moral example of her at the end of an episode.

'I hate those blow-job twins,' said Laura, pointing at the television, her mouth full of toast. She swung one long leg over the edge of the chair. 'They're even more boring than Harold and Madge.'

'Blow-job twins?'

'That's what Sarah calls them.'

'Sarah Maxwell?'

'Yeah, she says they've both got real blow-job lips,' Laura pouted obscenely and giggled.

But Esther was not thinking of blow-jobs, she was thinking of Sarah Maxwell, the coolest girl in school, ever since her mum let her have a wet-look perm when she was in the first year, when everyone else still had plaits and ponytails. The perm had grown out, but the coolness remained. It stuck to whatever she touched, and whoever she hung out with, like she had dusted them with glitter. And now it stuck to Laura.

'Was that who you were *smoking* with?' asked Esther.

Laura sighed heavily and put her plate on the floor beside the chair. She licked her fingers where the butter and Marmite had made them shine.

'I knew you'd be weird about this,' she said.

'I'm not being weird.'

Laura rolled her eyes and leaned all the way back in her chair, like she was trying to get as far away as possible. 'Look, I'd have asked you, okay, but I didn't even know – it was just a last-minute thing, after ballet. It wasn't even a big deal.'

'So why didn't you just say where you were then?'

'Because – of this! You! I knew you'd make it into a whole big *thing*.'

'I'm not making it a thing, I just think you could have said.'

'What do you want, a written confession? God, it's

only a few Silk Cut, it's not like I was doing cocaine or something.'

'Oh fuck.' Esther leapt off the sofa, remembering that she hadn't picked up everything from the driveway.

'What? What?' Laura shouted, as Esther ran out of the room. 'Oh, I'm sorry, did you leave your *cocaine* outside?'

Esther slammed the front door when she came back in. She hoped it would make a point.

'I said, did you leave your cocaine outside?' Laura sneered, still in her leather chair.

'It wasn't funny the first time,' said Esther. 'I always keep my drugs in my oboe case, actually. I left my library book on the drive.'

'A library book? Rock and roll,' said Laura, tossing her head as she turned up the volume on the television, but the *Neighbours* theme tune was playing already. The episode was over.

Esther cracked her book open to the page she'd reached when it got too dark to read outside. She held it right up to her face to block Laura out. From behind the paperback pages she heard Laura flick through other channels and settle on something with music – MTV, probably. She watched loads of MTV since they'd got a satellite dish. She always knew the lyrics to everything, and what was popular long before it appeared on the Chart Show.

Esther wanted to watch MTV herself, but then it

would be like giving in. Anyway, her mum would be here at seven to take her home. Maybe next Thursday she'd just wait in the library if Laura was going to be like this. Maybe they'd never be friends again. Laura would go off with Sarah Maxwell and the faceless boys from the High School and Esther would spend the rest of her school years stuck in the music room with Miss Coombe, watching everyone else be cool without her.

The phone rang in the kitchen and Laura got up to answer it, huffing and sighing in annoyance. Esther wondered if it was Sarah on the end of the line, or even a boy. But Laura was back after a few minutes.

'Okay, look, I'm sorry,' she said, standing in front of Esther so she couldn't be ignored.

Esther fixed her eyes on her book, not quite ready to forgive.

Laura threw herself down on the sofa next to her. 'I am sorry, Est, honest. You know what it's like, you get swept up in things. I just forgot I was meant to be back here.'

Esther did not know what it was like. She had never been swept up in exciting social plans. She made a 'hmph' noise that could have been an acknowledgement or it could have been a cough. But she did lower her book a fraction.

'Esther,' said Laura. 'Esther, come on.' She shuffled up alongside her on the sofa and nudged with her elbow until Esther lowered the book entirely.

Then Laura caught sight of the cover. She snatched the book from Esther's hands and read in a dramatic voice like a movie announcer, '*Little Girl Lost: A child star's descent into addiction – and out again*, by Drew Barrymore. What is this shit?'

'Shut up. Just because you don't read anything.' Esther tried to grab the book back, but Laura held it out of reach.

'I've read *Forever*,' Laura shrugged.

'*Everyone's* read *Forever*. Embryos still in the womb have read *Forever*.'

'Well, I don't know why you're being so superior,' said Laura, flicking through the pages. 'This isn't exactly Steinberg, is it?'

'Stein*beck*.'

'Whatever.'

Laura reached the picture section, and held the pages open so they could both see them at the same time. Despite herself, Esther leaned over her shoulder to watch her turn the pages.

'Oh my God, look at this,' Laura shrieked, stopping at a picture of Drew at the Oscars. 'Corey Feldman! She didn't really date him, did she? He's hideous.'

'Well, she *was* on drugs,' said Esther.

'You'd have to be. No way, *E.T.*! God, *E.T.* Do you remember we had a massive fight over that owl? And who was going to be Gertie?'

'I'm Gertie!' spluttered Esther, remembering.

'No, *I* am Gertie!' Laura pushed back with her shoulder.

'Well, you *have* started smoking. So, Drew, by my calculations that means you should be in rehab by the time you're, what – eighteen?'

'It is so not a big deal,' said Laura, setting down the book with an elaborate eyeroll. 'I mean, if you're going to keep going on about it, why don't you just have a cigarette yourself and then we're evens.'

'Oh, right, let me just go to the shops and buy some in my school uniform,' said Esther. 'I know, why don't I get Corey Feldman to drive me there in his Corvette, then maybe afterwards we'll go to the Oscars together?'

'You are *so* lame,' said Laura. She threw the book down on the sofa and got up. 'Wait there.'

Esther waited. She looked at the photographs again – Drew Barrymore on a New York nightclub podium in a pair of Converse high-tops, barely eleven years old. What was she doing when she was eleven? Messing about with Laura's Barbie and Ken, playing at being adults, while Drew Barrymore was being one already. It was hard to feel like she had anything in common with the little girl from *E.T.*; if anyone was Drew, it was Laura.

A movement by the door caught her eye, and when she looked up she saw two cigarettes beckoning her out of the room, like skeletal fingers.

'Laura! Where did you get those from?'

Laura poked her head round the door and waggled the cigarettes. 'Sarah gave them to me. Want one?'

'Won't Margie be home soon?'

'No, that was her on the phone just now. My dad's not feeling well, she's gone to pick him up from the dockyard so he doesn't have to get the train. She'll be ages. Come on.'

Esther's mum had warned her about peer pressure. She'd said the cool people will make you smoke – they'll tell you you can't be friends with them if you don't join in. They'll force you into it, even though you don't want to. Esther had imagined being pinned to the ground by someone popular like Sarah Maxwell or Amelia Wentworth, a cigarette pushed between her lips as she twisted her head away in desperation like a woman tied to the train tracks in an old movie – no! no! no! But this was different – she *wanted* to do it, she was glad to be asked.

It was as if Laura was getting into a car with her new friends, with Drew Barrymore even, and just as she was about to shut the door, instead she held it open and invited Esther to come along for the ride. Esther got straight in without any questions, and didn't even do up her seatbelt.

Laura didn't have a lighter, all she had were the two Silk Cut off Sarah Maxwell, so they took a big rattling box of Cook's Matches from the kitchen out to the patio with them instead. It took a lot more tries to light up than it ever seemed to on television.

First the matches kept blowing out, then Laura kept going on at Esther to inhale properly.

'I *am*.'

'No, look. Watch, let me do mine first, you've got to inhale right when the flame is on the end.'

Esther studied Laura's technique with more concentration than she had afforded Miss Coombe at her oboe lesson earlier. On her next attempt she managed to half-light the end, and inhaled a mouthful of acrid smoke that made her cough until she was doubled over.

'You've got to keep taking drags,' bossed Laura, over Esther's heaving back. 'Otherwise it's going to go out again. Though you know what? Amelia Wentworth says if it only lights halfway, that means someone's in love with you.'

Esther sat up, spluttering from the smoke and the preposterous idea that someone might be in love with Fat Fester. Her head swam in a way that was quite pleasant. She took another drag, and the end lit up properly, all the way. She felt like she was in a John Hughes film. This was what teenagers were meant to do, smoke cigarettes when their parents were out. Not stay at home practising the oboe for two hours every night.

It was properly dark now, and cold. A few bright stars were out, and as she smoked Esther wished on one, silently. Once she would have done so out loud, but she wasn't sure if it was something that Laura might have grown out of without telling her. Now that she was used to the taste of the cigarette, it wasn't that bad. She found she quite liked this swimming feeling, as if the air around them had turned to water and everything had slowed down.

'My dad was sick last week, too,' said Laura, suddenly.

Esther turned to look at her, but Laura kept staring straight ahead.

'Sick how?'

Laura inhaled on her cigarette before she answered. 'I don't know, his stomach, I think.'

'Maybe something he ate?'

'Yeah, maybe.' Laura ground her cigarette out on the low brick wall that separated the patio from the rest of the garden, and red sparks flew around them like fireflies. 'Margie's convinced he's dying, obviously.'

Esther stubbed her cigarette in the same place. It made a mark on the bricks and she tried to rub it out with her fingers so they wouldn't get in trouble.

'I'm sure he'll be okay, Laur,' she said.

'Course he will,' said Laura, briskly, as if she already regretted saying anything about it. 'Anyway. Hand over the butt, I'll put them in the outside bin.'

Esther dropped the squashed end of the cigarette into Laura's open palm and swung her legs on the garden wall, kicking her heels on the bricks while she waited for Laura to return from the side of the house where the bins were kept. She sniffed at her sleeve for the cigarette smell. Although it wasn't an especially nice smell, she liked it. She smelled like she'd sprayed herself with essence of socially successful adolescent.

When Laura came back from the bin she was smiling again. 'So,' she said, hesitating before they went in. Inside the glass patio doors the kitchen was brightly lit, and standing in the dark it seemed to Esther as if they were waiting in the wings of a stage. 'Now you've smoked your first cigarette.'

Esther bristled a little at this patronage, but decided to make a joke of it, rather than be accused of making another big deal. Laura had offered her an olive branch made out of nicotine and Cook's Matches, and it would be a mistake to take it for granted.

She clutched both hands to her chest in mock gratitude.

'Wow, I hardly know how to thank you, Drew. When do we start on the *drugs*?'

Laura snorted as she slid the glass doors back. The stage was set and Esther stepped onto it next to her best friend.

Laura linked an arm with hers reassuringly. 'The great thing is, Drew, now when we go to rehab, we can go there together. Maybe they'll let us share a room.'

5

October 2013

I'm here to save the day. I'm a strong and independent woman. I'm thirty-eight years old. I can't get the rental car to start.

I've tried everything I can think of with this stupid fob they gave me at the Hertz desk. The lights have gone on and off, I've blasted myself with the air-con, locked and unlocked the doors five times, and I even managed to set off a whooping alarm that made everyone else in the car park leap in shock, entirely simultaneously, like a flash mob.

Deep breaths. I can do this. My mission as Laura's saviour cannot be thwarted by a key fob.

There's no actual key, of course, that would be way too obvious.

I could go back to the rental desk for help, but it's miles across the car park and back through the airport, at least a fifteen-minute walk, and the worst of it is that the man at the desk made a point of demonstrating how it worked. I remember nodding and not really paying attention. Thinking, God, do I really look like the sort of idiot who doesn't know how to start a car? I can't face either the walk or the inevitable lecture at the end of it.

'Laura!' I say out loud, gripping the steering wheel and looking upwards. 'What are you doing to me?'

With the fob clutched in my hand, I thump my forehead against the steering wheel in frustration, and somehow this combination permits the car to cough into life. I quickly rev the accelerator to make sure it doesn't stall. Okay. I have no idea how I did this, but everything's working. I've programmed the address of the motel into the satnav, so now all I need to do is go.

Stay on the right, stay on the right, stay on the right, I tell myself through clenched teeth as I circle the car park looking for the exit. *Right, right, right*, I chant like a mantra, as I steer the car onto a road with two fast-moving lanes. We're off. I can do this.

I was dismissive before about Margie not driving any more, but the truth is, I barely drive these days either. Even going to get her from the airport felt out of my comfort zone. It's just so much easier to stick around your own neighbourhood when you have to take a buggy and all the baby stuff with you wherever you go. Everything I need is within walking distance of the house –

the park, the shops, all the cafés that will let you bring a buggy in. And if Linus does one of those astonishing full-body babygro-destroying poos and needs a full change right down to his socks, I know I'm never too far from home.

At the weekends (block your ears, Emmeline Pankhurst) I'm either in the back with Linus or, when my husband says that makes him feel too much like a minicab driver, I spend the whole time I'm in the front contorted to reach the back. I'm the Mummy-dispenser, twisted round to pass a bottle or kneeling to retrieve a dropped Benjamin Bunny from under the driver's seat. I have often thought that if the car crashed at such a moment it would be the most humiliating way to go – mum-jeaned and arse-first through the windscreen, waving goodbye with the ever-present wet wipe in my hand.

Only now that I'm driving again, facing forwards, gaining confidence with every mile – *look at me, on the other side of the road, in America* – do I remember I used to like doing this. I used to love it, in fact: driving with the radio on, singing as loud as I wanted without worrying anyone would hear me. Obviously the controls for the radio in this car are nowhere a reasonable person might expect them, but finally I locate them on the steering wheel and flick through the channels until I hear something familiar.

'Goodbye Yellow Brick Road'. It's enough to make me

stop the car, but I'm too afraid I won't be able to start it up again.

Laura and I knew the words to every song on *The Very Best of Elton John*, all of them, even 'You Gotta Love Someone'. We sang them endlessly in her ancient orange Beetle on the way back home from sixth form – her dad promised to buy her a car if she passed her test, he just didn't promise it would be a good one. The Beetle had had a radio once, but when the coat-hanger aerial fell off for the last time Laura replaced it with a red plastic tape deck and a handful of compilation cassettes bought from the garage, since all of her proper music was on CDs. Believe me when I say *The Very Best of Elton John* was the Very Best of the lot. While Laura screeched round corners on two wheels like a rally driver, I tried to ignore my impending death in a traffic accident and concentrated on pressing the clunky buttons of the tape deck on my lap to fast-forward to our favourites. This was the favourite of them all. Laura always said 'Goodbye Yellow Brick Road' is the number one car-singing song of all time. It's got everything: falsetto vocals, sweeping harmonies and baffling lyrics about horny-backed toads.

The only thing it doesn't have is Laura singing alongside me. She always was the stronger singer; my voice sounds thin and reedy on its own, even when I turn the volume up. If I really try, I can almost see Laura as she was back then, sunglasses on, her black hair bobbed like Louise Brooks, a cigarette between her fingers. It seemed like she was always laughing when we were in the lower sixth, seventeen and just able to drive; or maybe I only think so because she stopped laughing for such a long time afterwards.

It seems so wrong to be here in California without her. I've been to America before, of course, for work; flying visits to the East Coast to interview authors and the occasional celebrity who'd written a book. I even had a long weekend in Miami once, getting spa treatments while my husband was at a conference. But the West Coast has been the final frontier – forever Laura's alone. I always thought when I came here, it would be to see her; I didn't think I'd be coming here on my own to find her instead.

There's a sign for Napa, and I make sure I'm in the right lane for the exit, though just seeing the name written there, white on a green background, makes my heart jump. For as long as Laura has lived out here, every time I've seen anything about Napa I've thought of her. It happens surprisingly often, in that way that a newly-learned word seems to appear everywhere as soon as you're aware of it. Just the existence of Napa is a reminder of my best friend, so far away. And yet I've never come out to see her, not once.

Laura's invited us a hundred times. I thought it was because she wanted to show off her life in California – the vineyards and the mountains, the skiing in the winter and the fierce sunshine of the summer. Now, here by myself, driving alone from the airport as she must have done so many times, I wonder if she was just lonely and wanting to see some familiar faces in this strange environment. I'm the only family Laura really has apart from her mother, and I always told her I was too busy. I blamed work, being pregnant, having a baby. I said the flight is too long, the dates don't work for us. But really I think, I have to admit it, a part of me was worried that if Laura saw me here – her old, old friend in this new life she's built for herself – she'd begin to wonder, as I had, what we had in common any more.

Her emails were full of stories about parties and festivals, beach trips and spontaneous weekends in Las Vegas. Mine were bright and jaunty sanitized tales of motherhood; no-one but another mother really wants to hear the bad stuff, do they? Her world was international and glamorous, mine domestic and bland. I wouldn't have swapped our lives for anything, couldn't imagine going back to a life before Linus, but it is a bigger person than me who can look at the path not taken without a single pang of regret.

It felt so much safer to keep our friendship preserved in the past – secure in do-you-remembers instead of trying to negotiate something new and uncharted. Laura could come home to see us instead, home where everything stayed the same and we slipped easily into the roles we'd occupied for decades. Sensible, settled me, and free-spirited Laura. I was so committed to my idea of her as independent and carefree and thrilled with her Californian self, that I realize now I rarely actually asked her how she was, without already priming her answers. 'Tell me about your amazing weekend in Tahoe,' I'd say. 'Who is this hot Australian you're seeing?' I only asked the questions that supported the stories I told myself about Laura. I think I so wanted to believe she was happy out here that I wouldn't give her a chance to tell me she wasn't. Maybe disappearing was the only way she knew to say that something was wrong.

There is another road running alongside this one, both heading up into the hills. Sometimes I can see it very clearly, and other times it recedes – I think it must have gone, but then it is back again. In and out of view, all the time. It makes me think that the past must be like this – always there, every strand of it running alongside you, sometimes clear, sometimes distant. Every possible life you might have led, every choice you didn't make, even if you thought it gone forever. I remember a programme I saw once, a documentary in a home for people with dementia. The residents had forgotten their husbands and their wives; they looked at their own children with incomprehension. They no longer remembered how to feed themselves, or even how to hold a spoon. But when played the music of their youth, their faces lit up with joy. Entire songs came back to them, word-perfect, and they clapped in time the hands that had been so uncoordinated just moments before.

The past is always there, always, it's just a matter of finding a way in.

POISON IVY, 1993[3]

Sylvie Cooper: I always seemed to be looking at life from the wrong side of the window.

6

When Laura first christened their sleepovers Two Virgins and a Video, back when they were thirteen, it was about the funniest thing Esther had ever heard. It sounded like a band name or a TV show, like *The Hitman and Her*. Two Vs and a V, they called it in front of their parents and when questioned as to what the Vs stood for they giggled so much that no-one made them explain it.

Like they would say 'virgin' to their parents! Or to anyone else. Not out *loud*. Everyone at Portsdown, boys and girls, knew that the only response to the question 'Are you a virgin?' was a flat denial. Even if you were eleven. That's what made it even funnier.

But now they were eighteen. Two Virgins and a Video was still factually accurate, and Esther wasn't laughing any more. When Laura sounded like she was about to say it as they walked into the Video Palace, Esther shushed her furiously and then tried to look nonchalant.

Video Palace was hardly palatial, being little more than a corner shop with a dusty carousel display of videos with an emphasis on sex and horror. Video Nasties, Esther's mother would have said, but at Laura's house Esther had watched more of them than her mother could have imagined. They'd seen all the *Nightmare on Elm Streets* and *9½ Weeks* and *Blue Velvet* and pretty much everything else.

What else were two virgins to do when Laura hadn't wanted to go out for six long months? Esther was certain that if they had been going to all the parties Laura had been invited to, neither of them would be virgins by now. Or at least, Laura wouldn't. She'd kissed boys before, lots of them, and they still rang the house to ask her out.

The two of them stood on either side of the wire video carousel and scanned the racks like they didn't already know exactly what was on them. They could have gone to Blockbuster instead, with its shelves and shelves of new releases and fridge crammed with Häagen-Dazs, but then they'd have missed the main attraction of the Video Palace. The attraction that wasn't on sale.

'Did you have a brain tumour for breakfast?' Esther asked, holding up an empty video case next to her face, like a lady in an advert.

'Not *Heathers*,' said Laura. She kept rotating the carousel as if something new would suddenly appear there.

'But,' Esther pouted, 'I love my dead gay son.'

And Laura loved films with Winona Ryder in them, ever since a guy from the High School said she looked like her at a party last year. There was a certain resemblance in the big dark eyes and the elfin dancer's frame. And also, which the guy from the High School pointed out just before Laura slapped him, the unexpectedly big breasts.

But Laura wasn't having it. 'What is your damage, Heather? Isn't five times enough? *Lost Boys*?'

'Really? I feel like I'll stab *myself* through the heart with a stake if I have to watch that again.'

'God, this is so boring. We've seen *everything*,' Laura sighed, stagily loud, like Scarlett O'Hara. It was a sigh that hoped for an audience.

She leant back on the glass-fronted cabinet of soft drinks, shrugging so that the unbuttoned neck of her floral dress slid down to expose one shoulder and a bright pink bra strap. Once she'd arranged this accident, she glanced casually across the room to see if it had been noticed.

'Oh my God, Laur, why don't you just flash your tits at him and be done with it?' said Esther.

'Shut up!' mumbled Laura, but she did pull her dress back up.

Behind the counter of the Video Palace sat Ricko Struthers, home from university for the summer, and back in his old holiday job. He looked up briefly from leafing through a copy of the *NME*, his long dark hair brushing the pages as he turned each one with a beautiful, intriguing scowl. Every girl at Portsdown had gone into mourning when he left school two years ago. His old locker had become a shrine of sorts: on passing it in the Science Block corridor, girls would briefly run their fingers over the keyed scratch of his name in wistful tribute. Even the first-years did it now, although they surely had no idea who Ricko was. Esther felt this was probably how religions began, the mindless aping of a ritual until its meanings were obscured and only the ritual remained. She wondered if she should write an essay about this – it was quite postmodern really.

Laura returned to the carousel and spun it crossly, too hard. As the wire frame wobbled on its spindly stem, videos started to fly out of the top shelf and crash onto the floor. Esther scrabbled to collect them all before anyone else came in and saw her handling the dodgiest-looking over-18 videos that the Palace had to offer.

'Laura! You've got to help me! They've gone everywhere.'

'You okay over there?' called Ricko, and they chorused yes before bursting into laughter, both of them crouched on the floor next to the Pot Noodles with their hands full of soft porn films.

The dream of Ricko hadn't faded in his absence; if anything, absence had intensified the collective obsession. During breaktimes the sixth-form girls used to gather in a shelter formed by some scrubby bushes behind the gym, furtively passing round Silk Cut as they recited their memories of him like Hail Marys. Inhale – blessed art thy heavy, expressive eyebrows that can be raised one at a time to express interest, amusement or – please not at me – contempt. Exhale – blessed art the wrinkles of thy forehead, like Christian Slater's.

'No way, look, it's Gertie,' said Laura, picking up an over-18 video that had fallen under the ice-cream freezer. 'In an "erotic thriller".'

'No, it's not,' scoffed Esther, taking it off her, but it was.

Drew Barrymore scowled on the front of the video case, in a jacket with terrible 80s shoulder pads and a tight red skirt that almost showed her knickers. A slash of bright lipstick looked incongruous on a chubby face which was still clearly recognizable as that of the cute little girl from *E.T.*

'It's a *sign*,' said Laura, eyes shining with mischief. 'It's Video Palace *destiny*. We're watching *Poison Ivy*.'

Esther tried to argue against it, but Laura was insistent. She crossed her arms, and shook her head with her eyes closed, refusing to even look at any alternatives. Not even *The Lost Boys* would sway her.

'I've seen everything else,' she said. 'I want something *different*.'

Esther stood her ground until Laura elbowed her in the ribs, nudging her towards the counter.

'Oh, I'm sorry,' she said, pretending to be a stranger. 'I didn't see you there.'

Esther shoved her back. 'Excuse me. So sorry, my mistake.'

'No, excuse *me*.' Laughing, Laura jostled her again in the direction of Ricko. 'I didn't mean to get in your way when you were going up to the *counter*.'

'You're not making me do this,' hissed Esther. 'You chose this, you have to get it out.'

'Didn't bring my Video Palace card,' said Laura, holding up her hands. 'Sorreeeee.'

'You can use mine.'

'Can't. Ricko knows who I am.'

The truly annoying thing was that she was right. All the boys knew who Laura was, and Esther knew it. Laura pushed her again, and this time Esther reluctantly let herself be propelled in the direction of the cash register.

Laura had always been persuasive, but in the last few weeks there was a new recklessness to her, a sense that she was constantly on the verge of doing something shocking. When her dad got sick she shut down, just got really thin and stopped going out. She didn't even answer the phone any more, and sometimes Esther wondered if the only reason she carried on seeing her through all of it was that their parents were friends and she couldn't escape Esther as easily as she could everyone else. But the old Laura was coming back; she couldn't stay shut in forever. Yesterday she'd shouted back at some lairy builders out of the car window, telling them to get their bums out. And the week before that she'd turned up at Esther's with a half bottle of vodka nicked from Margie – on a Tuesday – and got hammered. Esther worried that if she didn't get the video for her, Laura would show her up in some way, though she couldn't have said how.

Maybe by saying *virgin* really loudly.

That was enough to get her moving. You see, thought Esther, this was the difference between the two of them. Esther's virginity was mortifying, the shameful proof that no-one wanted to sleep with her, while Laura's was the purity of a princess in a tower, untouchable and yet desired by all. Of course she had no need to be embarrassed by it.

Esther had read *The Beauty Myth* – twice – so she understood how the patriarchy used idealized images of female beauty to punish women. She really did. But even so, sometimes, standing next to Laura, it was hard not to feel inferior.

Even though everyone at school longed for huge bouncing curls like Amanda de Cadenet's on *The Word*, hair that was styled proudly high above the scalp, so heavy it had to be flicked back away from your face with a forearm, every girl at Portsdown had sighed with envy over Laura's unfashionably straight dark bob. Other girls crimped their fringes, slept in plaits, coloured their hair with Shaders and Toners and Sun-In, but no-one ever saw Laura do so much as run a comb through hers. This was, Esther felt, the power of beauty, no matter what Naomi Wolf said: to be blessed with the gift of effortlessness, while for other girls the struggle to not be entirely and repellently hideous was all-consuming.

And if the girls felt envy, the boys felt something else altogether.

Ricko looked up, unsmiling, as Esther approached the counter, covering the video case with her hands, and hoping her stomach didn't stick out too much underneath her Wonder Stuff T-shirt. He glanced behind her, to where Laura appeared to be deeply absorbed in a display of soft drinks.

When the boys at school surrounded Laura in the fifth years' courtyard one breaktime, and sang her that song out of *Top Gun* – *you never close your eyes, any more when I kiss your liii-iiips* – half of them on their knees, arms outstretched, Ricko wasn't among them. But he was watching. Ricko never chased after girls; he never had to. He just held himself aloof enough to draw them in, like a Venus flytrap in red Converse and flannel shirts.

Esther handed Ricko the empty video case and saw one of his much-swooned-over eyebrows rise as he read the front.

'How old are you girls, anyway?' he said. She suspected he was trying not to laugh, and cursed Laura once more. 'This is an 18.'

'We *are* eighteen,' she said, mortified that he couldn't tell.

She blamed her moon face, which kept her looking aggravatingly babyish and had her turned away from Peggy Sue's the one time she'd tried to get in with Laura last year. Esther's mother always said, 'You'll be grateful when you're older, you'll want to look younger', but that was just so annoying. No-one cared about what would happen when you were *forty*; you wouldn't even be going to nightclubs then.

Ricko smirked, turning the video case over in his hands to look at the back.

'You're in the lower sixth now, yeah? I remember you.'

But he was looking over her shoulder again and Esther knew he wasn't really speaking to her.

'Er, we left,' said Esther, and then realizing that could be misunderstood, rushed to explain. 'I mean, finished, done our A-levels, I mean, not dropped out. Or moved. Just, yeah, we're just hanging out for the summer and then we're off to university. Like you – well, not like you, because neither of us is going to Manchester, I mean. I'm going to Leeds and Laura's going to Nottingham.'

There was a spark of amusement in his eyes, and he lifted one corner of his mouth into a sardonic smile. 'Well, it certainly is good to have all that information.'

Esther burned with mortification – why had she just kept on *talking* like that? Like she couldn't stop. God. Laura appeared next to her at the counter. She put a two-litre bottle of Pepsi Max by the till, and tossed her fringe away from her face with a shake of her head. She still didn't look at Ricko, but when she spoke it was for his benefit.

'I'm not going to university,' she said.

Esther turned to stare at her, but Laura wouldn't meet her eye either. Did she think *lying* was going to impress Ricko Struthers?

'Er, what? Yes, you are.'

'I'm taking a year out,' she said, so casually it was like she was talking about taking a day off instead of an entire year of her actual life. 'I deferred.'

She picked up a packet of football cards from a box next to the till and fanned herself with them, her elbows resting on the counter so Ricko could see right down the front of her dress. It was so embarrassing; it might be summer, but it wasn't even hot in the Video Palace.

'But you never said–' Esther started.

'You didn't ask,' said Laura.

But they had talked all through the sixth form about how Laura would drive over to Leeds in her orange Beetle for visits when they both started university – it wasn't even that far from Nottingham – and then they'd both graduate at the same time. Afterwards they were going to move to London and share a flat together. Of course Esther hadn't asked. It was all *planned*.

'Cool,' said Ricko. 'Going travelling?'

Laura shrugged. 'Maybe. Have to earn some money first – you know what that's like.'

Ricko laughed, and their eyes met at last. Esther felt as if she could hear a sizzle in the air between them, like cartoon lightning bolts. Ricko looked away first.

'Let me get this for you,' he said, turning his back on them as he looked for the video on the shelves that lined the back wall.

Esther made a face at Laura, who answered by crossing her eyes and sticking out her tongue. She picked up a packet of Maltesers and propped them up next to the Pepsi Max, which was unfair because she knew Esther was on a diet. Again.

When Ricko gave them their erotic thriller it was thankfully camouflaged in a generic Video Palace case. Esther handed him the money and waited for her change, while Laura twisted a strand of her dark hair around her finger and made a show of intently reading the back of the Maltesers packet like it contained mysterious and fascinating hieroglyphs about her future.

'If you girls can tear yourselves away from erotic videos tomorrow night, I'm having a party,' said Ricko as he dropped the change into Esther's palm. Laura wasn't looking at him so he said it to her instead. 'My parents are away. You should come.'

Esther glanced at Laura, aware that this was an invitation being offered through her rather than to her. Laura propped her chin on the heels of her hands and looked up at Ricko through her lashes. Esther wondered where she had learned this from, and when.

'What *kind* of a party?' she asked, as if they had hundreds of others to choose from.

Ricko's smile turned wolfish. 'It's whatever kind of party you want it to be, Laura Thomas,' he said.

She flushed red and stepped away from the counter. 'We'll think about it,' she said, with another toss of her head. 'Come on, Esther. Let's go.'

She strode away, dangling the Maltesers from her fingers, her dress billowing behind her as the door opened out onto the street.

'Bye,' Esther said to Ricko.

'Yeah,' he said, staring at the shop door, which was already swinging back from where Laura had pushed through it and gone, always one step ahead.

7

Laura insisted on holding Esther's hand when they walked into Ricko's party together. Esther didn't want to – what if people thought she was a lesbian or something? Those weird bits in *Poison Ivy*, with Drew Barrymore and the girl from *Roseanne*, were fresh in her mind. It was fine for Laura, the boys were all too busy lusting after her to question her heterosexuality, but Esther had never even been kissed. She had no proof. She didn't *feel* like she was a lesbian, but if you'd never kissed anyone how could you be sure you weren't? She felt like the Schrödinger's cat of virginity, suspended by inexperience in a state of perpetual asexuality.

They'd arrived late on purpose; Laura wouldn't let them get there until nearly ten o'clock. As soon as they turned into the close they could hear the music pounding out through the open windows and doors, and if they hadn't known already which house was Ricko's they could have identified it by the people who had spilled out from the party onto the front lawn. Although they heard calls of Laura's name as they went inside, she wouldn't let go of Esther's hand all through the hallway and the living room. She was still holding on tight when they reached the kitchen, where Ricko sat on the edge of a table, the undone laces of his Converse dangling above the brown linoleum. If he was anyone else but Ricko Struthers someone would have tied those laces together so he tripped when he stood up – they begged for it – but no-one dared. Jamie Porter was there; Esther remembered he was the one who Sarah Maxwell gave a blow-job to at a party in Hayling Island, and Joey Collins, and some others whose names she didn't know. Everyone seemed to be smoking. The air was thick with the smell of dope, and Ricko's eyes had gone all small and weird, like a hamster's.

Esther had smoked dope exactly once, seven months ago (she'd noted it in her diary), before Laura stopped going out and her own social life dried up accordingly. One of the High School boys had handed her the last burning embers of a joint in the garden of the White Horse, aka the Shite Horse, the only pub in Southsea where they never asked for ID. She'd been so happy to be acknowledged as someone worthy of receiving it – someone who looked cool enough to be smoking more than just boringly legal cigarettes that anyone could get from the newsagents – that she'd held onto it for a bit too long after her first tentative drag, waiting to see if she felt high, and she'd burned herself. Not that she admitted it, not even when a matching pair of Rice-Krispie-sized blisters mushroomed instantly and painfully between her fingers. Laura kept asking if she was okay, so everyone turned to stare at her and made it loads worse.

'Hiya,' said Ricko, his face lighting up at the sight of Laura. He slid off the table, and smiled lazily. 'You came.'

Esther felt Laura squeeze her hand tighter and it made her annoyed. She didn't need this reassurance, like she was a tame chimp being released into the wild or something; being acclimatized slowly to a frightening environment. She didn't consider that maybe it was Laura who needed the reassurance that night.

'Well, a girl can't stay in watching videos every night,' said Laura, coolly. She didn't even go red.

Ricko's lazy smile turned into a proper grin. 'Oh yeah,' he said. 'How was *Poison Ivy*? Erotic enough for you girls?'

His friends started laughing, and Ricko joined in. It wasn't an inclusive sort of amusement. Esther felt he must have told his friends about their over-18 video already, made a joke of it at their expense.

'It was awful,' said Esther haughtily, trying to look above it all. 'Not erotic at *all*.'

The boys laughed even more, guffawing and slapping their legs as if she'd said something hilarious.

It *wasn't* erotic, thought Esther crossly. Why were they laughing? In fact, horribly and unexpectedly, there was loads of stuff about a girl's mother dying. Esther couldn't even look at Laura in those bits, knowing her dad was in the next room. No-one said Laura's dad was dying, but no-one had to. He didn't have a movie disease like the mother in the film, looking beautiful and tragic; he had the real kind, that made him lose all his hair, that bloated him with steroids. And sometimes he smelled, actually smelled of shit from the colostomy bag, and didn't even seem to notice. It was so awful – he tried to act like everything was normal, teasing them about school and boys, and Esther hated herself for not being able to be normal back.

Laura let go of her hand and joined in the boys' laughter, throwing her head back, as if she too thought Esther had said something brilliantly funny. When the laughing had subsided, Laura spoke in a low voice, and all the boys leaned forward to hear her.

'*I* thought it was kind of sexy, actually.' She dropped her eyes to the kitchen floor and caught her bottom lip with her front teeth, as if she had admitted more than she meant to.

But Esther knew she had done it completely on purpose. It was a move straight from the film – the only difference was there wasn't any brown lino in *Poison Ivy*, or any Ricko Struthers. She nearly gasped out loud at the treachery of it. The film wasn't even slightly erotic, they had howled with laughter through all the sex scenes – hiding behind pillows, pointing and shrieking at the corny blue lighting and grand pianos and the flabby buttocks of the old man Drew had been shagging. He wore a toupée, for God's sake – how could Laura say she found it sexy?

'Yeah?' said Ricko softly, moving a little closer to Laura, separating himself from the pack.

'Maybe it's just me,' said Laura, lifting her chin and looking at him directly. 'I'm very suggestible. So, what are we drinking?'

Esther never got to find out, because Ricko draped his arm possessively over Laura and led her away, whispering in her ear. She didn't look back. Esther waited for a minute, hoping that one of the other boys might talk to her, but they all turned to each other and resumed their conversations as if she wasn't there. She and Laura had drunk a cocktail of spirits before they came out – a little splash from each bottle in her parents' drinks cabinet, all topped up with orange juice to hide the taste. It was enough to give a buzz, but she could feel it wearing off, and she knew she would need to be drunk to get through the rest of the night on her own.

There was an open bottle of vodka on the kitchen draining board, and a load of dusty Panda Pops that she'd last seen on the offers shelf at the Video Palace. As she tipped the vodka bottle into a plastic cup, she realized it was nearly empty. She shook it to get the last drops out and then she felt it snatched from her hand.

'Shit McGinty, don't tell me we're out of vodka?' declared a posh voice.

Esther started in surprise as Amelia Wentworth held the bottle between them accusingly. Amelia swayed as she scanned the array of bottles for a replacement. Even though they'd gone to the same state school, Amelia had cultivated a voice that wouldn't have put her out of place at Roedean. If she wasn't so pretty she'd never have got away with being such a fake.

'Call this a fucking party?' Amelia said. She grabbed Esther's arm and laughed far too loudly. Esther realized she was very drunk. 'No vodka? Panda Pops? Plastic cups? Are we seven years old? I said call this a party? Wait a minute. I know you.'

Amelia's delicate nose wrinkled with the drunken effort of placing Esther, and she staggered backwards. She put one painted fingernail to her lips, as if considering, then cackled loudly and shrieked.

'Hahaaaa, just kidding, Fester, who's gonna forget you? Did Laura bring you? Where *is* that bitch? I haven't seen her for fucking ever.'

Esther mumbled something about Ricko. Amelia had called her Fester in front of everyone, in front of all those boys. Maybe no-one had heard – she wasn't about to go round the room with a clipboard checking – but *she'd* heard, and that was bad enough. Amelia had never actually bullied her when they were at school, never done anything worse than not really have any interest in her. Somehow it was worse to hear the hated insult from an unexpected source.

'She's with *Ricko?*' said Amelia, looking disgusted. 'God, I wouldn't have thought sloppy seconds were her style, would you? If you lined up all the girls Ricko's shagged you'd have a bridge over to the Isle of fucking Wight.'

Esther stared as Amelia grabbed a bottle of Thunderbird and drank straight from the neck, wiping her mouth with the back of her hand when she'd finished. Was she really going to call her Fester, call her the worst possible name, and then think they'd just segue straight into a chummy conversation about Ricko Struthers? Esther shrugged by way of an answer.

Amelia leaned close, and cackled again. 'And I'd be *on* it, Fester, I'd be right on it with the rest of them. But at least I can say I was young enough not to know better, can't I?'

'My name's not Fester,' Esther said quietly.

'What?' bellowed Amelia. She cupped her hand to her ear like an old lady.

'My name isn't Fester.'

Amelia frowned. 'Isn't it? But that's what everyone calls you – isn't it like a nickname?'

'No. It's Esther.'

'Oh, right,' Amelia shrugged, and looked around the

room, unperturbed. 'Sorry, I'm useless with names. Total idiot, *drunk* idiot. Esther. Esther Esther Esther. Got it. Here, have a Thunderbird.'

Amelia sloshed a measure into a plastic cup and pressed it into Esther's hand. Esther didn't drink it straight away. She was still thinking about what Amelia had just said. Could it really be that people like Amelia and Sarah didn't actually call her Fat Fester? Might they truly just think Fester was a jokey nickname amongst friends? Did Amelia see her not as a figure of fun, but as Laura's friend, someone you might talk to at a party? Have a drink with?

'But where have you beeeeeeeen?' asked Amelia. She leant heavily back on the sink and drank from the bottle again. 'You and Laura – I must've called her a million times since exams finished.'

There it was again – you and Laura. Not just Laura.

'Oh, she's had some family stuff going on,' said Esther warily. She didn't know how much Laura had told people about her dad.

Amelia grimaced. 'Families. Nightmare.' She sloshed more Thunderbird into Esther's cup, and clashed the bottle against it. 'Well, Esther, ESTHER, it's good to see you two bitches back.'

By the time Amelia passed out on Mr and Mrs Struthers' bed, she and Esther had drunk the entire bottle of Thunderbird and half of the Lambrusco. And Esther was well on her way to actually enjoying Ricko's party. She didn't need Laura, she had talked to loads of people, not just Amelia but Sarah Maxwell and Joey Collins and some of Ricko's friends from university who'd come down especially.

But now she felt a bit sick. So she pushed her way through the crowds in the kitchen and stumbled out into the garden for air. She wasn't alone. A tangle of limbs lying down on the garden bench suggested an unidentifiable snogging couple, and beyond them some of the boys were playing a game of football in the weak light from the kitchen window. It mostly seemed to consist of tackling each other drunkenly into the flowerbeds, and chanting 'Lin-e-ke-er' at appropriate intervals. They glanced up when the door opened, saw Esther, and then went back to their game.

Sometimes Esther felt glad she was invisible to boys like that; she remembered the thrown chips back when she was in the fifth year, and knew that invisibility was a better alternative. Perhaps this was maturity, she thought, to accept this about oneself instead of wishing it was different. She knew now that she would never be a Laura. There were two white plastic chairs underneath the window and she lowered herself into the nearest one, holding the arms carefully, unsure of her legs after all the Thunderbird. Or maybe it was the Lambrusco. Just before Amelia passed out they'd been mixing them together – Thunbrusco, Lambird. She giggled and a loud hiccup caught her by surprise as the back door opened again.

A shadow turned its head to look at her.

'You okay?'

Esther hiccupped again, and nodded, not trusting herself to speak.

The shadow detached itself from the square of light at the doorway and came towards her. It was a tall, thin boy with hair longer than Esther's own, and an amused look on his narrow face.

'This seat taken?'

Esther shook her head and held out her hand in the circus ringmaster gesture that means *please, take it*. She was holding her breath and swallowing to make the hiccups go away.

The boy stretched his long legs out in front of him when he'd sat down. Esther didn't know him – he was tall enough to be distinctive, she'd have remembered. He had a bit of an accent; Northern, she thought. He reached into a pocket in his combat trousers and pulled out a packet of tobacco and some Rizlas.

'Never met a mute before,' he said, and Esther couldn't help herself, she let out all the air in her lungs in a burst of laughter and hiccups.

'Hiccups,' she said, pointing at her throat idiotically. What did she do that for? But he just smiled and carried on building his joint, pulling a little corner off the Rizla packet and rolling it up on his lap.

When he'd finished he lit up and leaned back, his head against the kitchen wall, blowing a plume of smoke from his pursed lips like he was kissing the night sky. Esther stared at his profile until he turned to look at her, raising his eyebrows quizzically.

'Want some?' he asked, and Esther nodded again.

She was at Ricko Struthers's party. She'd hung out with Amelia and Sarah as an equal. And now she was sharing an actual joint with a boy who hadn't sneered and walked off as soon as he'd seen her sitting there. Tonight she felt not only like she had every right to be here, but like she'd always had the right, like the invitation had been there in her pocket all along, and she'd only just noticed it.

'Are you at university with Ricko?' Esther asked, politely passing the joint back after only a few draws.

He smirked. 'I do like a nicely brought up girl. At least you didn't ask me what I do.'

Esther felt wrong-footed: she had said the wrong thing, and she didn't know how.

'Oh, don't make that face,' he said, laughing. 'I'm just kidding. Yeah, I'm at Manchester with him. You know him from school?'

'Yes. Well, through my friend Laura.'

'Laura?' he squinted at her with interest, smoke rising up from the joint between them. 'That one dancing on the table? She's your friend?'

Esther felt herself freeze. She'd caught glimpses of Laura all night, always with Ricko's arm around her like a headlock. Downing shots and singing along to the music in the living room. She had steadfastly ignored her, waiting for an apology that never came. But now she thought about it, she hadn't seen her for ages. More than an hour.

'On the table?'

The boy whistled before he answered, the sort of whistle builders did from their vans at girls like Laura, and never at girls like Esther. 'She looks pretty wild, your friend Laura.'

'Wait – it might not be her. Laura Chelwood's here, I saw her, maybe it's her. What did she look like?'

'Dark hair. Short, like.' He raised his hand, horizontal against his jaw to show exactly where Laura's bob stopped. 'Miniskirt. Pink bra.'

'Pink bra!' exclaimed Esther, disgusted. 'God, trust a boy to notice her *underwear*.'

'Hard not to,' said the boy, laconically. 'Seeing as she had her top off.'

Oh shit. *Shit*. She pushed the chair away from her as she staggered upright, hearing the plastic legs scrape on the concrete like nails on a blackboard. She should have known Laura would do something like this. She'd felt it bubbling up for days and done nothing. It wasn't normal to just shut yourself away for months on end and not expect trouble afterwards. Laura was the leak you ignored for months, until you found everything underwater.

Esther had to force herself into the living room, so packed was it with bodies cheering and clapping, their backs to her as they watched something or someone in the middle. The music was loud enough that she could hear her whole body pulsing with it, the floor seemed to bounce with feet stamping in time. It was all men in here: suddenly she didn't think of them as boys, they felt big and threatening, and all of them were so much taller than her that she couldn't see what they were looking at. But over their heads she saw a swirl of patterned fabric being waved. Esther knew that pattern. She knew that top. She was with her the day she bought it in Pilot. Shit.

There was a roar as the top was flung into the crowd, and hands reached up to grab it. She pushed harder now, she didn't care any more about being invisible or being cool, or anything other than getting to Laura. Angry faces turned on her, she was shoved back but she kept going. The singing had stopped and the crowd started baying, 'Off! Off! Off!'

At last she broke through and there was Laura, eyes half-closed on a low coffee table in the centre of the room, her hair stringy with sweat and her eyeliner running in streaks down her face. Jamie Porter was using her top to whip at her legs as he led the chanting. Laura swayed on the table, and took an uncertain step to the left, and the boys cheered as she righted herself. Elated at her renewed balance, Laura dipped her knees and dropped one of her bra straps down her shoulder.

'Off! Off! Off!' Jamie led the chant again, pumping his clenched fist in the air.

'Laura!' Esther shouted, and Laura stopped and looked around, confused. Then she looked down and a silly smile smeared itself across her face.

'Esther!' She bent down to fling her arms around her, and Esther could smell vomit in her hair. 'Esther, where you been? I missed you.'

'Get out of the way, you fat bitch,' one of the men snapped, pulling at Esther's shoulder and dragging her away from Laura.

'Hey, thass my friend,' slurred Laura.

'Laura, get down!' shouted Esther. 'Get down, we're going home.'

Laura shook her head so hard she nearly fell again, toppling into a sea of hands that helped her up. She smiled sweetly at them for helping, and then at Esther.

'I don't wanna go home,' she said, pouting. 'Don't be boring.'

'Yeah, Esther, don't be fucking boring,' shouted Jamie Porter. 'She's having a great time, leave her alone.'

Esther felt the crowd turn against her, jostling aggressively and trying to push her back away from the table. She looked desperately for someone who might help – Amelia was passed out upstairs, and there was no sign of Sarah, but what about the boy from outside? Or Ricko? He must want to help, he wouldn't want to see Laura do this. But there he was, just standing there at the back of the room, angled against the wall and smiling, actually smiling. He'd looked just the same when all the boys sang at Laura back at school – it was a bit of fun, nothing serious, but not something he'd lower himself to. Esther caught his eye, trying to get his help, and his smile didn't falter. He looked straight through her.

Esther looked back to the table. Laura's hands were behind her back now, on the clasp of her bra, and the chants were getting louder. She turned nearly all the way around, smiling her sloppy smile, with her hands unmoving on the clasp. Then she stopped. Her face went pale and serious, like she was trying to remember something. The crowd flinched momentarily and then surged forward when her smile returned, and she started her clumsy dance again. But it gave Esther an idea.

'She's going to be sick!' she shouted.

'No'm not,' objected Laura, but she staggered again and Esther caught her this time, clutching her tight as she fell from the coffee table.

'She's fine,' hissed Jamie, pushing his way towards them, his big red face right up close to theirs.

Laura gasped, and started crying. 'Don't *shout*, Jamie,' she wailed.

'She is, I know she is,' said Esther, as loudly as she could, so everyone would hear. 'She always cries right before she pukes, she's done it since she was little. Step back, *back* before she gets it everywhere.'

Jamie glared at her, suspecting she was lying but too worried about being thrown up on to risk it. The crowds parted like the Red Sea, and Esther led Laura, as floppy and unresisting as a sleeping puppy, to the front door. She only realized that she'd forgotten to pick up Laura's top when she heard the door slam behind them.

'*Not* gonna be sick,' Laura said weakly, sinking down to sit on the lawn. Behind her Esther could see the faces of the people inside, crowded at the window to see what was happening. 'Not gonna be sick, Est. Already *been* sick.'

'I know,' said Esther. She took the flannel shirt that was tied around her waist and put it on Laura gently, one arm at a time, like she was a child who didn't know how to get dressed.

'Sick on *Ricko*,' said Laura, crying even more as Esther did up the buttons one by one. 'In his *bedroom*.'

'Good,' said Esther.

It took a long time to walk back. Once she stopped crying, Laura made two futile attempts to return to the party. The second one ended with her lying in a municipal flowerbed with her legs twisted up in a swinging fence chain, and from then on she meekly leaned on Esther and was silent the rest of the way.

They were nearly at Laura's house when she mumbled into Esther's shoulder.

'What?' said Esther, tensing in case she was going to be sick again.

Laura lifted her head up. 'No more Two Vs and a V nights, Est.'

'Okay,' she agreed. 'We'll go out more, it's a good idea. We've been in a lot.'

'No.' Laura stopped still, wavering a little in the sickly orange light of a lamppost that cast her eyes into deep shadow. She frowned with the drunken effort of making herself understood.

'No – I mean we *did it*, Est. Before I was sick. Me and Ricko Struthers.'

'Oh,' said Esther.

'I *know*,' said Laura. She grinned suddenly. It was as if, now she thought about it, with her eyeliner streaming down her face and vomit in her hair, it had been a very successful evening altogether.

'I'm not a V any more,' she said.

Of course you're not, thought Esther, trudging onwards, leaving Laura to catch up with her. You're barely even Laura Thomas any more. Gertie's all grown up now, and turned into Poison Ivy.

8

October 2013

Have you ever played that game What I Think You Do All Day? Laura and I played it when she was back at Christmas, the week I'd gone on maternity leave. We sat together on the sofa, with our bare feet resting on the little stool in front of the fire, and I tried not to notice that hers were tanned and pedicured, while mine were pale and swollen like the underside of a fish. It wasn't just the two of us, of course. My enormous stomach rose up from the sofa, and Laura rested her head on it to see if the baby would oblige by poking her with an elbow or a foot. But we already knew what the baby did all day. Not much.

I'd played the game with friends before, on a villa holiday in Puglia, all of us shrieking with indignation at the assumptions and misunderstandings. Everyone thought I just sat at my desk and read books all day, apparently, and went to parties in the evenings where men with goatee beards stroked their chins and talked urgently of iambic pentameter. One mother stormed off to bed when her husband guessed she spent most of the day eating cake and denting the car. No-one really understood what the bankers did all day, even some of the bankers.

I thought playing a game like that would help me to really understand what Laura's life was like in California, since it felt so far away and foreign. Don't they say that it's what you do every day that tells you who you are? It's not the label that's truly revealing – winemaker, journalist, banker – but the details underneath it. Now, though, I think that all I did was highlight, with each precise detail, the differences between us.

Laura was confident that now I wasn't working, I must spend my days lovingly folding small white babygros in the newly-painted nursery until my husband came home bearing a bunch of flowers for the mother of his unborn child, which made me splutter and protest. It wasn't her fault, though. We hadn't talked much about me being pregnant; I think we were both a little afraid. I was too superstitious to believe it was happening until I saw the baby in my arms, and Laura – well, I don't know what she felt. I worried that she might feel left behind, as I once had done when it seemed like her life was taking her somewhere I couldn't go. I was wary of talking too much about it, in case it felt like I was showing off. In case it put more distance between us.

For all my indignation, I did even worse. I blame that picture Laura sent me from Napa in her first harvest season, the one where she's standing in a huge metal vat half-full of grapes, wearing yellow oilskin trousers that come nearly up to her neck. She is laughing, splattered with juice, and she holds her purple palms up to the camera, fingers outstretched in jazz hands. 'You think I went to college and did a degree to just *tread on grapes*?' she kept saying, outraged at my assumptions. And then she bombarded me with science – malic acids and enzymes and sugar levels and yeasts. She talked about test tubes and pipettes and testing parameters. So now when I think of Laura at work, I'm afraid I still think of the oilskin trousers – I can't help myself – but over the top of them I imagine she is wearing a pristine white laboratory coat.

This is what happens when you live thousands of miles apart. You only know about the big things – the telling details all get lost, and that is why I'm struggling to work out what might have happened to Laura. We played that game nearly a year ago. That was the last time we sat down together and talked face to face in the same room. And now that I really need to know the details, I can hardly remember what she said.

What strikes me now is that when I asked about her life, what she talked of mostly was work. That was always her focus. I know she mentioned a relationship back then, nothing serious (it never was), but she ended it soon after she got back to California and I don't remember his name now. It wouldn't surprise me if Laura didn't either.

In the months since we played that game together my life has changed so much that I hardly recognize it. Perhaps Laura's has too.

I know nothing of her day-to-day any more, really. I've seen the inside of her living room in the background of a Skype conversation, but I couldn't pick out the house she lives in if it appeared on a news bulletin. Does she know her neighbours? I don't know what car she drives to work. I don't know where she goes out – is there some regular place she visits where they might know what's happened to her? What does she do after work? Who does she do it with? When you lose the details, you don't know what questions to ask. You miss the signals that might tell you something is wrong.

And then there is the detail of what she is doing now, day to day, since she disappeared.

The landscape is adding to the unsettling sense that this American Laura is unknown to me. I was sure I'd recognize California somehow, even though I've never been here – I've seen Laura's photographs on Facebook, I've watched everything from *L.A. Story* to *Baywatch*, surely it would all be familiar? And yet it's not. It's not like I thought I'd be rollerblading on Venice Beach or anything; I knew I was going inland, but my mind turned to Yosemite, Joshua Tree; landscapes of magnificent natural beauty. No-one ever said that all the rolling hills above San Francisco would be covered in wind turbines. Or that from the freeway you can see nothing more scenic than massive superstores called things like Staples and Trader Joe's. And it's cold. Not as cold as back in London, but colder than I thought California would be. As I turn the car temperature up, it makes me wonder what else I might be wrong about.

When I emailed to tell Laura I was coming to California I hadn't even booked the flights, so sure was I that just the threat of it would make her break her silence. I was certain she'd tell me not to come, say I mustn't possibly leave Linus behind on her account, but she didn't. Or she couldn't. I don't want to turn into Margie, who is now all but certain that Laura is manacled in the basement of a crazed maniac, but it's impossible not to think the worst. What if Laura *can't* answer? What if she wants to, but someone or something is preventing her? The longer it goes without any word, the closer I edge towards joining Margie in her paranoid Cold War bunker.

It's getting dark by the time the automated voice of the satnav directs me to turn left for the final time. I want a bath now, and a bed. I want to call home, even though I can't – it's well past midnight in London now.

The motel Stanley recommended is at one of those American addresses that are all but incomprehensible to Europeans, just a list of numbers; an equation rather than a direction. He said everywhere else was booked up at this time of year. The only other places available were four hundred dollars a night.

I suppose I could have spent that, if I'd wanted to. It's only two nights. If I was coming here on holiday I know we'd happily have blown the budget on one of the posh boutique hotels of which Napa seems to have an abundance. But it felt wrong to think about high thread counts and free toiletries at a time like this. A cheap motel feels like a penance, and a spur. There will be no luxuriating in bubble baths, or hot stone massages. There will be only an incentive to get out and find my friend and get back home to my family as fast as I can. If only all the old Spanish missions out here hadn't been turned into wineries I could have found myself a spartan monk's cell for the truly penitent experience. As it is, this place feels like punishment enough.

The Sonoma Motel turns out to have put most of its emphasis on the motor part of its name, being at first glance nearly all car park, with a two-storey horseshoe-shaped fringe of rooms around the edge. It has a sign that must be straight from the Sixties, angular with the name picked out in contrasting pastels, back from the days when driving was a glamorous activity and motels the last word in modern living. You could imagine Rock Hudson and Doris Day motoring into the car park on some madcap adventure. You could also imagine this place has not been decorated since they left. It's not that it's awful, exactly, more that it's so obviously faded that it can't even claim to be nostalgic; just neglected.

I park the rental car in a corner of the wide tarmac courtyard which has, incongruously, a small kidney-shaped swimming pool in the middle, just in case you'd ever longed to go for a dip surrounded by pick-up trucks and exhaust fumes.

Another assumption is shot down in flames when I go to the check-in desk: I had been led to believe that all Americans would find my accent charming and remarkable, but when I say hello the tired-looking woman at reception barely glances away from the television that is mounted up near the ceiling, showing a local weather report.

I give her the confirmation email and she reaches behind her for the key without looking, an automatic gesture she must have done a hundred times, and then stops to frown. She turns to see what is in the way of her grasping hand and when she twists back from the wall of pigeonholes, she holds a brown padded envelope as well as the room key.

'This you?' she asks with suspicion, reading my name very deliberately and looking from me to the envelope and back again, as if she expects she will have to repeat it to the police later, when they burst in to arrest me.

'Yes,' I say, brightly, holding out my hand for the package. 'Thank you.'

She stares back without handing it over.

I'm not used to this. I've been spoiled by the kind of hotel that greets me by name, by doormen who take your bags, by, let's face it, a husband who usually deals with this sort of shit. He knows how to charm a grumpy receptionist, and how much to tip the person who shows you to your room, not that there's any sign of that happening here. He knows how to coax room service when the kitchen is already shut, though it looks very much like the closest this place gets to catering is the vending machine outside, which promises hot *and* cold drinks.

'Is there a problem?' I ask. I make my voice frosty and British, as intimidating as possible, but I've never been much good at this sort of thing. I've spent too long wanting people to like me to be convincing as a bitch now. Perhaps you have to be born into it, like my mother-in-law.

'Two nights?' the receptionist asks. Her small eyes are made even smaller by her squinty suspicion and, as she squeezes the envelope, blatantly trying to work out what's inside, I can see that her meaty fingers have left damp marks on the paper.

I nod. I want to snatch the packet away from her but I won't give her the satisfaction of seeing me beg for it. I'm sure it's from Laura. It has to be. Who else would have left something for me at the front desk of a motel in Napa? I gave her the address, I told her when I'd be here. If she can't face emailing me, maybe she has written.

I try to be patient while the receptionist inspects my

passport and driving licence with maddening slowness. It takes longer to pass her security checks than it did to get through customs at the airport. Only when she is satisfied that she has everything short of a retinal scan does she hand over the envelope and the key to my room.

She narrows her eyes at the packet. I wonder if she thinks it's drugs or something. I won't give her the satisfaction of opening it in front of her, nosy cow, so I tuck it under my arm as if it's all the same to me whether I open it now or in a few days' time.

I'm almost tearful when I get outside. The confrontation has unsettled me. It's jet lag, I know that. And stress, probably, from leaving Linus and from worry. But it's also relief, because if Laura's left me something then she must be okay, mustn't she? For the first time I admit to myself that my greatest fear is not that someone has done something awful to Laura, but that she might have done something to herself. I haven't said so to anyone, as if to say it out loud might make it real. And I'd never voice any suspicion to Margie without proof – she has enough conspiracy theories to fret about already. But if dead men tell no tales, dead women leave no Jiffy bags at seedy motel receptions.

Under the artificial light of the car park the handwriting is hard to read. It doesn't look like Laura's, but I cling to my hope – handwriting can change, can't it? It could be that along with saying 'washroom' and 'awesome', Laura has also picked up a different way of writing. Heightened emotion can change your writing. But I think I know before I open it that nothing short of a hand transplant could have changed Laura's handwriting from its usual scrawl into the neat copperplate cursive that spells my name.

When I lift the flap of the envelope and reach inside, my fingers close around a set of keys.

SCREAM, 1996[4]

SIDNEY PRESCOTT: But this is life. This isn't a movie.
BILLY: Sure it is, Sid. It's all a movie. It's all one great big movie. [pauses] Only, you can pick your genre.

9

Ricko Struthers was at Laura's dad's funeral, dressed in a black suit and a skinny black tie like he'd popped in on his way to the bank heist in *Reservoir Dogs*. What was he doing here?

Perhaps it wasn't as weird as it seemed, thought Esther, sat between her sister and her mum on a hard wooden pew at the front of the church. There were lots of people from school here. Katie Long was over by the font with her parents, and behind her were some of the girls Laura had been with on the netball team. Amelia Wentworth and Sarah Maxwell had come together, massively overdressed in black suits and heels and sunglasses. Sarah even had a ribbon choker on, like she was going to a party instead of a funeral. They waved at her across the aisle and she waved back hesitantly, glancing at her mother to see if this was allowed.

It wasn't so much Ricko's presence that was odd, she decided, craning her neck to look towards the church entrance, it was the way he was acting. Standing at the door with Esther's own father and a couple of other older men in their naval uniforms, handing out orders of service, guiding people to pews. He was acting like an old, old friend, or even a member of the family.

He'd given a little start of surprise when she came into the church, but Esther was used to that lately. And then he opened his mouth as if he was about to say something, but of course her dad came rushing over as soon as he saw they'd arrived, and took them to their pew. So she couldn't have asked Ricko, even if it was polite to: why are you here?

She had been thinking of Laura the night that Edward died. She'd gone with Jane and Claire to see *Scream* at the university Film Society, and they'd stayed for the discussion afterwards, led by an eager postgraduate with a woven ethnic waistcoat and matching skullcap. Jane wrote notes next to her – exams were over, but the habit was hard to break – and Claire sat with her head attentively cocked, but Esther didn't listen much. She picked at her flaking blue nail polish and thought about Drew Barrymore, and decided she'd call Laura when they got home, ask if she was still insistent on being Gertie now that meant being murdered in the first ten minutes of the film.

But when they got back to the house, one of the boys had left a note Sellotaped to the house phone in the hallway so she couldn't miss it.

ESTHER!!!!!!!
CALL YOUR MUM!!!!!!!! ED DIED (SORRY).

For a moment she wasn't sure who Ed was, though she had been expecting this call for years now. He had always been Edward to her. She had a strange sense of being outside herself, of observing herself taking in the news, while next to her Jane read the note over her shoulder and asked if she was okay.

Esther nodded, but she was surprised to find that she was shocked. Hadn't Edward been given twelve months to live back when she was at school? No-one had ever imagined he could live this long – nearly three years. And yet the news of his death in her hand, in green felt-tip letters, the reality of it after so many false alarms, was almost as shocking to her at that moment as if he had died suddenly in a car crash.

Was this how Laura felt? Had she known that this time was different? Did she and Margie understand that this wasn't another one of the crises that saw Edward rushed into hospital and then, miraculously, terribly, brought back home to continue dying?

Esther still didn't know how Laura felt, even now, sat here waiting for her father to be buried. The phone was engaged every time she'd tried to call from university, and when she got home her dad said to just leave it, Laura and Margie had so many other things to think about right now. Esther's mum had sorted out the food for the wake, her dad was giving the eulogy and was the executor of the will. Next to the practical adult efficiency of her parents, Esther had become a child again, dependent and passive, riding in the back of the family car and squabbling with her sister like they'd never left home. Esther knew her dad was right, that it was selfish of her to expect a response from someone who had just lost a parent, but it didn't make her feel any better to arrive at the funeral without having spoken to her best friend.

When Laura and Margie came into the church with Edward's aged parents, following the coffin, it was Ricko who led them to the front pew. And when he'd done so, he sat down next to Laura, just like that. Esther nearly gasped out loud. Sophie pinched her leg, and cast her eyes over at Laura and Ricko – *did you know?*

No, she didn't. All the hormonal passion she had once felt for him, as a teenager who didn't know any better, had curdled into dislike at his party all those years ago. And when he ignored Laura afterwards, turning his back on her in the Shite Horse just a week later to laugh with his friends, her dislike calcified into loathing. She wasn't a silly schoolgirl any more, easily impressed by a good-looking older boy. Esther was twenty-one, an adult. She knew about Life these days. She knew about Men. By which she meant she wasn't a virgin any more.

The funeral passed quickly. Esther's father delivered the eulogy with a military briskness that thankfully precluded mass weeping, and she only knew it was difficult for him by the whiteness of his knuckles as he held onto the lectern. The vicar talked for a long time about God, and Esther, who was an atheist, felt it was Too Much. Margie stared mutely in front of her through all of it, as if she didn't hear a word. *Tranquillizers*, Esther's mother mouthed to her daughters when she saw them looking. Only when the final hymn was played did Margie begin to cry. She cried as a statue might, stony-faced and quite still, while tears poured down her face like rain. It was the sailor's hymn, and as Esther tried to sing the words she felt her throat thicken so that no sound came out. *Oh hear us when we pray to thee, for those in peril on the sea.*

She knew Edward almost as well as she knew her own father. There were times when she was little that she'd accidentally called him Daddy when her own was away at sea. He had sat in his Vauxhall Astra outside village halls waiting to pick her and Laura up from parties, knowing (unlike her own dad) that he should stay in the car and not embarrass them by coming in. He did the *Telegraph* crossword every morning. He loved sailing. And now he was gone forever.

Her mother passed her a tissue without being asked, and only then did Esther realize she was crying. It felt like she was grieving not just for Edward, and for Laura, but for the illusion she had held until then that somehow these things happened to other people. She had thought that Edward's death was bad luck, a terrible tragedy arriving from nowhere, but now she saw that it was worse than that; it was inevitable. She understood that at some point in the future this hymn would be sung at her own father's funeral. That she and Sophie would be the ones in the front pew, and that there was no escape from it.

Laura, as ever, was just the one who did it first.

Back at the Thomases' house, Esther's mother ran around the kitchen like six people at once. Too busy for weeping, she tore cling film off trays of prepared sandwiches in the kitchen, and emptied crisps into bowls. Esther felt like a waitress rather than a mourner, circulating with the plates that her mother had pressed efficiently into her hands.

Some of the guests just took sandwiches without noticing her, others paused their conversation to ask polite questions about university, or to compliment her father's eulogy. Esther kept to the back rooms where the older people had congregated, letting Sophie do the front room, where their own friends had ended up. It was as if the party had been segregated, she decided gravely. Esther, with her new awareness of mortality, had chosen to side with those who were nearer to the end. Though she wouldn't have said so to their faces; she imagined it wouldn't go down that well.

'Oh hi, Commander Betts, may I offer you a cucumber sandwich to go with your impending sense of DEATH?'

Margie had been put to bed with more of the pills her doctor had prescribed, leaving Laura as the sole representative of the family other than her father's parents, who were mutely huddled together on the sofa. She was in constant demand, thanking people for coming, saying goodbyes, listening to stories of her father that guests were suddenly driven to share with her, as if only her ears could validate them.

Esther still hadn't spoken more than a few words to her, but as she watched Laura circulate politely around the wake, she winced at how pale and angular she was in her funereal black. Grief seemed to have sharpened all of the bones under her skin, and her hair was cut short now, like a boy's, which made her red-rimmed eyes look enormous. She moved through the crowds with a sense of being apart from all of them, gracefully elevated by mourning. It made Esther think of Jackie Kennedy after JFK was shot. Only Jackie wasn't followed everywhere she went by Ricko Struthers.

He stood just behind her, one hand on the small of her back, and when he judged she had been talking to one person for long enough he would offer a few excusing words and move her on to the next guest. Esther could not understand if this was something Laura had asked him to do, to save her from the unrestrained grief of others, or if he had chosen to do it. Either way, he stood between Laura and anything other than the briefest of exchanges with her guests. Esther, hampered by her sandwich plates, tried repeatedly to get near enough for a proper conversation, only to find herself facing Ricko's back or Laura's as he ushered her considerately away.

When at last she got close, and saw Laura's mouth open in greeting, her way was promptly blocked by friends of her mother's, exclaiming over her weight while their beringed fingers grasped at the salmon and cucumber triangles. She felt as if she was in a very polite, domestic version of *Gladiators*, trying to get to the finish line against the clock while everyone around her leapt out with foam cudgels, determined to hold her back.

At last she admitted defeat and retreated into the corridor with her almost-empty plates. But even there she was not safe.

'Fuck me,' said Amelia Wentworth, grabbing a sandwich as she appeared out of the front room. 'Let's have one of these, I'm starving. When did you get so *thin*, Esther?'

Amelia and Sarah looked like they had learned how to dress for a funeral entirely from Hollywood movies. Their skirts were short, and their sunglasses were now pushed up on their heads. Amelia had red lipstick on.

'Yeah, God, I barely recognized you in the church,' said Sarah Maxwell. 'No offence.'

Since she'd lost weight, Esther had frequently fantasized about seeing her old school friends again. It would happen after she'd graduated, when everyone was home for the summer. The pub would hush as everyone turned round to see her; jaws would drop. The memory of Fat Fester would be permanently erased from the collective memory. She had never imagined it would happen at Laura's dad's funeral, and now it felt all wrong and tainted to be commented on like this.

'What happened?' pressed Amelia, through a mouthful of tuna mayonnaise sandwich. 'How did you do it? I'm *dying* to lose five pounds.'

'You can't say dying at a *funeral*!' hissed Sarah, swatting at her arm. 'Oh my God, what is *wrong* with you? But seriously, how did you?'

Esther had thought this through long before she came home. Weight Watchers was not cool. She hadn't even admitted to her university friends that she went to meetings every Tuesday night – they thought she went to the library. Not that that was cool either, but at least it wasn't actively humiliating. The important thing was to control the narrative, she felt. How she presented her weight loss was crucial – no-one needed to hear 'my fat girl struggle'. She had decided it was best presented as if this was her natural size – it was her old, larger self who had been the impostor.

'It just kind of fell off,' she shrugged, as if it had happened without her noticing. Without her noting every point in her Weight Watchers notebook, and tracking her measurements obsessively.

'Was it drugs?' said Sarah. 'One girl at college lost *so* much weight when she started taking speed.'

Esther smiled a Mona Lisa smile which she hoped suggested conspiratorial agreement. She had never been offered speed in her life.

'Ugh,' said Amelia, curling her lip. 'Speed's a dirty drug. I only ever take pills. Don't you?'

'Have you seen Laura?' asked Sarah, ignoring her. 'We've got to go and I've not even spoken to her yet.'

'Me neither,' said Esther, looking over her shoulder to see if Laura was maybe behind her. 'She's kind of busy talking to all her dad's friends, I think.'

'And what the fuck is Ricko Struthers doing following her around like a bodyguard?' asked Amelia. 'I mean, it's one thing to *lose* it to him, but since when were those two actually together?'

Sarah huddled in closer, and lowered her voice.

'Well, I was just talking to some of her friends from Oddbins.'

'Oddbins?' asked Amelia.

'God, Meels, you have a brain like a fucking colander. Do you retain *any* information? She's been working there *forever*,' said Sarah, with exasperation. 'It was meant to be a summer job, but then her dad and everything . . .'

'Shit, yeah, sorry.' Amelia slapped her forehead apologetically. 'Idiot.'

'Apparently he just started coming in, every day, would only be served by Laura.'

'Attractive,' said Esther. 'The alcoholic seduction.'

'What's he doing now?' asked Amelia. 'Since uni, I mean? He must have graduated by now.'

'God knows,' said Sarah. 'I heard he's back living with his mum and dad, *on the dole*. But *anyway*, this girl said that Laura wasn't having any of it, and then one day he came in with this *erotic video*–'

'What?' Amelia exclaimed, reeling backwards in horror. 'Porn? Actual porn?'

'I don't know! It can't have been. But it definitely was *erotic*, because Wendy, that's the girl from Oddbins, she said that Ricko made a point of saying he'd brought her an *erotic video* he thought she'd like. They all heard him say it.'

'Ugh, God, Ricko Struthers always was a fucking perv,' said Amelia.

Sarah shrugged. 'You should know. But Wendy said Laura took one look at this video and that was that. They've been going out ever since.'

'And she didn't say what the video was?' asked Esther.

'Might have done, I don't remember.'

'Was it – do you remember if it was *Poison Ivy*?'

'Yeah, that was it – how did you know?' asked Sarah, looking surprised.

Before Esther could answer, her mother appeared from the kitchen, wiping her hands on a striped apron. Her hair, so like Esther's, had escaped from its chignon and frizzed around her head like the halo of an angel who had never heard of the taming properties of Studio-line gel.

'Esther!' she said. 'There you are! Hurry up. I need you to pass round the cheese.'

'I've got to go,' she grimaced.

As they said goodbye, awkwardly trying to hug around the sandwich platters, Esther couldn't help thinking that her fifteen-year-old self would be astonished to see her now, about to graduate from university, embracing the two most popular girls at school as if they were all dear friends. And thin. Thinner even than Amelia Wentworth.

At last the house was nearly empty. Just a few friends of Esther's dad's were left telling gruff naval stories around the dining room table while she and her mother stacked the dishwasher and wrapped up leftovers for Laura and Margie. Sophie had already escaped, picked up by her boyfriend an hour ago.

Esther's mother looked up, and dropped the bin bags she was holding to rush over to the kitchen door, where Laura and Ricko were standing together.

'Darling girl,' she said, pulling her into the kitchen. 'You've been wonderful, have you eaten anything? Do you want me to make you a plate up?'

Ricko was forced to release Laura as Caro swept her into her arms.

'Now look,' she continued. 'The fridge is absolutely full to bursting. You and your mum shouldn't need to go to the shops for ages. But when you do, you give me a call, okay? I know your mum's not keen on driving at the moment.'

Laura nodded, but said no to any offers of food. Esther's mother's eyes swept from her to Ricko and back again.

'Ricko?' she said. 'I wonder if I could ask you to help me with the empty bottles. I need to stack them by the bin and they're quite heavy. Esther, you can take Laura upstairs, she doesn't need to hang around with those boring old sailors any more. The two of you should get out of the way.'

Ricko glanced at Laura. 'I'll take her upstairs–'

'I'm fine,' Laura said firmly. 'Help Caro, she's hardly stopped all day.'

He acquiesced with a narrowing of the eyes that was so swift and fleeting that Esther wondered if she had imagined it. Seconds later he was charming her mother with practised flirtation, hefting a plastic sack of bottles over his shoulder.

'He's good with mums,' said Laura, as Esther followed her up the stairs. 'I said to him it should go on his boyfriend CV. Good with mums. Everyone likes that, don't they.'

Esther tensed a little at the confirmation of her suspicions. 'So – he's your boyfriend now?'

Laura sighed. 'Don't, okay?'

'Don't what? I'm just asking. You'd think you might have mentioned it.'

Laura pushed open the door to her room, and when she sat down on the bed her eyes glittered with tears.

'There's been a lot going on,' she said quietly.

Esther sat next to her on the bed and put her arm across Laura's rounded back. She could feel the bones of her spine, each vertebra as sharply distinct as if she was hugging a skeleton. Laura dropped her head onto her shoulder, and Esther could feel the shuddering breaths lifting her ribcage as she tried not to cry.

'You should cry, Laur, it's fine. You can cry as much as you want, it's good for you.'

Laura wiped her eyes with the back of her hand and shook her head. 'I'm just sick of it, Est. If crying made you feel better I'd be on cloud fucking nine. And Margie would be delirious.'

She sat up and sniffed, then caught sight of herself in the mirror and went over to examine her face. She ran her index finger under her eyes to get rid of the make-up that had settled there, and then she grimaced over her shoulder at Esther.

'Ugh.'

'You look fine.'

'No, I don't. You do, though, Est, you look great. I meant to say before.'

'It was Weight Watchers,' admitted Esther straight away. She knew Laura wouldn't tell. It would be years before she could accept that a compliment about her looks wasn't always a reference to her weight. 'You cut your hair.'

'Yeah,' Laura came back to the bed and sat down. She

rubbed her hand over her cropped hair. 'I did it last week. Everyone at work kept saying I looked like that one out of the Spice Girls.'

'What?' laughed Esther. 'The sulky one? You don't look like her at all.'

'I know,' said Laura, one corner of her mouth lifting into a wry smile. 'I'm Drew Barrymore, for fuck's sake. How dare they?'

Esther wanted to ask if she'd seen *Scream* yet, but then she remembered how the entire film, once you got past the murders and the po-mo references, was about the fallout from the death of a parent. Was *every* Drew Barrymore movie destined to remind Laura of her dad? Anyway, probably Laura hadn't had time to go to the cinema lately. It would be a stupid question.

Instead they sat quietly for a while, the way only old friends can. Laura's room hadn't changed since she was at school. The posters on the wall were still of Johnny Depp and Mark Gardner from Ride, even though everyone fancied Leonardo DiCaprio now. Or Ewan McGregor, if you were cooler than that. There were dance certificates Blu-tacked around Laura's mirror, and the shelf above her bed held the *Ballet Shoes* and *Sadler's Wells* books as if she hadn't read anything since. Knowing Laura, she hadn't. On the wicker nightstand next to her bed was a clear plastic photo cube. Esther knew the pictures in it off by heart, they hadn't changed for a decade. The photo facing her now was her favourite –

the infant Laura lying on her father's chest, both of them fast asleep.

'Has it been awful, Laur?' she asked.

There was a long pause before Laura answered. 'Yes,' she said. That was all.

Esther reached for the photo cube, and turned it over in her hands. There was the wedding picture of Margie and Edward. A grainy yellow-toned baby picture of Laura lying on a tartan rug. That awful photograph of her and Laura in leotards and legwarmers, doing Esther's mother's Jane Fonda video when they were eleven Another of Edward. And one of Ricko. She nearly dropped it.

It was a recent photo. She could tell by his hair, which was shorter now than when they were at school, though still not as short as Laura's. He smiled lazily into the camera, reaching towards the photographer. It was very obviously taken in bed.

Laura leaned over and took the photo cube from her.

'He was so great with Dad, Est. You can't even imagine.'

'Oh.'

'I know you don't like him,' said Laura.

'It doesn't matter if I don't like him – I thought *you* didn't like him. That's what matters.'

Hadn't they bitched about him for years now? Giggled and run out of pubs when they saw he was there? Mimed puking up on him now that, retrospectively, he totally deserved it?

'He's said sorry for being a dick back then.'

'He *was* a dick.'

'He was. But he's not now. I didn't believe him at first, but he's been so wonderful to Margie and me. He's driven her everywhere after she had a panic attack in Sainsbury's car park, he's even taken me to work and picked me up every day.'

'But you've got a car of your own,' said Esther, and her objection sounded petulant even in her own ears.

Laura looked at her. 'Sometimes I just like the company,' she said. 'It's been lonely, Est. Everyone else away at college, getting on with their lives while I was stuck at home.'

'Does he work near you, then? Is that how you ran into each other?'

'He doesn't work right now,' said Laura, not quite meeting her eyes. 'He could have done all sorts of things, he had loads of offers since he graduated, but he says this is more important. He's given up a lot for me, Esther. He's really changed.'

So have you, Esther thought. But what did she expect? Everyone changed after school. Just because Laura never moved away or went to university it didn't mean she stayed exactly the same. Did she think Laura would be suspended forever at home, like Rosencrantz and Guildenstern, only reanimated when her old friends came back to see her?

'He even carried Dad upstairs, every night,' Laura continued. 'You know how much Dad hated having to sleep in the sitting room after his legs went, but Margie and I couldn't get him upstairs ourselves. Ricko could. He came round every night and took him upstairs to bed, and he came back every morning and brought him downstairs. You can't know what that meant to Dad, right at the end. To have a bit of his dignity back.'

Esther reached over and grasped Laura's hand. What help had she been? Far away in Leeds, sending letters and making phone calls while she concentrated on her finals. It wasn't the same. Ricko Struthers, for all that she still believed he was a cock, had helped, really helped, not just said 'if there's anything I can do' and left them to it.

'I'm glad he helped,' she said. 'I – I tried calling – I left messages on the answerphone.'

'It's okay,' said Laura, squeezing her hand back. 'I know.'

Downstairs they could hear the back door opening again, banging against the outside wall, and the clink of more bottles. Esther's mother had switched on a radio and the reassuring murmur of BBC voices floated up to them from the kitchen.

'So, what are you going to do now?' asked Esther.

Laura frowned. 'Now?'

'I mean – you can go to university now, can't you? I suppose you'll have to reapply, though.'

'No.'

'Or you could do clearing? Is it too late for clearing? Then you could get a place this year – you wouldn't have to wait.'

'I'm not going to university.'

'But – why not?'

'It's too late,' Laura sighed and shook her head, picking at the chenille bedspread. 'I'd be the oldest by miles. I wouldn't even graduate until I was *twenty-five* or something. That's halfway to *fifty*.'

'It's not too late,' Esther said. 'There were loads of mature students on my course. There was even a man in his seventies.'

Laura snorted. 'Mature students? No thanks.'

'Then look, I know,' said Esther. She was desperate to do something, to show that she too was practical and helpful. She could do a different sort of heavy lifting.

'Jane and I are getting a flat together, after graduation. We're moving to London, Islington probably, or Stoke Newington, when Jane starts her law conversion. We could get a three-bedroom place, there are loads of them in *Loot*. We could live together, Laur, just like we planned it back at school.'

Laura looked at her, head tilted to the side as if she saw her for the first time. She smiled and Esther had the oddest feeling that Laura actually felt sorry for her, instead of the other way round.

'School was a long time ago.'

There was a heavy tread on the stairs, coming up towards Laura's room.

'But what will you do instead?' asked Esther. She felt rushed. She hadn't asked half of the questions she wanted to, and now they were going to be interrupted.

Laura opened her eyes wide in surprise. 'Well, this,' she said, as if her childhood bedroom held everything she could ever want. 'I've got a good job, and a place to live. Margie can't be on her own yet – she needs me. She doesn't know how half the remote controls work, for a start. If I wasn't here she'd just be sat in the dark.'

The bedroom door opened and Ricko stood there, handsome and suited, framed by the door like a Ken doll in a cellophane box. Laura's face softened as he came towards them.

'And I've got Ricko,' she said, holding out her hand.

'Course you have,' he said, taking it.

'He's moving in here next week,' said Laura. 'Margie says we can't do without him.'

Ricko sat down on Laura's other side, where the pillows were. The bed felt very small and Esther was embarrassed to be on it with both of them, right where they probably did it. She had a thousand questions at this revelation, not least – how will you both fit in a single bed? She knew that Laura had waited to tell her until

Ricko was in the room, hoping his presence would stop her from challenging this whole stupid idea.

'Don't you want more than this?' she blurted, unable to stop herself.

Laura leaned backwards onto Ricko's chest, wrapping his arms around her front like a seatbelt, their hands making the clasp at her waist. She smiled at Esther, and her eyes were half-closed, as if she was about to go to sleep. Esther wondered if she, too, might have been tranquillized.

'When you fall in love, you'll understand,' she said.

Ricko stared at her over Laura's head. He didn't lower himself to sneer or make his dislike obvious, but he didn't need to. His disdain was like a physical thing, a hand pushing her backwards out of the room and away from them forever.

'Right,' Esther said, standing up and brushing down the cheap black skirt she'd bought especially for today. 'Okay. Right. I'd probably better go. I expect you're tired.'

'Yeah,' said Ricko. 'She is. All of these people crowding her, they don't understand it's too much.'

'I do feel tired,' said Laura, stifling a yawn. 'I'm sorry, Est, we'll catch up properly another time, won't we?'

She reached up her arms, and Esther bent down to hug her. Ricko didn't let go, so she found herself huddled in an uncomfortable scrum of three, as if she and he were both tussling for possession of Laura. It reminded Esther all of a sudden of the owl that had lost its head, and been destroyed from being fought over. She saw that resisting Ricko's control would only mean trouble for Laura. She was too fragile to be pulled between them both without it hurting her.

'Of course we will,' said Esther, straightening up. 'Come up to London. When I've got a flat – you should come up and stay.'

Laura glanced up at Ricko, who shook his head just the smallest amount, a tiny twitch of disapproval. 'I don't like London,' he said. 'Full of pretentious idiots.'

It was clear that he already counted Esther amongst their number, even though she was yet to move.

'Well, Laura could come,' suggested Esther. 'On her own.'

Ricko squeezed Laura tighter by way of an answer. To Esther it looked almost like he was giving her the Heimlich manoeuvre, but Laura just snuggled in closer against him. His black suit and her black dress made it hard to see where he stopped and she began.

'Why would she want to do that?' he asked, raising an eyebrow.

'Right,' said Esther again, biting her tongue. 'Just think about it.'

'I'll see you and your mum out,' said Ricko, and it sounded more like a threat than a courtesy. He stood up and loomed over her. Behind him, Laura sank down on the pillows, closing her eyes like Sleeping Beauty falling into a swoon.

As Esther descended the stairs with Ricko far too close behind her she had a horrible, panicky sensation of wanting to run away from him, away from this house where Edward was gone, Margie was tranquillized by drugs and Laura stupefied by grief and loneliness into a relationship with a man she once professed to hate.

Before she got to the kitchen, where she could hear her mother still tidying up, Ricko grabbed her arm to hold her back. Not hard enough to leave a bruise, but hard enough to let her know that he could leave one if he wanted to. The demonstration of his restraint was almost more frightening than if he had lashed out and hit her.

'Listen,' he said, in a low voice. 'I know you're jealous.'

Jealous? thought Esther, struck by the idea as if by a slap. Is that it? Is it not about Ricko at all? Am I just childishly jealous that I've been replaced as Laura's best friend?

'I get that,' Ricko continued, a slow smirk stealing over his face. 'Laura told me how much you used to fancy me back when you were at school.'

'She told you *what*?'

'She said you used to go on and on about me looking like Christian Slater, was it?' He gave a throaty chuckle, and Esther felt sick. 'Used to drag her to the Video Palace when I was working there, so you could see me.'

How could Laura have told him that? How could she

have made it seem like it was just silly Fat Fester who fancied him, instead of *all* of them, Laura included? She imagined Laura and Ricko lying together in bed, all beautiful and cool like a Calvin Klein advert, facing one another on a bank of snowy white pillows, laughing and laughing at Esther and her adolescent passion for a man who would be forever out of her league.

'I didn't–' she started, but Ricko had let go.

'Don't be selfish,' he said. 'Let her be happy. Leave her alone.'

Esther's mum came out of the kitchen then, her hands full of empty Tupperware, and asked if everything was all right. Esther's face burned red but she just nodded, and said a terse goodbye to Ricko.

On the way home she stared miserably out of the car window. She remembered the boyfriend in *Scream*, how he turned out to be the killer in the end. How he'd wanted to destroy his girlfriend and everyone around her. Somewhere in the back of her mind she had cast Ricko in this role as soon as she saw him with Laura. He'd been the focus for all of her suspicions – the explanation for Laura's silence and distance, the reason she couldn't get close to her all day. Esther wasn't wrong exactly, she just hadn't understood the full story.

Ricko might have been an accomplice, but his wasn't the betrayal that hurt. Because when the villain's mask was whipped off in the hallway of the Thomases' house it wasn't Ricko's face she saw there, but Laura's.

10

October 2013

After hours of restless insomnia under the scratchy hotel sheets, I wake from a brief sleep at dawn, disturbed by a strange dream in which I was sure I could hear Laura laughing just outside the motel door. It seemed so real that I get out of bed and lift a plastic blade of window blind to scan the car park, but of course there is no-one there. Only the dead headlights of the cars stare back, their metal bodies surrounding the swimming pool like animals at a water hole.

I know I won't get back to sleep now; these early mornings are not new to me. Once I'd have cursed jet lag, pulled the covers over my head and tried to will myself back into oblivion. Now I'm used to being awake when everyone else is asleep. While Linus dozes after his early-morning feed, I've often done a load of laundry, caught up with the ironing, made and frozen batches of vegetable puree, ordered a supermarket delivery, sorted the recycling and unloaded the dishwasher before I cast a glance at the kitchen clock and see it is still only 8 a.m.

My husband calls it Benny Hill time – he says he can hear the speeded up music every time I start running around like a maniac, though he can dream on if he thinks I'll do my errands in tight tops and hotpants like the Hill's Angels. And let's face it, he's usually as fast asleep as the baby at that time in the morning. He comes downstairs yawning and scratching, and grabs a clean cereal bowl from the cupboard without ever seeming to understand that it is Benny Hill time that got it there. I wonder if he realizes it now that I am thousands of miles away.

Although it's early in California, it's the middle of the day at home. He'll be at work, or maybe at lunch. I send him a text to let him know I'm still alive, and one buzzes straight back. As if it's a charm, the magic phone that always elicits a reply, I send another text to Laura, but of course there is no answer. I'll call my mum later, when Linus is in bed, and I can ring her on the landline, since a call on her mobile flusters her in even the most serene of circumstances. Alone with Linus it may send her into Margie-style hysterics.

Being awake at home, with a million things to do, is not the same as being awake in a nondescript motel bedroom in the middle of California. If I was in England by myself, without responsibilities, I'd take the chance to go for a walk, but the streets outside the motel are made for drivers, not pedestrians. I don't think I even remember seeing a pavement since I turned off the freeway. Anyway, it's still a little dark. I might be an independent lady traveller, but I'm not an idiot. It could be dangerous. And I couldn't bear the irony of something happening to me when I am here to find out if something has happened to Laura.

I wonder what she's doing now? I know where she should be. They start work in the small hours at the vineyard when harvest is on. She's told me that she takes her first break at sunrise, climbing to the roof of the lab with her mug of coffee to watch the fog burn off the hills. And yet Stanley has agreed to meet me this morning. At the busiest moment of the year, he is taking time off to talk to me about the renegade employee who has left him short-handed. It says a lot for Laura that he is willing to do this. Or perhaps a lot for Stanley.

The keys from last night are on the bedside table, along with the note that fell out of the envelope when I shook it over my motel bed. Of course they weren't from Laura. I should have known they wouldn't be. She might be mysterious, but she isn't crazy. If she wanted me to find her, she'd tell me, not lay a treasure hunt around Napa with herself as the prize. No, the note was from Stanley, to say that if the motel was too horrible I should go and stay at Laura's instead. He'd left me her keys.

I couldn't do it. I know it's cowardly of me, but I

couldn't go there by myself at night and let myself into the strange, empty apartment from which my best friend has disappeared. I couldn't do it last night, and I can't do it now.

I know I should use this time to go there, before anyone else is up. Start the search immediately, not wasting a minute of my few short days of playing detective. I only have one night left. I could let myself in and wander from room to room looking for clues; take crime scene photographs, and then quiz Stanley professionally over breakfast about what I have found, if anything. But for the first time I admit to myself that I'm scared. Not that I will discover anything terrible – Stanley has already told us that everything seems normal – but that I won't discover anything at all. That Laura will remain as distant to me when I am here in California as she was when I was in London.

I'm afraid I'll fail. I'm afraid that I'll discover she was a stranger all along.

Stanley has chosen to meet for breakfast at a restaurant near Laura's apartment, so that we can walk there together afterwards.

It's already packed, even though it's barely nine o'clock. After the basic motel that Stanley selected, I had expected something similar – cheap and functional. But this place is gorgeous – tables at the door are piled high with pastries, cookies and gourmet breads. A blackboard above the cash register lists a French toast special, and five different kinds of pancake. The whole room smells of fresh bread and coffee. I realize that I haven't eaten anything since I was on the plane; my stomach growls loudly and I put my hand over it, like I am placating an animal.

When the woman on reception takes me over to the table that Stanley has reserved, I think at first that she has made a mistake. Although I've never so much as seen a picture of Stanley, Laura's described him to me, and my imagination has filled in the gaps. The man I am meeting is a vineyard owner with a kindly and paternal interest in his English employee. That makes him old, I'm certain of it, if not actually elderly. The Stanley I'm expecting will be wearing a checked shirt, and a Stetson of some kind, with the brow pulled down low over his weathered face. He will be slightly bow-legged from his years on horseback. I realize with deep embarrassment that I somehow believed I was meeting the Marlboro Man.

Instead, the man who stands up to shake my hand is young. Not young as I'd have defined youth as a teenager, but young as I define it now, which is to say, surely not more than fifteen years older than me. His hair is silvered at the temples and lines fan out from the corners of his eyes, but Stanley is no more the Marlboro Man than I am. He is wearing a crisp blue shirt, like a businessman rather than a cowboy, and the only weathering on his face is a light tan.

Although he smiles when he says hello, his dark eyes are grave, and he clasps my hand in a determined way, as if we are making a solemn vow together for Laura's sake.

'You found it okay?' he asks, sitting back down.

'Yes, it was fine. Thanks, Stanley, thanks so much for meeting me.'

I'm flustered by the difference between the man I was expecting and the man I've met. Laura's talked about hot Australian harvest interns, and Californian surfers, but she never once said Stanley was good looking. She hasn't lied exactly – she never said he's old, but she's implied it. Why?

I settle in my chair and he passes me the menu.

'It was good of you to come,' he says. 'To leave your boy at home.'

'It's only a few nights,' I say, though my voice betrays me with a little throaty wobble on the last word.

He smiles sympathetically.

'You got a picture?'

I grab my phone and scroll through the photographs to find a good one. It's kind of Stanley to make the effort. I'm sure he can have very little interest in babies, especially babies belonging to total strangers. But he takes the phone and makes all the right admiring noises, even enlarges the picture and asks if Linus is teething – the red cheeks are a giveaway.

'Do you have children?' I ask.

He pauses for a moment. 'No.'

He hands my phone back abruptly, and it's clear he'd like to change the subject, so I ask him what he's having for breakfast.

'I already ate,' he says.

'Sorry, you must have been up for hours.'

'Yep.'

He hadn't been exactly Mr Chatty on the phone when I was still in England, but then I had been peppering him with questions, and all he had to do was answer them. Now, in person, Stanley is practically monosyllabic; I can't tell if this is exhaustion from harvest, or discomfort at being here with me.

'Did you go to her place yet?' he asks, two furrows deepening between his eyebrows as he fixes his eyes on the coffee mug in his hands. He has worker's hands, rough and calloused, at odds with his neat shirt and brushed hair.

I shake my head. 'I thought I'd wait to go with you,' I say. 'If that's okay.'

He glances up. 'But you got the keys?'

'Stanley,' I say, tired of tiptoeing around the reason we are here. 'What do you think has happened to Laura?'

He takes a sharp breath in. I thought Americans were famously direct and upfront about things, but he seems horrified by my question.

'I guess I hoped you were coming here to tell me. Thought she might have confided in her best friend if – ' he hesitates – 'if something was troubling her.'

A waitress bustles up to the table with a coffee pot in her hand and a pencil tucked on top of her ear. She turns over an empty cup on the table and fills it to the brim before I can tell her I'd rather have an espresso.

'Well, hi, Stanley's new friend,' she says, looking from him to me. One of her drawn-on eyebrows rises in blatant interest.

'Now, what can I get you?' She takes a notepad from a pocket in her apron, and holds the pen over the paper expectantly.

'She only just sat down,' says Stanley, scowling. 'Don't rush her, Kathy.'

'Tetchy this morning, aintcha?' She rolls her eyes in my direction. 'Someone needs more coffee, am I right?'

He puts his hand silently over his half-full cup, his expression pained. The waitress laughs, inviting me to share the joke. I know Stanley will have been up for hours already at the vineyard. I know he should be there still, and that he is meeting me here, at the worst possible time, just to be kind to a friend of Laura's. I decide to spare him the wait while I consider every one of the five pancake varieties.

'I'll just have toast, thanks,' I say, slamming the menu shut and handing it to the waitress.

'Oh, you're from *England*,' she exclaims, taking the menu and clamping it under her arm next to her generous bosom. 'I love that accent, you talk *just* like Laura.'

I feel as if all the air has left my body. I don't know

why I'm so surprised – this place is near Laura's home, Stanley said so. Of course she must have been here. And yet, hearing her name so casually on the lips of a complete stranger unsettles me for reasons I can't quite explain.

'I guessed you must know Laura, right?' the waitress continues, oblivious. 'If you know *Stanley*?'

He seems to wince a little, as if her very presence is painful to him.

'Yes, I do,' I say evenly, looking from him and then back to her. 'I do know Laura, very well. You do, too?'

'Sure, honey, that little English muffin is in here all the time. Isn't she?' she says to Stanley.

'So when did you last see her?' I feel like Margie, launching straight into paranoid questions. Like I will grab the waitress's notebook off her and go around the entire restaurant forcing answers out of people. *Have you seen this woman? When? May I take a DNA sample?*

The waitress taps her pen on her teeth thoughtfully, eyes cast up to the ceiling. 'Well, now, let me see. I don't think I've seen her for a couple of weeks, not since she went on holiday.'

'Sorry?' I say.

'I said I haven't seen her since she went on holiday.'

'On holiday?'

'Yes, honey. To the Bay Area, I think?' She looks to Stanley for confirmation.

'When did she tell you that?' I demand, a bit too

aggressively. She takes a startled step back, and holds her notebook high up on her chest in self-defence.

She looks confused, and her head swivels from me to Stanley as she answers. 'Well, she didn't.' I notice she has dropped the 'honey'. 'Stanley told me himself, didn't you?'

I look at Stanley and he has visibly paled, but he holds my gaze as he answers.

'Holiday, that's right. She went on holiday.'

'See – there you go. Holiday! I knew I was right,' laughs the waitress, her good mood restored instantly. 'At harvest! Some girls have all the luck. I dream of a holiday, I really do. Toast coming up, honey.'

A silence stretches between us after the waitress leaves. I wait for Stanley to speak. He pulls at the cuffs of his shirt, picks at imaginary threads, says nothing. Around us the pitch of conversation is high, and happy. I don't know why I thought I'd get answers from these people about Laura. Look at them. They're not locals, they're tourists, far away from the concerns of daily life, determined to have a good time. Couples pose for photographs; laughter drifts over us from adjoining tables.

Next to them Stanley and I sit like two vultures in a flock of vibrant parakeets.

'Why did you say Laura's on holiday?'

His eyebrows sink down over his eyes, and he looks down at the table. His mouth twists a little at one side, like he's chewing on the inside of his cheek.

'Why?' I say again. 'You said it to the waitress. It's a lie.'

'Well,' he says slowly, turning the blade of his knife over and over so that it flashes in the overhead lights like a distress signal. 'Laura's kind of a private person, don't you think?'

I nod to keep him talking, but I think, *not if you really know her*.

Until she disappeared, I always thought Laura couldn't keep a secret from me for long. Even when she tried to hide things, I knew what was happening, or I guessed. Ricko. Her dad. Malcolm. But I remember Amelia Wentworth running up to me in the street the Christmas after we'd left school to ask if it was true that Laura's father was dying. I'm sorry to say I felt an unedifying little stab of satisfaction to hear that though Laura had hung out with the popular girls, she hadn't entrusted them with anything truly important. It didn't occur to me to wonder if she would have told me about her father either, if I hadn't already known. It occurs to me now.

Stanley continues.

'It seemed to me that she'll be back soon, she won't have gone far. And when she gets back, she's not going to like it if people have been talking about her, speculating on where she's gone.'

'So you think she's gone away on purpose?' I ask. 'You think it was her decision?'

Stanley's eyes narrow a little as he looks at me, like he's wondering if he can trust me.

'It's not the first time she's run out on me at harvest,' he says carefully, as if he's offering a bait to see if I'll take it.

I say nothing. It's impossible to know what Laura told him about before.

'There was some family emergency,' he says. 'I guess you'd know more about it than me. But that time she told me before she went.'

'Okay,' I say, non-committal. I don't think Laura would have told him why, so I'm not about to disclose everything. Anyway, it's irrelevant. We're here to find where she's gone now. 'But she didn't say anything this time. That's suspicious, isn't it?'

He rubs at the side of his jaw, looking uncomfortable.

'She's not the type to get in a car with a stranger, or take a crazy risk. I don't see it being suspicious. I figure she just needed some space.'

'But *why*, Stanley?' I ask.

The waitress interrupts us with a basket of toast, four different kinds of it, each of which gets its own detailed introduction; pumpkin and cinnamon, multigrain, rye, gluten-free. Stanley shrugs apologetically when she finally leaves us. Everywhere in Napa has gourmet ambitions, he says – even when it comes to bread. I reach for the butter and leave space for Stanley to talk.

I've dispatched two rounds of toast before he clears his throat to volunteer more information.

'It just felt to me that it was better to give her a way

out, for when she comes home,' says Stanley. 'If she wants one.'

I must look sceptical because he sighs. 'The way I see it, she *has* taken a kind of a holiday. Maybe she's lying on a beach in Hawaii and drinking cocktails, maybe not, but she's taken a holiday from herself right now, okay? And maybe we need to respect that.'

'So you think she's going to come back by herself?' I ask.

'Don't you?'

'What if she can't?' I say.

'We have to believe she will,' he says, as if believing it will make it happen. 'We have to, Esther. I believe it with all my heart.'

He actually puts his hand on his heart as he says this, like he is in an ageing boy band, making hand gestures as they sing hackneyed words about hearts and angels. It infuriates me – what use are Californian platitudes right now? I haven't flown thousands of miles, abandoned my family, holed up in an awful motel, just to hear that Stanley, who is only her boss after all, not her soulmate, *believes* Laura will come back, with his *heart*. I want cold, hard facts. I want mobile phone records and incriminating photographs and a trail that will lead me directly to my best friend.

'I just don't see how lying about where she's gone is going to help us find her – don't we want people to be looking out for her?'

Stanley twists a pink packet of Sweet'n Low between his fingers. 'Not if that's not what she wants.'

'But we don't know what she wants.'

'That's right,' he says.

On the phone from England I found Stanley's certainty that Laura would be okay reassuring, but here it is frustrating. He seems so certain she's left because she wants to, and yet he doesn't know why. If you don't know why, you don't know anything. I want to shake him.

'Is that what you've told the people at the vineyard?' I ask. 'That she's gone on holiday?'

'Yep.'

'Don't they think it's weird, though? For her to leave in the middle of harvest?'

'Maybe.'

'So people will be talking about her anyway,' I say.

'People are always talking about Laura,' says Stanley, looking up at me with narrowed eyes. 'She knows that as well as anyone.'

THE WEDDING SINGER, JULY 1998[5]

JULIA: *May I ask what happened with Linda?*

ROBBIE: *She wasn't the right one, I guess.*

JULIA: *Did you have any idea she wasn't the right one when you were together?*

ROBBIE: *I should have. Uh, I remember we went to the Grand Canyon one time. We were flying there and I'd never been there before and Linda had, so you would think that she would give me the window seat but she didn't and . . . not that that's a big deal, you know. It's just there were a lot of little things like that. I know that sounds stupid . . .*

JULIA: *Not at all. I think it's the little things that count.*

11

Esther didn't need to get dressed up for work. Tony Simms, newspaper editor of twenty years' standing, considered himself to be looking pretty sharp if he managed to make it through the morning without a mustard stain on the brown tie that he wore over his summer shirts, light blue with sleeves short enough to show the dispiriting tideline of a farmer's tan on his upper arm. Ancient Colin from the postroom rotated just two pairs of shorts all year, regardless of the weather, both sporting hems so frayed he appeared to be wearing some sort of Country and Western fringing as he pushed his squeaking trolley through the corridors. Every single day since Esther started at the *Gazette*, Bob from Classifieds would look up from his cubicle at Colin's approach and shout, 'Oi, Colin, looks like there's a couple of threads hanging down from your shorts – no, wait, they're your legs.' Colin would laugh the teeth-gritted laugh of one who hoped to someday smash in

Bob's skull with the franking machine. But even they were as sharply groomed as Boyzone in comparison to Al Webster, her boss on the grandly-named culture desk.

Privately, Esther felt that thirty-one was far too old to be sporting a hairsprayed horn of bleached yellow hair on either side of one's skull, not to mention the heavily kohled eyes of a silent movie star, but there was method behind Al's sartorial madness. Without the hair and make-up, his doughy features did little to impress themselves on the memory; he would have been just another music journalist of a certain age, resting his pint on his expanding beer belly as he repeated that story about hanging with the Manics way back before they were big. He and Richey were like *that*, apparently, which was a safe boast, since no-one had heard from Richey Manic for years.

Al's idea of suitable workwear was a threadbare pair of tartan bondage trousers and a T-shirt featuring whichever band he liked best at that moment – usually Black Flag or The Ramones, since modern music was shit. He had no time at all for Blur or Oasis, and he would often wag a podgy finger at Esther and warn her that she shouldn't even ask him what he thought about dance music. She never did.

Esther had realized some time ago that she didn't feel the way most people did about music. For her, that sort of passion was reserved for books. It was not to say she didn't like music. There was a stack of CDs as high as her head balanced up next to her bed, but ask her why she liked any of them, ask her to write a review of the Chemical Brothers for the culture pages, and she'd run out of adjectives in five minutes. Talk to her about a book, though – she was reading *Morvern Callar* for the second time, obsessed with the coldly mesmerizing heroine – and she could hardly stop the words from gushing out of her. 'Like sick,' said Al in her interview, but she got the job anyway.

A job for which she did not need to dress up. And yet, every morning, she did, as far as she was able. The more successful of her friends, like lawyer Jane, wore neat Jigsaw skirt suits to work, with shoes from Hobbs. Esther's poorly-paid version of dressing up was to top a pair of stretchy black trousers from French Connection with one of her brightly coloured thermal vest and cardigan combinations, the ones with a thick matching lace trim around the décolletage. At publishing parties all the proper editors wore them, though Esther knew theirs were the posh ones, the real kind from shops like The Cross or Voyage, where you had to ring a bell to be let in, not Camden Market knock-offs like her own. The publishing women flitted brightly around the parties in their twinsets like expensive and well-read parrots, pecking kisses on each other's cheeks, and Esther knew herself to be an impostor in their midst, cheap dye leaking onto her bra.

She dressed up for David. He was coming with her to the Penguin summer party tonight. The idea of it was somehow thrilling and annoying at the same time. The proximity was more than she'd dared hope for, the travelling there, just the two of them on the tube, the introductions that would link them together in people's minds – perhaps even in David's mind – 'David and Esther, Esther and David, David and Esther from the *Camden Gazette*'.

Esther counted it a personal triumph that at last she'd been invited to Penguin's annual summer party on her own merits, after battling to be noticed at all. Now that she was a respected books journalist, she'd maybe make conversation with Salman Rushdie or Sebastian Faulks. Someone said Nick Hornby might be there. Yet here was David, not even a *Gazette* employee, just work experience, who turned out to know Fiona, one of the publicity assistants, and who therefore received an invitation without even trying.

His desk was empty when Esther got to the office, and so was Al's, but that wasn't unusual; she was normally the first one there. She hung up the dress she'd brought for the party on the coat stand near her desk, hoping the creases from being shoved in a plastic bag for the tube journey would drop out by the time she put it on. It was borrowed from Jane, a pewter-grey bias-cut slip with little silky straps and a scattering of dull silver sequins, like a glamorous nightie. She hoped David might comment on it approvingly when he arrived, or perhaps he would just silently notice it and begin to anticipate the night ahead with pleasure. The night together. She felt her cheeks flush pink. Not like that, of course. Not yet, anyway.

Al's entrance to the office was announced this morning by the fatty odour of a McDonald's cheeseburger and fries snaking its way into the office ahead of him. This usually indicated a late night, a hangover and a boring story which he'd insist Esther wasn't to ask him about, but would then tell her anyway. She hoped the burger smell wouldn't get into the fabric of Jane's dress, especially since she hoped to be able to return it to her wardrobe without having to pay for dry cleaning.

He landed in his chair with an 'oof', and then made a big show of looking in his desk drawers for the stash of painkillers and Alka-Seltzer he kept there. When he caught Esther looking at him he gave a wry chuckle and said, 'My head. Seriously, don't ask!' She wondered if he'd ever notice that she really never did.

Al finished his breakfast, screwing up the paper bag and walking over to drop it in her wastepaper basket. He never left any kind of food wrapper in his own bin. It was as if he felt he might be able to transfer the calories to someone else, as well as the rubbish. He sat heavily on the edge of her desk, first licking his fingers, then twisting his horns of hair back into points. Smelly points, she thought, with a tiny shudder that she hoped he didn't notice.

'Esther, Esther, Esther,' he said. In his hand he held a piece of A4, a few paragraphs of text scribbled over with red notes. She recognized it as her own review of the new Ian McEwan, for publication this Friday.

She turned the swivel chair to face Al and crossed her legs tightly at the knee, tucking one foot behind her calf. He brought out her inner librarian and she hated herself for it.

'I thought we'd talked about the house style?' he said.

'Yes, I know we did,' Esther said, and she heard her voice as Al must hear it: female, hesitant, easily intimidated by people in authority. Even if their hair smelled of cheeseburgers. 'I just wondered if it might not work for book reviews as well as it obviously works for you in the music ones. I mean, you look at the *Guardian* Review or *The Times*, they're all in the first person.'

Al sighed, looking up at the ceiling. 'The thing about a house style, Esther, is, it exists for a reason. And that reason is, darlin', that no-one gives a toss what Miss Esther Conley, aged twenty-one–'

'I'm twenty-three.'

'Aged whatever, you ain't Martin Amis, no-one gives a toss what *you* think about – ' he stopped and peered at the paper in his hands, bringing it right up towards his face. Al needed glasses but felt they would compete with everything else that was happening on his head, so he went without. 'About *Enduring Love* or any other book, okay? But the *Gazette* is a different matter. The *Gazette* carries weight, you understand? What the *Gazette* says *means* something. I haven't spent ten years building up our reputation as an impartial judge of the cultural landscape of Britain for you to step in and start boring readers with what *you* think about stuff.'

Esther would have liked to laugh. Cultural landscape of Britain? Reputation? She wondered how many of Camden's residents even made it all the way to pages 40 and 41 for another of Al's pompous reviews, which always ended: 'The *Gazette* says . . .'

> The *Gazette* says allow The Tempests to suck you down into their swirling vortex of sound. You'll drown in delight. Four stars.

> The *Gazette* says in years to come Britpop will be long forgotten, but everyone will remember where they were when they first heard the fierce agonized howl of Asymmetric Pillow Machine. Five stars.

She spoke carefully. It was time she made a stand, in her own small way.

'But Al, it's the same review, whether it's me who's saying it or the *Gazette*. Five stars are five stars, surely? Isn't the rating what matters?'

'No, it isn't, darlin',' said Al, shifting his buttocks worryingly. Esther had an awful moment of wondering if he might be preparing to fart – it wouldn't have been the first time – but the only sound came from her desk, creaking under the strain. 'It's the voice. The authoritative voice is what matters. First rule of journalism. But maybe they didn't teach you that at *university*?'

Al spoke of university with the same disdain that Ricko Struthers did. You didn't get your hands dirty at university. You didn't grow up with printer's ink on your hands and in your veins in a stuffy classroom. Esther made a point of never telling people she had a first class English degree, just like she never mentioned that she thought she had nice eyes; it would be showing off. But Al had seen her CV and had never let her forget that good marks were worse than meaningless when it came to actual experience. All that intellectualizing got in the way of decent copy. If the final decision had been up to him instead of Tony Simms, he'd have appointed someone way more rock and roll – someone who'd be rolling out of clubs with Irvine Welsh instead of writing considered critiques of Anita Brookner's genteel heroines.

As much as Esther felt that Al was an idiot, she was too recently out of university to be immune to the opinions of those in authority. Analysing a novel or a film had always come as second nature to her, picking out narrative themes from the whole like extracting the meat from a nut, but Al's constant criticism was beginning to make her doubt herself. The worst of it was that he didn't care about the books at all, and never had; he made it clear that he resented giving up any of his music pages for Esther's superfluous literary waffle. Often she opened the paper on a Friday to discover he had edited a five-hundred-word book review down into a mortifying and meaningless fifty-word soundbite with her name on it.

The *Gazette* says . . . Esther Conley, you sound like a dick.

When David started, though, just two weeks ago, he had read an unedited review of hers and whistled through his teeth.

'This is good stuff,' he'd said.

That was all, but it was enough. Esther was by now so parched of praise that these few words seemed as thrilling as if she herself had received a glowing review in the pages of a national paper. And David had gone to Oxford, actual Oxford, so the pleasure was burnished with awe and respect.

When he finally walked into the office at ten, David did so as if he was joining a thrilling party, hesitating at the entrance with a half-smile on his lips, ready to be delighted by the day ahead.

Al glanced up from the notepad on which he was excoriating in blue biro the band he'd seen last night – yeah, excoriating, good word, he'd use that – and failed to stop a sneer curling his lip. He had repeatedly expressed the opinion that David Carrell was working, no, *playing*, at the *Camden Gazette* for no other reason than being the nephew of Jolyon Carrell of Carrell

Media. It was the worst kind of work experience placement, said Al, the imposition of a spoiled rich kid, along with the clear insinuation that David must not be employed doing anything actually useful such as photocopying or filing.

Esther had noticed that Al had squirrelled away all of his expenses receipts in a drawer of his desk, as if he thought that in addition to being a Carrell nephew, David might also be a spy. She quite enjoyed the idea that Jolyon Carrell, while running his network of national newspapers, had nothing better to do than investigate whether Al Webster on the *Camden Gazette* culture desk regularly expensed his hangover McDonalds.

There was nothing ostentatious about David, though his clothes had that expensive sort of dishevelment only the truly wealthy can get away with. There may have been holes in the elbows of his jumpers, but the jumpers themselves were pure cashmere. David didn't even have the floppy Hugh Grant hair that usually identified a former public school boy; his was dark and cropped short. Deeply uncool, said Al, who asked what sort of a statement David thought he was trying to make with that? No, his privilege was all in the way he moved, his confident saunter through the office, the comradely wave to Tony Simms as if they were equals, the unhurried chat to Patience the cleaner about her daughter's upcoming wedding. No sense of urgency that he was half an hour late, no apology. Just a slow progression through the corridor, stopping briefly every few steps for another greeting, like a young prince on walkabout. He had a physicality to him that spoke of ski seasons and tennis matches, sailing regattas and cricket teams.

When David finally made it to his desk – actually a corner of Esther's that had been temporarily cleared of Jiffy bags – he put down a paper bag from the Pret a Manger that had recently opened by the tube station. She knew he liked to have a cappuccino every morning and felt this was a sign not just of his urbane sophistication, but also his unthinking wealth. Every penny of her meagre salary was accounted for – she knew a takeaway coffee could not be a daily indulgence until she'd been promoted at least once.

'Morning,' he said, taking another paper cup out of the bag and offering it to her. 'I wasn't sure what kind of coffee you'd want, so I got you a cappuccino, Esther, same as me. That okay?'

She stammered gratefully as she took the cup from him. He had got her the same coffee as his *own* – was that a sign that they were meant to be? Before she could thank him properly, he'd turned to give a cup to Al.

'Now you, Alster, I thought would be more of a latte man, am I right?'

Esther knew for a fact that Al was a strong tea with three sugars man, but for all of his principled dislike he was temporarily dazzled enough to claim in a high, surprised voice that there was nothing he liked better than a piping hot latte.

As David sauntered back to his desk, Al mouthed 'Piping hot?' at himself in disgust.

'Cheers, mate,' he called after David, adopting a significantly more gruff and manly tone. 'That'll compensate nicely for you being late again.'

David laughed good-naturedly and Esther could see Al's transparent confusion that not only had his criticism failed to hit home, but that it made him seem petty and point-scoring next to David's largesse.

The day passed slowly. No matter how much Esther tried to keep herself occupied, her thoughts kept returning to the Penguin party. She congratulated herself on remembering to take her socks off after lunch so there wouldn't be a pair of red manacles imprinted around her ankles later, and decided against the lunch special in the canteen in case the cheese and onion pasty gave her bad breath. She told herself this was because she would be talking to important people at the party, but really, she was thinking about kissing.

In her head she rehearsed conversations with David. She imagined herself delicately leading the conversation towards the subject of his romantic life. He hadn't mentioned a girlfriend, but a man like David would surely not be without some sort of love interest? Tonight she would find out. If anything was going to happen between the two of them, it would surely happen then, when they had slipped the bonds of the *Gazette* together.

Esther felt like the last year on the culture desk had been little more than a series of trailers for the actual feature film that would begin as soon as she put on Jane's silver dress and became a heroine at last.

Her work phone rang infrequently enough for it to be a surprise when it blared at five. She was just about to take her outfit to the loos to get changed and do her make-up, and she considered leaving it; but Al raised an eyebrow, and though he ignored his own phone most of the time, she didn't dare do so blatantly in front of him.

'Culture desk,' she said, which was how Al insisted she answer the phone, as if there were hundreds of them sat there instead of just three. Esther was simply grateful he didn't make her speak in the third person. 'The *Gazette* says please send us the press release as soon as possible. The *Gazette* says thanks very much.'

At first all she could hear was heavy breathing, and she wondered what sort of sicko could possibly be bored or perverted enough to get a thrill out of making a dirty phone call to a north London newspaper. Then it became obvious that the person on the other end of the phone was crying.

'Hello?' said Esther.

The crying continued. She cast a glance over her shoulder. Al was typing out last night's review with two fingers, while David sat behind her, his feet on the desk, turning over the photocopied pages of a manuscript they'd been sent from Faber. He winked.

'Est?'

Esther hadn't heard her voice for months. She hadn't seen her since Christmas.

'Laura?'

There was more crying. Esther turned around and cupped her hand over the receiver to shield the conversation from David and Al.

'Is it Ricko? Has something happened? Did he hurt you?'

She sniffed. 'No.' There was a pause. 'It's over, Est.'

'What?'

'I broke up with him.'

'But what happened?'

Laura's answer was a fresh burst of crying.

'Where are you?' Esther asked. She could hear heavy traffic in the background, and a police siren.

'In – a phone box,' said Laura. Esther could tell from the hesitant way she said it that she wasn't giving her the full story. There was the sound of traffic behind Laura's voice, and the far-off wail of a police siren.

'Where's the phone box?'

'It's – it's the one outside Camden tube station.'

'You're here in *London*?'

'Esther, I've been a shit friend. I know I have. But please, please, I had to get away. I didn't know where else to go.'

Esther looked over her shoulder again. David sat in profile, frowning over his novel. In the strip lighting of the office, Jane's silvery dress shone behind him like a ghost. The Spirit of Parties Not Attended. The Spirit of Davids Unkissed.

She left it hanging there and picked up her coat instead from the back of the chair.

'Wait there,' she said. 'I'm coming down.'

12

Laura was pacing outside the tube station looking lost and hopeless and yet, somehow, even in her moment of desperation, also undeniably cool. Her hair was long now, past her shoulders, and she wore an old black jumper over a miniskirt and a pair of biker boots. Esther looked at Laura before she had been seen herself, pausing on the corner and looking at her as a stranger might. Yes, she saw damage, but damage like Elizabeth Wurtzel on the cover of *Prozac Nation* – damage in a pretty package, everyone's favourite kind. Damage that draws the approving eye even when the fingers dragging the cigarette away from her parched lips are yellowed by nicotine, even when her once-beautiful hair is unbrushed and dull. Esther didn't want Laura's terrible ex-boyfriend, she didn't want her dead father or her hysterical, unpredictable mother; but the delicate fragility of her glass coat-hanger collarbones, the enormous shadowed eyes –

Esther longed for those, she wanted them desperately, all of the fragility without the difficulty.

She felt guilty for thinking so; it was like envying a famine victim's protruding ribs, and yet it was so ingrained in Esther to compare herself to Laura that she couldn't help herself. Even as she hugged her hello and led the way to the World's End across the road, pushing open the doors to the saloon bar, she found herself noticing that every head still turned towards Laura, just as they had always done.

Laura drank two bottles of Rolling Rock in ten minutes, refusing a shared packet of Frazzles in favour of smoking a series of cigarettes with a shaking hand, lighting each from the embers of the last. Esther couldn't be bothered to tell her she'd given up since the last time they met, it felt irrelevant, so she smoked with her and the unexpected head-rush made her feel like they were teenagers again, sitting on Margie's patio wall.

'Marlboro Reds?' she said, coughing. 'God, they're strong. When did you start smoking these?'

Laura offered a wan smile. 'When Silk Cut weren't strong enough any more?'

'So come on. What happened?'

Laura sniffed, and wiped at her eyes with the tattered sleeve of her jumper.

'If you say I told you so, I'm leaving. Just so you know.'

'Laur, when did I ever say that?'

'You didn't have to.'

It wasn't like they'd been fully estranged. They'd seen each other at Christmas. Laura sent an occasional postcard, silly ones for tourists, with Pearly Kings and punk rockers. And Esther heard snippets of news from her mum, relayed through the unreliable filter of Cold War Margie. There had been fights. Ricko was dealing drugs from their house, though no proof of this was ever offered. The difficulty of translating Margie-speak into reality was that her worries and predictions always seemed to fall into the category of whatever scare story she had most recently read in the paper. After Princess Diana died, Esther's mother told her that Margie would not allow either Ricko or Laura to get in a car for weeks, despite the complete lack of paparazzi in the Portsdown area. Laura never offered any clues to her life with Ricko, so it was impossible for Esther to know if any of this was true.

'So,' said Esther. 'It's over.' She hoped that sounded non-judgemental, with not even a suggestion of told-you-so.

Laura took a big breath in through her nose, and it seemed to straighten her up, fill her with purpose. Just as she was about to speak, a long-haired man with leather trousers leaned over the railing that separated their table from the rest of the room and offered to buy her a drink.

Laura dropped her eyes to the table and murmured 'No, thanks', and the man shrugged and left, his trousers squeaking slightly as he walked away, like the sound a leather sofa makes when you move around on it.

'What happened?' Esther persisted. 'What made you do it?'

Laura's hair fell over her face, obscuring it. 'It wasn't just one thing,' she said, her voice quiet enough that Esther had to lean forward to listen. 'It was lots of things.'

'Like what?'

Laura tucked a piece of hair behind her ear and looked up at the ceiling, as if a list of Ricko's misdemeanours might be written there to jog her memory.

'He just never wanted to *do* anything, you know?' she said, her hands waving helplessly in front of her. 'He didn't want to get a job, and he didn't want to go out. He just wanted to stay in smoking all the time, and playing video games.'

'Hey,' said another long-haired man, approaching the railing with an indulgent smile, like Laura and Esther were exhibits in a petting zoo. 'Video games, huh? Sounds fun.'

Laura smiled politely. 'We're just – excuse us, we're just in the middle of something.'

He held out both hands apologetically and retreated backwards.

Laura leaned forward with her elbows on the table, holding her beer bottle between both hands like a microphone.

'Then Margie found a bag of weed, so you can imagine what *that* was like. She was convinced Ricko was a drug dealer and that he was about to force me into a lifetime of crack whoredom. I told him we should never have let her watch *Trainspotting*. Honestly, Est, you know how she is, I swear she thought it was a documentary.'

So that was one rumour dealt with, thought Esther. She wouldn't have put it past Ricko to have dealt a few pills or some weed to his friends, but she had doubted his ambition to do anything bigger.

'Anyway, after that she wanted him to move back to his parents', but I persuaded her he should stay.' Laura glanced up at Esther. 'I know. Look, even I thought I was being stupid by then. I don't know, it's hard to explain. I think having him there, on the dole and reliant on me – I think it sort of let me ignore the fact I'd fucked up my own life completely.'

Esther tried to interject, to say that Laura's life wasn't a fuck-up, but yet another man had approached the railing to interrupt them. This one, as long-haired as the others, gave a sheepish grin as he offered Laura a giant jester's hat with bells on it.

'I don't think so,' said Laura. 'Thanks, though.'

From across the room there was a burst of laughter from his friends as he turned away from the railing, the rejected hat swinging sadly from one hand.

'You know what this is?' said Esther.

Laura frowned.

'These guys coming up here?'

'What? You've brought me to some pick-up joint for miserable women? They can't resist my red eyes and streaming nose?'

'Laur, they think you're one of them. They reckon you're a Goth.'

She snorted through her nose, and looked nervously around the room. 'Fuck me,' she said. 'Everyone here is in black except for you. What is this place? It's like the Spice Girls never happened.'

'And you're the new Goth babe in the hood,' said Esther.

'Shit. Though I guess if I wanted to hide from Ricko, this would be the perfect witness protection scheme. He'd never think to look for me in the underground Goth network.'

'You'd probably have to get your nose pierced,' said Esther, considering the few other women in the pub. 'And buy some stripey tights.'

Laura laughed.

'Stop smiling,' Esther warned, wagging a finger. 'They'll realize you're a faker. You've got to look serious all the time. Suicidal, even.'

'Especially when I move to Whitby to write my bad poetry about ravens and graveyards.'

'Especially then.'

'Bad poetry?' said a man's voice.

'Fuck off,' said Laura amiably, smiling up at him.

'David?'

'You know this one?' asked Laura, checking with Esther. 'I thought he didn't look like one of them.'

'My leather trousers are in the wash,' David grinned.

'David,' Esther said, scooting her chair across the floor so he could sit down with them. 'I will give you a million pounds if you actually own a pair of leather trousers for real. Two million if you'll wear them to work.'

There was a great muttering and staring as the rejected Goths of the World's End, watching David pull a chair up to the table, wondered what he had that they did not.

He just laughed and sat down, crossing his legs in that posturing way men do where they cross an ankle over the opposite knee. Esther always wondered if they understood they were effectively making a triangle that said 'here's my crotch'. He had changed out of his moth-eaten jumper and into a suit and a white shirt with a fine blue stripe that matched his eyes. He held a tie in his hand, as if uncertain whether or not he should wear it. The Goths watched him with suspicion. Esther thought he'd never looked more handsome.

'David,' he said, reaching out a hand to Laura. 'I work with Esther.'

'Laura,' she said, shaking it solemnly. 'Accidental Goth, bit drunk, might cry.'

'Ah,' he said, bemused, and looked at Esther for an explanation. 'You just ran out of the office, I thought we were going to the Penguin thing together?'

Laura looked at Esther, then at David, then back at Esther. She put a hand over her mouth. 'Oh shit. You were going out. Why didn't you say something?'

Esther shook her head. 'It's fine. It was just a work thing, this is more important, I promise.'

She turned to David apologetically. 'Sorry, I think you're going to have to go by yourself, it's a bit of an emergency.'

'Don't tell me,' said David, surveying the Goths around them. 'The Damned split up? There's a world shortage of latex corsets?'

'Funny,' said Laura, grimacing. 'I'm the emergency.'

He grimaced back sympathetically, and Laura blushed a little, like colour appearing in a black and white photograph.

Esther couldn't help herself; she was watching them both for signs of attraction to one another. But David turned straight back to her.

'Sure you won't come?' he asked. 'Not even for an hour, just to show your face?'

Next to pale and waifish Laura he seemed more vital and outdoorsy than ever, like he was about to leap onto the rigging of a yacht instead of getting on the tube to South Kensington.

'You should go, Esther,' said Laura, lifting her chin bravely. She stubbed her cigarette out in the overflowing ashtray. 'I'll be fine. I can meet you later or something. Or I'll – I'll find somewhere to stay.'

'Laura, when were you last in London?'

'Um, why?'

'Have you actually been here since we came to see Bros at Wembley in the second year?'

Laura shook her head, shamefaced.

'Exactly. You're clueless. You'll be carried off by a troupe of horny Goths before you know what's happening. I'm staying with you.'

'A troupe?' said David. 'You reckon that's the collective noun for horny Goths, do you?'

'Well, what do you think it is?'

He scratched his chin, considering. 'Flock? Like bats?'

'No way,' said Laura, with certainty. 'That's New Romantics. Seagulls. Obviously.'

'Okay, a troupe of Goths it is.' He sighed and looked at his watch. 'If I can't persuade you to come, I guess I'll just have to represent the *Camden Gazette* all by myself.'

He stood up and shoved his hands into his pockets, managing to look both pathetic and horribly gorgeous at the same time. Esther nearly cracked then, and she could tell he knew it; there was a smile on his lips that dared her to change her mind. She thought of the glamorous editors swarming around him, imagined Fiona turned from innocent publicity assistant to fierce vamp, wrapping herself around his upper body like a boa constrictor.

'You can have double the canapés if I'm not there,' she said by way of compensation. 'I bequeath you my share.'

'Double the booze,' he agreed.

'The *Gazette* says . . . don't forget to speak in the third person all night.'

He smiled and, unexpectedly, darted forward to kiss her cheek. As he pulled away Esther felt the sharp graze of his stubble against her jaw.

'The *Gazette* says . . . standing up your colleague won't be forgotten, Esther Conley. You owe me one night in your company – soon.'

He raised a hand in farewell to Laura and left them, parting the crowd of Goths as if he'd roared through them all in a speedboat.

Laura swirled the last dregs of beer in her bottle and studied its contents. 'Anything you want to tell me?'

'About what?' Esther asked, innocently.

Although she knew she would be replaying David's chaste kiss for the rest of the night, possibly for the rest of her life, it was all too new and undefined to be shared. Especially with someone who had hidden so much for so long.

'Excuse me? Mr Hotness tracks you down to the pub to beg you to go to a party with him and there's nothing to tell?'

'It's work, Laura.'

'Come on, you can't hide it from me, Est. I know you too well.'

Esther looked at her, really looked at her. Past the pallor and the tatty black clothes to the girl she once knew. All of a sudden her relief that Laura had left Ricko turned into resentment for the years she had wasted with him. And now Ricko, or the legacy of him, was messing up Esther's own life.

'You don't, you know,' she said, pushing her half-empty Rolling Rock bottle away from her and leaning back in her chair. 'You really don't get to say that you know me well after all this time. Just like I'm not sure if I know you right now. '

Laura blinked in surprise at the abrupt change of tone. She held her bag on her lap like she was about to make a swift exit from the pub, and twisted its strap around her fingers.

'I don't even know if I know myself right now, Est,' she said, and her big eyes filled with tears. 'I keep thinking of what my dad would say if he knew what I'd done with my life since he died – nothing. Absolutely fuck all.'

Tears fell onto Laura's bag, and she wiped them away crossly as if they'd caught her unawares.

'I'm sorry I've been such a terrible friend.'

Esther didn't know how to answer.

'See?' Laura sniffed. 'You're not even denying it.'

'Well, you *were* a pretty terrible friend. You told Ricko I had a mad crush on him, for starters.'

Laura goggled at her. 'I did what?'

'He told me, Laura, don't deny it. He said you told him I fancied him madly, and I was massively jealous of your being with him.'

Laura's mouth fell open. 'He said that? When?'

'At your dad's funeral.'

She slumped back in her seat like someone had drained the air out of her. 'I can't fucking believe it, Est.'

Esther wasn't sure what Laura couldn't believe – that Ricko had told her the truth, or that it wasn't the truth at all.

'So did you say it?'

Laura gave a bitter little laugh. 'You see? You've never let me bullshit you, Est. That's what I've missed. Everyone else goes along with what I do – even Margie. But you always call me on it. That's why I couldn't face seeing you. I knew you'd make me see my life for what it was.'

'So you did,' said Esther. She should have known it.

Laura squirmed on her chair, avoiding Esther's accusing gaze. 'It's not like that – well, okay, it was a bit. He thought you didn't like him, Est, I was trying to make him see that you *did*. I told him that all of us used to fancy him, even you.'

'I didn't like him, though.'

'I thought I said you weren't allowed to say I told you so.' Laura's jaw jutted out mulishly. It was the same expression she'd worn when they fought over the stuffed owl.

They stared at each other, and Esther wondered if this was it, if actually the rift in their friendship was too big and too wide for them to be able to close it. It happened all the time; she'd already lost contact with people from university who she'd sworn undying allegiance to in the first year. And now it was happening with Laura.

Two men strode confidently up to the railing, seeking safety in a unified attack. Before they'd even opened their mouths Laura and Esther chorused, 'Fuck off!', caught each other's eye, and collapsed in hysterical laughter. The aggrieved Goths departed.

Laura wiped at her eyes, and looked up with an apologetic smile. 'Est, can I tell you something completely awful?'

Esther tensed in anticipation.

'About what?' she asked.

'About why I made him move out.'

Esther took a swig from her beer bottle for courage.

'It was because of Drew Barrymore.'

Esther spat beer all over the table.

'You did *what*? Shut up,' she spluttered.

Laura shrieked, and pushed her chair back. She wiped down her front where beads of beer had settled like tiny jewels.

'I know it sounds mad, Est, I know it.'

Esther was still laughing. 'What, did she visit you in a dream or something? Did you get a visitation? Did Poison Ivy come to see you from *beyond the grave*?'

Laura folded her arms across her chest. 'Well, I won't tell you, then. If you're going to be like that.'

'Oh, no. No no no, you can't say *Drew Barrymore* told you to split up with Ricko and then not tell me why.'

She sighed and rolled her eyes. 'God, okay. It's not as mad as it sounds, Est, I promise. You know how I said it was lots of little things? Well, Drew Barrymore was one of them.'

Esther nodded silently, so as not to spoil the flow by saying the wrong thing again.

'Have you seen *The Wedding Singer*?' asked Laura.

'No,' said Esther.

She didn't want to admit that going to see a Drew Barrymore film when she and Laura were all but estranged would have felt like going to Margie's house and pressing her nose against the window to see what Laura was doing without her. Even if she'd gone with Jane or Claire or, in her dreams, David Carrell, just seeing Laura's celebrity totem there on the screen would have made her feel lonely and cast out all over again.

'Me neither,' said Laura. 'But I asked Ricko if we could go. He didn't want to.'

'Okay.'

'I said I'd pay – I always bloody paid. And he said it wasn't about the money, it was because Drew Barrymore was a tragic has-been.'

'Well, maybe he just didn't want to see the film,' said Esther, taking another crisp from the packet. It felt alien to take Ricko's side in anything, but she wasn't surprised a man of twenty-five didn't leap at the chance to watch a romantic comedy.

'No!' said Laura, with intensity. 'Don't you get it? This

is from someone who actually got together with me over a Drew Barrymore movie. We always joked about her, how she was our matchmaker. It was like he was pissing all over everything we'd ever had together.'

'Which is a lovely image.'

'Thank you,' said Laura, with a smirk. 'And I said, you can't exactly call her a has-been when she's starring in a Hollywood blockbuster. So he said, "With any luck she'll get murdered in the first ten minutes like in *Scream* – I'll go and see it if you promise me that happens."'

'Well, that's fighting talk,' said Esther, now safely siding with Laura again. 'He can't talk about Drew like that.'

'Exactly! But he said that everyone has a peak point in their lives, and for some people it's earlier than for others. He said you had to deal with that and accept it.'

'Really?' said Esther, wondering when her peak point might be and desperately hoping that she hadn't already had it without noticing.

'He reckoned it was embarrassing for Drew Barrymore to be running around chasing an acting career – she should just give up gracefully and accept no-one cares about her any more.'

'Well, *we* care,' said Esther, loyally.

Laura scooped a handful of crisps into her palm, and chewed on one thoughtfully.

'The thing is, Est, I realized he wasn't talking about Drew Barrymore, he was talking about me. He was telling me that I was a has-been, that I'd passed my peak and it was downhill all the way from here. Stuck with my doley boyfriend and my mum in the house I'd grown up in. And it just came on me like a holy visitation, I swear. I just thought, fuck you, Ricko. This is not anywhere *near* my peak, and don't you dare tell me it is.'

'Right *on*.' Esther raised her beer bottle to clink it with Laura's in congratulation, and Laura swung hers back with such enthusiasm the bottles nearly smashed. Esther held hers up to the light to check it for cracks.

'You know what, Drew Barrymore could have totally given *up*,' Laura threw her arms wide as if she was addressing crowds of supporters instead of one long-distant friend. 'She could have not gone to rehab and stayed a headcase, or she could have, I don't know, coasted on being a former child star forever. Or carried on making shitty pornos like *Poison Ivy*. But she didn't give up, did she?'

'No, she didn't,' Esther agreed. 'Nuh-uh.'

She felt like she was in one of those American church choirs, standing behind the preacher in a purple gown, offering words of spiritual encouragement to support the evangelical truth. 'Mmm-hmm. You said it, sister. Praise be.'

'She just kept going and I thought, *I am Gertie*. I thought, Ricko thinks I'm washed up, but I'm not having it. I'm Drew fucking Barrymore, Esther. There is something better than this for me.'

Esther remembered the sleepy, grief-struck Laura in her childhood bedroom after Edward's funeral, claiming to be happy with nothing more than 'this'. Now she was stirring, inspiring. Esther felt like clambering onto the pub table in tribute, like the boys in *Dead Poets Society*.

'You're Drew fucking Barrymore,' she said, laughing. 'I love it.'

'From this day forth,' said Laura, pushing her hair back and lifting her face decisively to the yellow pub light, 'I am following the gospel according to Drew Barrymore. And it will lead me to my *peak*.'

'Well, you've converted me,' said Esther. 'I could do with a peak of my own. Where do I sign up?'

Laura grinned at her, and the last two years fell away. There she was, her old friend. She had never really gone away at all. Ricko had been just a smokescreen between them for a while. Laura hadn't changed – she had been there all along.

'You've always been signed up, Est,' she said, reaching across the table for her hand. 'There's no gospel without you. There couldn't be.'

Esther felt she could say amen to that. So she did.

13

October 2013

When we leave the café to walk to Laura's apartment, Stanley leads the way down a tree-lined side street. He implies that in doing so he is indulging me in a quaint European custom that will make me feel at home. When I ask what he means, he says that it was a source of considerable amusement to Laura's colleagues that she insisted on walking whenever possible. She had even chosen this neighbourhood, on the wrong side of town from the vineyard, because it was full of shops and restaurants, so there was no need to drive all the time.

'I kind of loved that,' he says, with clear admiration for Laura's independent spirit and refusal to conform. 'It's so British.'

I don't tell him that it took three expensive attempts for Laura to pass her driving test, or that she was famous for handing her car keys to total strangers and begging them for help when faced with the threat of parallel parking. One of the things she had liked most about America, she told me when she first moved here, was that the roads were wide and the parking spaces plentiful. So much harder for anyone to tell that she was a terrible driver. And yet, wherever she has gone, she must have braved driving there. Her car is gone; Stanley said so.

I can see why Laura liked walking around this neighbourhood. The streets are lined on either side with old-fashioned timber-clad houses, no more than two or three storeys high. There are white picket fences and American flags flying, just like in the movies. Wooden steps lead up to porches where carved pumpkins bare their square teeth ready for Halloween. Children's paintings are pinned up in windows. A stooped old man looks up from raking leaves on his lawn and, after nodding a greeting, rests his chin contentedly on the top of the rake to watch us pass.

It is cosy – friendly, even. It doesn't have the brash urban energy of other American cities I've visited, ruled by freeways and flyovers. Instead it feels quieter and more gentle; the sort of place where even a foreign stranger could put down roots, and feel at home. But the closer we get to Laura's, and the more homely the surroundings, the more uncomfortable I feel. Stanley falls quiet, too, confining his speech to directions – right, right again, just round this corner – until at last we are there.

Laura's is a house exactly like all the others on the

street: painted white, with a square of garden in front. Perhaps hers is a little shabbier than some, in the way of rental properties. Paint peels from the window frames, and the swing seat on the porch hangs at a reckless angle that suggests it's either broken, or will be the moment someone sits on it. But this place isn't the worst house on the block; you don't look at it and immediately imagine that it hides a terrible secret. It just looks normal, and its very normality feels like a let-down. I thought, and I realize now how deluded I was, that seeing where Laura lived would be a clue in itself. As if it would be like a haunted house in a movie – you'd know just by looking at it that something inside was wrong.

There's an entrance on the lower floor of the house where a dreamcatcher floats serenely in the breeze, but Stanley runs briskly up the steps of the porch to the upper level. He pushes the front door open, and as he crouches down to collect the junk mail that has accumulated on the doormat, I go past him into Laura's home.

I have no idea what I am supposed to be looking for. It feels strangely like I am in some sort of performance, playing a detective. Laura and I used to pretend to be Cagney and Lacey when we were little, borrowing our mothers' handbags to swing from our shoulders as we strode confidently across the playroom solving crimes, with Sophie unhappily pressed into service as either a greasy Manhattan hoodlum or long-suffering husband

Harv. I can't be Lacey without your Cagney, Laura, I think. I don't know how to do this without you.

The dark hallway leads to a living room at the front of the house, where a big window looks out onto the street. The room is painted a pale mushroom colour, and there are two framed pictures on the far wall – one of some mountains, the other a forest. They are the kind of generic pictures a cheapskate landlord puts up to make a place look homely, but they have the opposite effect. More than anything they remind me of the posters you see in a dentist's office, or some kind of medical waiting room. They seem wrong in a domestic setting; I can't shake the feeling that someone is going to open a hidden door and invite me in for an appointment, or to deliver bad news. I appreciate Laura wasn't going to have an apartment plastered with film posters and pictures of her favourite bands – we're not fifteen any more – but I'm surprised there is so little of her apparent here. She's lived in this place for years, yet it looks like she's just moved in.

Stanley comes in behind me, sorting through the mail, and goes straight to the tiny kitchen that has been built at the other end of the room. He puts the envelopes and keys on the counter that separates the kitchen cabinets from the rest of the room and starts opening doors, as if he's looking for something.

'Is everything okay?' I ask.

He looks up, as if I've surprised him. 'Sure. Just

thought I'd make some tea. I know how you British girls like your tea. You have a good look around.'

The kitchen is little more than two rows of pale wood cabinets on the back wall, one at head height and one on the floor, and on the counter stand a microwave and a kettle. Nothing else, not even a toaster. I think of my kitchen counter at home, with its stainless-steel coffee machine next to the bottle sterilizer, the juicer we never use slowly gathering dust. You can infer so much about us from our appliances, and I suppose that is the intention; these are the pop-star posters for adults, aren't they? The Gaggia and the Dualit are invitations to make assumptions about us – middle-class, affluent, smug. You know that when you open the cupboards they will be full of organics and expensive olive oil. Laura's kitchen is the opposite. It's almost hostile in its anonymity.

'Do you mind if I look in here quickly?' I ask.

Stanley shuffles backwards obligingly, so I can open the fridge. It's spotless. There are a few jars at the back, mustards and jams, but apart from that it's completely empty. The cupboards above turn out to hold some noodles, rice, cans of tinned tomatoes and a stack of Heinz baked beans and Bird's custard powder that look more like an art installation than something to eat – as if they are there for nostalgic reassurance rather than sustenance. I imagine Laura opening the cupboard door when she felt homesick, and it makes me sad.

Stanley catches my eye as I shut the doors and says, 'She ate out a lot. I guess.'

'I guess,' I say back, echoing him by accident, and the words feel alien in my mouth, like I'm trying to be someone I'm not.

I leave him there and go back into the living room, which means only that I take one step from the tile floor onto carpet, and there I am.

The weirdest thing about Laura's apartment is the tidiness of it. Nothing is out of place, and there is a strong smell of bleach, like a municipal swimming pool. It makes me realize that this is the first time I've ever visited a place she lives in entirely by herself. I've only been to houses that she's shared with other people, usually boys – houses where there are sports socks drying on the radiator and crusted saucepans growing mould in the sink. You could always tell her room by the fairy lights strung everywhere; she said they were an effort to be feminine amongst all that testosterone, but I always suspected the real reason was that harsher bulbs would have revealed the floor-nests of knickers and abandoned plates. But that was long ago.

Now striped cushions are plumped against the sofa, two on each side, with all of the stripes lined up horizontally. Magazines have been fanned out on the glass coffee table, reinforcing the waiting-room feel: two copies of *Decanter* from England, and one of *People* with Catherine Zeta Jones on the cover. Laura's always loved her celebrity gossip – when she lived in France she bought copies of *Voici* every week, despite not knowing any of the French television stars – but when I pick this magazine up, I see it's a few weeks old. I don't know if that's significant. It might mean she's been gone for longer than we think, or it might mean that she just doesn't buy a trashy magazine very often these days.

People change. Perhaps living alone has made Laura houseproud and meticulous; or maybe she's developed some kind of OCD, unable to leave the house if the sofa cushions aren't perfectly straight. I don't know. What do I expect to discover about where Laura has gone, when every moment seems to bring a new reminder that I know so little about who she is?

A table and chairs are set up by the window to make the most of the light from outside. They're pushed right against the sill so there is room for only three people to sit down. I imagine Laura here in the mornings before work – would she have sat facing the street? Or in this chair on the side? Was she alone then, at breakfast? Or was someone else with her, pouring her coffee and sharing her cereal? She hasn't mentioned anyone for a while, but that doesn't mean anything. When Laura refers to herself as single, she means nothing more than that the current man sharing her bed doesn't yet deserve the title of boyfriend; she is rarely alone for long. Stanley said she was private, and perhaps she is even more private than I had suspected.

I run my finger along the table as I move towards the hallway, feeling the rough wood under my fingertips like Braille. I wonder what this table would tell me if it could talk.

What if there is someone new, and significant? Someone who's more than just one of her usual flings? Laura never minds talking about those, that's how I can tell they're not serious – she offers up all the details without even being asked. But it would be just like her to say nothing if she'd got involved with a man who actually meant something to her. I think of how she was with Ricko, how she disappeared then, too, in a different sort of way. He didn't have to shut her away from her friends that time – she did it to herself. Far away from family and her old friends, Laura is vulnerable, even if she doesn't feel it. Who is here to see the old signs, to warn her if she is letting herself get drawn into something that might be hard to get out of?

I can hear Stanley behind me in the kitchen; the gentle chime of clinking china and the rumble of a boiling kettle.

'You look around,' he says when he sees me looking over at him, urging me out of the room by waving his hands. 'I'll have the tea ready when you're done. It's not big, won't take you long.'

I can feel myself hesitate at the doorway, nervous about going further into Laura's home. There is something so wrong about sneaking around a friend's place when they are not there. It's like reading a diary, or going through someone's text messages. The living room and kitchen are places where any casual visitor might go, but the rest of Laura's apartment feels more intimate, and the sense of intrusion stronger. I think of how I would feel if I found a friend of mine rooting around in my private belongings without my permission. I can't shake the feeling that Laura might appear suddenly, her key in the front door, staring in horror at her best friend, who should rightly be thousands of miles away, picking through the contents of her bathroom bin.

Thinking of bathrooms, I suppose that's a good place to start. They say no man is a hero to his valet, and it's also true that no woman is a mystery to someone who has seen the contents of her bathroom cabinet. Back when we used to have big house parties when I was first married, I used to rigorously edit the bathroom before guests arrived. The hair removal cream, verruca treatment and nose hair trimmers (my husband's, I should clarify) were temporarily hidden in a box under the bed so that any nosy visitors would find nothing more under the sink than expensive organic face creams and body scrubs – evidence of a life of serene perfection in which nothing needed curing or removal, only indulgent enhancement. Since Linus was born, of course, I don't bother. Once you've bellowed like a cow in front of a roomful of strangers who are all staring at your nether regions, your notions of personal modesty change somewhat. Nowadays I've discussed my mastitis with enough people not to bat an eye if they discover the tube of nipple cream sitting out in the middle of the kitchen.

Laura's bathroom is as pristine as one in a hotel room (though sadly not like the one in my dingy motel on the other side of town). There is nothing left by the sink, not even a toothbrush. And I need not fear for Laura finding me rifling through her bin; there isn't so much as a cotton-wool ball to be seen when I lift the lid. The bathroom cabinet looks just like mine used to before a party; like it's been expecting someone to open it, and is quite prepared to give nothing away.

There's a bottle of bright pink liquid that calls itself Pepto-Bismol and claims to be a cure for indigestion, though I've never once heard her complain of heartburn. Painkillers. A tub of jojoba hand cream that looks like the sort of present women of our age receive from people who don't know them very well – not something Laura would buy for herself – and sure enough, when I pick it up I can see it's never been opened. There's a packet of Q-tips, some spare loo roll, a bottle of bathroom cleaner and that's it.

It's what is not there that is more interesting. No washbag, for someone who travels all the time. No toothbrush or toothpaste, no razor, no face cream, no sunscreen. Laura told me she wore sunscreen religiously in California, terrified into it by the weather-ravaged faces of the grape-pickers she'd met at the vineyard. There are none of the products here that a woman uses every day – this is the bathroom of someone who has taken things with her, wherever she's gone.

I hear Margie's voice in my ear. 'What if someone just *wants* you to think that? What if they've taken Laura's things with her so you think she left voluntarily?'

The worst part about looking for Laura is that I don't know how seriously to take things. One moment I'm amused at the idea of myself playing both Cagney and Lacey; the next I've become Margie, fretting about the logistics of shipping a body back to England. I have a vision of Laura sitting on the edge of the bath and watching me from under her blunt fringe, shrieking with laughter at the idea that I'm trying to divine her whereabouts by means of a bottle of Pepto-Bismol and a missing toothbrush.

But the more I look around, the more I think that Laura has gone away because she wanted to. This apartment is no Marie Celeste, abandoned unexpectedly with a meal half eaten, or a diary left abandoned at a critical moment (*Dear Diary – wait, what is that spooky sound outside? I will just go and investigate*). It's clear that no-one was dragged out of here, protesting. No-one scratched a plea for help on the wall. Someone emptied the bins, cleared the fridge, mopped the floors, and packed a washbag. Someone prepared to leave this place. And who else could that someone be but Laura?

It worries me to realize that in some twisted way I have

preferred to imagine that there might be a sinister reason for her disappearance – a mysterious lover, a masked stranger – rather than the more likely scenario: that she could so easily walk away from her life and everyone in it without a word of explanation. Is this how Margie feels? That it's better to imagine Laura abducted and detained, than simply just not that concerned with us any more?

I finish my fruitless search of the apartment with Laura's bedroom, which is dominated by a high double bed with a row of pillows propped up against the wall. There's a quilt on the bed that I remember from Laura's bedroom at home. It's a child's quilt, too small, really, laid lengthwise across the end of the bed and folded over on itself to show the pale silk lining of the underside. I sit down and run my hand over the faded material. It's beginning to wear through at the corners. I slept under this quilt a hundred times when I was little, before Laura and I got too big to share her single bed and I moved onto the camp bed on the floor of her room. She must have brought it with her, or maybe Margie sent it to remind her of home. It is the first thing I've seen here that admits any kind of history before she arrived in California.

The rest of this place is so devoid of a past that it's as if she doesn't want any reminders of the places she's left behind. It's funny, because I never thought of Laura as running away from things until now. I only ever saw her running towards bright new futures. There was always an exciting job, a new frontier, an album of envy-inducing photographs for everyone to like on Facebook. But now I look at this apartment, her most recent fresh start, and I see that of course it is somewhere a person could leave without difficulty. It would be easy if that person had never really allowed herself to feel at home here, or anywhere else.

The bedroom has few other secrets to reveal, other than the telling lack of a suitcase. She must have taken it with her. I've had her wheeled red suitcase in my hall often enough to know what it looks like, and it's nowhere to be seen. I even look under the bed, which is as clean as the rest of the apartment. Clothes are hung neatly in a built-in cupboard, shoes lined up underneath. I don't know Laura's wardrobe well enough to be able to tell what's missing, but the clothes left inside give me hope. If she wasn't planning on coming back, wouldn't she have taken everything?

I'm about to leave the bedroom when, on impulse, I look behind the bedroom door, which has swung back on itself against the wall. I nearly leap backwards at the sight of a figure there, but it's only my own reflection in a long mirror that has been hidden out of view. The mirror itself is of little interest, being of the same throw-away cheapness as everything else in the apartment – but around the edge of it, tucked into the frame and Sello-taped on top of it, are photographs, more than I can count, at least fifty of them.

When I go closer to look, I am touched to see that several are of Linus; printouts from emails I've sent to Laura. I reach out a finger to stroke the cold, printed cheek of my newborn boy, resting in a clear hospital cot. There's a photograph of Margie, looking away from the camera, her grey hair twisted up into a strip of woven cloth, in profile like Whistler's mother. Here I am, with Laura, in a photo booth back at the tail end of the eighties, sucking our cheeks in and pouting into the lens. I look like the schoolgirl that I am, round-faced and unsophisticated, while Laura looks like a supermodel slumming it in a Portsdown uniform for the day.

There is a picture of Edward, too, of course. At the top of the mirror, watching over Laura. It's her favourite picture of him – this must be a copy, since I know the original is still in its silver frame on top of Margie's piano in England. He's in the uniform of a Lieutenant Commander, which would make him in his forties when it was taken; so handsome and smiling, it's unimaginable that within a few years he would be dead.

The photographs are all clustered around the top of the mirror, as if it's some sort of totem pole with her father at the top and then the rest of us in descending order of importance. If there is a new man in her life, he hasn't made it to her photograph mirror yet, because I recognize most of these people from Facebook – other interns from Laura's first Napa harvest season, that Australian guy she had a thing with, I can't remember his name – Trent, I think? Laura with a group of girls in a bar, holding a bottle of wine up to the camera and pointing to a label that's too blurry to read – it must have been one they'd made themselves. Laura and Stanley, staring with concentration into a baffling arrangement of test tubes and bottles. Stanley in a restaurant, laughing and reaching out a protesting hand to the camera. Laura and Stanley again, both in shorts and sturdy walking boots, standing together high up on a hill somewhere with rows and rows of vines receding into the distance behind them. Her hand shields her eyes from the sunshine as she smiles at the photographer. His arm is around her waist.

Laura and Stanley. I stand rigid in front of the photographs; my breath stops still.

I never asked why he would have a key to his employee's house. I never questioned how he knew exactly where to find the tea, or the cups in Laura's kitchen, opening cupboards and drawers with the easy confidence of a regular visitor. It didn't occur to me to wonder why Laura might hide personal photographs where no-one would see them unless they were in her bedroom with the door shut. Unless they were invited there. I didn't press Stanley when he said that Laura would be used to people talking about her at work; of course they would, if she was sleeping with her boss. Again.

Laura and Stanley. Some detective I am.

NEVER BEEN KISSED, SEPTEMBER 1999[6]

JOSIE GELLER: That thing, that moment, when you kiss someone and everything around becomes hazy and the only thing in focus is you and this person and you realize that that person is the only person that you're supposed to kiss for the rest of your life, and for one moment you get this amazing gift and you want to laugh and you want to cry because you feel so lucky that you found it and so scared that it will go away all at the same time.

14

Esther bloody knew there was something between David Carrell and Fiona from Penguin. She had detected the incipient romance before it was apparent to either of the participants, like one of those dogs she'd read about that could sniff out a cancerous tumour in advance of an X-ray. Fiona and David had been officially going out for six months now, and if Esther had to hear one more sickening story from David about the weekend they'd spent at Jolyon's cottage in the Cotswolds, or the meal they'd had at the River Café, or how Fi (Fi!) had this really adorable way of sneezing, like a little baby mouse, she was going to be forced to strangle him to death with a pair of opaque black book publicist's tights. If only Al was still here she knew he would gladly have joined her. They could have made a satisfying tug of war of it.

Esther should have been pleased Al was gone. He and the horns had left to 'pursue new opportunities'. Which everyone knew was code for 'got sacked', even as they wrote perfunctory messages in his leaving card wishing him good luck. David sat at Al's desk now. David did Al's job now, as Esther's boss.

This morning he came into the office shaking water from his hair like a wet dog. He slung his jacket onto the back of his chair and threw an umbrella under his desk where it joined a pile of shoes, football boots and a gym bag that rarely left the office. It was a mystery to Esther how David maintained his appearance of sporty endeavour when his idea of strenuous exercise was lifting an arm to hail the taxi that would take him to lunch.

'Alright, Est?' he said in the mockney accent he was trying out lately, despite the fact his education had come via a trust fund rather than the state.

Any hint of their former flirtation had gone, flattened into submission by this new and resolute blokeishness. Each jocular 'alright' that he uttered, each matey punch to the shoulder, made Esther want to weep for the opportunities that had passed her by. She couldn't say for sure that if she had gone to that Penguin party David would have been her boyfriend instead of Fiona's, but she knew that if there had been no flirtation between them at all, if she had just imagined the whole thing, he wouldn't have been so careful to rid himself of any hint of it now.

It wasn't just that he had a girlfriend, either. She realized that much of their camaraderie had come from sharing the lowest rung of the ladder at the *Camden*

Gazette, and yet it was apparent that David had always been destined, as the heir apparent, to tread on this rung with only the lightest and most fleeting of steps. He'd hesitated on it just long enough to launch himself further up the Carrell Media ladder, where a mere Esther Conley could not reach.

Esther thought of her teenage self, who would have railed at the injustice of it all, claimed it as nepotism, another victory for the patriarchy, and demanded an inquiry. She was more sophisticated now, but it didn't make her any happier. She understood that making a fuss would only turn her into an Al Webster, obsolete and redundant, the printer's ink on his fingers now a mark of shame instead of pride in this brave new media world of websites and email. It wasn't like David was a bad boss, she told herself. Wasn't this growing up? Learning to work with the world as it was, rather than as it should be? And in the world as it was, David would be neither her boyfriend nor her work experience minion. To bleat about unfairness would only make her unhappy.

'You coming to the pub for the football later?' he asked, as he reached under his desk to turn on his computer. 'Fi's at a work thing tonight and I'm heading there with some of the boys.'

'Yeah, great,' Esther said. She pulled her hair back into a knot and fixed it in place with a biro from her desk to keep it out of the way. 'Let me just scratch my balls while I think about that. No, thanks.'

She may not have been the high-heel-wearing sort of girly girl who sipped cocktails and demanded to have doors opened for her, but even so, Esther took offence at David's latest attempt to further neuter her into some kind of pint-swilling, footie-discussing Denise van Outen clone. She bet he wouldn't have asked Fiona to the pub. Fiona got the Cotswold cottage and the Atlantic Bar instead.

'What?' said David, holding his palms out in supplication.

'David, have I, in all the time we've worked together, ever once expressed an interest in football?'

He shrugged, wiping his face clear of rain with his sleeve. 'You've come before. In fact,' he pointed an accusing finger at her as he recalled contradictory evidence, 'if it wasn't you who used a packet of Barbecue Beef McCoys to prove to Classifieds Bob that she understood the offside rule, then it was someone who looked very like you. Who went by the name of Esther Conley.'

That was last year at the Goose and Grapes. When David nicked one of the explanatory crisps straight from Esther's hand, winking as he ate it, she was certain it must be a sign. Though now she thought it was probably just a sign that he fancied a crisp, rather than her.

'That's not because I'm interested in football,' she said. She wasn't about to admit she had only ever gone to watch the football just to spend time with David. Instead she answered with, if not the exact truth, an element of it. 'That's because Bob is a patronizing idiot. The offside rule is general knowledge, it's hardly evidence of a deep interest in the beautiful game.'

David inched closer on his wheeled chair, clasping his hands together mock-pleadingly. Esther couldn't stop herself from noticing that, despite his jacket, the rain had soaked through and made his white shirt cling to his shoulders. He looked like Colin Firth as Mr Darcy emerging from the lake, if the lake was composed of stain-resistant office carpet tiles.

'Come on, Est, we can talk periods and handbags if you want, it doesn't have to be about the football. It's just an excuse to go out to the pub and get shitfaced together. It'll be a laugh.'

'I'm busy, you sexist arsehole.'

'Doing what?'

'Reading Andrea Dworkin.'

'Andrea who? Come on,' he said. 'What are you doing really?'

'Stuff.'

Esther picked up her Filofax and flicked it open, waving it around so David could see that many important events were written on its pages, but fast enough that he couldn't read any of them. It was a general impression of intriguing busyness she was after – and that impression would be ruined if he was able to make out the words 'step aerobics' on the entry for today.

'Are you on a date?' he asked. A slow sideways smile

began at one corner of his mouth. 'Is that why you've gone all mysterious on me?'

'No,' she answered immediately, realizing too late that she should have been aloof instead, let him think she had an intriguing love life of which he knew nothing.

'It's that Laura, isn't it?' he said, ruefully. 'Leading you astray with her fine wines and her fancy restaurants. You just don't have time for your old friends like you used to. Classifieds Bob was saying only yesterday how you never give him one of your special neck rubs any more.'

'I've never given Classifieds Bob a neck rub!'

David raised an artful eyebrow. 'That's not what *he* says.'

He scooted his chair away and picked up the ringing phone before Esther could answer back. As soon as she heard him say 'Hello, mousey' she knew he was talking to Fiona and blocked out his conversation. She'd got very good at that lately.

Bloody David and his rodent-sneezing girlfriend and his far-too-see-through shirt. Esther wished Laura had email at work so she could fire off a five-hundred-word rant and get it all out of her system. But there was just one email address at her office in St James's, and only one computer; Laura had shown it to Esther when she went there to pick her up once, both of them giggling hysterically as Laura opened the doors of a brass-handled antique cabinet, as if she was about to reveal comprom-ising photographs of her boss instead of an ancient

Amstrad. The computer was switched on twice a day, and was shut away the rest of the time like an embarrassing relative that everyone pretended didn't exist.

Instead she took out her Nokia and texted Laura. Suddenly she didn't feel like step aerobics after all.

Esther had thought the *Camden Gazette* was old-fashioned, but Laura's office made hers seem like something out of *The Matrix*. Even the frontage of Bewes Brothers Vintners hadn't changed for two hundred years, the thick Georgian glass windows obscuring the inside from view. If she had walked in to find Regency bucks perusing the wares in breeches and topcoats, Esther wouldn't have been a bit surprised. But the customers in the ground-floor shop wore disappointingly modern clothes as she passed the racks full of wines that cost more than she earned in a week, heading towards the stairs to the offices above. The receptionist recognized her and, with the phone clamped to her ear, waved her on inside to where Laura sat.

The office walls were wood-panelled, the interconnected rooms saved from being oppressively dark only by the ceilings that towered over her head. Each vast claw-footed desk was illuminated with its own green-glass lamp, so that the few people working late were each marooned in separate pools of light. In the corner there was a very old man scratching at a vast leather-bound ledger with a fountain pen. Esther had to look again to make sure he wasn't actually using a quill.

Laura was the only one left in the PR department, the very last room that Esther came to. She looked up when she heard her friend's approach, and slammed shut the desk diary she had been writing in.

'God, I thought you were never going to get here,' she hissed in a low whisper. 'Fucking Malcolm's been sleazing around for half an hour, trying to get me to go for a drink with him. Everyone else's gone to a tasting.'

Esther looked nervously over her shoulder as if the mysterious Malcolm Bewes might emerge from under a desk.

'Sorry, tube got stuck,' she said, her eye caught by an imposing portrait of an Edwardian Bewes high up on the wall, one foot resting on a tree stump while two spaniels gazed up at him in devotion. 'Don't you get spooked being here by yourself in the dark? It's so creepy.'

'You should see the cellar,' shrugged Laura, picking up a pile of papers from her desk and dumping them in her in-tray. 'There are bottles down there going all the way back to Waterloo.'

'And probably the skeletons of all the girls the Bewes men have ever touched up,' shuddered Esther. 'Over *centuries*. You should watch out.'

'Skeletons?' boomed a voice behind her.

She whipped round to see an extremely tall man standing behind her with his legs akimbo – his ruddy cheeks and his reddish-blond hair were identical to those on the oil painting above his head, declaring his Bewes lineage. His eyelashes were pale like Boris Becker's. It was hard to tell his age – he could have been anything from a rugged thirty-five to a well-preserved sixty. Esther had expected someone more repellent from Laura's descriptions; if it weren't for his awful clothes, he would almost have been attractive. He wore a green tweed waist-coat over mustard-yellow corduroy trousers. Combined with his outdoorsy complexion, this country-squire ensemble made Esther anticipate that at any moment he might shout 'Tally-ho!' and go galloping around the desks, making horsey noises.

He didn't.

'Esther, can I introduce you to my *boss*, Malcolm Bewes,' said Laura pointedly, stepping out from behind her desk.

Malcolm harrumphed with delight and held out his hand for Esther to shake. He took hers between both of his palms and squeezed tightly. 'Good lord, Laura, they make them fine where you come from, don't they? What a pair.'

Esther, already on her guard, was horrified; was he referring to her *breasts*? She must have shown it on her face because he hurriedly let go of her hand.

'What a pair *you both make*,' he said, his smile only faltering for a second. 'One dark, one fair. Marvellous.'

'Anyway,' Laura said, pulling on her coat. 'That's me

done. We're off to the cinema, Malcolm. I hope you have a good evening.'

Esther nodded a polite farewell, keeping her arms crossed so that she both covered her chest and kept her hands free from being squeezed again. But Malcolm stood between her and the door, as immovable as a tweed-covered tree, and almost as tall.

'Cinema, eh?' he said, his rosy cheeks shining like apples in the dim light. 'Are you quite certain I can't persuade you both to join me at the opening of Roland's wine bar instead?'

Laura answered quickly. 'You know I'd love to, Malcolm, it's always such a treat to be taken out. But I'm afraid Esther's already booked the tickets, haven't you, Est?'

Esther had done no such thing, they had loads of time to get tickets, but she looked at her watch as if she was in a terrible rush. 'Yes, seven-thirty at the Odeon Leicester Square. We'd better get a move on.'

Never Been Kissed wasn't really on until nine. And in any case, they were going for a drink at the Cork and Bottle first, so she could vent off about David and Fi before the cinema demanded silence. Wine, a rant, and a dose of Drew Barrymore to finish the evening. It was exactly what Doctor Laura had prescribed.

'Still,' he said, looking thoughtful. 'Always a bloody half hour of adverts before the film starts, eh? Won't be on until eight at least. And Roland's is just around the corner, edge of Chinatown. So why don't we all share a taxi over there and you can come for a drink first?'

Laura and Esther looked at each other, before Laura answered for both of them. 'It's just – you're going to think this is ridiculous, Malcolm, but Esther really doesn't actually like wine. So I think we'll have to give it a miss.'

As someone who spent most of her Saturdays drinking Pinot Grigio with Laura in the pubs around Finsbury Park, Esther was surprised to hear this. But she shrugged apologetically under Malcolm's astonished stare.

'Sorry,' she said.

'Not a problem,' beamed Malcolm, unperturbed. 'I supplied Roland's cellars myself, and I happen to know he's serving nothing but champagne tonight. Everyone loves champagne.'

Laura widened her eyes at Esther just enough for her to pick up the cue. 'Not me,' she declared loudly. 'I'm afraid I really don't like champagne at all.'

He frowned. 'Not like champagne? Extraordinary. What on earth do you drink?'

Laura answered for her. 'Alcopops,' she said. 'She loves them. Or Sea Breezes, that sort of thing.'

'Yes,' lied Esther, all innocence. 'Anything pink and sweet gets my vote. Would Roland have that sort of thing at his wine bar, do you think?'

Malcolm took a step backwards, and his face fell, literally. At least an inch. Esther saw that when he wasn't smiling his face became much narrower, and his cheeks sagged down just slightly below his jawline. No-one could deny that he looked good for his age, but now she could see that age quite clearly. Fifty at least.

'Well,' he said, shaking his deflated face sadly. 'I am most disappointed that you would prefer, Laura, to drink *alcopops* rather than attend an evening with one of our most prestigious clients.'

'Another time, Malcolm,' she promised.

He didn't move, just stayed there, blocking their exit, no longer smiling. Esther felt the coldness of his stare as it travelled over both of them, his bonhomie suddenly vanished.

'Perhaps there won't *be* another time,' he said.

'Oh, I'm – well, I'm sure there will,' Laura faltered, glancing at Esther. 'You go to so many parties.'

'I do,' he said. His voice had gone very quiet for such a large man. 'But the invitations begin to dry up for girls who always say no to me.'

Esther felt like she was watching one of those snakes that hypnotizes its prey, as he ignored her to focus all of his attention on Laura. She gazed up at him helplessly, and Esther could see her resolve drain away. His threat was clear, but subtle enough that he could have easily explained it away if challenged. Even if he wasn't the boss, even if there was someone to whom Laura could have reported him, what would she have said? Malcolm made me go to a wine bar with him to drink free champagne? Who would have seen this as anything other than the act of a benevolent and paternal senior figure to an insignificant office junior?

'Well, it's far too generous of you, Malcolm,' she said at last. 'I really don't see how we can say no. Just a quick drink before the cinema. If that's okay with you, Est?'

Esther wasn't sure how to answer. It felt to her like she was complicit in Laura's defeat whatever her reply. And she knew that Malcolm had already won. 'If it's what you want, Laura,' she said.

'Of course it is,' Malcolm beamed, his jovial smile returning instantly. 'A good decision. I'll have Arabella call us an account car.'

As he finally turned away towards his office, Laura's shoulders slumped and she dropped her bag onto her desk with a heavy thud.

'What the fuck?' whispered Esther. 'How did that happen?'

'I'm *sorry*,' Laura hissed back. 'I tried. But I can't afford to piss him off, I just can't. You don't understand.'

'I understand he's a pervy old weirdo,' said Esther.

'He's my pervy old weirdo *boss*,' said Laura, sinking her forehead onto her palm like she was taking her own temperature. 'Who fired the last PR girl with no warning and no pay-off. I *need* this job, Est. I don't have a degree like you. All I've got is too many years at Oddbins, and the fact that Malcolm Bewes likes a bit of an ego massage.'

'I don't think it's his ego he wants massaging, Laur.'

'Fuck off,' she said, resignedly. 'Not all of us can be as noble as you.'

15

Roland's wine bar was full of men exactly like Malcolm, booming and confident and moneyed. They looked at Esther and Laura appraisingly, as if they had been brought there as the entertainment – roll up, roll up! Gaze in wonder at women decades younger than you! Brought here against their better judgement! There were few other women in the room, just a knot of expensively highlighted older ladies who gave tight smiles as cursory introductions were made. Their eyes were flinty with lack of interest, and they quickly turned back to continue their interrupted conversations. Malcolm immersed himself in a group of back-slapping chums, and left the girls standing awkwardly beside him. Next to Malcolm's extreme tallness, Esther felt like they were children again, allowed to join their parents' party for an hour before bed, admired for their youthful cuteness but somewhat getting in the way of grown-up business.

'Champagne?' asked a dark-haired waiter, holding up

a tray in front of them. He looked their own age, and though his face was impassively professional, his eyebrows twitched a little as he looked from Esther to Laura, trying to work out why they might be there.

'Is that a *biro* in your hair?' asked Laura, as Esther reached forward for a glass.

She straightened up, and her hand flew to the back of her head, *oh shit, probably*. She'd never taken it out.

'You nearly took my eye out,' Laura said, taking a glass from the tray. She bent her head and put her whole nose inside the rim like she was going to inhale the champagne instead of drink it. As Esther watched she made a really loud sniffing noise.

'Sorry.' Esther shrugged. Why was Laura being so embarrassing? No-one else even seemed to notice, in fact, loads of them were doing it. Exclaiming over the champagne and tipping their heads back to get the full flavour. Idiots. She turned back to get a drink herself, but the waiter had been swallowed up by the crowd already, leaving her thirsty.

'A biro in your hair! Just because Dreamy David's gone off with some other woman doesn't mean you should stop making an effort, you know.'

Esther stopped searching for the waiter and glared at Laura. 'Stop making an effort? Well, excuse *me*, Cindy Crawford's *House of Style*.'

Laura laughed gaily, and flicked her fringe out of her eyes. Esther was reminded of Ricko Struthers's party back when they'd just left school. This was a laugh for the benefit of the people around them, it wasn't for her. She'd seen the change steal over Laura in the taxi on the way here, as if the moment she had agreed to come, to relinquish her own evening for Malcolm's, she'd had to adopt a different personality. One that was harder, and sharper.

This laugh of Laura's was dangerous. It meant a reckless sort of gaiety that never ended well.

'Oh, come on, darling,' Laura said. 'I don't understand why you don't fight for David if you really like him that much. Put on a tight dress, rub up against him by the photocopier, make him see what he's missing.'

'Since when did you call me darling?' asked Esther, refusing to even acknowledge Laura's insulting suggestions.

Even if she'd lower herself to go fully *Poison Ivy* on David, vamping him away from Fi, she would only think the worse of him if he succumbed to that sort of thing. Laura didn't get it – it wasn't that Esther was noble, it was that she wanted to believe that David was. She would rather be without him forever than with him and disappointed by the manner of it.

Laura raised one eyebrow. 'I call everyone darling, darling. I'm in PR, for fuck's sake.'

'Of *course* you do, darling,' sighed Esther. It was hard to have a proper conversation when Laura was so determinedly 'on'. It made Esther feel like a client rather than a friend, her audience instead of her equal.

'Oh, come on, don't be like that,' chided Laura. 'I'm only trying to help.'

'Because you're so sorted yourself?'

'I *like* being single,' hissed Laura. 'I'm focused on my *career*, Esther. Love is for suckers, didn't you know?'

Suddenly her face broke into a huge smile that was all teeth and lips. It never reached her eyes, but you wouldn't see that unless you were really close up. Esther turned to see Malcolm elbowing his way towards them with a bottle of champagne in each hand.

'Girls, girls,' he shouted, above the din of the crowd. 'Roland's getting us somewhere to sit, can't bear the bloody crush here in the bullpen – sorry, Penny, darling, not you! Wonderful to see *you*. Just got to get the weight off, you know.'

A tall woman inclined her head to allow Malcolm to kiss the air next to her pale cheek before he tried to push onwards.

Esther noted his 'darling' and wondered. She remembered how quickly Laura had lost her American accent back when they were children. Once the novelty of being the exotic new girl had worn off, it had taken her mere days to shed the years in California for the playground sayings of an English primary school. She was still quick to observe, and even quicker to copy when she thought it was to her advantage.

Laura took the bottles from Malcolm efficiently, insisting that helping out at parties was what he paid her for. As she led the way to the alcove from where Roland waved at them, indicating the table he had saved, Malcolm's hand was now free to give her a playful slap on the bottom. Esther was astonished to see that Laura did nothing but laugh at him over her shoulder.

Malcolm followed Laura into one side of the booth, nestling next to her as if someone might be coming to sit on his other side. Esther took the opposite side alone and sat in the middle of it. The dark-haired waiter came over with ice buckets and fresh glasses, and began removing the wire hood from the first champagne bottle. At last, thought Esther. I need a drink.

'Got Roland to give us a couple of bottles of the good stuff,' said Malcolm. 'No point wasting it on the masses, eh?'

The waiter handed Esther a glass of the champagne and she lifted the glass to her nose as she'd seen Laura do. It was dry and yeasty. The bubbles popped on the underside of her nose; it smelled expensive and delicious. Just as she was about to take a sip, Malcolm pressed her hand down away from her mouth and took the glass away from her.

'No need, young lady, no need. Got to admire you for trying it, but hang on – yes, here he is.'

Esther looked up and saw another young waiter manoeuvring through the crowd with a lurid pitcher of bright pink liquid in one hand and a martini glass in the other.

'Sea Breeze for madam?' he asked, with only the faintest sneer on his lips. 'We appear to be out of alcopops this evening, Mr Bewes.'

The waiter with the dark hair winked at her. Malcolm stifled a guffaw behind the back of his hand, and then picked up his glass of champagne to toast Laura, who giggled obligingly.

Great, thought Esther. Just great. Not only do I have to sit here in a roomful of people my parents' age, not only must I watch my best friend be pawed by a dirty old man, but I don't even get to drink the good stuff while I do it.

She took a mouthful of her cocktail and tried not to wince. Laura mouthed at her over the table.

'I owe you.'

Esther just nodded grimly. At least they'd make their excuses for the cinema soon.

Her drink had come with a white plastic straw that she felt sure had been added by the disdainful waiter to make her feel even more like a silly little girl. She stirred it around in her drink, watching the ice cubes melt as Malcolm droned on about champagne producers he had known, and other such fascinating subjects. She would have liked to get properly drunk, but all the fruit juice was making her feel full up before the alcohol could have any effect.

Laura didn't seem to be having that problem. She was already pink in the face, though not as pink as Malcolm, at whose latest joke she was laughing uncontrollably. The first bottle of champagne had been upended, empty in its wine bucket, when Esther's straw pinged out of her fingers and fell under the table, splashing her skirt on its way. She bent down to retrieve it, not so much because she wanted to put it back in her drink covered in floor-germs, but because it would make a change of scenery from watching Laura appear to hang on Malcolm's every word. Didn't he see it was an act? How could he really think she was interested in an old man like him?

Underneath the table the sound was muffled, and it was dark enough that Esther had to squint to see. As her eyes adjusted, the white straw shone on the floor like a fluorescent tube. Like an arrow. She looked where it pointed, away from her. Laura's legs on the leather seat opposite were crossed at the knee, and on the top knee, clamped there like an octopus on a rock, was Malcolm's large hand. How long had it been there? Why hadn't Laura pushed it away? Why could she still hear Laura giggling as if nothing was happening?

When Esther sat up, with the straw in her hand, her face was hot.

'What's up?' said Laura. Her eyes were glassy with champagne. 'You've gone all red.'

'I think it's time to go,' said Esther.

'Loads of time yet,' boomed Malcolm. 'Whole other

bottle to get through yet – we'll have that waiter make you more cocktails.'

'No, thank you,' said Esther primly. 'Laura, *Never Been Kissed* is going to start soon.'

'Never Been Kissed?' Malcolm laughed, slapping his own leg with his free hand. 'I don't believe it of either of you. I bet you've both done a lot more than *kissing* in your time. Filthy little mares.'

'Oh, Malcolm,' said Laura, and pushed playfully at his chest with both hands. Esther could not believe what she was seeing. Not even an hour ago Laura was complaining about his sleazy ways, and now she was encouraging them.

'Wait a sec,' he said, peering into the crowd. 'There's Roland, wait there, all the more reason not to go. I'll bring him over to say hello. I'm sure he'll want to get to know *you*.'

He scooted along the seat of the booth, calling after his friend and vanishing into the crowd.

'What are you *doing*?' Esther hissed at Laura, as soon as he was out of earshot.

'What?'

'His hand was on your *leg*.'

'Pffft.' Laura reached over to the ice bucket and took out the fresh bottle, refusing to answer. She started to peel off the foil, then the hood, then she twisted the cork out of the bottle with practised ease.

'*Laura*. We should *go*.'

Laura filled her glass, drank half of it in one long gulp, and put the glass back on the table heavily, as if she'd expected to find the tabletop a few inches lower.

'Don't *judge* me, Esther.'

'I'm not judging. It's just time to get out of here. Come on, let's go.'

Laura didn't quite meet her eyes as she answered. 'You go, I'm going to stay.'

Esther stared at her, aghast. 'You're going to let me go to the cinema on my own?'

'You can stay if you want. Up to you.'

'Is this your *peak*, Laura?' she asked. '*This* is your Drew Barrymore moment? Letting some rich old pervert feel you up under the table?'

'I know what this is about,' sneered Laura. 'You *wish* your boss would feel you up. You wish he would and you're taking it all out on me. We're no different, Esther.'

'This has *nothing* to do with David,' gasped Esther.

'Oh, really?' Laura crossed her arms over her chest, and glared back. 'Lover-boy who took the job that should have been yours? And you just rolled over and let him? Never even told him what you felt about it – or about him? You and I are both compromised as fuck, darling, but at least I know it.'

'*Don't* call me darling.'

They had both been too involved to notice that Malcolm had reappeared with Roland.

'Now, now, girls.' Malcolm chuckled, swinging an arm

over Roland's shoulders. 'Bit of a catfight, is it? Meow.' He mimed a cat's paw, scratching in the air.

Laura tittered, and somehow that was enough to push Esther over the edge. She stood up.

'Thank you for the drinks, Malcolm. I'm pleased to have met you, Roland. I'm afraid I have to leave now.'

'Oh,' said Malcolm, looking crestfallen. 'Come on girls, no need to be silly, kiss and make up. Roland and I will watch.'

They both laughed heartily. Esther saw that Laura didn't join in, for once.

'I need to go,' insisted Esther, and she pushed past them, past the entire crowd of them, until she was out on the street, trying not to cry.

She wasn't quite sure where she was, she hadn't paid attention in the taxi, and it took a few minutes before she worked out that she was in one of the narrow streets to the north of Leicester Square. Malcolm hadn't lied about that, at least. She could still go to the cinema if she really wanted, but she didn't feel like it any more. Just as she turned in the direction of the tube, a man stepped out of the shadows where he'd been smoking a cigarette. It was the waiter from earlier, the dark-haired one with the champagne.

'Hey, Sea Breeze,' he said, dropping the filter on the pavement and grinding it under his heel. 'Leaving already?'

He was quite good-looking, now that she saw him

properly. Or maybe it was just the comparison to Malcolm that made her think so, gilding the waiter with the glow of youth that Laura's boss lacked.

'I don't even like Sea Breeze,' she snapped. 'Not that I need to explain myself to you.'

He just laughed.

'Okay,' he said. 'You leaving your friend in there?'

'What's it to you?'

He looked over his shoulder towards the bar like he could see through the walls to every person inside. 'I've seen that tall guy in here before – with other girls. He's a right sleaze. Your friend seems pretty drunk. She gonna be okay?'

Esther turned to face the waiter square on, planting her feet on the pavement as if she was readying herself to punch him. All of her anger at Laura channelled itself towards this innocent stranger.

'I am not her saviour, okay? Do you understand that? She is a grown woman, who makes her own decisions, and I am not responsible for them. Thank God.'

The waiter stepped backwards, an uncertain smile on his face. He shrugged, and pushed the sleeves of his white shirt up towards his elbows. 'Okay, whatever, it's none of my business.'

'No, it's not.'

'Have a good night,' he said, heading back towards the entrance.

She got to the end of the road when she heard footsteps running after her. 'Sea Breeze! I think you should give me your number.'

'Oh, do you?' she said haughtily.

'Yeah.' He grinned. 'I'll keep an eye on your friend. Call you if there's a problem.'

Esther paused, fiddled with the shoulder strap of her handbag, looked up into his laughing eyes.

'I'll let you have it on one condition,' she said, tossing her head. She felt brave all of a sudden. What did she have to lose?

'Anything,' he smiled.

'You absolutely promise not to call me about my friend.'

'No?'

'No. She'll be fine. She always is. You can call me about me.'

16

October 2013

Stanley is standing at the window when I go back into the living room, staring out into the street. He turns when he hears me and makes a rueful face at the two cups that sit steaming on the table between us.

'No milk,' he says, nodding at the unappealing black tea. 'Didn't think of that. You all done?'

'Oh, I think so, Stanley,' I say coldly.

He goes to pull out the chair nearest to him, and then stops with his hands on the back of it, waiting for me to do the same before he sits down. So he's considerate enough to wait for me to be seated first, but it hasn't occurred to him that he should consider telling me the truth about him and Laura. Nice priorities.

'Aren't you going to – ' Stanley indicates the other chairs, but his voice dries up as he looks me in the eye.

I don't know what he sees there, but it's enough to shut him right up.

I just stare back at him, saying nothing. His face is impassive, giving nothing away, but his hands twitch, once, gripping the chair back like someone has given him an electric shock.

'Is everything okay? Did you find something?' he asks. I see him swallow, his Adam's apple lifting and then falling.

'No,' I say. 'And yes.'

Although he doesn't move, it is as if that same electricity is running through him all of a sudden, no longer a single shock but a live current. He is tensed, humming with expectation, like he's ready to run out of the house and follow whatever clue I give him.

'So what is it? Do you know where she is?'

'You tell me. Or do you like keeping secrets, Stanley?'

'What do you – ' He sees the challenge in my expression and his mouth shuts suddenly, as if he's afraid of what might come out of it.

'You and Laura,' I say, and his blue eyes flash with something I can't identify before he looks away. Was it anger? Guilt?

'I'm right, aren't I? You're having a relationship with her.'

Stanley looks back at me and then he nods once, almost unwillingly, like someone behind him has pushed his head forward and down. I get a glimpse of the top of his scalp, where the hair is beginning to thin, and I'm surprised to find it makes him seem vulnerable. I don't want to feel sorry for him, I'm too angry.

'For how long?'

He rubs his hand over his face, pinching his eyebrows together, and his answer is muffled in his palm. 'Not long.'

'What does that mean?'

He drops his hand down by his side.

'Three months,' he says. 'Nearly four.'

'Was it serious?'

He laughs harshly. 'Was it *serious*? Maybe you should ask Laura that.'

'If I could ask her, neither of us would be here, Stanley. Stop dicking me around. Why didn't you tell me you were seeing her?'

'Why didn't *she*?' he says bitterly, and we stare at each other accusingly across the table. He breaks first, turning his head to look out of the window where there is nothing to see but the empty street.

'I knew she hadn't told you,' he says at last, addressing the window instead of me. 'She must have had a reason for that. If she didn't tell you, then—'

'You didn't think *you* should tell me?' I demand, hearing my voice go high and hysterical. 'Laura is missing – isn't that more important than keeping some stupid fling a secret? Don't you see how that makes you look?'

He turns around from the window and his face is

hard, angry. 'It's not a good idea to make assumptions about people.'

'For fuck's sake, Stanley, Laura's gone, you're hiding things from me. Of course I'm making assumptions. What else haven't you told me?'

His face darkens with anger, and when he answers his jaw is so tight that he seems to speak through his teeth. 'You wouldn't even know she was gone if it wasn't for me.'

I find that I'm edging backwards, out into the corridor that is the colour of blood. But he is right, of course. He called Margie, he raised the alarm.

'You think she didn't tell me how you never came to visit, no matter how much she asked?' he says, pacing slowly and dangerously from the living room to where I'm standing with my back against the wall. 'Never called? Too busy to ask what's happening in her life until it's too late?'

I can feel my heart beating against the cage of my ribs, like it's trying to get out.

'What are you saying? What's too late?'

'I thought, let her come, this so-called best friend, maybe Laura confided in her more than she said. Maybe she knows more than you think. But you don't. You don't know anything at all, do you?'

Stanley takes three long strides towards me, and just when I think he is about to grab me by the shoulders, he pushes past and opens the front door. The sun from outside casts him into shadow so that all I can see is the outline of him, filling the rectangle of light.

'Why is it too late?' I shout after him. He can't leave like this.

'I don't have to explain myself to you,' he says, and slams the door in my face.

I slide down the wall and burst into tears on the floor of Laura's hallway. I stop abruptly when I realize that I have no idea how to get back to the restaurant without Stanley to guide me. Scrabbling to my feet, I run out of the front door and down the wooden steps, but already he's gone. Which turning did he take?

Before I can run after him there is the sound of a door opening behind me, and a shout.

'Hey, Lara! What did I tell you about making all that goddamned noise?'

My accuser is standing under the opened door to the downstairs apartment, underneath the waving feathers of the dreamcatcher that I saw earlier. She has grey hair in a long plait that dwindles sparsely over her shoulder, and a tie-dyed dress billows over purple leggings. It is very evident that she is not wearing a bra. She looks like someone who went to Woodstock and never properly left.

'Lara?' I say.

'Oh, you're not her,' she says, scowling with suspicion as if I have tricked her on purpose. 'You just moved in?'

'No,' I say, surprised she might think so. 'I'm a friend of hers.'

'Hmph,' she says, still wary. 'If you're staying for long I'd appreciate if you took your shoes off when you're inside. Wooden floors are real noisy if you live underneath. And anyway, shoes carry toxins into the house. It's better to leave them outside.'

She points down to her own bare and gnarly feet to show she is setting an example. An example of what feet might look like if left unwashed for about twenty years. There is an actual tide mark on her heel.

'Can I ask you – excuse me, but do you know Laura well?'

She leans back against the wall of her house, and crosses her arms over her tie-dyed chest. She surveys me from head to foot with a practised eye.

'You seem kind of anxious,' she says. 'Do you eat sugar?'

'Sugar?'

'Mmm-hmmm. Stresses the adrenals. Creates highs and lows. Makes a person real anxious.'

'It's not *sugar*,' I snap. How absolutely ridiculous – my best friend's gone missing, I've left my only child in another country and the apparently helpful Stanley turns out to be a deceptive arsehole who's been shagging Laura on the side, but of *course* the reason I'm stressed must be the jam I ate with my toast this morning.

The woman looks sceptical and a little disgusted at my denial, as if she has pointed out an unsightly blob of food on my lip and I have chosen to ignore it.

'I know Lara just about as well as I need to,' she says. Not well enough to pronounce her name properly, I note. 'But I know *all* about her. Oh yeah. I hear a *lot*.'

'What sort of thing?' I ask, trying to be polite since I've clearly offended her with my sugar denial.

She smirks, and twists the sparse end of her plait around one finger. 'Your friend Lara's pretty popular.'

She raises an eyebrow so I won't have any trouble interpreting her meaning. Give me strength. Single woman has sex life: it's hardly a shocking revelation, is it? Anyway, isn't Laura's neighbour from the free-love generation? Who is she to be making judgements?

'She always has been,' I say defensively. 'Laura's always had a lot of – friends.'

'Funny,' says the woman, pushing herself back up to standing straight, as if she's had enough of this conversation and is preparing to leave. She sighs and flips the grey plait so that it hangs down her back. 'All of that loving for a girl whose heart chakra's so blocked.'

'What does that mean?'

She holds out her hands in a 'don't-blame-me' gesture. 'I *offered* to do a chakra cleanse for her. You could see just by looking that they were all misaligned. I said I'd give her a discounted rate, seeing as how we were neighbours. There wasn't any need for her to be so rude about it.'

I can just imagine Laura's reaction. After five minutes in the company of this woman I'd like to strangle her with her own plait. Living in close proximity to her would drive anyone to madness.

'Anyway, all that crying didn't surprise me.' She has the air of an aggrieved martyr, outwardly sorry to have her dire predictions proven right, but secretly quite pleased.

'People think they keep themselves safe by hardening their hearts, but they don't. A hard heart,' she puts both hands on her heart, linking the fingers and thumping her chest to make her point, 'is more easily broken.'

She lets her fingers fly into the air as if they have exploded out from her chest, and wiggles them as they fall, like a really lame human firework.

Homily delivered, she opens the screen door back into her apartment. A waft of incense reaches my nose.

'Wait,' I say, taking a few steps towards her and grabbing the outside handle so she can't shut me out. 'All that crying? What did you mean, all that crying?'

She looks up and tugs at the door crossly to get it away from me, but I have my foot against it. Her bare feet don't stand a chance against my leather boots, complete with their load of toxins. When she realizes I won't let go she speaks begrudgingly.

'Oh, for *days*. She cried so much she even made herself throw up. More than once. I *heard* it. You can hear everything in these apartments. If she'd only listened about the chakras. I could have helped.'

I let go of the door and she retreats inside, where her house is dark. The door bangs behind her and I can't help but see the mesh, through which she is dimly visible, as a web from where this plaited spider is enjoying pulling and releasing threads, toying with me.

'Wait – you said you thought she'd moved out?' I call out, as I see her shadow recede further into the house. 'Why did you think that?'

She steps up close without opening the door, so close that her tie-dyed chest is touching the mesh.

'The thing is,' I start to babble, trying to get it all out before she goes again. 'Laura's gone, and no-one knows where. So if you know anything, anything at all, it would really help me to find her, to make sure she's okay.'

The woman breathes heavily behind the screen, squinting at me, deciding whether she will help this friend of Lara's.

'She *woke* me,' she says, sulkily, as if this is the pertinent fact. 'She packed up the car in the middle of the night and drove off. That suitcase of hers bumped down every step, boom boom boom. She should've lifted it. Inconsiderate.'

'When was this?' I ask.

Her face scrunches up with the effort of remembering. 'Around the time of the full moon?' she says. 'Yeah, it must have been. That's how come I saw her so clearly – it was bright out.'

'The full moon?' I echo, disbelieving. 'Can you be a little more specific?'

'Nope,' she says brightly, and disappears from view.

'Wait,' I call after her, into the black hole of her lair. 'Was she upset? Was she alone? I need to ask you more questions!'

There is no answer.

I'm nearly at the pavement when I hear the creaking sound of the screen door opening once more.

'Hey, there is one more thing.'

I twist my head round to see her. She's smiling. It's obvious she's enjoying this. The power, the attention, the captive audience to whom she can complain to her heart's content about the noise from upstairs.

'That guy came and cleared everything away. That's why I thought she'd gone for good. Because of all the trash he threw out.'

'The trash?' I ask, turning around to face her properly. 'What guy?'

Her smile widens as she sees she's caught me once more, reeled me back in.

'The guy that left just now, before you, with the blue shirt on. He's been here a lot. You get to know the way people sound after a while.'

'And what exactly did he throw away?'

She shrugs. The brief window of helpfulness has passed, as if she can only stand to be cooperative for an allocated time, and it has already run out. 'Well, I wasn't about to go through the trash bags. I'm not a meddlesome neighbour, no matter what Miss Hoity-Toity says.'

I assume this must be Laura.

'All I know is he was up there a long time, pushing the vacuum around, moving the furniture. Then up and down, up and down the steps with all those bags of trash. It *disturbed* me.'

She looks at me for sympathy, but I have none. It feels as if someone is squeezing my lungs, my whole chest is tight and it is hard to breathe. Didn't I know it from the first moment? That everything was too tidy and clean in there?

'And this – was this around the time of the full moon, too?' I say, in a voice that has become small and anxious.

'No,' she shakes her head, definite this time. 'This was just a few days ago.'

'Two days?' I suggest, trying to pin her down. 'Three?'

'It was the night I came back from the crystal healing workshop in Sedona,' she says, already heading back towards her dreamcatcher.

'Please,' I shout at her retreating back. 'Where did he leave the bags? Where's the trash now?'

She stops with her hand on the door and frowns over her shoulder, where the plait rests like a living thing.

'Well, the refuse collectors came round yesterday. It's all gone now.'

I let out a scream of frustration, and bury my face in my hands.

'Seriously, young lady,' I hear Laura's neighbour say. 'You really need to quit the sugar.'

And then she is gone.

DONNIE DARKO, MAY 2001[7]

[MS POMEROY (Drew Barrymore) is fired by the Principal. She steps outside the school through an emergency exit. She stares out at the beautiful forest. Her eyes are filled with tears.]

MS POMEROY: *FUUUUUUUCKKKKKK!!!!!*

17

Esther would have liked it if Charlie had stayed for dinner with Laura. It was the first time she had been to their new flat, and Esther had had it planned even before they moved in. She and Charlie would open the door with their arms around each other, barefoot on their immaculate Victorian tiled hallway, while delicious smells of a homemade supper wafted from the kitchen. A single white orchid would be framed in a hall window behind them. Laura would go from room to room like Kevin McCloud at the end of an episode of *Grand Designs*, exclaiming over all the well-thought-out touches that made this rented flat a home.

Okay, so the hallway wasn't actually tiled. And she wouldn't dare tread on the worn and filthy carpet of the communal entrance without shoes. There was no orchid either, and fine, no hallway window, if you were going to be picky. But it was their first home together. They had a joint household bank account, and both of their names were on the bills. Esther could invite people round to 'our place', she had someone to come home to: at the age of twenty-six, she was officially part of a 'we'.

She carried a picture of Charlie in her wallet, from a photo booth at the station the glorious Sunday last summer when they'd been to Whitstable. Her shoulders were pink from the sun, he had a ketchup stain on his shirt, and their smiles were as wide as the seaside horizon they had just left behind. Sometimes she wanted to flip the wallet open and wave it at people like a couples' identity card – look! See that I am validated! Witness that I am loved! Charlie Meynell was, she felt, the living proof that she had finally left Fat Fester behind for good.

So to show Laura around the flat herself, without Charlie by her side, would be to miss out on its biggest and most important asset. It would be like taking someone around the Palace at Versailles without showing them the Hall of Mirrors.

But the Hall of Mirrors had other plans.

'Come on, Sea Breeze,' he said, pinching her chin affectionately to hold her face still for a kiss. 'Just tell her I'm at work.'

'But you're *not* at work,' said Esther. 'I specially chose a Wednesday night so you'd be here.'

'It's not like Laura knows the rota at Roland's,' he laughed, and hoisted his sports bag onto his shoulder. 'She won't care anyway. You girls will have more fun without me here getting in the way.'

'Can't you just stay to say hello?' she asked, pulling at his sleeve and looking up at him through her lashes. 'Andy won't mind if you're a bit late.'

He just kissed her again, and opened the door out to the corridor. '*I'll* mind if they start without me,' he said. 'Maybe I'll see you both later, if she's still here. Have a good time.'

When he left Esther sighed, but it was a sigh of resignation rather than real disappointment.

Until she moved in with Charlie, Esther had had no idea how profoundly unsociable most men were. He had plenty of friends, but he'd never think of seeing them without a reason – a gig or a game or a film about fast cars and people with ridiculous names like Vin Diesel. It was as if there had to be a focus that was bigger than all of them, or else they might actually be forced to talk to one another, and that could never happen. Even the plans for these occasions, made over the phone, appeared to be conducted via a series of insults and grunts that were finished in five minutes. 'Wassup, wanker! Yeah? Uh? Seven? Fuck off. Cool.'

Maybe he was right; they probably would have more fun without him. He and Laura had been awkward around each other from the start. It was all bloody Malcolm's fault.

Esther opened up her copy of *The Naked Chef* in the kitchen – Laura had sent it to her as a housewarming present and this was the first time she'd cooked from it.

The recipe called for a big glug of olive oil to be poured over the salmon and vegetables before they went in the oven. She had only discovered half an hour ago that there was no baking tray in the flat. Now the salmon was resting at a bit of an angle in a too-small foil takeaway container that she'd washed up instead. All of the cherry tomatoes seemed to have rolled down to one end of the container, even though she'd done her best to block them with a dam of green beans. Probably it wouldn't matter once they were all cooked. Esther paused nervously with the olive oil bottle in her hand, holding it up to the light to see how much was inside the dull green glass. How much was a glug, exactly? Maybe Laura would know.

Wait, was that her phone? Where was her handbag? She could hear ringing from inside it, muffled. She ran into the sitting room and straight into one of the flat-pack boxes that held her Billy bookshelves from Ikea, not yet unpacked.

'Ow, fuck.' She hopped on one foot around the room and collapsed on the sofa, and there was the bag, exactly where she'd thrown it when she got in from work and ran into the kitchen to try to be all domestic. The text message envelope blinked at her as she thumbed the button to answer.

'Est, didn't you get my texts? Where have you been? Get the front door open,' shouted Laura. Her voice came in ragged bursts, it sounded like she was running.

'What's going on?' Esther sprinted to the front door and opened it, but there was no-one there. She peered down the road towards the tube station. Still no-one. 'Where are you?'

'Just fucking hurry – I'm nearly there. Christ, I never thought she'd follow me all this way.'

'Who?'

'Is the door open?'

'Yes, but I can't see you.'

Esther stepped out onto the pavement so she could see further down the street. At the point where the road curved up the hill, she could see two figures approaching, both at speed. One was gaining on the other.

The figure in front waved, but not in a friendly way. It was more like the wave that someone might give if they were trapped in a burning building. It was Laura, her other hand clamping the phone to her ear. She had something tucked under her phone arm – a plant? – and she was moving incredibly quickly, with her free arm pumping at her side like one of those speed-walkers you see in athletics competitions. She looked over her shoulder and, without warning, threw the plant behind her and started running. The pursuing figure speeded up. She had a pale narrow skirt on and heels, and though it looked at first as if she'd cleared the pot plant with a determined skip, her heel caught on the edge of the obstacle and she stumbled, grabbing a wrought-iron fence for balance. Laura had the advantage and she took it with a final sprint, flinging herself into the front garden and slamming the gate.

'Get inside!' she yelled, pushing past Esther in panic.

With the front door safely shut behind them and the flat door bolted, Laura edged towards the bay window that faced the pavement. A thick green privet hedge blocked most of the view, but over the top of it the crown of an ash blonde head could be seen, pacing back and forth, unsure which house her quarry had disappeared into.

'Laura, what the fuck is going on?' Esther demanded.

'Shh! Don't say my name so loud!' Laura stationed herself behind the curtain, clutching at the edge and drawing it around her as she peered out of the window.

'She saw you come in here. Who is that woman?'

Laura kept her face turned to the street, but swivelled her eyes back towards Esther.

'It's Alice Bewes!' she hissed. 'Malcolm's wife.'

That was it. Esther had had enough. She marched over to the window just in time to see a pair of blue eyes squinting through a bare patch in the privet. The eyes registered surprise, and then moved, fast, heading towards the garden path. Esther snatched the curtain from Laura and drew it across the window so they were suddenly cast into gloom.

Seconds later the hammering began on the front door. It stopped momentarily, and they heard the metallic creak of the letterbox being pushed open on its springs.

A high, posh voice called out, 'I know you're in there, you little slut!'

Esther pulled Laura down onto the sofa by her sleeve. 'You said you'd stopped sleeping with Malcolm,' she whispered furiously.

'I *have*,' Laura whispered back, through gritted teeth. 'It was only ever a few times, Est, it's not like I was his *mistress* or something. You don't have to make a big deal of it.'

Esther glared at her friend through the artificial darkness. 'His wife is trying to break into my house, Laura. It's not *me* who's making a big deal of it. Why's she followed you here?'

'I don't fucking know!' Laura glanced nervously towards the flat door, cringing away from it.

The hammering got suddenly louder and then it stopped.

Esther and Laura stared at each other, eyes wide, as they heard the clip-clop of heels moving from the front step. Silence.

'I think she's gone,' Laura whispered, leaning forward and straining to hear. Esther leaned forward, too. Nothing.

Then the bay window shook as it was battered from outside. Laura threw herself down on the floor of the living room commando-style, as if she expected

Malcolm's wife to come clambering through it, but the glass held.

'I'll smash this window!' An irate shriek came from outside. 'Don't think I won't smash it!'

'Fuck!' hissed Laura. She grabbed at Esther's ankle and tried to pull her down to the ground beside her. 'Fuck, she's gone completely mental. Get down!'

Esther wrenched her leg away. It wasn't just pride that kept her from lying down, it was the knowledge that Charlie had dropped half his Chinese takeaway on the carpet last night. But mostly it was pride. She was not about to be intimidated in her own home.

'Right, that's enough,' she said. 'If she smashes that window I lose my deposit – and I'm not about to lose money over your stupid affair.'

'It wasn't an affair!'

Laura swung manically for Esther's ankle again, but she stepped away too fast. Behind the curtains, the window rattled ominously.

Esther paused in front of the curtains, took a deep breath in and flung them wide open. Malcolm's wife stood in front of her, both arms raised ready to hit the glass again, her face contorted into a gargoyle's mask of fury.

'Stop this right now!' Esther shouted, as commandingly as she could.

She had never spoken to someone older than her this way, and she wasn't sure what was going to happen, but she had to say something. Alice Bewes froze perfectly still with her arms above her head, as if Esther had pointed a gun at her and might shoot. Her hands were clenched in fierce little fists, ready to pummel at the glass again.

'You need to go before I call the police,' Esther called through the window.

Alice dropped her arms by her sides, and pulled at the front of her navy blazer to straighten it, aware at once of how she must look. She pressed her lips together and shook her head so that her blonde hair fell obediently back into its hairsprayed bouffant under a padded velvet headband. From the other side of the window it was like watching a silent movie actor go through a series of emotions: rage, resignation, shame.

'*I* should call the police,' Alice called, lifting her chin to make her voice carry. Even so, it had a defeated sort of sound to it. She looked only a little younger than Esther's own mother, too old to be running down the street after silly young women.

'What for?' Laura muttered from the floor, where she was still hidden. 'It's not like shagging your boss is illegal.'

'Shut up, Laura,' Esther snapped at her. She turned back to Alice.

'No-one needs to call the police if you just go home, Mrs Bewes,' she said, as kindly as she could while shouting to make herself heard.

Alice's chin wobbled. She pressed under her eyes with

manicured fingers, blinking hard, as if she thought she might be able to stop herself from crying by pushing the tears back in.

'I – I don't suppose you could call me a taxi?' she asked.

It really wasn't the evening Esther had planned. She spent half of it on the doorstep with Alice Bewes, repeatedly calling the minicab firm to chase the promised car. Alice accepted a glass of chardonnay, and then another, and then she asked for another, but she refused to come indoors where that slut was hiding, and that slut wouldn't come outside either. Esther shuttled between the two of them dispensing sympathy, alcohol and tough love and wondering how she had got herself involved in this.

By the time the maroon estate car turned up, a forest of air freshener trees hanging from its dashboard, Alice's anger had dissolved into tears. Esther put her in the back of the car with a promise that no-one need ever know of her detour to Finsbury Park. And then she went inside to face Laura.

But before she had even reached the kitchen it was clear there was a more urgent matter to be dealt with.

'What the fuck is that smell?' she said, fanning her hand in front of her nose.

Laura screamed as she cast her phone aside, leapt to her feet and ran to the oven. From inside they both heard two muffled pops, as if small bombs had been set off.

'Shit, shit, shit!' Laura threw open the door and black smoke billowed out to hover above their heads like a malevolent spirit. They both reared back as they heard another explosion, which was followed by a blaze of orange flame at the top of the oven, where the takeaway container had been placed on the highest shelf.

Esther looked around desperately for an oven glove, only to remember she didn't have one. She grabbed the first thing she could see, a piece of fabric that was draped over the back of a kitchen chair, and covered her hands to pull the takeaway container out of the oven.

'That's my cardigan!' shouted Laura, making a lunge for it and then skipping neatly out of the way when the entire burned salmon slid off the foil and splatted onto the floor next to her feet.

'Fuck your cardigan – are you trying to burn my flat down? Why did you put the fish under the *grill*?'

Esther threw the container into the sink, where it hissed and crackled. All that remained of the exploded cherry tomatoes was a pyre of blackened skins, and the green beans looked like a pile of spent matches.

Laura's eyes widened. 'The grill? I thought it was the oven. I was trying to help.'

'Can you just open a window?' Esther snapped, flinging Laura's cardigan onto the table behind her and inspecting the damage in the sink. 'God.'

Laura shoved the sash window up as high as it would go and waved her hands to disperse the smoke. She snatched up her cardigan and shook it out of the window.

'I'm sorry, okay? I thought it would be a good thing to do.'

'I bet you didn't even add the glug of olive oil, did you?' Esther muttered, using a fish slice to poke at the incinerated remains of her perfect Jamie Oliver recipe.

'What glug?'

'It doesn't matter. The whole thing's ruined anyway. The whole *night's* ruined.' She dropped the fish slice into the sink with a clatter, and stalked over to the fridge to see what else they might be able to eat.

'Look, I just didn't want to *sit* here while you were outside,' Laura pleaded, wringing her cardigan in her hands. 'I wanted to *do* something.'

Esther grumbled into the vegetable drawer, 'Oh, I think you've already done quite enough.'

At first she wasn't sure if Laura had heard her. She wasn't even sure if she'd meant her to – the words had come out before she could stop them. But the silence from the other side of the fridge door told her she'd hit home. When she closed the fridge she saw that Laura had put her cardigan on and held her bag in her crossed arms, ready to leave.

Her cheeks were flushed, and her voice was high as she said, 'I'm sorry, okay? I think I'm just going to go.'

Esther positioned herself between Laura and the door. 'You don't get away with it that easily.'

Laura blinked hard up at the ceiling. She pressed her lips together tightly before she spoke. 'You're right, though, I ruined the whole evening. Let's do this another time. You can come round to mine and torch the curtains or something. Payback.'

Esther stayed firm.

'I know you'd love to walk out, Laura, but I'm not letting you.'

They stared at each other for a long moment which would have been meaningfully silent were it not for the faint hiss of the ruined fish steaming in the sink.

Laura made a sudden break for it with a feinting manoeuvre to the left and then a dart to the right, but Esther caught her by the shoulders and didn't let go. They grappled next to the fridge for a few seconds like a pair of thoroughly inept wrestlers.

'Laura!' Esther started laughing despite herself. 'Don't make me play a game of fucking kabaddi with you!'

'Oh my God,' Laura spluttered, falling backwards into the kitchen and out of Esther's reach. 'Kabaddi! Do you remember when Katie Long passed out from holding her breath too long when we played it in the fifth year?'

Esther clapped her hand over her mouth at the memory of Katie lying there unconscious, with Mr McDonald running across the playground tarmac towards them in panic, his trouser-legs flapping in the wind.

'And when we told Mr McDonald it was because of kabaddi he thought we'd been doing drugs!'

'*Who gave her the kabaddi?*' intoned Laura, in a deep manly voice.

Esther wagged a teacherly finger. '*How much did she take? Tell me!*'

Laura laughed so much she had to sit down. They'd all had detention for a week, and their whole year had to sit through an assembly on the dangers of unsupervised sporting activities on school grounds.

'God, Katie Long,' said Laura, wiping hysterical tears from her eyes. 'Do you ever hear from her any more?'

Esther could see that Laura hoped this was it – she'd successfully diverted the conversation away from herself, and now they could fall into fond reminiscences of Portsdown for the rest of the night.

'Come on, Laur,' she said, sitting down next to her. 'We need to talk properly.'

Laura hung her handbag over the back of the seat. She inched the cardigan sleeves, one by one, down over her hands, taking her time settling herself.

Esther saw with surprise that there was a bowl of Doritos on the table. She'd put them there hours ago, ready for a pre-dinner snack after the house tour that never happened. Oh well. She took one and nodded to the bowl so Laura would see it too.

'There you go. Supper,' she said, with her mouth full. 'And if you say anything about this being unhealthy I swear to God I will make you eat the fish instead. All of it.'

'I wasn't going to say anything,' Laura protested.

'I know,' said Esther. 'That's why I wouldn't let you leave.'

Laura hesitated with her hand hovering over the Doritos.

'What's that supposed to mean?'

'Oh, come on, Laura, will you stop trying to act like nothing's happened? You said you weren't sleeping with Malcolm any more.'

'I'm not!' She slumped in her seat like a sulky teenager.

'His wife doesn't seem to think so.'

'It's not even a big deal,' Laura muttered.

Esther sighed. She felt incredibly tired. 'Did you *see* his wife?'

'Of course I saw her,' she snapped back. 'That crazy witch chased me all the way from the office. I even changed tubes to try and lose her. She just kept on coming, like the Terminator with an Alice band, running up the escalators. If it hadn't been so crowded I think she'd have caught up with me.'

Laura gave an experimental smile, testing to see if Esther was ready to laugh about this yet.

Esther wasn't. 'Laura, she was devastated.'

Laura grabbed at her wine glass and drained it in one fierce gulp.

'Would you have told me if I hadn't found out?' asked Esther.

Laura considered her over the rim of her empty glass. 'I did tell you,' she said carefully.

'You only told me because Charlie saw you get in the cab with Malcolm that first time, and he told me. Can you imagine how that felt, Laur? My first ever date with Charlie, a total stranger, and he tells me something about you that I'd probably never have known otherwise.'

'I *did* tell you,' Laura repeated obstinately. She poured herself more wine, and left the bottle next to her glass as if she anticipated an immediate refill.

'You told me because I asked you. I'm saying, would you have told me about Malcolm if I hadn't asked you the direct question? If Charlie hadn't told me – would you?'

Laura crossed her legs, tucking her top foot around the lower calf in the way, Esther remembered from her school days, that only thin girls can. Even though she could sit like this herself now, if she wanted to, there was something about that gesture from Laura that always made her feel excluded.

'I would've,' Laura muttered, almost under her breath.

'Really?'

She huffed, and flicked her hair away from her face. 'It's not like I'm proud of it, Est. It's just something that happened. But – when you've done it once, it's harder to say no the next time.'

Laura picked up a Dorito, and then seemed to think

better of it. Instead she turned it over and over between her hands like a poker chip.

'So if you've stopped sleeping with him, what made Alice Bewes chase you all the way here?'

The Dorito stopped still, an ominous orange shark's fin in Laura's fingers.

'It was after the cricket at Lord's last week,' Laura said, in a quiet voice. 'We took a load of clients and he gave me a lift home afterwards. That was the first time in months and months, I swear to God, Est. I'm not going to do it again.'

Esther noticed Laura couldn't look at her, or wouldn't.

'How do you think she found out?'

Laura sniffed, considering, and ate the crisp that she had been handling.

'I don't know,' she said, chewing thoughtfully. 'Malcolm's been texting me. Maybe she saw.'

'Have you been answering?'

Laura's eyes blazed. 'You don't understand! You've never understood. I need this job! I'm not like you, with your perfect degree and your perfect job at *The Times* and your perfect flat with your *boyfriend*.'

It was only afterwards that Esther remembered Laura did not say perfect boyfriend.

'Oh no, wait,' she said, feeling her temper rise. 'Don't you dare turn this around and make it about me, Laura.'

'Everything's just easy for you, isn't it? It's like – you've got your whole life mapped out, haven't you? You've always known what you wanted to do. Well, no-one gave me a map, Esther, okay? I didn't get a map, and I just keep ending up in stupid fucking dead ends.'

She burst into big, noisy tears, hiding her face behind her hands.

'What if Ricko was right?' she wailed into her palms. 'I thought Malcolm was the *anti-Ricko*, I wasn't going to get distracted by an actual relationship again. I was going to focus on my career, and look. It's just like Ricko said, I peaked too long ago. Everything's been a disaster ever since.'

Esther saw her glance, just for a second, between her fingers to see the reaction she was getting. As exasperating as Laura was, for all of her histrionics, it was that little glimmer of self-awareness that made her both ridiculous and forgivable.

'It's not a disaster, Laur,' she said, patiently. 'It's worse for Alice Bewes. She's actually married to that arsehole. You're only twenty-six. You can leave this job, you can get away from Malcolm. Start again somewhere else.'

Laura laughed bitterly. 'Start again? You don't understand what it's like in the wine trade, it's a tiny world. And everyone in it knows Malcolm.'

'Do they know Malcolm in Australia? New Zealand? Didn't you say you'd always wanted to try a season in a vineyard? Get closer to the production side of things? Why not do it now, while you're single and free?'

'Yeah,' said Laura sarcastically, rolling her eyes. 'Let me just access my trust fund and I'll book the tickets first thing tomorrow. Like I can afford to just walk out on my job.'

She reached for more wine, but this time she topped up Esther's glass too, and Esther saw this as a good sign that they were on the same side again, at least.

'Come on, Laura,' she persisted. 'Make a plan. Save up. Get the hell out of Dodge. It's never too late.'

Laura slumped in her chair. 'Easy for you to say. I've already had one fresh start and look where that got me.'

'Do you reckon Drew Barrymore would give up right now?' Esther asked, in desperation.

'Oh, would you fuck off,' muttered Laura. She swirled her wine around in the glass. 'Who cares what Drew Barrymore would do?'

Esther gasped in mock horror. 'Laura! What about the gospel?'

'You never really believed that, did you?' Laura sniffed, lifting her red-rimmed eyes. 'It was just a stupid joke. You weren't meant to take it seriously.'

'So you've become an infidel. You understand you're going to have to be burned at the stake now?'

She gave a reluctant smile, an I'll-indulge-you-for-old-times'-sake smile. 'An *agnostic*,' she said. 'I'm not an infidel, I'm – I'm a doubting Laura Thomas.'

Esther shook her head sadly. 'So you doubt the gospel

of Drew. I've got to say, I never thought I'd hear those words from Gertie herself.'

Laura stuck her tongue out at her, like they were seven years old again. 'Whatever. Drew has let me down lately. Look at me, my whole life's turned to shit.'

'And that's Drew Barrymore's fault?' Esther snorted into her wine glass. 'I don't remember her telling you to shag Malcolm. In *fact* – ' she suddenly sat forward on her chair. 'We were meant to see one of her movies that night we went to Roland's. *Never Been Kissed.*'

'The night I went home with Malcolm?'

'Exactly.'

'Yeah? So?'

'So we *didn't go*.'

Esther's eyes were wide as the theory formed in her head. It wasn't so much that she actually believed it, but she could see it was working as a distraction to drag Laura out of her sulk.

Laura raised an eyebrow, and smirked. 'So what are you saying – shagging Malcolm is a punishment? For not going to see a Drew Barrymore movie?'

Esther grinned and shrugged. 'Maybe Drew is a vengeful deity. Strictly Old Testament. Thou shalt have no other gods but me.'

Laura spluttered at the idea. 'You are a stone cold lunatic.'

She cackled back. 'You have to *believe*, Laura, it only works if you *believe*.'

Laura put down her wine glass and stood up, brushing Dorito crumbs off her front.

'Okay,' she said, standing ramrod straight like she was about to begin a gymnastics routine there on the kitchen floor.

She lifted her arms, gazed at the ceiling and assumed an expression of holy wonder, as if she saw the painted ceiling of the Sistine Chapel up there instead of swirly white Artex.

'Drew!' she called, into the heavens. 'I need a sign! I beg your holy forgiveness for neglecting you! Please give me a sign to make me believe in your gospel again!'

Two days later she got fired.

18

October 2013

My hands are trembling as I get my phone out of my bag. I have proof, I have to call the police. Stanley knows something about Laura disappearing, something more than he's telling me, and I don't think this is something I can deal with on my own.

'Napa Police Department, how may I direct your call?' asks a nasal female voice.

'I need to report a missing person. In suspicious circumstances.'

'Missing Persons, thank you, please hold.'

I should have got back to the car first, I realize. Now that I'm on hold, I can't check GPS to work out where I am. The neighbourhood that seemed so friendly and charming when I first walked through it with Stanley, is no longer. All of these streets are confusingly similar, like a maze – the same wide roads, the same green street signs with square white letters. It's like they don't want you ever to be able to get out. I wonder who else is hiding secrets here, who else has seen things about their neighbours and told no-one?

I hesitate on a corner while I wait for the call to be transferred.

'You want to report a missing person?' says a male voice on the other end of the phone. He sounds paternal and reassuring, and I immediately feel better. I am not alone. I can get help for Laura.

'Yes,' I say, crossing the road in what I hope is the right direction. 'In suspicious circumstances.'

This seems to me the crucial point. They said before that they had no reason for concern, but I have uncovered hidden secrets. There is evidence now. They have to do something.

'May I take the name of the missing person, please?'

I tell him and there is the sound of a keyboard being tapped at on the other end of the line. He asks for a few other details – her date of birth, my relationship to her. It feels official. At last, something is being done.

'Okay. We already have a file for a Ms Laura Katherine Thomas, ma'am. I believe her mother reported her missing a week ago and the matter was investigated then.'

'Well, she's still missing,' I say, as I march purposefully down the pavement, past the white-painted houses, the identical lawns. 'I have come all the way from England to find her, and I've discovered new and very important information.'

'And what might that be?' he asks. He sounds kindly but a little perfunctory, like he is taking down a car registration number, instead of important details on a person who might be in danger.

'I've discovered that she was seen just before she disappeared,' I say triumphantly, proud of my detective work.

'She was reported missing on – October 25th,' the policeman reads from his files. 'What date did you say she was seen?'

I hesitate, realizing I should have looked this up before I called.

'I don't have the exact date,' I say, 'but it was the night of the full moon. Her neighbour saw her then.'

He coughs uncomfortably. 'I beg your pardon?'

'I *know* it sounds mad, I'm sorry,' I say. 'Her neighbour didn't remember the date, all she knew was it was the night of the full moon. Can't you google it? It's important.'

I stop in the shade of a tree. The sun is now high in the sky and though it is a mild day, my angry strides and confusion over directions have made me too hot. Sweat trickles uncomfortably down my back, and it feels like my face is burning up.

'I will certainly investigate the moon cycles later. And what was Ms Thomas doing when seen by her neighbour on,' he pauses, possibly to add just the right level of sceptical amusement to his tone, 'the night of the full moon?'

'She was – apparently she was packing up her car, but that's–'

He interrupts before I can go further.

'Excuse me, ma'am, but I need to have all the facts straight before we proceed. Ms Thomas was seen packing her own car before she went missing?'

'Well, that's not the suspicious part – don't you understand that no-one has seen or heard from her since, and – *and* it turns out that she had a secret lover.'

There is another pause on the other end of the phone. 'A secret lover, ma'am?'

'Yes. She was sleeping with her boss. Stanley Hoffmann, of the Foothills Vineyard. H-O-F-F-M-A-N-N with two Ns. Neither of them had told anyone about it – doesn't that seem strange to you?'

'Stanley . . . Hoffmann. Two Ns.' He says it carefully, and I feel pleased: this must mean he is recording it somewhere. Writing it down, or typing it into some important police database. Stanley is in the system now, his name linked to Laura's, suspiciously.

'Okay, ma'am, is this behaviour out of character for your friend?'

'What do you mean?'

'Is it unusual for Ms Thomas to be reticent about her personal life?'

I find I've started stammering, it feels like he's tricking

me with every question. 'No, I mean, yes, I mean – disappearing is completely out of character. She's never done it before.'

'Is Mr Hoffmann married? Is this what you mean by secret?'

'No, he's – ' But then I stop. How had I not thought to ask this before?

Of course that would explain why Stanley wanted to keep his relationship with Laura a secret. And why she would hide all photographs of him so that no casual visitor might see them. I don't remember seeing a wedding ring on his left hand, but then, I wasn't looking for one. And wouldn't that be exactly Laura's style? The easiest way to avoid a real relationship is to pursue a man who is already in one.

'Ma'am?'

'I don't know if he's married,' I admit. 'But please listen, there are other things – I went to her apartment, and it had been scrubbed clean. There was a very strong smell of bleach.'

I take a turning to the right, where the road appears to open out a little. The twin rows of trees on either side stop abruptly up ahead.

'Ms Thomas's apartment was – clean?'

'*She* didn't clean it!' I shriek, and even I cannot help hearing that my voice has become squeakily hysterical. 'Stanley Hoffmann cleaned it after she'd gone! Her neighbour said he spent hours there. She said he took bags of rubbish – I mean trash, bags of trash to the kerb. Don't you think *that's* suspicious?'

The man on the other end of the phone chuckles, actually chuckles like this is funny.

'I don't get a lot of calls complaining about a man taking out the trash. You got any more of these suspicious circumstances or are you done?'

'Isn't that enough? A woman is missing! You're not even taking it seriously!'

I hear the policeman draw breath before he answers. 'Ma'am, it sounds to me like your friend's just taken a trip away. You said yourself she was seen packing her own car. I'm sure there's nothing to worry about.'

'But it's not like that!' I plead. 'I know something's wrong, I just know it. You need to talk to Stanley Hoffmann.'

I hear more tapping on the keyboard before he speaks again. 'There is a record of a previous Missing Persons report for Ms Laura Thomas,' he says, slowly, as if he is reading it as he speaks. 'Over a year ago now. And – yes, says here she was found safe and well after a trip to a spa.'

'Yes, I know about Calistoga Springs,' I snap. 'You don't understand, this is different. Would I have come all the way to America if I thought she'd gone to a *spa*?'

'Ma'am.' The policeman is firm now. 'The report says that Ms Thomas was, and I'm reading the quote here, "embarrassed and apologetic" when the police spoke to her last time. It says she is of sound mind and does not present a risk to herself or others.'

'But that was *Margie* who called you then, not me.' Even as I say it, I know that it is hopeless. He doesn't believe me and, worse, he's decided I'm as hysterical and paranoid as Laura's mother.

'Yes,' says the man. 'The caller was a Margaret Elizabeth Thomas, from Sussex County, England. And may I take your name, ma'am?'

I hang up immediately and stare at the phone in horror, wondering if they can trace me to this very street with their law-enforcement technology. If I put my name on record, I lose any chance I might have to call again with credibility. Once I'm identified as the crazy full-moon woman who rang to complain that Laura's apartment was too clean, no-one at the police department will ever take me seriously again, no matter what new evidence I uncover.

The facts came out all wrong. I'm too jet-lagged and sleep-deprived to formulate my thoughts properly. I made it far too easy for the policeman to dismiss me, and I've blown my best chance at getting real help in finding Laura.

The irony is, of course, that it is only now the police decline to be involved that I have become certain something bad has happened. Until a few hours ago, although I had momentarily entertained some worst-case scenarios, I'd mostly been expecting to come out here and find that there had been a simple misunderstanding. I'd thought that Laura would appear at any point, horrified to have caused such drama.

But now I can see that my reason for thinking this was Stanley, who has done everything he can to try to persuade me that Laura would come back without our interference. He said she wanted a break from everything, and I, though I wanted to believe him (because then Laura would be safe), I didn't want to believe him (because then she would have left us on purpose). I told myself that I was manufacturing outlandish suspicions of abduction or worse, to take away my own guilt for neglecting Laura lately – but what if Stanley has been the guilty one all along?

Yes, he was the one who told us Laura was missing, but isn't that a classic double bluff? The very best way to draw suspicion away from yourself would be to pose as the helpful employer and friend. Although I appreciate that I am making this assessment based on episodes of *Columbo* rather than actual detective experience. But still, if Stanley had admitted their relationship straight away, I would have less reason to suspect him right now. And if he had nothing to hide, why all the lying?

Thank God I took the right turn; at last the residential district is coming to an end, the houses being replaced by bed and breakfasts and small touristy shops as it leads back to the shopping precinct. The car is just where I left it, near the entrance to the café where I met

Stanley just a few hours ago. It makes me sick when I think of how grateful I was to him then, when all along he knew he was getting in the way of finding Laura. It feels like days have passed since I sat there innocently eating toast and thanking him for his help.

Inside the window, right up by the reception desk, I can see the waitress who served us, the one who called Laura an English muffin. She frowns with concentration as she taps orders into a computer with a pen, and it makes her look older than she did this morning, like the demands of the day have dragged her down already. The sight of her makes me stop still with the car key in my hand. *She knew*, I think. She knew about Laura and Stanley. That would explain why she was so pointed about Stanley being in the café with a new 'friend' while Laura was on holiday. The biggest clue was right there in front of me and I missed it.

When I push open the door, I'm hit with a blast of air-conditioning that makes me shiver. It blows my cotton scarf to the side, and I have to catch it with my hands and hold it down over my chest. The café is quieter now: just a few tables are still occupied, people taking their time over late breakfasts. Most of them are in their sixties or older, retirees, I suppose. People in no hurry to get anywhere. Busboys are laying the rest of the tables for lunch.

The waitress sees me standing by the door and comes

over with a look of friendly concern. I can see that she recognizes me.

'You okay, honey?' she asks. 'You leave something behind?'

I shake my head. 'No, I just wondered if you had a minute to help me with something.'

She looks quickly over her shoulder and laughs. 'I guess. Manager's out back, what do you need?'

'It's about the man I was here with,' I say, and at once her face becomes guarded. I see it happening, the easy friendliness falling from her eyes.

'Yeah?' she says.

'How well do you know Stanley?' I ask.

'Better than some,' she says. 'Not so well as others. Why?' Her lower jaw juts out defensively.

'Does he come in here with Laura a lot?'

She frowns a little. 'Yeah, sometimes. They're friends, but I guess you know that already.'

'What kind of friends?' I ask.

'Honey,' she says, with patent disapproval, her lips pursing, 'I just serve people breakfast. I don't make it my business to ask personal questions, and neither should you.'

Strands of her fine grey hair have been blown into her eyes by the air-conditioning vent above us. She pushes them away impatiently with the back of her hand.

I try one last question before her patience runs out.

'Is Stanley married?'

She gasps, and her hand flies to her mouth. It is far more of a reaction than I was expecting, and clearly more than she meant to give away. She composes herself quickly, and pulls her notepad out from her apron, as if she must rush to a table of invisible customers.

'He said he didn't have children,' I say, moving closer before she can get away from me. 'But I never asked if he was married. It's important. I know you know he was seeing Laura.'

'Don't,' the waitress says, holding out her palm to me and backing away. She looks oddly like she is about to cry. 'Don't come round here stirring up trouble.'

'What trouble?'

'Some things are best left alone,' she says, and before I can ask her anything else a tall man appears from the kitchen and shouts her name. She almost breaks into a run in her hurry to be gone.

50 FIRST DATES, JUNE 2004[8]

HENRY: I just want to try something that will make her remember me.

19

The only good thing about the weekend was that Esther could give up any pretence that she was fine. No-one knew the effort it cost her to go in to work every weekday morning with a smile on her face; to answer the phone, file her copy, to go out to lunch with contacts and interviewees and force herself to eat even though her stomach had shrunk to the size of a shrivelled food-repelling pea. Her boss had given her two days off when it first happened – compassionate leave, she called it, as if someone had died, and it really felt to Esther like someone had.

On Saturdays she didn't have to brush her hair, or get dressed, she didn't have to eat at lunchtime – she didn't have to eat at all. Instead she lay in bed and smoked, intensely, as if she was in training for the freestyle smoking Olympics. Charlie had left a packet of Marlboro Lights behind, abandoned under a sofa cushion, and she had lit just one leftover cigarette for the smell of it. With her eyes closed she could inhale and imagine he was still there, sitting on the kitchen windowsill, his feet on a chair, blowing the smoke outside with that guilty grin on his face. She had taken one tentative drag of his leftover cigarette, felt the familiar teenage head-rush, and that was it.

Why had she ever given up? How had she forgotten that smoking was the greatest way ever invented of feeling like you were doing something when you were actually doing nothing at all? She smoked sitting up in bed, with a cigarette dangling from her lips like the hero in a French New Wave film. She smoked lying down, balancing the ashtray on her chest. She aimed for a gold medal in leaving the longest possible unbroken tube of ash at the end of her cigarette. When, inevitably, the ash crumbled all over the duvet, falling apart like (she felt) the cremated remains of her formerly contented life, Esther, who had once washed her sheets every single week, simply rolled over and ignored it.

She also ignored the doorbell, which had been ringing for at least five minutes. It was eight-thirty in the morning. There was no-one she wanted to see at that time and nothing that might be delivered that could possibly interest her. Unless it was more fags, but as far as she knew the Turkish corner shop did not make home deliveries, especially not speculative ones. Though perhaps she should suggest they did in future. It would save having to put proper clothes on to replenish her supplies.

The doorbell was ringing continuously now, like someone was leaning on it. Charlie had bought one of those stupid musical ones, not a sensible *ding-dong* that anyone could ignore, but a tinny tune that ended on a wildly aggravating high note.

At last it stopped, and Esther stubbed out her morning cigarette with relief. Then it started again, erratically. One ring, then three, then four in a row and then one again. Two. One. Intermittent doorbell torture.

Her mood, which had been less than sunny to begin with, had hardened into a deep and fierce blackness by the time she opened the door.

'Why the fuck aren't you answering your phone?' asked Laura, with her finger still on the doorbell. She wore a blue silk dress and bright red heels, unusually smart for this time of the morning, and Esther remembered at once why she was there.

She turned around and went back into the flat, knowing Laura would follow. Knowing already that it would be impossible to get rid of her.

'I told you I was coming at half eight,' said Laura. Her scarlet high heels made their way along the dull carpet of the communal hallway, and she glanced at her watch as she shut the flat door behind her. 'You were meant to be ready. Come on, jump in the shower or we'll be late.'

'And I told *you* I wasn't coming.' Esther slumped onto the sofa, into the nest of blankets she'd left there for when she wanted a change of scene from the bedroom.

'Well, you obviously have a magical weekend planned instead,' said Laura, casting her eyes around the sitting room, where full ashtrays nestled up against glasses in which the sludgy red wine dregs of many solitary evenings had solidified.

The curtains were half-open and, trying to see the room through Laura's eyes, Esther noted that the morning sunlight illuminated a fine layer of dust and ash that had settled over everything, Miss Havisham-style. She didn't care. Frankly, at least Miss Havisham had got as far as being proposed to. At least she got to show off her engagement ring to her friends, and choose a wedding dress. Esther hadn't even managed that before Charlie fucked off to find himself by travelling round the world. He was too young to be tied down, apparently.

'I wasn't properly invited,' she muttered. 'The invitation only came two weeks ago. Everyone knows what that means. Second-tier guest. Third, probably. She doesn't even want me there.'

'Don't look a gift toff in the mouth,' said Laura, delicately wiping ash off the sofa arm and perching there to look down at Esther. 'Amelia's fiancé is loaded – didn't you read the invitation? The reception is at his parents' *manor house*. The ceremony is in their own chapel, for fuck's sake.'

Esther huffed and rolled over, pulling the blankets over her face.

'So?'

'So? Esther, have you forgotten that I'm an impoverished student? You might be used to free booze with your fancy-pants job, but I have just finished four weeks of oenology exams, and I plan to celebrate on Harry Branwell's bar bill.'

'You should've taken Adam,' Esther mumbled, and from inside her hot tent of blankets she could hear Laura hooting with scornful laughter.

'Adam? He's already far too keen, God knows what he'd think if I invited him to a wedding. Anyway, Est, he may have the body of a Greek god, but he's got the wit of a Greek salad. He'd be no fun. I want to go with *you*. Come on.'

Laura nudged her with the pointy toe of her red shoe.

'I am not fun,' Esther growled. 'And I don't want to have fun either. Ever.'

She wouldn't have admitted it to Laura, but there was a part of her that luxuriated in taking to her bed each weekend. By Thursday afternoons she was already looking forward to the empty days alone; it was so much easier to give in than to fight her broken heart. Her hollow stomach and excess of cigarettes gave her an almost narcotic feeling. Slightly spacey, as if she didn't really exist; and if no-one saw her or knew where she was, then perhaps she didn't.

'Get up and get dressed, you selfish cow.'

Esther pushed the blankets off her face in outrage.

'*I'm* selfish? Don't you even have a heart? How can I face Amelia Wentworth's wedding when I've just been dumped by the man I thought I was going to *marry*?'

Her voice cracked on the last word. She sniffed loudly and wiped her nose on the blanket. A clean white tissue appeared in front of her at the end of Laura's fingers, and she took it. She had run out of boxed tissues weeks ago, and been reduced to loo roll ever since. This unexpected luxury made her want to cry even more.

'You can't stay shut away forever,' said Laura, more gently this time. 'I know you're heartsore, Est, but you've got to get out and see people again. Amelia's wedding would be good for you – just a few old school friends, no-one who knows Charlie. I promise it won't be too awful.'

Esther sat up on the sofa, swinging her legs back onto the floor. She could see that the first two fingers on her right hand had been stained a sickly yellow from all the nicotine.

'I saw Katie Long two weeks ago,' she said, staring miserably at the floor. 'In John Lewis on Oxford Street one lunchtime.'

'Kabaddi Katie?'

Esther nodded, blinking hard as she remembered seeing Katie across the aisles of bed linens, hoping she wouldn't recognize her. Of course she had, she'd come practically running over to tell her news.

'She told me she was engaged, and I didn't know what to say. I just froze – and then I ran into the toilets without even saying congratulations.'

'It's okay,' Laura said soothingly, rubbing her back. 'I'm sure she'd have understood if she'd known.'

'I haven't finished,' Esther insisted, pushing her hand away. 'Laura, she followed me all the way in and shouted that I must not have heard her properly. Then she shoved her hand under the cubicle door to show me her engagement ring.'

'She did *not*.'

'She *did*. It was like that disembodied hand out of the Addams Family movie, just groping around on the toilet floor.'

'That's revolting.'

'I nearly weed on it.'

'You *should* have weed on it. What a nutter.'

'But don't you see – she's not the nutter. *I* am. Everyone's getting married, Laur, or engaged, or having babies. I'm nearly *thirty*, you're meant to have this kind of thing sorted by thirty.'

Laura shrugged, unconcerned. 'I haven't got it sorted, either. Doesn't that make you feel better?'

'No,' Esther grumbled.

'Why not?'

'Because you've always got some new boyfriend, you're beating them off with a shitty stick. It's not like that for me. Charlie was *the one*, don't you understand? He was the one person who really, really got me and loved me.'

Laura didn't answer right away. She got up and collected a few glasses, wiped the worst of the ashy dust off the coffee table. Esther knew that things must be really bad if Laura thought they needed clearing up.

'I get you, Est. I love you, too,' she said.

Esther snorted with sarcastic laughter. 'So what, *we* should get married?'

Laura made a face of utter horror. 'No way. Not until you have a shower, anyway. Wash your hair, too, you stink like a pub floor. Then maybe we can talk about a first date.'

When Esther came out of the bathroom, with a towel wrapped around her clean hair and her face scrubbed pink, she was surprised by how much better she felt. Her life was still over, obviously, but she had forgotten the small and simple pleasures of massaging shampoo into her scalp, shaving her legs, putting on scented moisturizer. She had neglected herself for so long that it had felt as if she was doing these things for a stranger in her care, someone who had to be treated with infinite care and kindness.

In the kitchen Laura had made coffee and raided Esther's wardrobe for three dresses which now hung from the lock of the window, stirring in the morning breeze like patterned ghosts of the girl who used to wear them. So Esther thought, anyway. Laura had less time for introspection.

'Pick one,' Laura said bossily, from the sink where she was washing up. 'Then dry your hair. If we're out of here by ten we can still make it to Kent in time.'

'Laur,' said Esther, tucking the top of her towel in by her armpit to secure it. 'Look, I'm really grateful to you for coming here, and I know you're trying to help, but I've got to do this my own way. One step at a time. A wedding is too much – seeing everyone. Katie will be there – I can't.'

Laura frowned at her as she continued, as bravely as she could manage.

'I'm still – I think I'm just still grieving. Just leave me to deal with this myself. Please.'

She sniffed again, but more delicately this time. When she had washed her hair she had discovered something suspiciously like snot in her fringe. That was to be avoided in future. One step at a time.

'Sit down,' said Laura. She snapped off the rubber gloves with determination, and tossed them aside.

Esther felt her stomach plummet to her knees as she lowered herself obediently into a chair. She had been the person dispensing the tough love often enough to know the signs that it was imminent. It felt like she was in the wrong chair. Shouldn't she be the wise and sensible one?

'Do you think Charlie's *grieving* in Bali or Bangkok or wherever he is?'

'He'll be in Malaysia by now,' Esther said, accidentally betraying the fact she had memorized his entire planned itinerary. She quickly dropped her eyes down so she wouldn't have to see Laura's pitying expression.

'Est,' said Laura, sitting down opposite her. 'Wherever he is, he's probably up to his knackers in gap-year girls. I'm sorry, but it's true. No-one goes travelling to find themselves, they go to get laid, whether they admit it or not.'

Esther stared at her, aghast. Of course, she had thought so herself – she had lain awake night after night imagining Charlie copping off with leggy Swedish nymphomaniacs in Thai beach bars – but these were secret fears, not to be said out loud in case that made them true.

'I need a cigarette,' she said, trying to get up.

'No, you don't,' said Laura, putting a restraining hand on her knee. 'You've smoked enough. Listen, Charlie has moved on, I promise you. Now it's your turn. It's been months. You *have* to try.'

'I *have* tried,' wailed Esther, feeling fresh tears spring to her eyes. 'But I'm not like you, I can't just forget about three years together.'

Laura's jaw was firm. 'Yes, you can. You can't be sentimental about it, Est. Every time you feel your head going there you think about something else – train yourself. It doesn't just happen, you have to *make* it happen.'

Esther dabbed at her cheeks with the edge of the

towel. She wished she was as strong as Laura, who seemed to cleave her way forwards with such energy that she never had time to worry about what she had left behind.

'I wish – I wish I could just burn out the bit of my brain that has Charlie in it, so he'd be gone forever. Like he'd never existed.'

'Like in that film,' mused Laura.

Esther's eyes narrowed with annoyance. This was her moment to lose it, not Laura's, for once. 'Let me guess,' she said with heavy sarcasm, 'a Drew Barrymore film?'

Laura looked surprised. 'No. *Eternal Sunshine of the Spotless Mind*, Kate Winslet.'

'Oh.'

'Though now you mention it,' said Laura, thoughtfully, 'Drew's latest film *is* about amnesia. You could do worse, I suppose. Want me to thump you on the head and see if that does the trick?'

Esther scowled at her.

'Anyway,' said Laura. 'Think of the gospel – Drew Barrymore's not married, is she? She doesn't have kids. It's not the only thing that counts in life.'

'Fuck off, Laur. You can't Drew Barrymore me out of this.'

Laura tilted her head a little as she considered her friend. Then she leaned back in her chair and let a smile play on her lips. It wasn't a sympathetic smile, thought Esther, it was almost as if Laura was laughing at her, right in her time of need.

'Oh, I see how it is,' Laura said, nodding. 'Fine.'

Esther sniffed again. 'What?'

'You think you're too good for this, don't you?'

'Too good for what?' she mumbled.

Laura kept her eyes fixed on her as she answered.

'You think that this gospel of Drew Barrymore stuff is fine as life advice for poor old fucked-up Laura. You'll tell *me* to trust in Drew when things go tits-up in my life, but no, it's not good enough for *you*, because *your* feelings are far more deep and complex than mine.'

'That's not true.'

'Yes, it is, I can see it. Haven't I sat in this very kitchen and had you tell me to try and be more like Drew? But when it's your turn, you think you're above it. You think it's a stupid game.'

'It *is* a stupid game.'

'But smoking yourself to death is really, really smart?' snapped Laura. 'You need to know, Est, that just because people don't show all their feelings doesn't mean they don't have them.'

'I never thought–'

'Yeah, you did. I know you did. You think I can move on from things because I don't feel them as much as you do. You reckon I'm so shallow I can just chivvy myself out of feeling bad with a Drew Barrymore movie and an inspirational quote off a greetings card.'

Esther didn't know how to answer. She had been so lost in her own feelings. They seemed to her so unique and terrible, so specifically related to Charlie, that they could not possibly have been felt by anyone else. Of course she understood that other people had been heart-broken – didn't every song on the radio seem to have been written with her in mind? – but her heartbreak had been all the more shocking to her because she had believed she was someone who wouldn't fall apart. It horrified her to realize that Laura was right. She had believed she was better than that.

'You're just stronger than me, Laur,' she said, the closest she could come to an admission of guilt. 'I always thought it was the other way round, but it's not.'

'Do you know why I'm strong?' said Laura. She leaned forward with an evangelical light in her eyes. 'It's not because of Drew Barrymore, but it's *like* her. I just keep going and so does she. That's all you can do, Est, you keep going until you feel better. And you *act* happier, even if you don't feel it. Sooner or later you find out that you feel happier, too. It's not magic, it's work. You've got to work to forget the bad stuff.'

'I've tried to do it. I'm trying so hard at work I don't have the energy for anything else. Please understand.'

Glancing up at her friend in hope of sympathy and forgiveness, Esther was taken aback to see a familiar smile on Laura's face. She recognized it instantly, like a snapshot in a much-thumbed photo album. It was the same smile she had worn wrapped in the arms of Ricko Struthers on the day of her father's funeral. The sympathy Esther had hoped for was there, but so was a kind of distant pity as if, yet again, Laura was some way ahead of her, looking nostalgically back.

'Do you really think,' she said, 'that I don't understand grief?'

20

Of course Kabaddi Katie was on their table, of course she was. Esther saw her straight away across the marquee, waving her left hand around as if it was possessed. No-one within a six-foot radius could possibly have missed her baguette-cut diamond ring or, standing obediently by her side, the handsome fiancé who had given it to her. Next to her was Sarah Maxwell, who turned around smiling as she saw them approach, to reveal an enormously pregnant stomach straining at the tie of her wrap dress. Esther felt she was on an episode of *Bullseye*, when Jim Bowen wheeled out the speedboat at the end to show what she would have won, if only she'd been able to keep hold of her relationship like everyone else. *Keep strong*, she told herself, fixing a smile of greeting to her face, *keep strong.*

She was too anxious to look around the marquee for other familiar faces from Portsdown; weren't Sarah and Katie enough? All the way there in the car, Laura had kept going on about how weddings were so great for re-connecting with people. She must have thought it was encouraging, but the very idea of it made Esther's insides turn somersaults.

It was fine for Laura to re-connect with people from the past – everyone remembered her as the most fancied girl at school. It was different for Esther. She had thought that being with Charlie had banished the spectre of Fat Fester forever but since he had gone, though she was aware she was thinner than ever, those schoolgirl insecurities kept springing back. Every time she thought she had banished one, another popped up. *You're only here as Laura's friend! You're always the afterthought! No-one will ever fancy you again!* It seemed that fatness had been not so much the cause of all of her teen anxieties, merely a convenient envelope for them all to fit into. Now those same worries buzzed around inside her like flies trapped in a somewhat smaller jar.

'Esther!' exclaimed Katie, with another unnecessary left-hand flourish. She inclined her head and pouted the way you would to a kitten or a puppy, something rather loveable but definitely on a lower evolutionary level than yourself. 'Awwww, I had no idea Amelia meant so much to you; you were sobbing your little heart out at the back of the church. So *sweet*.'

'Were you?' said Sarah, looking surprised.

'It was all very moving,' said Esther, who had been forced to gather herself after the ceremony by speed-smoking two cigarettes next to the gravestone of a Betty Mercer from Tankerton, who had died aged 72. A swift reapplication of face powder and mascara had mended the worst of the damage, and Laura had promised that no-one would notice.

'Oh, just ignore her, weddings always make Esther bawl like a baby,' said Laura. 'Wasn't Amelia's dress lovely?'

The conversation danced around this boring yet safe subject – were those real pearls on the bodice, did you think? Would you call that colour cream or ivory? – until Esther was interrupted by a posh female voice at her elbow.

'Excuse me,' asked a tall woman in a fuchsia skirt suit. 'Is this Dandy Dan?'

'Pardon?' she said, blinking and wondering if she was hearing things.

'Yes,' said Laura, answering for her. It made Esther feel a little like a bemused elderly relative who had been taken out of sheltered accommodation for the day. No matter how much she tried, everything seemed so overwhelming.

'This is Dandy Dan,' Laura continued, 'though I've no idea why.'

'Name of Harry's first pony,' said the hearty red-faced man at Esther's elbow, with a chuckle. 'All the tables are named after his horses. Jolly touching, I call it.'

'Just glad I'm not on Copper Bottom, frankly. Ghastly

little cob. A biter,' said the woman in fuchsia. Her large eyes were wide and far apart, and her face ended in a sharply pointed chin. This, combined with her long thin limbs and the waving feathers of her fascinator, gave her the appearance of a rather glamorous praying mantis.

She extended a hand to introduce herself.

'Barbara Weekes, do call me Bunty, and this is my husband Jonathan.'

Esther supposed that between them Bunty and Jonathan probably weighed the same as any average couple, but it looked like there had been a mistake in the allocation of their allotted pounds. Jonathan had received more than his fair share, and Bunty not nearly enough. Standing beside one another, they looked like an illustration of the number ten.

'Godfather of the groom,' said Jonathan, greeting each of them in turn with a crushing handshake. 'How do you do? '

'We're all old school friends of Amelia's,' said Esther, making a tremendous effort to be sociable instead of letting others carry the conversation. She suspected it might be easier to talk to strangers than to people who could ambush her with reminiscences or difficult questions about why she wasn't yet married herself.

'I was just saying to Sarah,' said Katie, leaning into her fiancé's side and gazing up at him adoringly, 'that at *our* wedding, we're going to name all of the tables after possible honeymoon destinations. You know, Amalfi coast, Maldives, Hawaii.'

Her fiancé nodded, with a slight air of resignation that suggested he had heard this more than once.

'The idea is – tell me if you've seen this before, because I haven't,' Katie continued excitedly. 'I won't know until the ceremony where we're going, John's planning it as a surprise. So after the speeches you'll look under the table and whoever finds the tickets–'

'Nicks them and flies off to Bora-Bora?' suggested Esther. The words were out of her mouth before she could stop them. Laura glared at her, and she felt like the bad fairy at Sleeping Beauty's christening, spoiling everything with her black thoughts.

Katie frowned, more puzzled than annoyed. 'No, they give them to us and reveal the destination. I mean, what? Do you think someone would actually take them? God, John, maybe we should re-think this.'

Laura laughed. 'Esther's only joking, you know what she's like.'

Esther forced a laugh in response. 'Yeah, just kidding, sounds amazing.'

Katie turned to her fiancé. 'I really think we should talk about that later, John. At least don't put the tickets on the same table as your Glasgow cousins.'

John's eyebrows flew up in alarm and he gave an abrupt cough.

'A charming idea,' said Bunty unconvincingly.

'Delightful.' She swivelled her pointy chin around, assessing the other tables nearby, no doubt wondering what she and her husband had done to piss off Harry enough for him to seat her with a group of strangers who were thirty years her junior.

When they took their seats, Esther was relieved to discover that Laura had been right – she made herself ask polite questions of Bunty to her right and Sarah Maxwell's husband to her left, she laughed at people's jokes, and it wasn't long before she found that even if she wasn't exactly enjoying herself, she could admit that it was better to be here than smoking alone in bed. She felt that if anyone were to look in her direction they would see a perfectly normal wedding guest; only she knew that she was hollow inside. Hollow, and dying for a cigarette. Laura was on sparkling form, flirting gently with Jonathan and teasing out old school stories from Katie to interrupt her ceaseless flow of wedding talk. Esther found herself wondering for the first time if Laura might be hollow on the inside too. It had shaken her to see how she'd mistaken her best friend's strong outside veneer for her real self – she had never imagined that brave, fearless Laura might be an act. Or perhaps, like she said, the act was over and she was truly happy now.

'At *our* wedding,' said Katie, considering the plate that had been put down in front of her, 'I've said no salmon, not even smoked for a starter. John doesn't agree but –

no offence to Amelia, it's always salmon, isn't it? At these things?'

'We didn't have salmon,' Sarah said, rubbing a contented hand over her belly. 'But then, ours was a winter wedding.'

'Very elegant,' Bunty murmured politely, but Esther saw her stab her salmon with unnecessary force, out of boredom or annoyance, she couldn't quite tell. 'Have you travelled far today?'

'I recognize this bunting from the Cox and Cox catalogue,' said Katie, interrupting. She pointed upwards to where triangular flags were looped from the central tent pole, and lowered her voice a little. 'At our wedding the bunting will be handmade by John's mother, won't it, John? It just adds more of a personal touch.'

John gave a tight smile next to her, and Esther imagined his poor mother imprisoned in her home with yards and yards of jaunty bunting, toiling away until it was all made to Katie's satisfaction.

Other subjects were broached, but the conversation at Dandy Dan was like a tennis volley with a relentless professional – whatever anyone attempted to serve was returned instantly with a wedding-related smash from Katie.

'And what did you do for wedding favours?' Katie asked Sarah. Her eyes were bright with interest, ready to take notes or make an unfavourable comparison to her own plans.

'I say,' declared Jonathan, valiantly stepping into a conversation which had until then been free from any male participation. Esther thought she actually saw John shake his head at him in warning. 'I thought the wedding favours were saved for the groom!'

'Well!' exclaimed Katie, and buried her face in her glass of wine.

Poor Jonathan went crimson, and Bunty glared at him with an 'I'll talk to you later' expression. Out of sympathy, Esther tried to engage him in a separate conversation.

'Isn't this wine nice?' she said. 'Cheers.'

She saw Laura roll her eyes, but 'nice' was the best she could do in her socially rusty state. She wasn't about to start talking about cat's pee and gooseberry bushes, or doing that awful ostentatious sniff that Laura used to do, like she was trying to drink the wine through her nostrils. She was just trying to help out a man her father's age who, through no fault of his own, was sharing a meal with Bridezilla.

Jonathan smiled at her gratefully. 'I'm very pleased you think so,' he said, beaming at his wife.

'At *our* wedding–' Katie began, but Laura interrupted her by picking up the bottle and loudly reading the label.

'A Picpoul,' she said, looking impressed. 'I wouldn't have expected Amelia to make such an interesting choice. Most people go for something safe and boring at weddings, Sauvignon, that sort of thing.'

Katie and John exchanged a stricken look in silence, and Esther bet that they had just decided to change the wine at *our* wedding.

Jonathan looked at his wife again with barely suppressed glee, his shoulders shaking.

'Jonathan bought the wine, dear,' explained Bunty, the feathers on her fascinator bobbing as she leaned forward. 'His present to the happy couple. He's a bit of a connoisseur.'

'Well, I think it's an excellent choice,' said Laura, and lifted her glass to toast him.

The others followed her example and they all sipped with suitably reverent expressions, even though they'd been necking it back obliviously just moments earlier. Except for Sarah, who placed a hand on her belly and shook her head, mouthing 'the baby', as if none of them had noticed until now.

'So did you drive to the Languedoc especially?' asked Laura, putting her wine glass down. 'I didn't think this vineyard sold outside of France.'

'I say,' said Jonathan, slapping his leg in the manner of a pantomime principal boy. 'You know your stuff, don't you!'

'Laura used to work in the wine trade,' said Esther, proudly. 'And now she's doing a degree in viticulture.' She felt pleased to have steered the conversation onto something more interesting to everyone other than

Katie, who was now assessing the table cutlery, turning over a knife with calculating eyes.

'Laura's going to be a winemaker,' she added.

'Are you now? Most impressive,' said Jonathan, as Laura demurred that it wasn't all that impressive really.

'Isn't that fascinating,' added Bunty, seeming to consider Laura with new interest.

Jonathan reached over for the wine bottle and held it in his hands as someone might hold a newborn baby; with pride and extreme care. 'Must confess I didn't drive there, bit of a cheat to tell you the truth.'

'Yes?' said Esther, politely.

'Yes, good chum of mine's in the wine trade. He got them for me on one of his trips. It's not what you know, eh?'

'Absolutely,' Laura agreed, sipping a little more.

'Matter of fact,' said Jonathan, leaning forward on his elbows. 'Maybe you know him? Wine's a small world, isn't it? Malcolm Bewes, Bewes Brothers – ring a bell?'

Laura looked like a cold metal spoon had been dropped down the back of her dress. She sat up very straight and her eyes widened a fraction. It was a reaction that was only visible to someone who knew her well, a moment's unease before she got control of herself.

'I've – well, I know *of* him, of course,' she said. 'He's very well known in the trade.'

As she answered, she reached forward for the place card on which her name was written, turned it flat onto the table, and covered it with her hand. While Jonathan continued to marvel at the coincidence that had led them to sit on the same table, Laura slowly inched the place card to the edge of the table and dropped it into her lap.

Esther was so concerned with watching this subterfuge that she failed to hear what Jonathan was saying until it was too late to interrupt.

'. . . bad business a few years ago. Had to get rid of some young girl in the office, work not up to scratch, you know the sort of thing. Anyway, she hit back with a lawsuit of some kind, claimed sexual harassment, which was utter tosh, of course. Malcolm's a gentleman, a complete gentleman.'

Laura nodded mutely, and ignored Esther's attempts to catch her eye.

'Anyway, bloody lawyers told him he was better off settling out of court than going through a trial. So the girl got paid off, small fortune, apparently. Poor Malcolm was destroyed by it, utterly destroyed. Felt his reputation had suffered, even though not a word of it was true.'

Jonathan refilled his own glass, seemingly too lost in memory to think of offering the bottle to anyone else. 'Bad business,' he said, shaking his head sadly. 'Bad business.'

Bunty had been watching the conversation with close attention. Esther got the impression that little escaped the beady eyes under the fascinator feathers. There was an intense expression on her face, as if she was doing complicated arithmetic in her head.

'*What* did you say your name was, dear?' she asked, leaning forward.

Esther leapt in immediately. 'I am absolutely gasping for a fag, sorry, terrible habit,' she said, standing up and giving Bunty an apologetic smile. She nodded at Laura, 'Coming?'

'Fuck's sake!' said Laura, panting and laughing as they dodged behind the far corner of the marquee. Although this meant they had a view of the catering tent instead of the Capability Brown landscape, at least they would be hidden from anyone who might come looking for them.

'What are you going to do?' asked Esther.

Laura shrugged. 'Nothing? I mean, what can Bunty really do? Christ, I never imagined–'

Before she could continue, a blonde head peered around the edge of the tent, followed by the rest of a slim and deeply tanned woman who picked her high-heeled way over the guy ropes, an unlit cigarette in her fingers. She was pretty in a harsh sort of way, with too much make-up on around her eyes, and a grim expression like she had just battled her way out of the wedding breakfast with a pickaxe.

'Got a light?' she asked, assessing them both with a flinty stare.

Esther handed over the lighter and introduced herself

while the woman inhaled an enormous, grateful gasp of smoke, as if she had just been saved from drowning.

'Lou,' said the woman. 'Shit table?'

'Sorry?'

'Are. You. On. A. Shit. Table?'

Esther and Laura glanced at each other and tried not to laugh.

'Well, of course you are. Why would you be hiding out here if you weren't?' Lou blew an angry stream of smoke up above her head. 'Me too. I said to Amelia, do *not* put me on some table full of other tragic single women, I said, make *sure* I'm sat next to a single man. Thirty per cent of women meet their future husband at a wedding, did you know that?'

Laura shook her head.

'Are *you* single?' Lou demanded. She clamped a cigarette between her lips and lit it.

'Not exactly,' said Laura.

'You?'

'Well – I'm–' Esther stammered.

'She just split up with someone,' said Laura, stepping in again.

Lou blew her stream of smoke in Esther's direction. 'Well, join the club,' she said. 'I am the fucking chairwoman of that club. I can't believe I got a spray tan for *this*. Amelia's wedding might as well be a lifeboat on the *Titanic* for all the romantic possibilities, it's all women, old people and *children*.'

She took another drag on her cigarette, and narrowed her eyes at Esther through a cloud of smoke.

'You get dumped then?' she asked.

'Yes, a few months ago,' Esther said quickly. She had to get used to talking about it, find a way of talking about it that didn't bring tears to her eyes.

Lou, sensing a possible display of emotion, gave Esther's shoulder a brief pat, the sort you would give to a dog if you didn't really like dogs but wanted to be seen by others as a sympathetic person. Esther wondered if Lou was afraid that her pathetic state might be contagious and incurable, like herpes.

'Nightmare,' Lou said, but moved swiftly on, as her real interest was not in Esther but in herself. 'I wasn't dumped, of course. I said, Alex, I am going to be thirty-one next month and either you propose or I'll find someone who will. And that utter, utter bastard – ' her voice shook – 'said that now I *mentioned* it, he'd been having second thoughts.'

Esther wasn't sure what to say. She attempted to return the shoulder pat, in solidarity, but Lou looked at her tentatively offered hand in horror and so she retreated.

'Are you dating again?' Lou snapped.

'No,' Esther said. It didn't feel like the time to admit she hadn't even been leaving the house unless it was absolutely necessary.

Lou's eyes narrowed. 'How old are you?'

'Twenty-nine.'

'Well, you'd better get on with it,' Lou said. 'It's all over at thirty-five.'

'What is?' asked Laura, with genuine interest. She was looking at Lou with fascination, like she was a creature in a zoo. The conversation seemed to have quite distracted her from her own situation.

'Everything!' exclaimed Lou, exasperated. 'Fertility, looks, chances of ever getting married. Trust me, you've got to act fast.'

'Act fast,' Esther echoed. She wasn't sure how to respond to this rather terrifying woman. Lou seemed not just like a different sort of person from her, but like a different species. A species that lurked around the back of marquees giving unsolicited advice in a rather aggressive tone.

'Do you know how many dates I've been on this year?' Lou demanded.

Esther and Laura admitted that no, they didn't.

'Fifty!' she said, her expression inviting them to join in her astonishment.

Esther heard Laura inhale sharply.

'Fifty dates, wow,' said Esther, unsure whether she was meant to congratulate or commiserate.

Lou cocked her head suddenly, listening to something inside the marquee. 'God, here we go, they're starting the speeches. Like it couldn't get any worse. We'd better go back inside.'

She stalked off ahead of them, her fake-tanned legs striding around the corner before they'd had time to move.

'Fifty dates,' said Laura. 'It's a sign.'

'Of what?'

'That's the Drew Barrymore movie – *50 First Dates*.'

Esther ground out her cigarette on the grass. 'Not everything is about Drew Barrymore, Laur.'

'That's what you think,' grinned Laura, her good humour entirely restored. 'You never know what miracles Drew might be up to on our behalf.'

They got back to their table just as the speeches began, and any further conversation was thankfully impossible. Esther noticed Bunty looking over at Laura more often than seemed coincidental, but Laura seemed quite oblivious now, and perfectly relaxed. She joined in the sweepstake that Sarah's husband had set up on how long the speeches would last, she whooped and cheered as Harry Branwell praised his beautiful bride. Whether it was an act or not, Esther was astonished how quickly Laura could recover herself. Just as she said, she pushed the bad thoughts away and moved on. But weren't the bad things you thought about still there, even if you ignored them? Just because Laura didn't like to think of her affair with Malcolm didn't mean it hadn't happened. Esther was afraid there would always be a Bunty of some sort, ready to drag up the past just when it seemed safely buried.

The sweepstake winnings were claimed by Katie's fiancé, who had suggested a bum-numbing forty-five minute total, and was sadly proven correct. Now coffee was being served and guests were beginning to get up from their tables and move around the marquee. From outside came the sound of a band embarking on a bossa nova version of 'Crazy in Love'.

Bunty was distracted from her continued scrutiny of Laura by Jonathan, who stood up with some effort and said that he fancied stretching his legs after the speeches. And anyway, they should really try to see Harry's parents before it got too late. The two of them stood, and while Jonathan placed a pashmina around his wife's shoulders, Esther and Laura said polite and non-committal good-byes. But Bunty wasn't that easily diverted. She cocked her head at Laura, like a bird regarding a worm.

'Remind me, dear, just what did you say your name was?'

Laura began to stammer and Esther was wondering if she should knock something over as a distraction, when two hands covered her eyes, plunging her into sudden darkness.

'I say,' she heard Jonathan exclaim, with a throaty chuckle. 'What's going on here?'

A voice whispered in her ear, 'The *Gazette* says . . . fancy seeing you here.'

Esther was glad she was still sitting down. She felt her

knees turn to jelly. She had told herself she was over David Carrell years ago; it had been an infatuation, not the real thing she'd had with Charlie. But her body told a different story, and she felt her breath quicken as she realized who stood behind her.

She reached her own hands up and touched his tentatively. 'Al?' she asked, making her voice hesitant. 'Is that you, Al Webster?'

'Oh, fuck off,' David laughed, pulling his hands away so that she could see him standing right there.

'It *is* you, Al! I'm so pleased you changed your hair,' said Esther, and David Carrell swept her into a hug right there in front of everyone.

With his arms around her, she realized they had never once hugged before, only pecked each other politely on the cheek on the rare occasions they'd met since she left the *Gazette*. Surely any moment Fiona would come over to reclaim him with a possessive mouse-sneeze, so Esther made sure to remember every last second that she was pressed to his chest. She thought of Winona Ryder licking the boy's leather jacket in *Mermaids* – she would have done the same to David's shirt front if she'd dared.

When they let go, David kept his arm over her shoulder as he waved across the table. 'Well, hi there, Laura Thomas,' he said, and Esther heard Bunty's sharp intake of breath.

'Let's go and dance!' Esther said.

'What, now?' said David, laughing.

'Right now,' she insisted.

But it was too late. Jonathan introduced himself and his wife, and there followed several painful minutes in which they discussed mutual acquaintances while Bunty stayed silent and watchful. Esther and Laura stayed silent and worried. At last Jonathan declared he was going outside to the terrace to see the band. Bunty looked back over her shoulder a few times as she was led away, like Lot's wife; only she and the fuchsia fascinator never turned into a pillar of salt, as much as they might wish she would.

'Let's dance later,' said Laura, with a look of relief. 'I think it's better to catch up with old friends first.'

'This is just such a surprise,' said Esther to David. She felt like nothing could wipe the foolish smile off her face. She had to get a grip before she made a total tit of herself. 'I can't believe it. How's Fiona?'

'Oh, yeah,' he pulled his arm away from her as if he had just remembered his girlfriend. 'She's good. She's in New York.'

'Oh, right,' said Esther, feeling herself blush as she made a little respectful distance between herself and David. A space for Fiona, if she had been there physically. 'Nice. Lucky her.'

'Yep.' He rubbed bashfully at the side of his neck, looking down at the floor. The band switched to 'Toxic' by Britney Spears.

'Oh, for Christ's sake, you two,' said Laura, putting

her hands on her hips and glaring at both of them like they had just run over her cat. 'Esther – David and Fiona have split up. She went to New York for work and she has been living there since Easter with a lawyer called Mario. David – Esther and Charlie broke up three months ago. He was a wanker, and never good enough for her, if you ask me. You are both single. Need I make myself any clearer?'

Esther stared at her open-mouthed. 'Did you – did you know about this? You knew he'd be here?' She glanced up at David, who looked equally nonplussed.

'Of course I knew!' Laura said, throwing her hands up in exasperation. 'Amelia told me about some single friend of Harry's that she was trying to set up at the wedding, and I realized who it was. God, the nightmare I had trying to get you to come here at all, Esther! I thought I was going to have to drag you by the hair.'

'So you're – ' said Esther, looking up at David, hardly daring to believe it was true.

Before he could answer he was pushed aside roughly by an unseen hand, and there was Bunty, escaped from her husband and back at the table, glancing anxiously over her shoulder in case she had been followed. The feathers on her head flicked a fuchsia warning, and everyone stepped back in alarm.

She pointed an accusing finger in Laura's face, and though her cheeks were a fiery red, her voice was very calm. 'I know exactly who you are, Laura Thomas, and just what you did to Malcolm Bewes.'

They all froze, even David, who knew nothing of Malcolm Bewes, waiting to hear what she would say next. They looked like they were playing a game of What's the Time, Mr Wolf, each of them stock still while Bunty prowled around them, snarling.

'I know you took his money and went to college with it. I guessed it was you as soon as you said you were studying viticulture. And then your face when Jonathan said Malcolm's name. Well, that gave it all away.'

Laura gulped, and Esther went to stand next to her in case Bunty's attack got physical. David placed himself alongside them in solidarity. Behind them, their old school friends watched with open mouths.

'And I just want to say – ' hissed Bunty, coming closer. They all flinched back as one, leaning their upper halves away from her like limbo dancers.

'I just want to say,' she continued, 'that it was about *time* someone took that disgusting old pervert to the cleaners.'

She sniffed once, briskly, and her fascinator feathers dipped and quivered. 'Malcolm Bewes had it coming. He bloody well had it coming.'

21

October 2013

Memory hates a vacuum. It fills in the gaps like a slapdash builder – that'll do. You can have a perfectly clear recollection of your holiday romance the summer that Laura had split up with Ricko, when you both went to Mykonos on a cheap package deal from Luton Airport. You can remember everything about that Greek god, from his deliciously heavy accent right down to the gold tooth that glinted in the back of his mouth when he laughed. And then Laura will scoff and get out the photo album that proves your delicious Greek was actually a roofer from Billericay who was known to his friends as Naughty Barry, and you know that she is right. The gold tooth was from Essex, not Athens, all along.

Without that friend who has known you forever, your memories are unreliable, and so are theirs. Every new discovery about Laura's life makes me question the facts

I thought I knew for certain – who she is, who I am, who we are to each other.

Before I came here I wouldn't have hesitated to call Laura my best friend – and I hoped she'd have done the same for me, but now I am beginning to wonder. A shared past can't sustain a friendship forever, or God knows I'd be best friends with Amelia Wentworth and that is very much not the case. There has to be something more to any relationship than just memory. Friendship is like a shark: it has to keep moving forwards to survive.

I thought Laura and I had done this, I thought we'd navigated our way through the bad stuff together. It seemed to me testament to our friendship that it had survived not just distance, but differences. But maybe I've been kidding myself all along. Laura has been crying – for days, her neighbour said, and I don't have the first idea why. She's packed up her car, and I don't know what she was running from. Or if she was running at all. Isn't it possible she was going to Stanley's that night? Isn't it likely that the last person to see her was not her crazy neighbour, but her secret lover?

The police won't help. All of the messages I've sent to Laura have been met by silence. There is only one person who can answer my questions, and this time I'm not letting him get away.

The Foothills Vineyard is a twenty-minute drive out of town, towards the distant mountains, and the turning off the freeway is signposted by an enormous full-colour billboard that advertises winery tours, tastings and family days out. For the family that likes to drink together, I suppose.

I crest the hill and there is Foothills, looking as if it has been brought over brick by brick from the Tuscan countryside and reconstructed here in the Californian sun. It is a huddle of low stone buildings, with small arched shuttered windows pitting the sides, and red-tiled roofs that pitch steeply downwards. There is a square tower to the east with ivy growing up it, and a riot of bright pink bougainvillea over the entrance gate. Grape vines run parallel to the road, right up to the walls, as if they are marching themselves there in orderly rows, ready to be crushed. The whole vista is picture-perfect and, as if to prove it, there is a gaggle of Japanese tourists taking photographs outside.

When I get out of the car, a young girl in a green shirt with the vineyard name on a crest points me towards a side entrance and tells me that the tour starts in five minutes. I'm about to tell her I'm not here for the tour when it occurs to me that there is no better way to approach Stanley unnoticed than under cover of a large group. I let myself get swept into a crowd of passengers who are disembarking from a Napa Wine Tours coach, and follow their leader's upheld folded umbrella into the place where Laura has worked for three years.

We pass through an arched door and find ourselves in

a courtyard, where another red-tiled roof covers a veranda that runs across three sides of the square, supported by a wooden frame. The yard is full of visitors exclaiming over the old stone buildings and posing for senior citizen selfies next to the fountain in the centre. Around the edges of the yard are old wine barrels that have been cut in half and planted with flowers.

I move into the cool shade of the veranda where it is quieter, and where I hope the darkness will make me less conspicuous. Laura called the vineyard a small family concern, but it seems highly professional, with uniformed staff and a tour timetable painted on a sign by a big glass door that seems to lead to a shop. There are three more doors visible in the walls of these buildings, each of them closed. The one on the other side of the courtyard opens for a moment, and I see a flash of white tile as it swings shut. A man emerges, wiping his hands on his trousers, and I know I can rule that door out.

Like any other tourist, I look around, taking in my surroundings as I walk along the length of the veranda, close to the wall. Unlike any other tourist, I keep an eye on the staff to make sure I am unseen. When I see they are beginning to usher everyone into a queue in front of the main entrance, I take my chance and slip through the nearest door, which is marked 'Private'.

The Tuscan villa vibe disappears as I find myself in some sort of waiting room, with a squashy leather sofa and chairs gathered around a coffee table full of magazines called things like *Napa Valley Life* and *Inside Napa*. As if no-one could possibly have interests outside of the wine valley. Behind the sofa is an illuminated cabinet full of awards and framed certificates. I'm just about to look closer when a door opens in the side of the room and a woman gasps, her hand flying to her chest in surprise.

'Oh!' she says. 'Are you here for the tour? You'll need to go outside. No visitors in here.'

'I have a meeting with Stanley Hoffmann,' I say, as smoothly as I can manage. I know that looking flustered will give me away instantly as someone who shouldn't be here. I learned this staying in posh hotels for work; look like you belong, and people believe you.

The woman looks confused. She is middle-aged with a kind face, and thick fair hair in a plait that goes over the top of her head. She looks anxiously towards the door that she came from. *So that's where he is*, I think.

'I didn't think he – that is, I keep Mr Hoffmann's diary, and I don't believe he has a meeting right now.'

'Well, it wasn't a formal thing,' I say, turning away from the display cabinet. I take a few steps towards her, drawing too close on purpose, and just as I hoped, she is distracted into moving backwards away from the door. Now I am closer to it than she is.

'We met this morning and agreed I could call by later to continue our interview.'

I'm astonished at how easily the excuses flow. If you

had told me just a week ago that I, harrassed parent of one, would be calmly forcing my way into the private offices of a Californian vineyard, I would have thought you were crazy. And yet here I am, acting as if this subterfuge is all quite normal. You don't know who you might become until you're tested. And today I have been tested severely.

'Interview? Are you a journalist?' she asks, trying to place me.

'Yes.' It isn't a lie. It's just not exactly the truth either.

She looks at me with suspicion, and her nostrils flare a little, almost as if she is trying to sniff out my motive. 'This morning–' she says.

'I can show you my Press card if you need it,' I say, reaching into my handbag, though I know it isn't there. I haven't used it for months.

'No.' She holds out her hand to stop me. 'It's okay. If you wait here, I will go and ask Mr Hoffmann if he has time to see you. It's a very busy time for us here at Foothills.'

But I'm not about to give Stanley a chance to get out of this. My hand is on the door handle and I've pushed it open before she can move.

'You can't go in there!' I hear her shout, but I slam the door behind me.

Stanley isn't here either. There's just a small, cramped room with a desk and a computer set up outside yet another door. What is this place – a labyrinth? I move fast, but not fast enough – the fair-haired woman has the advantage of knowing where she is going, and my hesitation is her advantage. She grabs at my arm as I lunge forward, so that both of us burst through the doorway at the same time.

Stanley sits at a desk, quite composed, as if he has been waiting for me all along.

'She pushed her way in!' the fair woman exclaims, and I can hear she is near tears.

He stands up, unsmiling.

'It's okay, Amy,' he says in a quiet voice. 'I was expecting her.'

Stanley's office is dark. There is a window high up on the wall, but it is shuttered against the sunlight and the only illumination is artificial – an Anglepoise lamp squatting on his desk. The room is almost cell-like in its lack of decoration; not a picture or poster, nor a rug nor a cushion to soften the stone walls, which are the same inside as they are outside. There is not one family photograph or telling personal effect. I realize at once that it reminds me of Laura's apartment – it's a place that wants to give nothing away.

When Amy has been persuaded to leave us alone, insisting loudly that she will be waiting right outside, I sit down on the swivel chair in front of Stanley's desk and cross my legs. He sinks down into his chair so that we are level.

'I shouldn't have run out that way,' he says, and I am shocked to see that his eyes are brimming with tears.

He wipes his eyes with the back of his hand quickly, embarrassed, and I seize my advantage while his defences are low.

'I called the police,' I say.

It is his turn to be shocked. I can see how much he is trying to regain his composure. His mouth works as if he is trying to chew his lips from the inside. Before, his face was cleared of all emotion – now it is as if everything is trying to come out at once. He is fighting against himself, and losing.

'The police? But Laura would hate that, I already told her mother–'

'I know what you told her mother, Stanley,' I say calmly. 'And I know what you told me, but it's what you're not telling me that's my concern right now.'

He drops his head down into his hands and mumbles something down at the desk top, more to himself than to me. When he looks up I can see he is nervous, and suddenly I realize that I am not. The power balance has shifted. I might be suspicious of him, but I'm not at all afraid.

'The police will have questions for you when they get here,' I bluff. I want him to be scared. I want him to know how it feels to panic. 'But first, you need to answer mine. Why didn't you tell us about you and Laura? Surely we had a right to know what was going on?'

'Yeah,' he says, wiping his cheek roughly with the heel of his hand.

'Do you know why she's gone? Did you two have a fight or something?'

Stanley shakes his head.

'No fight.'

I don't know whether to believe him. Isn't it always the husband or the lover who is to blame when a woman goes missing? And it seems all the more suspicious when that lover is her married boss.

'So why did you clear out her apartment?' I demand.

He shifts in his seat, and his eyes dart over my shoulder to the door, before he looks at me again.

'How do you know I did that?'

'Her neighbour saw you.'

Stanley rolls his eyes to the ceiling and sighs heavily.

'I can see you're mad about it, but Laura would be madder. She hated me fussing – that's what she used to call it. Quit fussing, Stanley. Leave the spilled lasagne on the floor, Stanley. Step over the laundry, Stanley, it doesn't matter.'

He tries to imitate her accent at the end – 'mattah' – and smiles a little, inviting me to share his amusement, but I'm not finding it funny.

'So why did you do it?'

He blinks at me as if he is surprised by the question. 'In case you wanted to stay there,' he says, like it is obvious. 'I couldn't let you stay without cleaning the place first. It wouldn't have been right.'

'You think it was right for me to look around her apartment without knowing that you'd thrown out bags of rubbish and scrubbed the floors with bleach first? What else did you hide from me?'

His face pales, and he shifts on his chair.

'Nothing!' he says. 'I didn't want you to think badly of Laura, when you saw how she'd been living.'

'Why would I think badly? I know what Laura's like, she's always been messy.'

He sighs again, and chews at his thumbnail before he answers. 'I know she's not much of a housekeeper, but it got worse lately. She said she was too tired. Said she got in from work and just went to bed, didn't have the energy to clear up after herself. And it seemed like all she ate was pizza. There were boxes and boxes of it on the floor, some of them empty, some of them not. I thought there might be bugs – roaches – if I left it. I didn't want you to see that – or tell her mother, make her worry for no reason.'

I think of Margie's chaotic Sussex cottage, with chickens wandering in and out, as injured hedgehogs breathe their last beside the Aga. I can't imagine her caring one bit. Who is this stranger to judge Laura – or any of us?

'Well, it wasn't for no reason, was it?' I say.

Stanley shakes his head, his eyes almost closed. 'I thought it was because of me,' he says. 'Because of us.

I thought the – situation was making her depressed. That's why I kept it from you. Because she didn't tell anyone about us, and neither did I.'

His mouth has gone into a straight hard line, white at the edges, and his eyes are pained.

'Is it because you're married?' I ask.

He actually pushes his chair back away from his desk to put distance between us, and gulps for air like he's running out of oxygen. He looks as if he would run out of here if he could. I knew it.

'Now listen,' Stanley says at last. His voice is shaking. 'It's not for her sake that she's kept this from you, it's for mine. Knowing she was a girl who could keep a secret, well, that might have been part of her attraction for me. Not a person who'd run all over the vineyard telling tales. I've been talked about enough.'

He looks up, as if considering whether I, too, can be trusted to keep a secret.

'So Laura didn't tell you about my family?' he asks, almost choking on the last word.

'No,' I say. Though as he starts to speak again, I think I do have some dim recollection of Laura mentioning his wife in an email. But I had no reason to remember it, so I haven't.

He brings his chair forward again now, resting his elbows on his desk and clasping his hands tightly together.

'I got married late,' he says, slowly, not meeting my

eyes. 'Forty-four. Never thought I'd get married at all, or have kids. Men aren't meant to be sad about that, are they? But I was.'

He looks up, lifting his chin and breathing in deeply.

'Summer 2004 Monica came to work on the vineyard and that was it. She was twenty years younger than me, up from Arizona for the season, meant to go back to Phoenix in the fall. No fool like an old fool. I fell right into it like a lovesick teenager. We were married in six months, parents in a year.'

I'm not sure what he wants from me here: sympathy that he married too fast and regrets it? Poor Monica, that's hardly her fault. And I thought he said he didn't have children?

'I loved my wife,' he says, and I note the past tense. 'But my boy – that's another kind of love. A whole other kind.'

I press my lips together hard to stop my eyes from filling up. I have been trying not to think of Linus today. Whenever I do it's like a physical pain in my chest, I miss him so much. I didn't think this short time away from him would be so hard.

'He was a beautiful, beautiful baby. Black hair just like mine.' He lifts a hand to his head and chuckles at my expression. 'Like mine used to be. It's a funny trick nature plays, making a baby look just like its daddy when it's born, so you can't stop staring and wondering at your own features in that brand new face.'

'Do you have a picture?' I ask.

Stanley looks shocked, and shakes his head.

'No,' he says. 'At home, I mean, no, no, I don't have a picture.'

A slow and horrible awareness begins to dawn on me as Stanley ploughs on with his story. Before his speech was hesitant, slow, but now he is speeding up, racing to get to a conclusion that I do not think I want to hear.

'We called him Ned after my dad, and when he got bigger you couldn't keep him away from the vineyard. He rode on the tractors with the pickers, he played hide and seek in amongst the stills, we even picked him up so his little baby feet could step in the crush – the grapes, you know? – we don't do it that way any more, it's all machines nowadays. But it felt like a link with the old ways to have my son put his feet in the grapes like my father and his father. My son.'

Stanley coughs into his hand, then steadies his elbows on the desk, like he is bracing himself for an impact, and goes on.

'It was his first day at kindergarten. You know we start work early, three, four in the morning. So Monica brought Ned in to see us before he went – he wouldn't let me hug him because of his new backpack, just kept turning round to show it off and to tell us it had his lunch in it.

'That afternoon we were all waiting for him to come back, tell us about his day. I hoped maybe he'd let me hug him now. I can't say I watched the clock for it, too much happening to keep track of the time – but each time the door opened I hoped it would be my boy.

'I wasn't worried at first – thought Monica must have taken him out for ice cream or something, run into another mom she knew. Even thought maybe she was keeping him out of our way on purpose, knowing we'd stop work if we saw him.

'But when the door opened at five, it was Amy from the office telling me to get to the hospital.'

Stanley stops and takes a shuddering, jagged breath.

'They wouldn't tell me over the phone. I had to drive all the way to the hospital not knowing if they were alive or dead.'

He waits for a moment before he carries on.

'Ned died. It happened on impact, nothing they could do, internal injuries. When I went to see him you would have thought he was sleeping, not a mark on his face.'

'I'm so sorry,' I say. What else is there to say? It is meaningless but it is the only thing there is.

Stanley shakes his head. 'Monica was in theatre,' he says. 'It took hours but they saved her.'

'Thank God,' I say. 'Was she okay?'

Stanley shakes his head again. 'She made a full recovery, that's what the doctors said. Even though her leg was shattered, she walked again, everything. But I don't think she ever did truly recover from it.'

'You can't recover from something like that, can you?' I ask. 'Not really.'

I can't imagine it. I mean that quite literally, my mind won't let me imagine that happening to Linus or me. Not to my living, breathing, laughing boy.

'No,' says Stanley. 'You can't. We didn't. Monica couldn't be here any more – driving that same route, seeing the other kids going to kindergarten like nothing had happened, running into their moms in the store. One day she just left.'

'Where is she now?'

Stanley looks towards the shuttered window before he answers, as if she is behind it.

'Portland,' he says. 'Oregon,' he adds, in case I didn't know where it was. 'Before that, New Mexico. She moves around a lot.'

'You keep in touch?'

'Kind of.'

'Is – is this what Laura – ? Did she – ?'

I don't know what question to ask. It has obviously cost Stanley a great deal to tell me about Ned and Monica – the story hasn't come out of him smooth and practised, but halting and painful. He wouldn't have made himself tell it if there weren't some connection to Laura, but I can't see what it might be.

Stanley gives a curt nod. 'Laura knows. Everyone knows. Ever since it happened Amy takes it upon herself to tell anyone new at the vineyard. She does it to be kind, doesn't want anyone saying something that might hurt me. I can see when it's happened. One day it's, "Hi Stanley, how's it going?" and the next day they've got sympathy eyes.'

'Sympathy eyes?'

'You know, not saying anything out loud, just sympathy eyes. Nearly a frown, head to the side a little, sympathy eyes. Can't stand it when it happens. Laura didn't do it.'

'Didn't she?'

'Nope,' says Stanley. 'Just marched right up to me one morning, she'd only been there a week. Said, "Stanley, I've just been talking to Amy and she told me about your son. It's awful and I wanted to tell you I'm so sorry, you must miss him so much."'

Stanley sniffs sharply. 'No sympathy eyes. Just told it straight. That's brave.'

'Laura always was brave,' I say.

Stanley looks up. 'Laura *is* brave,' he says. 'Not was. Most people are afraid of grief – they don't mean to be, but you scare them. It's like you carry death with you and they can't get away fast enough. Laura wasn't like that. She faces up to things. That's how I know she'll be okay. Wherever she is right now.'

'But – do you, I mean, if this is something Laura knew about already – why now? Why would it change things now?'

Stanley takes a long breath, so deep I can see his chest lift under his blue shirt.

'There's a world of difference,' he says, and as he speaks he seems to deflate and shrink, like a balloon losing air, 'a whole world of difference between knowing about it, and waking up next to a man who's still crying over it most nights.'

'You said she's brave,' I say. 'That wouldn't scare her away.'

He looks sad, and old and disappointed, not just by Laura, but by everything.

'But it did,' he says. 'I woke up one morning and she was gone.'

MUSIC AND LYRICS (IN FRANCE: LE COME-BACK), JULY 2007[9]

RHONDA FISHER: *Look, hon, you don't fall a lot. And I've seen the way you look at him, so if you are falling for him . . . Just please, please make sure he's passionate about you.*

SOPHIE FISHER: *Well, you know, I mean, I'm not falling. We're just working together, you know? And besides, the one time we slept together, it's been totally professional.*

22

Until Laura moved to France to take up a work placement, the only thing that Esther knew about Épernay was that the First World War had been especially fierce there. She remembered it from history at school: trench warfare began right where the champagne vines grew. Didn't Churchill make one of his blustery Churchillian comments about it at the time – we're not fighting for France, gentlemen, but for champagne? Something like that.

Outside the window of the train from Paris, the French summer shone yellow in fields that flickered past like an old film reel. Esther had two proofs for work on the table in front of her, and half a printed-out manuscript in her overnight bag, but all she had read so far was a copy of *Heat* magazine, and she'd paid very little attention to that. Instead she thought of David, waving her off from the platform, even though she'd told him he didn't need to see her onto the Eurostar.

He'd claimed to be unable to resist the romance of the railways, though there was little romantic about the Waterloo terminal at six in the morning.

He had his own overnight bag with him, ready to go down to the Isle of Wight to stay with his grandmother for the weekend. Or so he said. She wasn't sure why she didn't believe him – she'd been to visit his grandmother herself, at the house in Bembridge, so that part at least was true. But she knew him too well not to be able to tell when he was excited, even if he was trying to hide it.

He had an almost childish way of chewing on the bottom corner of his lip when he was trying to keep a secret, like it was trying to get out of him and he had to remember to bite it back. She had already got on the train when an impulse made her stop and lean back out of the door to blow him one last kiss. She caught him just turning away to leave, a smile breaking over his face, and his lower lip caught by his teeth for a moment. It was a look she knew as well as her own face in the mirror, but this was the first time she had seen that expression when it wasn't directed at her.

There was no-one else there, though. She waited to check, despite the patent annoyance of the French family that was trying to board behind her. She waited and saw that he walked away alone.

She told herself she was being ridiculous. He needn't have come to the station at all, let alone got up early and shared the taxi. He could have had a lie-in, gone to the

Isle of Wight later, if he'd wanted. Yet somehow she couldn't shake the feeling that he had come to see her off not out of devotion, but out of a desire to make sure she had truly gone.

It took an almighty effort, and a small plastic bottle of white wine from the buffet car, to get herself out of her morose mood by the time the train arrived at her destination. She was determined that this would be a great weekend; she hadn't seen Laura for months and she wasn't about to let her down by being paranoid for no reason. Anyway, there surely wouldn't be time for self-indulgent introspection. Laura had already told her about the houseful that awaited her – crammed with seasonal workers, with blow-up mattresses in the sitting room and two people sleeping on the sofa. She was going to have to share a bed with Laura – it would be just like the old days, staying up late, gossiping.

When she stepped off the train, Laura was waving frantically from behind a barrier, beaming a red-lipsticked smile. She wore a long striped sundress and enormous sunglasses, like she had stepped out of a magazine feature about how to be chic and French even if you actually came from Portsdown. Under her arm was a paperback, in French, by Balzac, which was odd because the last book Esther had seen Laura read, in English, was one by Jilly Cooper.

'You're so brown!' Esther exclaimed, hugging her. 'Look at your tan!'

'Pfft.' Laura dismissed her with a burst of laughter. 'How was the journey? Were you okay changing in Paris?'

She grabbed Esther's overnight bag from her and hoisted it over her shoulder, despite Esther's protests.

'Let me show off,' she begged. 'You wouldn't *believe* my muscles. Feel my arm, go on, feel it.'

Esther squeezed the thin brown arm that had been extended, and admired, as she was meant to, the knotted muscles under the skin.

'I'm lugging crates and pushing carts full of bottles all day, it's the best exercise. Now look – ' she stopped outside the station entrance, and pushed her sunglasses up on her nose. 'There's been just a very little bit of a change of plan.'

'Change of plan?' asked Esther.

She felt suddenly nervous. Laura's perky brightness was so often a front to cover up something difficult, and she wondered what it was this time. Did Laura have to work this weekend after all? Was she going to spend the weekend alone?

'It's just, the house is so full, Est. It's a nightmare. And with all those boys, it's such a state, I can't let you stay there.'

'I don't mind,' said Esther. She didn't. It would be fun to doss around with a bunch of young guys again, like being a student. Sometimes she worried that she was prematurely old compared to Laura – going to dinner parties and work functions, talking about mortgage rates and visiting DIY shops on the weekend. Laura's life seemed so much more exciting.

'Well, I mind,' insisted Laura. 'It's just too revolting. There's always a queue for the bathroom, and the boys are getting up and coming in at all hours. So, I've got a surprise!'

'Ye-es?'

Laura linked her free arm into Esther's and pulled her away from the station entrance towards a line of waiting taxis. The drivers were all standing outside their cars, smoking and looking bored until they saw them approaching. Then there was a mass straightening-up and stubbing of cigarettes on the ground, and the door to the taxi at the head of the queue was held open by an extravagantly moustachioed driver.

'You're going to love it,' Laura said, handing the bag over to the driver. 'I've booked you in to a hotel right in the centre of everything. It's gorgeous. My treat.'

Before Esther could say that she'd still rather stay at the house, Laura had begun a rapid conversation with the driver in French, both of them gesticulating wildly in good-humoured disagreement over something she couldn't quite follow. Esther had time, standing mutely to the side, to consider that the most likely reason for the change of plan was a new man, or a potential one. She knew Laura liked to keep her options open and having her best friend taking up the other side of the bed closed certain options down. Esther couldn't help but be a little disappointed. She didn't care about sharing the bathroom, or being woken up. On top of David's odd behaviour, a hotel room all on her own in a strange town seemed more of a banishment than the treat that Laura promised.

'Since when did you speak such good French?' asked Esther, as they got in the back seat.

Laura gave a Gallic shrug. 'Just picked it up, I suppose.'

She leaned forward to add a further instruction to the driver, laughing coquettishly as he said something in reply. If Esther hadn't known that Laura was English – if she hadn't seen with her very own eyes the eating of Marmite and the picnicking in the rain that proved it – she would have assumed, as anyone would, that she must be French. The red lipstick, the practised flirtation, the complete fluency in the language. Laura's capacity to adapt herself instantly to any environment should not have surprised her by now, and yet it did. Esther thought that she must be like a Russian doll, able to step straight out of her old self, shiny and new and perfectly at ease wherever she happened to be. What happened to the discarded shells of former Lauras, she wondered. Did they just cease to exist, or did they shrink back down to be tucked inside the doll again, in case they were needed?

With a small amount of grumbling the driver took the turning that Laura wanted, down the Avenue de Champagne, and Esther saw that Churchill's war had been won. Champagne was more than victorious here, it was ubiquitous. On each side of the wide street were grey-roofed mansions, imposing behind high gates and formal structured gardens, each bearing the name of a legendary champagne house. Laura clutched at her sleeve, pulling her towards the window to see, 'Look!' she exclaimed, pointing with her battered paperback. 'Pol Roger! Perrier-Jouët! Isn't it fabulous? I had to bring you this way, it's the *best* introduction to Épernay.'

When they got to the hotel, at the moment one might expect to be offered tea or coffee, the matronly proprietor instead handed each of them a glass of champagne and made encouraging gestures with both hands, like she was persuading two naughty children to drink their effervescent medicine. Only when they had both finished would she show them to the room.

Laura went straight to the bathroom. 'Didn't I tell you it would be great? Caudalie toiletries!' she shouted, her voice echoey from inside. 'This is good stuff, will you nick it for me when you go? It's all made from grapes, you know, they've got their own vineyard somewhere in Bordeaux.'

'There's even a mini-bottle of fizz in the wardrobe,' said Esther, wonderingly, as she opened the doors to put her case inside.

Laura emerged from the bathroom with another. '*And* one in here,' she said. 'You know how in London you're never more than six feet away from a rat? Well, here you're never more than six feet away from a bottle of champagne. They wouldn't want you to go into Laurent-Perrier withdrawal on the toilet, Est. Imagine the scandal.'

'Truly they have thought of everything.'

'And so have I,' said Laura, popping open the bottle with a mischievous smile.

'Are you going to stay here too?' asked Esther. She sat down on the bed and bounced a little, experimentally. 'This bed's enormous, there's loads of room.'

Laura looked up from pouring the champagne into two plastic cups. Her expression was carefully innocent. 'Oh, I can't, all my stuff's at the house. We're going straight out from here. I didn't think.'

'Maybe tomorrow?' Esther suggested. 'We can have a sleepover just like we planned. Two Vs and a V, and hey, no queue for the bathroom!'

She sounded a little pathetic even to herself. She hoped Laura didn't think she was ungrateful for the expensive hotel room, but she had come here to see her best friend, not to get her hands on a load of free toiletries and some fluffy bath towels.

'Yeah, great.' Laura handed her a cup and went to look out of the window. 'This view! Isn't it amazing?'

More than ever, Esther was certain that a man must be involved. She knew better than to push it just yet. With Laura it was always best to give her time to reveal things at her own pace, even if that meant not getting the full story until after she was back in England. Laura was certainly hiding something, keeping up an incessant stream of tour-guide chatter so that there was no chance for Esther to ask any real questions about her new French life.

At least they would be able to slow down and catch up over a drink, thought Esther; but Laura had forestalled her there, too.

Her friends from the vineyard were waiting for them in a bar off the main avenue, a cellar that was reached down a brick-lined tunnel with steep stone stairs. In the underground room, racked with bottles as high as their heads, tables had been wedged at unexpected angles that suggested the priority here was the storage of wine rather than the comfort of patrons. The tables were lit by candles and the light was dim, but that didn't stop Laura from pausing in the doorway, holding Esther back, before they went in.

Esther thought she wanted to tell her something – maybe whisper a warning that one of her vineyard colleagues was a terrible bore, or finally admit that she was sleeping with one of them – but then she remembered that Laura always did this. A little pause before she went into a room, a moment for people to see she was there and react favourably. She'd done it since she was a child – it must be almost unconscious by now. Esther still marvelled at the idea that you would voluntarily give a room of people the chance to stare at you, instead of scurrying in quietly so as not to be noticed. Some part of her, no matter how she looked these days, would always be Fat Fester, expecting the worst.

The bar was hot and rowdy, and it seemed to Esther that everyone there greeted Laura by name as they passed. She introduced Esther to so many people that it wasn't clear which table they were joining until Laura led them right to the back of the room. Four men sat around the table, an opened bottle of champagne in front of them. They stood up as the girls arrived, raising their glasses as if to toast their arrival.

After all the other introductions, and the champagne she'd already drunk, Esther had to really concentrate to remember who was who. There was Pierre-Yves, who was older and distinguished-looking, and pimpled Georges, who was barely out of his teens, then pretty blond Thomas pouting moodily in the corner and, twice the size of the rest of them, Dirk, who turned out to be not French at all, but South African.

Dirk pulled out a chair for Laura, but she ushered Esther towards it and sat instead next to Pierre-Yves, who greeted her with a kiss on both cheeks and an approving exclamation over her copy of *Eugenie Grandet*. Laura said something in French to him that Esther couldn't follow, clutching the book to her chest as if she couldn't bear to let it go.

Dirk smiled welcomingly at Esther and poured her a drink, but she saw how his eyes flicked constantly back to Laura whenever he thought she wasn't looking. It felt like she had wandered into a play halfway through the second act; everyone knew what was going on but her. She wondered if Laura really wanted her there at all; was she just getting in the way?

'So you are the Esther we hear so much about,' said Pierre-Yves, leaning across Laura to speak to her. 'The journalist, yes? Laura tells us you are very big.'

Esther felt herself go red. It was true that she had put on a few pounds since living with David, but she never imagined her size was something Laura might have shared with her work colleagues. Had she told them, too, about the days when Esther was the fattest girl in school?

Laura shrieked and slapped his arm. 'Very big and important at her *job*, I said, you idiot. Not very big – I didn't say you were very big, Est, not ever.'

Georges asked, in hesitant English, 'You write for the newspapers?'

Laura leapt in to answer, trying to make up for Pierre-Yves's faux pas. 'Esther's got an amazing job at *The Times*, haven't you? She's always leaping on a plane to interview someone famous, and having dinner with celebrities.'

'Just writers,' Esther insisted to Laura's colleagues, embarrassed. 'I work on the books pages, it's not that glamorous.' She buried her face in her champagne glass, still wondering if they were all looking at her and thinking she was big.

'Oh, come on, you're always like this, doing yourself down – you met Madonna, didn't you?'

'Madonna!' exclaimed Thomas, suddenly roused from lassitude at the end of the table. He leaned forward eagerly. '*J'adore* Madonna! "Lucky Star"! Did she sing for you?'

'No,' said Esther, and he immediately looked less interested. 'She wrote a book – a children's book. There was a sort of tea party in Kensington, I went along for work.'

'Oh,' he said, disappointed. 'Not even one song?'

Esther shook her head and he sank back in his seat. She felt she was making a terrible impression.

Pierre-Yves considered Esther carefully. 'So we hear from Laura how she describes you – the big journalist from London. But how, I would like to know, does her best friend describe Laura?'

Although Laura laughed gaily, Esther saw a flash of warning in her eyes: don't embarrass me. It infuriated her. She was being asked to maintain the illusion of a Balzac-carrying version of Laura that she had only known for a matter of hours. New French Laura had banished her to a hotel. New French Laura had introduced her to a group of male colleagues without forewarning her that there was clearly some tension between them. New French Laura was a pain in the arse.

'Before I do,' she said, deciding to make Laura sweat a

little, 'why don't you tell me how *you'd* describe her. Dirk?'

He looked startled and cleared his throat, coughing into his cupped hand delicately for such a big man. If Laura's eyes had warned Esther, they practically burned Dirk as he prepared to answer. Esther expected to see scorch marks appear on his polo shirt.

'She's tough,' he said carefully, addressing his response to Esther alone. 'She can keep up with the boys.'

'Steady on, Dirk,' said Laura, though she seemed relieved. 'You'd better not be making me an honorary bloke. No girl likes to be an honorary bloke.'

Thomas pursed his lips, and appeared to think about what she had said. He cocked his head to one side. 'You are not a "bloke", Laura. But you are like a man in some ways, I think.'

'What, you fancy me?' teased Laura with a provocative pout.

Thomas made a face of exaggerated horror. 'Never! You lack – equipment. But you have this drive like a man, no? The career focus like a man? You do not allow yourself to be distracted by – emotion?'

Dirk laughed harshly and tipped his head back as he poured the rest of his champagne down his throat.

Laura's eyes narrowed. 'You think I'm unemotional?'

She asked all of them, but her eyes rested on Pierre-Yves as she finished speaking; it was clear his was the opinion that mattered most. Esther remembered Laura on the day of Amelia Wentworth's wedding; her insistence that just because she didn't show her emotions didn't mean she didn't feel them. And yet she seemed to want the impossible: to be seen as capable of deep emotion while hiding any evidence of it.

'*Non, non, non*,' Pierre-Yves said, shaking his head as if it was a subject to which he had already given some thought. 'You are emotional, of course. You are not cold. He means, you are practical in your life. You are not a romantic.'

'Oh, that's where you're wrong,' said Esther, and every head turned towards her, including Laura's. She gave another look of warning.

'Really?' asked Pierre-Yves, his eyes twinkling with amusement.

'Really. Laura is very romantic. More than you might know.'

Thomas gave a sarcastic 'oooh', and Laura aimed a half-hearted kick at him.

'Stop it!' She was still laughing, but in a high, nervous fashion.

Laura nudged her paperback book towards Esther, as if to say, this is who I am now, don't you understand? Esther wondered if it was showing someone up to remind them who they were, instead of playing along with who they were pretending to be. She could not be loyal to a Laura that she didn't know.

'How is she romantic?' asked Pierre-Yves.

'Well, her heroine – more than heroine, her spiritual advisor, you might say – is the queen of romantic comedy. In Hollywood, anyway,' she added, just in case there was a French queen of romantic comedy of whom she was unaware.

'*Non!*' exclaimed Thomas, clapping his hands together. 'Sandra Bullock! *J'adore* Sandra Bullock.'

'It's not Sandra Bullock,' said Esther. He curled his lip; first the Madonna let-down and now this.

'Meg Ryan?' suggested Pierre-Yves, with a sideways look at Laura. It was a glance that said, *I am not sure I know who you are any more.*

'Not since the last decade is Meg Ryan the queen,' said Thomas with contempt.

'Not her either,' said Esther. All of them were staring at her, she felt she was holding them in suspense. All except for Laura, who looked a little like Esther was about to rip the cover off her Balzac paperback and reveal it was actually a Sweet Valley High novel.

'Are you ready?' she looked from face to expectant face. 'Laura lives her life according to the gospel of Drew Barrymore.'

'Really?' asked Dirk, curling his lip in disbelief. 'From *Charlie's Angels?*'

Georges looked baffled, Thomas muttered something in French in amongst which Esther distinguished the insistent words 'Sandra Bullock', and Pierre-Yves raised a questioning eyebrow at Laura, waiting for her to confirm it.

There was the briefest of shadows across Laura's face, an almost imperceptible creasing of her brow, and then it lifted as if it had never been there at all. She broke into a broad and confident smile. Esther knew Laura well enough to see that in that moment she had decided it was better to claim the story and take charge of it than to try to deny it and possibly lose control of the narrative altogether.

'Of course,' she said, offering a shrug so Gallic that Brigitte Bardot would have envied it. 'No-one better disrespect my girl Drew. She taught me everything I know.'

'This is very interesting,' said Pierre-Yves, steepling his fingers on his chest like a university professor chairing a tutorial. 'What is this gospel?'

'Yeah,' said Dirk, sniggering a little. 'What life lesson did Charlie's Angels teach you? How to high-kick in a catsuit?'

'That female friendship is more reliable than any man,' said Laura sharply, and Dirk stopped laughing immediately.

'So,' asked Thomas, intrigue drawing him out of his Sandra Bullock sulk, 'her movies, they have – messages for you? This is how it works?'

Laura tossed her head, refusing to be embarrassed now that she had decided to admit to it. 'You have to believe in *something*,' she said. 'I choose to believe in Drew and it has served me well.'

Thomas's interest was piqued. 'Okay,' he said. 'I will try one. Your lesson from which film? Yes, from the film where she is – ' he couldn't think of the word and mimed stabbing. 'At the beginning, she is – *tué*.'

Esther identified it. '*Scream*.'

'That's easy,' said Laura. 'Don't trust the shitty boy-friend from school. If I'd listened to Drew back then I'd have saved myself years of heartache. Esther knew, though, she got the gospel even before I did.'

She winked at her, and Esther knew herself forgiven. Laura rarely held a grudge, even for a moment. However much she might insist her currents ran deep, on the surface it seemed that she could erase her moods like shaking an Etch-A-Sketch.

'Now you choose,' said Thomas to Pierre-Yves, who made a small expression of distaste, as if the subject was unpleasant to him.

'I have not seen a Drew Barrymore film,' he said. He seemed proud of it.

'Not even *Donnie Darko*?' asked Laura.

'This is an art film, it is not a Drew Barrymore film!' he exclaimed.

'Yes, it is,' Laura said. 'She even produced it. And the lesson is – expect the unexpected.'

'She is good,' said Thomas, to no-one in particular.

'*Le Come-Back*!' said pimply Georges, joining in.

'Le what?' said Esther.

'*Le Come-Back*. It is the most recent, I think.' He looked to Thomas for confirmation.

'Oui, oui, *Le Come-Back*,' agreed Thomas. 'With 'Ugh Grant. With the singing, you know?'

'Well, I haven't actually seen that one,' admitted Laura.

'I have,' said Esther. '*Music and Lyrics*. I saw it on a plane last month.'

'So?' asked Thomas, turning to her with interest. '*You* tell us, if you know this gospel also, what is the lesson?'

Esther considered it for a moment. 'Hugh Grant shouldn't be allowed to make any more films?'

Thomas clapped his hands together. 'This is true!' he exclaimed. 'He is *terrible*, no? But I think there is also another lesson.'

'What's that?' asked Esther.

'Drew learns it can be difficult if you sleep with your colleagues, no?' Thomas put a hand over his mouth to stifle his giggles, and winked at Esther. Dirk scowled at him and muttered something under his breath.

Laura pretended she hadn't heard, but the tips of her ears went scarlet and she checked her watch.

'Oh God, look at the time, we've got to go or we'll be late for dinner.'

Thomas looked surprised. 'Dinner?'

'Not for you,' scoffed Laura, swatting playfully at his

shoulder. 'You're having MacDo at midnight, if you're lucky. But *we've* got reservations at Les Berceaux.'

'Les Berceaux!' he exclaimed, his hand fluttering to his chest as if he was short of breath.

'What?' asked Esther, by now a little tipsy and confused.

'It has a Michelin star!' explained Georges, his eyes wide with awe. 'And, well, it is – ' he rubbed his fingers together in the international sign language for 'expensive'.

'I'm fine here, Laur,' said Esther. She was just beginning to enjoy herself with Laura's vineyard friends. The strange atmosphere had lifted and they were all having fun now. 'Honestly. Why don't we just stay here and get something? We don't need a fancy meal, it's enough just to be here together, isn't it?'

But Laura was insistent, pulling out Esther's chair and making her excuses.

'It's all planned,' she kept saying. 'It's all planned.'

23

When they emerged from the darkness of the cellar, it was a surprise to see that it was still light outside, the sky pinkish-blue and streaked with the high wispy clouds that predict fine weather. The streets were busy with people straight out of French central casting – leonine-haired men with lemon-yellow jumpers slung over their shoulders, and their elegant wives who had resolutely not got fat. Immaculate children played with a kitten under the awning of a nearby café, where old men smoked cigarettes and watched the world pass by. Everyone seemed prosperous and unhurried, taking their time on this beautiful evening.

Esther took Laura's arm, and their steps fell into a matching rhythm as they joined the accidental parade through the streets.

'Want to tell me what's going on?' she asked.

'It's a surprise,' smiled Laura, putting her finger to her

lips. She led the way down a pedestrianized alley, where the shade of the tall buildings cooled the air.

'I meant with Dirk and Pierre-Yves.'

She felt Laura stiffen a little as they walked side by side, her arm tensing just as it had when she'd told Esther to feel her muscles.

'God, Dirk. He's such an old woman.'

'Because?'

Laura gave an exasperated sigh. 'Look, I only slept with him once, and it was months ago, when I first got here. It was no big deal, I forgot about it straight away, but he's gone on and on about it ever since. I found out from Georges he'd been going around calling me his *girlfriend*, for fuck's sake.'

'Poor Dirk.'

'Poor Dirk, my arse. This is why I never get involved with younger men – they take everything so seriously. Older men are just so much more – I don't know – more sophisticated about things.'

'Older men like Pierre-Yves, you mean?'

Laura whirled around to look her in the eyes, grinning. 'I know! Isn't he gorgeous? Nothing's happened yet, Dirk's always hanging around getting in the way.'

'Yet. So this is why you didn't want me to stay at yours? I knew you'd have a man in tow, I bloody knew it, Laura.'

'No, it's – '

'What?'

'Nothing, you'll see.'

Laura squeezed her arm again, and all at once Esther felt that whatever had sprung up between them since she had arrived – this strange distance – had melted away. Perhaps it was the champagne, perhaps it was the beautiful evening, but she felt hopeful that she would have her old friend back for the rest of the weekend.

Buildings rose high above their heads, the walls broken by balconies and pots of red geraniums. Only a thin slice of the sky showed above them, where swallows – or were they swifts? – wheeled and dived in the last hours of light.

'Wait, your book!' she remembered suddenly. 'You left it behind in the bar.'

Laura snorted and kept going. 'Fuck Balzac. Pierre-Yves knew all along I hadn't really read it, he was just testing me. Now he knows my dirty Drew secret he'll have to take me with the gospel or not at all.'

'Do you really like him?'

Laura gave her a quizzical frown. 'Didn't I just say so?'

'No, you said he was gorgeous. I meant, do you really really like him? Properly.'

'Really really like him?' She laughed. 'Are we back at school or something?'

Esther was not about to let it go. Opportunities to ask Laura direct questions about her life were few, and fewer still were the chances to insist on an answer. She was an expert at avoiding emails that asked too much, and shutting down phone conversations when they strayed onto difficult subjects.

'You know what I mean: do you think it could be something serious? You seem so happy here in France – you seem so *French*. Like you're settled here, for good, maybe.'

'You're as bad as Margie,' scoffed Laura, and she adopted a high, fluting voice that was a poor imitation of her mother's. 'Oh Laura, first you deprive me of my only daughter by living abroad, and now you must deprive me of grandchildren too, you barren wench!'

'Did she really say that about grandchildren?' Esther could easily believe it, but she had credited Margie with a bit more sense than thinking demands on Laura's ovaries would bring her running home.

Laura nodded. 'She thinks it's all very well moving around when you're young, but now it's time I came home and settled down. Oh Laura,' she put on her high voice again. 'Why can't you be more like Esther? She sees her mother all the time, with that lovely boyfriend of hers.'

'God, you'd die of boredom after a week of being me. Seriously. But – tell me really, don't you ever think of coming home?'

Laura gazed up at the sky. It hadn't yet started to get dark, but enough light had been lost for one solitary star to be visible above their heads.

'Where's home, though?' she said. 'I've never lived in

Margie's house in Rackham and I'd never want to. London's not home. Nor's Portsdown, not any more.'

She didn't sound sad at all, but Esther was sad for her. She thought of her own parents' house at the top of Portsdown Hill, the same house she had come home to when she skinned her knees in the playground at primary school. The upstairs bathroom where Laura had guarded the door while she was sick after Katie Long's sixteenth birthday party. The playroom where she and Laura had first met was now her father's study, but in all other respects it was still the home that she had grown up in. Even though she was now thirty-two, with a house of her own, if she thought of 'home' it was the house in Hampshire that came to mind first. She couldn't imagine it any other way.

'Do you think it would be different if Margie was still in your old house?' she asked. 'That was home to you really, wasn't it?'

Laura frowned, like this was something she hadn't considered before. 'Maybe,' she said. 'But then I think of my dad there, when he was sick. And Ricko. It's like that blotted out all the good things that happened before. I don't know. It's so long ago, what's the point in looking back like that?'

They walked in silence for a few minutes. Although Laura had said there was no point in looking back, Esther thought they probably both were just then, remembering the house they had both known so well, with its remote-controlled curtains and state-of-the-art electronics that would now be hopelessly obsolete. It was rare for Laura to mention her father's illness out loud. She would tell funny stories about things that happened when she was little and Edward was healthy, but of the dark and terrible months where he was dying she had said almost nothing in all the years that had passed since.

'You know,' Laura said at last, 'the one place that has nothing but happy memories for me is the house in California. Isn't that funny? We only lived there for a few years, but I still dream about it sometimes. I think it's the last place I lived where I wasn't always thinking of somewhere else.'

'What do you mean?' asked Esther. She felt that Laura was opening up to her in a way she hardly ever did, as if a spell had been cast by their linked arms and synchronized strides in the fading summer light.

Laura shrugged a little. 'I just didn't know that we'd move away from there, I was little enough to think it was forever. I'd always have that bedroom with a laundry chute that went downstairs, I'd always go to the elementary school at the end of the road. And when we came back to England, I guess it was the first time I really understood that nothing in my life was going to last forever.'

Esther glanced at Laura's profile as they carried on walking. 'That sounds kind of bleak, Laur. Nothing?'

Laura lifted her chin up. 'I don't think it's bleak, it's

just true. I don't have a home but that gives me freedom, don't you see? I just make sure I like where I am right now and if I don't – ' she made a whooshing gesture with her free hand like a plane taking off – 'then I just move on.'

That kind of freedom did not appeal to Esther. She couldn't imagine not having somewhere to go home to. To be able to pack up your life in a few suitcases seemed to her not a freedom, but a status to be pitied, like a refugee.

'You do have a home, Laur,' she said. 'You've always got one with me if you want one.'

Laura laughed, and pointed across the road to show where they had to go next. They stepped off the kerb together. 'You going to move David out?'

'Noooo,' Esther smiled. 'I'm going to put you in the shed.'

'Thanks so much.'

'I mean it, though.' Once they had crossed the road Esther stopped to emphasize her point, forcing other people to walk around them. 'I really do. You mustn't think you don't have a place to go if you ever need one. You say things don't last, but come on, haven't we lasted as friends? Isn't that something?'

'I don't mean you, stupid,' said Laura, punching her arm. 'You're – well, you're probably my longest relationship. You and Drew.'

'I don't know if there's room for her in the shed, too,' said Esther. 'It's not that big.'

'She's an actress, Est,' said Laura, rolling her eyes. 'She'll be minuscule. We'll just tuck her up in the corner. Not a problem.'

A church bell chimed somewhere nearby, sending pigeons wheeling from the roofs above them, and Laura looked at her watch in panic.

'Shit, too much talking, not enough walking. We're going to be late. This way.'

She ducked down another small street, and Esther followed, trying to keep up. The sound of their shoes on the hard pavement rang off the walls around them. Esther couldn't see what the rush was about – surely the restaurant, however fancy, wouldn't mind if they were a few minutes late – but Laura was insistent that there was a plan that had to be followed to the letter. It was so unlike her to care about punctuality that Esther began to be suspicious there was some other agenda afoot.

Just as the small street was about to open up into a larger one, Laura stopped suddenly, like she had slammed into a wall, and turned around.

'You know what I said about forever?' She pushed her hair away from her eyes.

'Yes,' Esther answered, slightly breathless.

'Well, it's just – ' Laura looked upwards towards the diminishing light. 'That is me, okay, not you.'

'What's this about?'

'I just mean that one of the things I love you for, Est, is that you are good at forevers. You keep at things, you're loyal. You're forgiving.'

Laura's face was earnest, and worryingly sincere. Esther's suspicion turned to misgiving. 'What's going on? Are you about to tell me you're dying or something?'

'No!' she laughed. 'I think it's important to tell you that. Maybe you *are* home to me in some sort of way – not like I do actually want to move into your garden shed, but your happiness and stability make *me* feel happier, you know?'

'Not really,' admitted Esther, who was by now entirely confused.

Laura huffed in exasperation. 'Like – you're the football team, I'm the head of the fan club. Just because I can't kick the ball myself, doesn't mean I don't love to see it done well by someone who really knows how.'

'Laura, are you high?'

'Listen, it's important. What I mean is, forever after might not matter to me, but *your* forever after does. That's what I'm trying to say. I want you to be happy, I really hope you're going to be happy.'

She took Esther's hand and drew her out into the wider street where Esther could see a squat little building on a corner, with dark grey tiles that frowned over the stucco walls like a heavy and forbidding brow. There were green and white striped awnings at each window, and a chimney rising up from the roof lent the building the appearance of a country cottage even though as far as Esther could tell, they were in the middle of the town. The restaurant name was written above the door in Gothic script, and a suited figure stood below it with his hands clasped in front of him. Esther wondered if it was usual for a Michelin-starred restaurant in France to have a bouncer; it seemed a little excessive.

But then the standing figure lifted a hand to his forehead, shading his eyes to look across the street, and her heart skipped up into her throat and lodged there like a pebble. She knew that movement, she knew that figure.

It was the figure she had last seen turning away at Waterloo station this morning with a look of excitement on his face. He began to cross the road towards them and Esther saw that he was in his new suit, the one he said he'd bought to be a best man. His hair was wet, just washed, and as he got closer she could see the comb marks in it. Esther had a sudden premonition, a feeling that she would remember how David looked tonight for the rest of her life.

Laura squeezed her hand tightly, and then she let go. She put her palm on Esther's back and pushed her gently forwards.

'Go on, Esther,' she said. 'Go and be happy.'

24

October 2013

I want to call home more than anything. It is like a physical ache, right in my chest, and it makes my breathing shallow and agitated. I need to know that my boy is healthy and alive, and waiting for me to return. But it is nighttime in England already and Linus will be asleep, his perfect, round cheek turned towards his bedroom wall, hands either side of his sweet-smelling head, with their fingers curled in towards the palms like little shells. I will have to wait.

If I concentrate I can almost feel his solid little body in my arms, his heart held against my own, his head heavy on my shoulder. I can see the creases in his wrists, as if each has an invisible rubber band around it, and each perfect fingernail. I know this longing to hold him will be satisfied soon, and I can phone later, speak to David and find out how he is. It is impossible to imagine how it would feel if my son was gone from one day to the next, and yet the fierce and passionate longing remained. How would you fill the hours? How could you face the void? No wonder Stanley's wife has to keep moving.

I think of Margie suddenly. Does she feel this visceral longing for her missing daughter, even though Laura is grown-up? Does it overwhelm her like it threatens to overwhelm me? I didn't cry in Stanley's office, I couldn't. It would have felt obscene somehow, to cry over a child I didn't know in front of his bereaved father. As if I was claiming a grief that wasn't mine. But I cry now in the car park of the Foothills Vineyard, leaning my forehead on the steering wheel. I cry for Ned Hoffmann and Stanley, for Laura and Margie, for Linus and David and me.

Laura thought some people deserved domestic happiness, and others didn't, but I'm not sure she saw that it is more arbitrary than that. You can tell yourself you deserve your happy relationship, or your loving family or the life that you have so carefully built for yourself. You can even believe you've earned it – that people without the framework of loved ones are lacking in some way. But it can all be taken away from you in a moment, and that is what makes it so precious and so fragile. Stanley had a family, and now he doesn't. Margie too, but all she has left is a daughter who disappears without a word.

I am also crying out of shame, I realize, as I wipe the tears that are flowing so freely they've begun to run down my neck. How could I have mistaken the reserve of Stanley's grief for something more sinister? Especially when Laura has always admitted that she moves on as soon as she stops having fun. I thought better of her than this. The idea that she would add to Stanley's burdens by getting involved with him and then leaving without a word is all the more shocking now that I know the truth. As an employee she owed him an explanation, as his girlfriend even more so.

Would she call herself his girlfriend, though? When I asked Stanley if they were serious, all those hours ago in Laura's apartment, he said that I should ask her. I thought he was being flippant, but now I see his comment for what it was: an admission that he was the weaker partner. He couldn't define how serious they were because he didn't know how serious she was. The power in a relationship rests with the person who cares the least. And that person has always, always been Laura.

I dry my eyes with an old tissue from the bottom of my handbag and check my streaked make-up in the rear-view mirror, wiping away the black marks under my lashes. My face has gone puffy and my nose bright red. I look terrible, but I feel better for my torrent of weeping. And I am resolved.

So far I have relied too much on feelings to lead me to Laura. I've expected that I will somehow miraculously understand things just by being here, as if mere geography is a portal into Laura's thoughts. I imagined my visit to California like one of those Holy Land tours at the back of the Sunday supplements – Tread Where His Feet Trod. Understand Laura's Deepest Fears by Drinking Tea in Her Apartment and Harassing the Waitress in Her Local Café. I thought that the secrets of her life would reveal themselves to me, and only me, like a door that will open only for someone who has been taught the knack. But I've turned out not to have the knack at all, and worse, I've discovered it with everyone watching and waiting.

From now on, I am trusting only in the proven facts, and there are very few of them.

There's a sudden knock on the window, and I jump in my seat. The woman from earlier is bending down, the one who showed me the way to the vineyard tour.

'Is everything okay?' she mouths through the glass. Perhaps she says it out loud, but I have the air conditioning on and can hear nothing but the roar of it, like I'm in the eye of a tornado.

'Fine!' I say back, loudly, and jangle the car keys in my hand. 'Just leaving.'

She waves and steps back out of the way, and of course I stall the car straight away. But on the second attempt I drive away with the careful attention of one who knows she is being watched.

Only when I am back on the freeway to Napa do I realize that I have no idea where to go next. The clock tells me it is nearly lunchtime, though I am not hungry at all. But there is little point in returning to the grim motel before I have to, and at least if I found a place to sit down for a while it would give me a chance to think carefully about what I've learned. Since I arrived here I've been ricocheting from wild speculation to accusation and back again, barely staying still for long enough to absorb any of the information I've been given. And look where that's got me.

I take the first turning towards the town centre and it brings me into a quiet neighbourhood, not as tourist-friendly as the place where Stanley and I met for breakfast. These houses don't look like the clapboard kind that appear on postcards, they're less for show and more for living in. It is strange to my London eyes to see how much space there is here. The houses have gardens and driveways and garages and they're built low and wide instead of up, rarely bothering with a second floor. For some reason this makes the whole environment seem exceptionally foreign, or at least it makes me feel very foreign in it. A row of shops appears up ahead with a car park in front. There's a dry cleaner and a Rib Shack and a boxy white supermarket that advertises an espresso bar with free wifi alongside Produce and Specialty Foods. It seems to me as good a place as any. At least with wifi I can interrogate my paltry facts.

When I get out of the car I can hear the hiss of water sprinklers thudding as they rotate around the flowerbeds that separate the shops from the car park.

There is piped music inside, and the espresso bar is almost empty. Just one woman sits against the back wall, pouring sugar into her coffee from a glass jar with a metal spout on top. The space is functional rather than aspirational, and that is exactly what I need. I'm not sure exactly where I am, but it is far enough away from Laura's neighbourhood that I am sure no-one here will have known her, let alone appear to drop dark hints about where she might have gone. The waiter is an elderly Mexican man in black trousers that seem to be trying to escape his thin ankles and take refuge in his armpits, hoisting themselves up by his braces. The hems flap loosely around his calves as he shuffles to my table with an expression of deep weariness. I do not think he will be troubling me for conversation.

He takes my order without returning my smile and though I am quite content with a taciturn waiter – grateful even – it makes me realize how much my social interactions rely on Linus these days. I am used to talking to strangers every day, proudly telling them my son's age, or pointing out the two teeth that have just begun to push upwards from his lower gum. Of course people grumble if he cries in public, or tut when I try to take the buggy on the bus, but mostly they are kind and helpful, and I have grown to expect the smiles of strangers as my due in life. Without Linus, I feel like Clark Kent – my boy is the very best of me, and I am not myself without him.

It's an odd sensation, but also perhaps a little liberating to think that I can drink a coffee without having to provide entertainment and rice cakes, or even adult conversation. I can't honestly remember the last time I went to a café – or a supermarket espresso bar – entirely by myself.

I begin to have a sense of how Laura must have felt coming out here by herself, in those first few days abroad – a little anxious and disoriented maybe, but also free to do whatever she wants, and be whoever she wants. Not that she couldn't at home, but for someone who has always liked to keep things to herself, the opportunity to get far away from being the woman who slept with her boss, the girl who lost her father young, this is perfect. Isn't this the American Dream? To reinvent yourself? To pursue your happiness?

But also free to disappear, in a way that would be impossible for someone who has not made such an effort to keep herself free from ties of any kind. As much as I might envy Laura her independence at times, it gives me chills to think of her being able to melt away from her life without anyone raising the alarm for days.

The waiter reappears with my latte on a tray and then he takes from under his arm a stack of tattered celebrity magazines. He puts them on the table next to my coffee and pats them with his palm in an odd gesture that I don't quite understand – sympathy, perhaps? For being here alone? I want to tell him that I'm not lonely, he doesn't need to feel sorry for me. This isn't my real life,

I'm just a visitor in someone else's. But instead I ask him for the wifi code and he points it out to me, printed on the bottom of the receipt. Then he flaps his trouser legs slowly away.

I stir my coffee and try to think. If this was an episode of *Sherlock* there would be hundreds of complex calculations appearing in the air around my head – connections and clues that only the mind of a genius could unravel. But as an amateur detective I have been able to establish precisely two facts since I arrived in California – Laura was having a relationship with her boss, which is not only not unusual for her, but almost standard. And she packed up her car herself, which, for all my paranoid hypotheses, almost certainly means that wherever she went, she went of her own free will.

I get onto the espresso bar wifi and look up the date of the full moon. Although I am feeling despondent by now, there is a part of me that would love it if the policeman was wrong, if this was the concrete fact that changed everything. Of course it doesn't. The full moon was a Saturday. Laura didn't turn up to work on the Friday. It tells me nothing I don't already know. In desperation I even look up the crystal healing workshop in Sedona, double-checking to see when Stanley cleaned up Laura's apartment; but it's just as he said. He only did that when he knew I was on my way. If he was trying to hide something, he wouldn't have waited so long.

My suspicions have been attaching themselves to

everyone I can think of just to avoid facing the truth: the only person who has been behaving truly suspiciously is Laura.

There was her email to me, saying she needed to talk, with the Drew Barrymore reference that made no sense. I even google 'Drew Barrymore movies 2013' to double-check, but there's nothing. She hasn't even made a film since last year. It is another dead end.

There was the leaving in the middle of the night, and the crying that her neighbour overheard. If, as Stanley thinks, she was scared away by the full weight of his grief, then would she have cried over it? Crying suggests sadness to me, or despair, not the kind of cold-blooded selfishness that would make a person just walk away. The crying is the thing that gives me pause. It makes me think that either Laura felt guilt over leaving like she did, or there is something else that I am still missing.

I send a text to Margie while I finish my coffee, telling her I will call her shortly. The espresso bar is too quiet, and I'd rather ring her from the privacy of the car. It's hard to know if the few paltry facts I've uncovered will disappoint her, or just fuel more paranoid fantasies about what might have happened. But she is all alone and it is important that I keep her informed of the news, even when there is none.

Since there is nothing else to do while I finish my coffee, I pick up the magazines that the waiter brought me. The first one seems to be all about a reality TV star who's lost a lot of weight – 'dangerously skinny!', declares the headline – alongside a promise that you can find out just how she did it inside. I have no idea who she is, so I move it to the side. The cover of the next magazine is half-ripped and bent over on itself three times, like a paper fan. I smooth it out, and underneath my fingers I see Drew Barrymore beaming in delight, holding a very young baby up close to her face. Her baby.

It seems too much of a coincidence; I even look over my shoulder to see if someone is playing a joke on me, but the old waiter is engrossed in polishing the coffee machine and I'm not confident he'd even know who Drew Barrymore is. I know that Laura would say it is a sign. Even I think it must be, but when I scan the magazine cover for a publication date I see it can't possibly be relevant – it was published months ago. It can't mean anything. Except that Drew Barrymore's baby is only a few months older than Linus, which is sweet, but hardly an earth-shaking revelation.

I skip to the article and scan it – though it's mostly pictures, there are a few quotes about 'baby joy', nothing that is helpful. None of the facts I am so desperate to find. I don't know what I was expecting; that there would be a line at the end of the piece, 'If your friend has gone missing because of Drew Barrymore, please call this number'?

But then it hits me.

I've been so stupid. I thought when she mentioned

Drew Barrymore she was talking about the past. It was our shared joke, our secret shorthand. But what if Laura wasn't referring to the past at all? What if she was trying to tell me something about the present?

Drew Barrymore hasn't been making movies lately, she's been making babies.

Laura's neighbour said she had cried so much she'd made herself sick. But other things can make you feel sick. Stanley said she was tired all the time, had no energy. She was eating nothing but pizza; it wasn't so long ago I was craving carbohydrates. Feelings and facts seem to rush at me all at once. I pick up my phone.

Laura, I text her. *Are you pregnant?*

GOING THE DISTANCE, AUGUST 2010[10]

BRANDY: Where are you going?

ERIN: I'm 31. I'm an intern. I'm going to get wasted.

25

29 August 2010

From: laurakthomas@gmail.com
To: esther.conley@thetimes.co.uk

Estaaaaaaah!

So I'm here. You know you didn't have to come to the airport, but I am so so glad you did. Thanks for keeping Margie sane, did she tell you she texted me afterwards because she was certain she had spotted a shoe bomber checking onto my flight? Quite how a sixty-two year old woman from Sussex is better qualified to spot a shoe bomber than, I don't know, SECURITY, is beyond me. But anyway, I was relieved you and D were there to drag her away.

I've only realized now I've got here how lucky I was to get this internship. Mostly they go to Americans of course, but I think I'm a bit of a novelty to them – English and a lot older than the others and they like to condescend to me about English wine, which is totally fine as while they tease me I am learning shitloads which I shall take and use to build my British wine empire, muahahahaaaaa.

It's funny being the only English person here, though – lots of things they don't get. Like how the smell of the yeast food that will go in the wine is EXACTLY like Marmite, but when I said so there were blank stares all round. Maybe you'll have to send me a jar so I can show them what I mean.

We haven't really started on the winemaking yet – when I first got here they let me have a few days in the tasting room giving out samples to tourists who come on a brilliant boozing train so they can all get hammered. But since then it's all been lab & barrel room – labelling up the barrels (thrilling). Totally played the delicate female card when it came to moving all of the barrels & allowed Trent, an Australian who's been here all summer, to show off his muscles by moving them all himself while I said admiring and encouraging things. He paid me back by making me crawl inside the tanks to clean them – a job for a smaller person he claimed, but as some of the tanks are about the height of a house, I think I was being had.

Hurry up & write back! I miss you!

Xxx

1 September 2010
From: esther.conley@thetimes.co.uk
To: laurakthomas@gmail.com

Margie was fine, honest, we took her to a pub for supper before we dropped her home, got her quite pissed (on two glasses of wine), and deposited her back fairly giggly and happy about everything. I'll give her a ring in a few days, make sure she's okay. Don't worry about her.

Although – did you know she has a badger in her garage? With a broken leg? She wanted to show it to us, but we said we had to get back to London. Badgers are massive! Don't they bite?

Everything is exactly and boringly the same here without you. David's mother is coming to stay next weekend, which is nice for my self-esteem, ha ha. I've told David it's HIS job to iron all the monogrammed table napkins she gave us before she gets here. It took me nearly an hour last time and all Belinda said was that I ought to have a word with my housekeeper about her poor standards!! Apparently not only was the ironing not up to scratch but the floor under her bed was filthy. The housekeeper had to take a lot of deep breaths in the kitchen before she brought out the pudding, and the housekeeper's husband did not get laid for a week. I think he's learned his lesson.

Love you, Laur, and miss you tons. Please don't hook up with Trent the Australian and stay out there forever

– or worse, move to Australia. Remember you are British!
Have you got your American accent back? Gross!
Xx

4 September 2010
From: laurakthomas@gmail.com
To: esther.conley@thetimes.co.uk

I'm a little worried you might be psychic – what colour am I thinking of right now? Because Trent . . . aargh, I know! No danger of moving to Australia, or even staying out here, this has 'harvest romance' written all over it, over when the grapes are in. It's kind of a cliché, there are new couples springing up all over the place, amongst the migrant workers picking the grapes, on the forklift trucks, by the crushers.

Trent is a bit like one of those long-haired golden Labradors that's all bouncy and full of enthusiasm and (shhh) not quite the smartest. He's got that classic Aussie surfer boy look, though I have a secret suspicion he's given his blond locks a bit of a helping hand – remember Sun-In?? I'd bet my bottom dollar there's a bottle of something similar hidden in his bathroom, but we usually stay at mine since he's in some godawful shared house with six other men. Anyway, he's gorgeous and fun and he comes from a wine family in the Yarra Valley near Melbourne that has some ties with the vineyard. This is the third summer he's been out here because, er, he's still at university. I KNOW! He's a mature student though. Of twenty-six, haha!

Oh wait, did I tell you the film I saw on the plane over? A film starring – dun dun dunnnnn – Drew Barrymore. Est, she plays an intern. And she complains about being one at thirty-one. I laughed properly out loud. I thought Drew, love, try being an intern when you're thirty-FIVE. Of course I choose to believe it must be a sign, though I do not know what for.

It's funny to think of you all settled with a husband and a nightmare mother-in-law (what is she like?!). Sometimes I envy you, Est. You've always been so sure of what you want, and now you have it. You earned it all, you really did, and I'm so proud of you. Can you tell I've been drinking? Yeah, I blurry love you, you're the best, you're my BESSHHHHT FREEEEEEEEND.

Sometimes I think it's a bit ridiculous to be living like I am at my age, no mortgage, no husband – I don't even have a dentist for fuck's sake.

But the other morning I had a break after an hour of shovelling grape skins inside the tanks. The sun was only just rising, burning off the morning fog, when I went outside (it's always foggy when we start, and dark too). The early sunlight picked out the vineyards for miles and miles, rows going all the way up to the foot of the mountains, with faint remnants of fog lying low between them. I was sweaty and stinking of grape juice, my hands were stained purple and I was still wearing the yellow oilskin trousers you have to wear in the tanks. I could smell the bacon and eggs that Amy and Chase were cooking up, and suddenly I just had this really strong, clear feeling that I was exactly where I was meant to be. I can't explain it, maybe it's how you feel about David and being married? Just this sense that I am in the right place.

Even though I have no idea what I'll do when harvest is over, or where I'm going to be in five years or whatever it is they ask you in job interviews, for the first time since Dad died, I feel like everything's going to be okay. That's good enough for me.

God, sorry to go all weird and SERIOUS on you. I'm just exhausted, too tired to think up jokes. Need bed.

Xx

PS My American accent hasn't come back at all. In fact I've got more and more poshly English trying to make sure people can understand what I'm saying. Give it a few weeks and I'll sound exactly like the Queen.

18 September 2010
From: laurakthomas@gmail.com
To: esther.conley@thetimes.co.uk

Est? Have I scared you off with my DEEP THOUGHTS? Are you in prison for mother-in-law-cide? Buried under a pile of monogrammed napkins, unable to reach the keyboard?

I am immersed in wine – the purple hands are here to stay; they made a small child scream in the supermarket when I reached for the milk today. I've developed a deeply weird habit of going to the supermarket when I need to chill out. There's something about all those products and packaging from when I was little that is really calming. Lucky Charms and Sun-Maid raisin bread and Cool Whip – it's like walking through aisles and aisles of my childhood. Keep expecting I'll see my dad coming round the corner with an armful of beers, all ready for a barbecue. But not in a sad way. I like it.

I think I might see if I can go to San Diego when the season's over. I'll have a few weeks left on my visa and it would be good to go back and see the old house again. Maybe visit my school, see if things are still how I remember them.

But right now I'm out of the house at four-thirty, back at five, usually in bed by nine!! I dream of grape skins and juice hoses. I'd like to say the romance continues but Trent & I are both so knackered when I say we are still sleeping together I mean just sleeping. Snoring in his case. Like a slightly incestuous brother & sister. Very Flowers in the Attic.

Please write back & remind me there is a world outside of wine??

Xxx

24 September 2010
From: esther.conley@thetimes.co.uk
To: laurakthomas@gmail.com

Sorry, Laur, things have been a bit weird. I've been feeling totally shit lately, just exhausted. No energy at all. I thought it was the comedown from David's mum's visit, you know what she's like. Drains the life out of you like a vampire with a copy of Debrett's. Then I found a lump in my right breast.

The doctor sent me for a biopsy, but by then both of my tits were really sore and lumpy and I could tell the nurse thought it was all in my head.

They were about to do a pre-biopsy scan & the nurse said was there any chance I might be pregnant. I said nope, definitely not. And she explained very slowly, as if I was a total idiot, that what she meant was had I had any sex at all in the last few months. I wanted to say, thanks very much lady I am thirty-five years old not thirteen, I know how babies are made, but I just stayed polite and explained we used contraception.

She said, nothing's infallible, let's do a test just in case. And, Laur, I'm having a baby. Shit.

I don't even know how I feel about it. We weren't going to start trying until after Christmas. David is over the fucking moon but he would be since he's not the one who has twice thrown up in a carrier bag on the tube to work. Also actually at work though I passed it off to

Nancy as a terrible hangover. And the tiredness, I had no idea. When I get home I just crawl straight into bed at six – you thought nine was pathetically early! David brings me a sandwich or something when he gets in and I choke it down – it's worse if I don't eat, but it makes me feel sick when I do. All I can stomach is bread and pasta and anything that is starchy and processed. The mere sight of a vegetable makes me retch and fruit is worse (it has actually made me do a pre-pukey drool just typing the word 'fruit'), so now I've developed this wobbly doughnut of fat around my hips, like a lifesaving ring wedged there. And I can't tell anyone yet so I just look like I'm heading back towards being Fat Fester with a vengeance.

I want to be really happy and excited about this – I think I am – but honestly, Laur, it's just a total headfuck at this point. I guess that's why you're pregnant for a whole nine months, so you can get yourself used to the idea – oh, and grow a whole new person in your uterus, there's that. But maternity leave and a NURSERY, and babygros and baby SICK and breastfeeding and oh god, I can't even think of labour without having to sit down firmly on my as-yet-unripped perineum (I didn't even know I had a perineum until I read What to Expect When You're Expecting).

So, Auntie Laura, that is why I've been incommunicado. If you'll excuse me I now have to go and be quietly sick in my bin.

X

24 September 2010
From: laurakthomas@gmail.com
To: esther.conley@thetimes.co.uk

HOLY SHIT, EST, THIS IS AMAZING NEWS!!!! No wonder you're feeling crap, all those hormones and the vomming, but a baby! Oh man, Trent is asking why I'm crying, but I just wish I was there to feed you plates of pasta with a side of bread and tell you it's all going to be okay. IT IS ALL GOING TO BE OKAY.

Come on! It's not like you're seventeen. Or even twenty-three and with the wrong man entirely. You might not have planned it, but you're married! To a man who is really excited about this baby! You own an actual house with spare bedrooms and a garden for a kid to run around in! You're a proper grown-up, Est, you can do this. You're going to be an amazing amazing mother, I know it. You do everything perfectly, you always have.

I cannot wait to meet the actual baby you made!!

If I wasn't so entirely over wine I'd be toasting you right now. As it is, this Diet Coke's for you.

Xxx

26 September 2010
From: esther.conley@thetimes.co.uk
To: laurakthomas@gmail.com

I knew you'd know what to say. Thanks. I feel a bit better about it all now, and we've booked a scan for next month.

Maybe it will all feel properly real once I see the baby up on the screen, with fingers and toes and everything. You spend so much of your life trying not to be pregnant, it's so peculiar when you are. Even if it's what you want. It is what I want. I really really do. I think.

David told his mum – can you believe? Like the monogrammed napkins weren't bad enough, now she's apparently sent the Carrell christening gown to a special posh person's dry cleaners in preparation for the new heir. Apparently it's nearly a hundred years old. I feel like saying that it is a staunch Conley family tradition to only ever christen babies in poly-cotton blends, and I cannot permit antique lace near my child.

Obviously the own aged parents have been great. Dad went all stifled and silent on the end of the phone when we told him. I think he might have been crying. Mum just rings a lot 'to see how you are, darling' and sends me food parcels like I am back at university. Today's had a tin of treacle in it – for iron, apparently. Er, yum.

X

1 October 2010
From: laurakthomas@gmail.com
To: esther.conley@thetimes.co.uk

Oh good god, your mum told Margie you're up the duff. HOW COULD SHE?!!! Margie is throwing herself a massive pity party over being excluded from grandmotherhood. And apparently I am ruining not just her life, but my own as no woman can ever be truly happy without a child and my barren future will curse me.

Which is odd, because having me never seemed to make HER full of joy, did it?

For fuck's sake. How could I subject a child to Cold War Margie? She'd be filling its ears with stories of climate change and terrorism before it was out of nappies.

It is at times like these I am very glad she lives many thousands of miles away.

Yours, with a hollow womb,

L

X

5 October 2010
From: esther.conley@thetimes.co.uk
To: laurakthomas@gmail.com

Oh fuck, sorry. Mum is just far too excited to keep her mouth shut. Maybe we can grant Margie shares in this baby, she can be like a grand-godmother or something.

X

PS Scan next week. Excited.

11 October 2010
From: laurakthomas@gmail.com
To: esther.conley@thetimes.co.uk

I AM NO LONGER AN INTERN! Can you believe it? Was it the ever-benevolent power of my fellow intern Drew Barrymore, who can say? But some higher power convinced Stanley to give me a real job. He's doing the visa and the sponsorship and all the awful complicated paperwork that has put everyone else off employing me on a permanent basis.

You thought I might stay here for love and I have, in a way. Not for Trent, but for this place, and this job. I can't explain it. I just know it's where I'm meant to be.

When can you come to visit? You can bring the baby! I'm getting my own apartment!

Xxx

P.S how was scan?

15 October 2010
From: esther.conley@thetimes.co.uk
To: laurakthomas@gmail.com

Sorry I didn't answer right off, Laur, it's brilliant news. I'm so chuffed for you and David says congratulations too. You've worked so hard & I'm so pleased they've seen that and rewarded it.

We've had a strange old time. The scan showed a cyst

on the baby's neck, something to do with the 'nuchal fold'. There is a whole new and horrible vocabulary that we are having to learn very fast. Apparently the cyst might go away by itself. But if it doesn't they said it might impair the baby's development (that is such doctor speech, isn't it? Might impair the development, Mrs Carrell. I am an emotionless automaton with dead eyes, Mrs Carrell). It can be a sign of Down's and other serious problems. There is a link with maternal alcohol intake and this kind of cyst, I saw online – I keep thinking of all those weeks I didn't know I was pregnant. It's not like I was drunk all the time, but I was drinking (David's mother was staying, of course I was drinking).

I went into the scan thinking I could come out and tell everyone at last. Book in with a midwife, work out the due date, start thinking about maternity leave. It just seemed like an administrative thing, a box you tick. It wasn't meant to be like this.

I can't help wondering if it's a punishment for not being happy enough about the baby at first. Like I don't deserve to have a healthy child because I didn't want it enough. I know you'll say that's silly but it's what I feel.

More tests next week, for chromosomal abnormalities. Sorry to bring you down from cloud nine. Just wanted to explain silence.

Don't think I wasn't happy about your job. I am, and I'm glad of something to smile about right now.

x

15 October 2010
From: laurakthomas@gmail.com
To: esther.conley@thetimes.co.uk

Oh Esther, my poor girl. You must be so worried. ANYBODY'S mind would do a full Margie in the circumstances, but you must try to be positive. Worry can't make it any better.

When Dad was sick the worst worst bit was the not knowing, and the waiting for tests. But I honestly think it would have been even worse if we had been able to go online and guess for ourselves what might happen next. Our ignorance was kind of a blessing back then – we had no idea what was in store for us. And you know that the doctors were wrong about him so many times. They don't know everything, and neither does Google.

Don't look up anything else. You are not an alcoholic, you weren't downing bottles of vodka every morning. Some wine with your supper won't have harmed the baby, you have to remember that. And the doctor didn't say it was your fault, so who are you to start blaming yourself when the medical professionals aren't?

I know this is useless advice, I'm sorry. Can't even begin to imagine how long the wait for tests will feel for you and David, but I'm thinking of you both all the time.

Want to Skype tomorrow? I can call you early before

work – about lunchtime for you? Or will it just make you cry? I don't want to make you cry.

Love you the most.

Xxx

18 October 2010
From: esther.conley@thetimes.co.uk
To: laurakthomas@gmail.com

I know I shouldn't look things up online, but I can't stop myself. There are internet forums you can go on where people's babies have had the same thing – cystic hygroma – and I can't stay away from them, though I haven't joined in yet. Not sure if I can even comment on Mumsnet if I'm not even a mum. So many of these women have at least one child already – one of them wrote this long post about how hard it was to go through it all with two other children and I wanted to scream and shout at her that there are people who don't even have one baby yet.

Which is why I am not commenting, I think I'd go properly mad. I haven't even told David that I'm stalking these internet strangers the whole time I'm at work, he won't even contemplate the idea that it won't all be fine. He says we have to be positive, but it's driving me mad not being able to talk about what we do if it isn't fine.

I thought I was ambivalent about having a baby, Laur,

until it looked like I might not be able to have this one. Thirty-five seemed young to me when it came to getting pregnant, and now I keep remembering that mad woman at Amelia's wedding – do you know the one? With the fags? She said everything was over at thirty-five, especially your fertility. What if she was right? And it's all my fault for waiting too long.

Tell me funny stories, will you? Send me pictures. Get me off this fucking stupid treadmill of worry and blame.

X

19 October 2010
From: laurakthomas@gmail.com
To: esther.conley@thetimes.co.uk

Well if everything's over at thirty-five then I might as well shoot myself. Honestly, you're going to rely on a drunk stranger at a wedding – years ago – to tell you whether things are going to be okay with your baby? Come on, Est. I wouldn't rely on that woman to find her arse with both hands – she was MENTAL.

David loves you too much to be able to let himself think you or the baby might not be okay. Go easy on him.

I DO have a funny story for you and it is – you won't be able to believe the coincidence – all about wine. Sorry, but there is 0 else going on in the middle of harvest.

SO. Yesterday Stanley left notes on the work order

telling me to add 400 JU to Tank 4. Massively confusing, I had no idea what a JU might be – never came up at college and Stanley had gone out for the morning. In the end I tracked down Trent, and he told me it means Jesus Units, ie WATER. It takes down the alcohol levels. Why didn't they say so??? Jesus (literally).

Yes, Esther, I, your friend Laura, am turning water into wine. Please worship and adore me and possibly set up a religion in my honour. The blood of Laura, the body of Laura etc.

Love you the most, thinking of you all the time,

X

19 October 2010
From: esther.conley@thetimes.co.uk
To: laurakthomas@gmail.com

Esther Conley is out of the office until further notice. If you have an urgent query, please contact Nancy Campbell: nancy.campbell@thetimes.co.uk.

20 October 2010
From: david.carrell@carrellmedia.com
To: laurakthomas@gmail.com

Hi Laura,
I know you'd want to know that Esther is in hospital.

She's going to be fine, she will be home in a few days, but she lost the baby.

Sorry to send you bad news. There is nothing anyone could have done, the doctor says the pregnancy was not viable. They will do tests to find out why.

She was worried she hadn't called you. I know you'll understand.

David

20 October 2010
From: laurakthomas@gmail.com
To: david.carrell@carrellmedia.com

David my flight gets in tomorrow morning, I will come straight to the hospital. Which hospital? Is it Queen Charlotte's? Please tell Est I love her and please tell her it's not her fault, you know she will think it's her fault, it doesn't matter what the doctors say.

I'm so so sorry, it must be so awful for you both. I will stay with Margie, promise not to intrude on your time together, but I can't stay here knowing this is happening. Please don't be cross with me, Esther's all I've got.

Love,

Laura

26

October 2013

Of course it was all about asking the right question. Didn't I say so all along?

Laura is waiting for me this morning in Dolores Park, right in the Mission District of San Francisco. When I looked it up, I worried – even with my rudimentary Spanish I know that Dolores means sorrows. I think I've become so used to looking for signs in everything that now I see them even when they aren't there, because when I get to the entrance it's just a park like any other, with palm trees and a playground and a couple lying on a blanket on the grass even though there is a sharp autumnal breeze blowing up the hill. In the distance I can see the tall buildings of downtown San Francisco, and beyond them the blue-grey hills across the bay.

I think all along Laura wanted to be found just as much as she wanted to disappear. The two don't cancel each other out. She just didn't want to have to tell anyone the thing she was afraid to say out loud. I had to work it out first, as I've always done, and once I did, she answered immediately. There was nothing more to hide.

For a split second, I think it is Margie sat on the park bench at the top of the hill, her long neck drooping like a tulip stem as she looks down into her lap, ignoring the view below her. There is something about the slender stoop of Laura's shoulders that is just like her mother's. She is wearing a loose black jersey dress that billows around her ankles, with a denim jacket over the top, and leopard-print trainers. I wonder if I will ever get over my childish envy that, no matter what is happening in her life, no matter how old we get, Laura will always look cool. Her dark hair is pulled back into a loose knot at the base of her skull, and as I get closer, for the first time ever, I notice a few strands of silver in amongst the black.

'Laura,' I say, and she looks up, surprised although we had arranged to meet here. She has never worn much make-up – other than that brief flirtation with red lipstick in France – but she has never needed it. She needs it now. Her features are undefined, as if I am seeing her through a pane of frosted glass, her eyes dull and her mouth a pale ghost of itself.

She gives me a smile that is a diluted version of her real one, and holds out her arms. I remember hugging her when she was held so tightly by Ricko, the day of her father's funeral. It feels like that again now, as we sit with our arms around each other, that something is holding her back.

'I'm so sorry,' she whispers into my shoulder, and then she pulls away and wipes at her eyes roughly with the sleeve of her jacket. Perhaps this is why she's not wearing any make-up, maybe it's just more practical. She looks out into the horizon, blinking hard.

They say that words aren't necessary between best friends, but I don't think that's true. The longer that Laura takes to say anything, the more my mind races with possibilities. In her absence I have conjured up deaths and disasters, bodies and abductions and unborn babies. The least she owes me is an explanation.

'So are you still – ' I ask, not quite able to finish the question.

She turns her long neck, blinking her wet lashes in my direction.

'Yes.'

'Are you, I mean, do you want to be?'

'I'm trying,' she says, with another watered-down smile. There is a glimpse of the old Laura in the way she tries to lift her chin up like she used to, but she can't quite manage it. Ironically she reminds me of a new-born, struggling to support its head on a fragile neck.

It's been ten days since she left. That is a long time to be undecided on something as big as whether or not to have a baby. She told me about her dad that the not knowing was the worst, and yet she's suspended herself in that terrible limbo for over a week, all by herself. It makes me sad for her, but I can also recognize that alongside my sadness is a current of anger. She has taken all of this time, terrified the people around her, and for what? Nothing seems to have been resolved. If I hadn't worked out her secret, would she still be hiding from us even now?

'How far along are you?' I ask.

She closes her eyes as she answers, as if she can hide from the truth. 'Six weeks,' she whispers, her lips barely moving.

'And how long have you known?'

'Two weeks,' she says. 'Two weeks and a day.'

'But God, Laura,' I say, and the exasperation in my voice is unexpected even to me. 'Why didn't you *tell* anyone? You didn't have to go through this alone. We could have helped you.'

She looks at me sadly. 'You think I could just tell Margie I was pregnant with her grandchild, and then get rid of it? Or send you an email and wonder if you'd ever get round to reading it? Esther, I *wanted* a miscarriage – I wanted it to just be over without me having to do anything about it. How could I say that to you?'

'I would have understood,' I say. And I know I would have tried, but I also know she will remember me, hysterical after the third miscarriage early last year, railing against women who get pregnant accidentally. Women who don't even want their babies, I said, women who don't even care. But of course they all care; how stupid I was to think otherwise.

'I tried to tell you on FaceTime,' Laura says. 'But you had Linus with you, remember? I couldn't get the words out, with him there on your lap, trying to touch the screen, and you laughing. I couldn't say it.'

I remember it now, my head so full of the baby that I couldn't imagine Laura had called for any other reason than to see and admire him. I thought our conversation had been a little halting, but I blamed the connection – the slight delay that means one of you is always interrupting the other, breaking the flow. And when that wasn't happening Linus was pulling at my hair, or trying to grab my mouth as I was talking. I am used to fragmented chats, half-finished stories – I didn't see anything unusual in it. And then Linus hit his head on the side of the table and I had to go.

'But even if you didn't want to tell us *why*, you could have said that you were going away. So we weren't worried about you. Didn't you remember what Margie was like last time? You must have known she'd go completely mental.'

'I thought I'd be back so quickly,' she says quietly. The wind whips her words away and she shivers and pulls her jacket tighter around her. 'I never thought I'd worry everyone like this.'

'So where have you been?'

She shakes her head a little. 'All over,' she says.

Once I might have allowed her to get away with this. Glad to have found her safe, I might have granted her the benefit of the secrecy she has always loved so much. But not any more. The last few days have made me persistent, and they have made me cross.

'Laura,' I say firmly. 'You can't be all obscure like this. I've flown thousands of miles to find you, I thought you might be *dead*. How do you think I can help if you won't even say where you've been all this time?'

She looks away again, narrowing her eyes into the distance. The breeze blows her hair back from her face like she is standing on the prow of a ship, hoping to be the first to see land. The wind is beginning to pick up, and the couple on the rug appear to think better of it and pack their things away, preparing to leave.

'You can't help me,' Laura says.

I wait for her to say something more – that can't be it. But it is. She just sits there, in silence, her profile all tragic and noble as if no-one can possibly understand her pain, as if it elevates her above the plane of we mere mortals. More than anything, I would like to slap her. Really hard.

'Fine,' I say, slamming my handbag down on the bench next to me. 'Well, that's fine, Laura. You just stay all secretive and weird, as usual, and let everyone else drive themselves demented running around trying to work out what's going on. You're so fucking selfish.'

She gives a little gasp of shock, and her eyes are suddenly cold and dark as she turns them on me. 'I never asked you to come,' she says.

'*Thank you* might be a better thing to say,' I snap. I have started to shake, from the cold wind that is biting through my inappropriately summery cotton jacket, and from a fury that has been buried for far too long. '*Thank you* for leaving your baby for the first time ever. *Thank you* for picking my crazy mother up from the airport when they tried to arrest her. Thank you, Esther, for always sorting out my fuck-ups even when it ruins your own bloody life.'

'Margie got arrested?' Laura asks in a quiet voice. She looks horrified. I don't know that she has ever considered that her rash decisions might have consequences for anyone other than herself.

'Nearly,' I say. 'She was trying to get on a plane without a passport. She was desperate, Laura, I don't think you understand.'

She tucks her fingers into the sleeves of her jacket. The clouds above our heads have gone an iron grey and the air has taken on the chill that predicts rain.

'I didn't mean to scare her,' she says, and her eyes fill with tears. 'I didn't think.'

But she never does. Laura's life is about sensation and freedom, without ever seeing that there might be a cost – and she is not always the one to pay it.

'You have to think about other people – she was terrified something awful had happened to you.'

'I do think about other people,' Laura snaps back, suddenly defensive. 'That's not fair. There was just a lot going on, I wasn't thinking properly.'

'Laura, even if you think you're all independent, the things you do affect other people. You don't even seem to recognize that. There was a lot going on in my life too, and I had to drop it all to come and find you.'

She scowls, her face petulant, like a child's.

'I came to London for you – when you were in hospital. I did that for you, that wasn't selfish.'

I take a big deep breath to say what I have to say next. I have thought it for a long time but it has never felt right to say it out loud. It seems to me if I don't say it now then the chance will never come again.

'Laura, you came that time for *you*, not me,' I say. 'I know you did it for the best reasons, but you never asked if we wanted you there. You didn't think that maybe a miscarriage was something private that David and I might have wanted to deal with alone.'

She puts her hand to her mouth, pressing the thin white fingers against her lips as if she might be sick.

'Did you?' she whispers.

I nod. 'It was our baby, Laura, no-one else's. I know you meant to help, but you just made a decision based on how you felt, you didn't ask how we felt.'

'But I'm your best friend,' she says, eventually. 'How could I have stayed away when you needed me?'

'I didn't need you, Laura. I know that's hard for you to hear, and I was pleased to see you, but I didn't *need* you.' I try to say it gently, but I can see she is hurt. She hugs her arms around her waist and rocks very slightly back and forth.

'What are you saying?' she demands harshly. 'We're not friends? Why did you come here at all if we're not friends?'

I reach out to take her arm, but she shrinks away from me.

'Of course we're friends, Laura, but not like we used to be. It's not like we're seventeen any more. I love you, but you're not the front and centre of my life. Other people are there now, I have other priorities.'

'Linus and David,' she says, as if she is reminding herself of them.

'Linus and David and *me*,' I say. 'Laura, I put you first for too long. And you've got used to it – you think it's fine for me to drop everything and run out to America when you're having a bad time. But it's not. I can't do this, and you can't do this to me any more.'

She nods her head vigorously, pressing her lips together so the edges go pale.

'No, it's okay,' she says, wiping her cheeks with her denim sleeve, and then brushing down her skirt. 'I understand. Things can't stay the same as they were forever. Of course. You should get home to your family. I'll be fine.'

'Well, I'm here now,' I say, trying to reach out my hand to her again. 'And my flight isn't until tonight.'

She sniffs and stands up, swaying out of reach. 'Thanks for opening a window in your busy schedule for me,' she says in a tight, stiff voice. 'I appreciate the sacrifice. But I don't need you either, Esther, I never have.'

'Don't be like that,' I say. I stand up next to her, but she looks away. The sun has gone now, covered by cloud, and the park has become dark and unwelcoming.

'You've always followed me around like a little puppy dog, haven't you? Little Fat Fester, so desperate to be liked. And I felt sorry for you. So you don't need to pity me. The pity only goes one way, okay? You should be used to it by now.'

She's never called me Fat Fester before. Not even in our worst arguments. And even though the words lost their power to hurt me long ago, and despite the fact I know she is doing it because I hurt her first, my response comes before I can stop it, as if the teenage Esther is in there, speaking for me. I've had enough.

'Fuck you,' I say. 'Have it your way. Sort your own life out.'

'I will.'

27

Laura starts walking, taking the turning that goes up and out of the park. She has always been a fast walker, her legs are so long, but I thought morning sickness might slow her down. It doesn't. Her hair starts falling out of its knot, streaming behind her like she is swimming underwater. I could chase after her, but it seems to me that I've been doing enough of that, for most of my life. It's not enough that I came all the way to California to find her. Even when I worked it out, found out why she'd disappeared, it was me who had to come to San Francisco to meet Laura. We both had cars, one of us knows this place way better than the other. But no, the sacrifice must always be mine. Not any more.

I don't move at all, though a fat drop of rain lands on my shoulder, and then another. I watch Laura stride all the way out of the park, her black dress flowing behind her like the tail of a fish, until she has gone. The whole time I think she will turn around. Not to come back, but to see if I am following. I want her to see that I'm not, that I'm standing quite still, but she never looks behind.

The rain begins to fall harder, and I realize that I'm the only person left in the park. I pull my inadequate jacket up over my head and run in the direction of the car, but when I get out of the park gate I see a shop with an awning straight ahead, with dogs and their owners sheltering underneath, and I duck under it instead.

The dog walkers make room for me, laughing about the weather. 'Four seasons in one day,' says one, and another, whose poodle's claws have been painted bright green, says, 'The only thing a bitch can rely on, is that it's gonna be unreliable.' We all watch as the shower intensifies, gusting great splashes on the pavement, like someone's throwing giant bucketfuls from the sky.

I can't believe our friendship is going to end like this. Both of us stalking off in a strange city, hiding in a rainstorm amongst strangers. The odd thing is that I don't feel tearful or upset, I feel a numb sort of calm. I said that friendship was like a shark, and if it is, then ours has been swimming repetitive circles in an aquarium tank for too long. We've been moving without making any progress. But now the tank door has opened, showing the way out to the sea, and either we take it together or we say goodbye.

The rain stops as suddenly as it started and the sun comes out again, lighting up a fine golden mist that hangs in the air as the last clouds pass. One dog walker stretches a tentative hand outside the awning and cranes his neck upwards to see if it is really over. The heavy clouds have blown past and, says the Four Seasons dog walker, it'll be too hot again before you know it. Everyone disperses, waving and shouting goodbyes, and I am by myself again.

The streets around here invite a visitor to meander, it doesn't feel as reliant on cars as Napa did, and I decide to take a detour rather than go straight back to the car. What's the rush? I don't have to be at the airport until five, and it looks like I will be spending the rest of the day alone. The Mission District reminds me a bit of Camden, with its slightly seedy air. It has that same combination of expensive cafés and dirty dives; a place full of secrets and illicit activities, preoccupied professionals and lost souls with nowhere to go but the pavement. People don't look too closely at each other in neighbourhoods like this. It seems like a place where someone could disappear if they wanted; it shouldn't surprise me Laura wanted to meet here.

There are upscale teahouses next to coffee shops and Mexican taquerías, and every single person under the age of thirty seems to be pierced and extravagantly tattooed. I make myself spend half an hour seeing the sights with resolute dedication, if not quite enjoyment. I feel like I am playing a part in a film that is possibly being watched by Laura. Even though she can't see me, I want to prove that I am fine by myself. Not crying or despairing, but shopping. I might have been her follower once, but that was long ago. If we are going to move beyond this argument, things will have to be different.

I am looking in the window of a children's clothing shop, wondering if it is appropriate to buy an I Heart SF babygro for your child when you have come on a mercy mission for your pregnant and missing erstwhile best friend, when I feel my phone buzz in my pocket with a text.

'Sorry.'

Then another immediately. 'I was in San Diego.'

While I am digesting this, another text arrives. 'Where are you? Let me come find you.'

Laura wants to walk. She says it's easier this way, and I am trusting that she knows where we're going because I have entirely lost my bearings and am not sure I will ever see the rental car again. All I can tell is that we are going downhill, towards the glittering waters of the bay. And it is true that Laura seems able to talk better like this than when we sat facing each other accusingly on the park bench. Her words almost trip and stumble over themselves in their rush to be heard.

'I didn't mean to be selfish,' Laura says, and she swallows hard before she continues. It is like the story is pushing at her throat to get out, now that she has decided to tell it. 'I know you think I wasn't thinking about other people, but it was the opposite.'

She pauses while we separate to negotiate around an old woman with a shopping trolley full of tin cans, meeting again when we are past.

'I was only going to be gone a few days,' she says. 'I was going to call into work on Monday morning and tell them I was sick, and be back by Wednesday. No-one would have known I'd gone anywhere, they'd have just thought I was in bed.'

'What about Stanley?' I ask. 'Wouldn't he have come to see you if you were sick?'

She shakes her head, no, seeming quite certain.

'Stanley had heard me throw up the day before. I told him I'd picked up a stomach bug. He even went out and bought me a bottle of Pepto-Bismol. I was going to tell him I thought it might be contagious – make him stay away to make sure the whole vineyard didn't get it when we were so crazy with work.'

I look over at her, see her profile struck gold in the sunlight. 'You really thought of everything,' I say.

She hears the judgement that I tried to hide in my voice, and jumps on it, ready to take offence.

'You think I should have told him.'

'He has a right,' I say, and soften it with a question. 'Don't you think?'

But she answers with a question of her own.

'Did he – do you know about Ned?'

I tell her that I do. I haven't been able to stop thinking of it since Stanley told me. I even looked the accident report up online and saw a picture of Ned, with his black hair just like his father said.

'So you understand?' She puts a hand on my arm, pleading for me to agree that she was right to run away.

I shake my head, but I don't really mean no. What I mean is, what a fucking mess. What a total, awful mess for everyone involved.

'Could you really not have talked about it with him? You don't know how he would have reacted.'

'What?' she laughs bitterly, and her strides lengthen as she speeds up. 'Tell the man who lost his only child that I'm pregnant but I'm not sure I want his baby? How could I do that? How? If I was going to get rid of it he couldn't ever know. He *mustn't* ever know, Est. I couldn't do that to him. It would be the cruellest, cruellest thing.'

She looks desperate, her dark eyes are wild with the kind of panic you see in an animal that finds itself in a trap. The kind where it would gnaw its own leg off to get out.

'I thought about it for days and days,' she says, with a tremor in her voice. 'I just couldn't make myself believe that having a baby was the right thing to do. I couldn't be sure that I really wanted it. I wanted to want it. I know that it's meant to be the – I don't know, the ultimate happy ending for every woman. Isn't it? Like Drew Barrymore – you have a baby and then everything is perfect, all of your problems just melt away in the face of this great love.'

I begin to interrupt, to say of course it isn't like that, motherhood isn't a photoshoot in *People* magazine, but she silences me with a look. 'I tried, Est, I really tried, but I couldn't believe this was the happy ending. Finding out I was pregnant just magnified all my problems, made them a thousand times worse. What the fuck kind of mother would I make? Not married, not even in a proper relationship, no home, no healthcare, no savings. How could I bring a baby into that?'

'Laura–' I say, but she puts her hand out, palm towards me like someone stopping traffic, and carries on.

'So I booked an appointment. To – you know.' Laura won't look at me, she casts her eyes down to the pavement, and I think it is so strange that she can be brave enough to walk out of her home and her job, leave the father of her unborn baby, book in for an abortion, and yet she can't say the word out loud.

'I had an appointment for Monday morning and I got a motel room for the Sunday night so I'd be there first thing, but on the Saturday night I couldn't stand it any more. I had to do something – get out of Napa, just get away. So I left way too early; thought I'd drive around San Francisco until it was light. I wasn't sleeping anyway, it seemed better to do something instead of nothing. I was sick of doing nothing except thinking and crying all the time.'

She has begun to walk so fast that I have to almost

skip to keep by her side, but when she sees, she slows down a little and seems to steady herself, talking in a way that is more measured and less hurried.

'So I got to Walnut Creek, where you take the turning into Oakland.' She looks at me, knowing I have driven just that way this morning, and I nod a confirmation that I remember. It's the direct route into San Francisco, the road she should have taken.

'I saw the sign that pointed south and before I really knew what I was doing, I just kept on going. I told myself I'd turn back, that I was just taking a detour to lose an hour or so until it was morning, but I think I knew all along where I was going. The whole time I've been here in California I've said I'd go to San Diego, back to the old house to see where we used to live. There's always been some reason not to go. But by the time it was morning, I was there.'

I've seen it on a map, just the day before yesterday when I was trying to get my bearings in the airport car park. San Diego is hundreds of miles away, almost in Mexico. It is like deciding on a whim to drive from London to Aberdeen.

'Couldn't you have told someone?' I say. 'What if something happened to you?'

Laura stops and looks at me in disbelief. 'What? Something worse than this?' She points down at her stomach. 'Anyway, I'd switched my phone off by then. I didn't switch it back on until two days ago, and then there was this barrage of messages and calls and it just freaked me out so much I didn't know how to reply to any of them.'

She starts walking again, glancing at me apologetically. 'I didn't even know you were coming, Est, or I'd have told you not to. I promise. I would never have let you leave Linus and David if I'd known. None of this was meant to happen.'

'Did you see we'd be worried?' I ask. 'All it would have taken was one text or email.'

She shakes her head, as if the behaviour was a surprise even to herself. 'I can't explain it,' she says, 'it was like I was in a dream world, none of it seemed real.'

We stop at a crossroads to wait for a tram to rumble past us. Crowds of tourists surge around us, pushing as they try to take selfies with the photogenic tram in the background. It amuses me to think they may end up instead with a picture of grim-faced Laura and her anxious friend.

When the light goes green we cross the wide road and turn right, towards the sea, which is now just there in front of us, though it had seemed so far away from Dolores Park.

Most of the tourists turn to the left, where the signs point towards Fisherman's Wharf and Embarcadero, and so we turn right again onto a concrete walkway next to the water. There is a high iron bridge ahead of us, reaching impressively over the bay.

'Is that the Golden Gate Bridge?' I ask, and Laura looks at me just like she did when I didn't know who Barbie's boyfriend was, back when we were seven.

'Of course not. You drove over that bridge this morning from Oakland,' she says, barely leaving the 'duh' out of her voice. 'It's the Bay Bridge?'

'Oh, right,' I say. I suppose it's not the time for sightseeing anyway.

Although the traffic roars next to us, on the walkway there are palm trees interspersed with elegant Victorian lampposts, and ahead of us a giant sculpture of a bow and arrow, the point of the arrow buried in the ground so that just the enormous red flights are showing. We stop to look at it in bafflement for a few minutes, and leave without understanding why it is there.

'Did I ever tell you about when Margie and Dad left me on my own in a motel in San Diego?' asks Laura, when we've moved on.

'No,' I say, though I wonder what this has to do with her disappearance.

'It was when we first moved out there, so I was only five, I think. They were house-hunting and he thought she was looking after me, and she thought he was. So they both went out and left me alone by accident.'

She laughs, but I can't help thinking it sounds like the beginning of some terrible story about child abduction.

'What did you do?' I ask.

'I loved it,' she says, her eyes widening at the memory.

'I tried to use all the vending machines that Margie wouldn't let me play with, but I didn't have any money, and then I followed the motel cat and found she had these tiny black kittens hiding under the reception porch, and then the motel owner discovered me and took me to his wife, who let me watch cartoons and gave me Coke and crisps – and she was the first person who told me that you called them potato chips in America.'

It's odd to hear how she tells it in just the voice she must have related her adventures to her parents when she was five – all one sentence, too excited to stop and take a breath.

'Margie and Edward must have been sick when they realized what happened,' I say, and all at once I hear myself in direct contrast; anxious, responsible. I realize that I have crossed over to the other side; now I see these stories from the parents' point of view instead of just the child's.

Laura rolls her eyes, remembering. 'Margie went on and on about it for months, how it was all Dad's fault and I could have been abducted and taken south of the border, and all kinds of mental stuff. But I remember that I just thought it was amazing to be able to do exactly what you wanted, without a parent around, or anyone in charge. I thought it must be what it was like to be grown-up – you could eat potato chips and watch television, and do exactly what you liked all the time.'

I laugh at the idea. Only a child could imagine that

adulthood is a time of uninhibited pleasure and freedom. Laura smiles back.

'I know,' she says. 'But I think a part of me went back to being that little girl while I was there this time. Even though I had a car and a credit card and had paid for my own motel room, I didn't want anyone to know where I was. I wanted that freedom, and Est, I know it's stupid, but I honestly imagined everyone would be like Margie and Dad – just oblivious and too concerned with their own lives to notice that I'd gone.'

I think of the panicked phone calls, and the tearful accusations, the airport escape attempts and the marital arguments, the abandoned baby and the hysterical transatlantic flight. It is so exactly like Laura to have no idea of the chaos she leaves in her wake.

'Oh God, if only you knew,' I say, and Laura at least looks guilty about it.

'So what did you do, then?' I ask. 'All that time you were there, what were you doing?'

She looks even guiltier. 'I went to the zoo?'

I note how she poses it as a question.

'The *zoo*?'

'Well, not just the zoo,' Laura says, realizing she has pitched it wrongly, and rushing to correct herself. 'I went to our old house on I Avenue first, and to my elementary school and the park where they used to have the bands in the summer. I went to the beach, and the Hotel del Coronado, where my dad used to take me to drink Shirley Temples in the bar.'

She looks over at me, smiling a little, a real smile, sharing her fond reminiscences. But I don't understand what this has to do with her pregnancy. How is visiting her old school going to help?

'But did it help?' I ask. And I can't resist adding, rather pointedly, 'Did the *zoo* help?'

She is embarrassed, but rightly. All of us panicking and worrying, fearing the worst, while she was visiting hotels and beaches and, unbelievably, gorilla enclosures like she was on holiday.

Her eyes fill with tears suddenly. 'No.' She wipes the tears angrily away. 'I don't know what I expected to happen. I thought going back there would be some sort of revelation, but it wasn't. I didn't feel free and amazing, I just felt really really sad and alone.'

We walk underneath the Bay Bridge, and the sound of the traffic above us is enough to stop us trying to talk until we are out the other side.

'God, I'm sick of all this crying,' says Laura. 'How long do these hormones go on for, Est, I can't stand it. I'm crying at everything, it's fucking ridiculous.'

I think about how much more I cry these days. At adverts, at anything where a child might be distressed or ill, at any orphaned baby animal on a wildlife documentary. At leaving Linus behind.

'I don't know if you ever do,' I admit. 'But – probably

you're going to feel a lot better about everything when you make a proper decision about what to do.'

Laura stops walking and her expression is pained, like she really thought we could keep going over stories from her childhood and the situation would just resolve itself while we chatted. I see her trip to San Diego in exactly the same way: it was never a solution, only ever an escape.

'What do you think I should do?' she asks, hesitantly. She is facing into the sun now and it makes her squint as she waits for me to answer.

'Laura, listen to yourself. You want to run away from everything, you want other people to solve your problems for you. It's like you think the answers lie in being a child again, and you're wrong.'

Her squint turns into a frown.

'Don't you see that all your problems are coming from this desire to stay a child? You're nearly forty, for fuck's sake. You can't be a child any more.'

Laura's mouth opens and shuts while she thinks of what to say. And then she answers, angrily, like she suspects me of trying to trick her, 'So you're trying to tell me I should have the baby and be a *parent* instead? Is that what you think?'

'It doesn't matter what I think, Laura,' I say. 'You don't have to be a parent if that's not what you want. No-one can decide that but you. But it is time that you began to behave like an adult.'

She runs her fingers through her hair, almost clawing at her scalp. 'I just keep waiting to *know*,' she says. 'One way or the other, I just want to know what to do.'

'But that's just it,' I say. 'No-one ever knows anything for sure, Laura. That's just a child's fantasy about being grown-up. You might never *know*, but as an adult you have to make a decision and then deal with the consequences, however hard they get.'

Laura looks at me with her big, wide eyes. 'But a baby,' she says, almost breathless with the fear of it. 'That is one massive consequence to deal with. Years of consequences. You can't just change your mind and run out on a baby.'

'No,' I agree with her. 'But maybe you could pack away your running shoes, whatever you decide.'

28

There is more of Margie in Laura than she would like to think, and more than I would ever tell her. I had always believed Laura floated above the rest of us because she was elevated by being cooler, prettier, less conventional than other people. But now I think that she kept herself apart from fear of getting involved with the real, dirty business of being alive. She was trying to be the pristine and beautiful water lily without understanding that all of us, even her, have to have our roots in the deep, sticky mud.

After her father died, she saw catastrophe in every close relationship, ending them before they got serious. She ran from England to France and then she left Europe altogether for the New World.

But the frontier ran out at the Pacific Ocean, and it forced her to turn back. I didn't make her return to Napa, though when she talks about it now, that is how she tells it. She has me marching her to the car, lecturing her the whole time about facing up to her responsibilities. It is probably easier for her that way, to make out that the revelation came from outside, rather than from her own much-denied and dismissed emotional insides.

The way Laura has it, the way I heard her tell it to David once I was home, cackling with laughter on speakerphone, I barrelled into the state of California like a truth-seeking cowboy, bursting through the saloon bar doors and firing my pistols from both hips until she gave herself up.

The truth is more boring, as grown-up decisions usually are. I think we would all like our moments of revelation to be like the movies. We all want to be Drew Barrymore on the pitcher's mound at the end of *Never Been Kissed*, waiting for the moment that will change our life. But the truth is also more beautiful, as any decision that is life-changing and real is beautiful. And I will remember it for Laura, because I know that one day she will be proud of it and proud of herself.

Leaning on the railing that separates the Embarcadero walkway from the sea, her hair blown back by the sea breeze, crying and laughing, Laura called Stanley herself and told him everything, while I waited by the giant bow and arrow that turned out to be called Cupid's Span. I hoped it might be a sign. I didn't hear what Laura said to Stanley, or what he said to her, but after they had spoken she said she was ready to go home. She says she hadn't made a decision at that point – she went back and talked to Stanley some more, and they decided it together. But I think I knew what she would decide the moment I heard her call it 'home'.

Laura's makes a better story, I suppose. She loves the drama of it all – Margie's near arrest, my genuine belief that Stanley might have done away with her, our teen-aged screaming match in the middle of Dolores Park. The only story that could have pleased her more would be if Drew Barrymore herself, guru and spirit animal, had turned up in the Bay Area to dispense her gospel to Laura in person.

But Drew was in Africa making *Blended* with Adam Sandler, and we will, out of respect, end the story of her gospel before that film is released. Our lessons are already learned.

Laura Thomas and Stanley Hoffmann are
proud to announce the safe arrival of their daughter,
Drew Esther Edwina Hoffmann,
born on June 10th 2014.
She would have been a sister for Ned,
whose memory we honor.

Film credits

1. E.T. THE EXTRA-TERRESTRIAL (1982)
Kathleen Kennedy – producer • Melissa Mathison – associate producer • Steven Spielberg – producer • Steven Spielberg – director • **Production Companies** • Universal Pictures • Amblin Entertainment (uncredited)

2. LITTLE GIRL LOST (Drew Barrymore's Autobiography) 1990
Publisher: Pocket Books
ISBN 978-0-671-68923-0

3. POISON IVY (1992)
Katt Shea – director • Melissa Goddard – executive producer • Jana Howington-Marx – associate producer • Marjorie Lewis – co-executive producer • Peter Morgan – executive producer • Rick Nathanson – co-producer • Andy Ruben – producer • **Production Company** • New Line Cinema, MG Entertainment

4. SCREAM (1996)
Wes Craven – director • Stuart M. Besser – co-executive producer • Dixie J. Capp – co-producer • Cathy Konrad – producer • Marianne Maddalena – executive producer • Nicholas Mastandrea – associate producer (as Nicholas C. Mastandrea) • Bob Weinstein – executive producer • Harvey Weinstein – executive producer • Cary Woods – producer • **Production Companies** • Dimension Films (presents) • Woods Entertainment

5. THE WEDDING SINGER (1998)
Frank Coraci – director • Richard Brener – co-executive producer • Jack Giarraputo – producer • Brad Grey – executive producer • Michelle Holdsworth – associate producer • Ira Shuman – co-producer • Robert Simonds – producer • Rita Smith – associate producer • Sandy Wernick – executive producer • Brian Witten – co-executive producer • **Production Companies** • Juno Pix • New Line Cinema • Robert Simonds Productions

6. NEVER BEEN KISSED (1999)
Raja Gosnell – director • Drew Barrymore – executive producer • Jeffrey Downer – co-producer • Sandy Isaac – producer • Nancy Juvonen – producer • **Production Companies** • Fox 2000 Pictures • Bushwood Pictures • Flower Films (II) • Never Been Kissed Productions

7. DONNIE DARKO (2001)

Richard Kelly – director • Christopher Ball – executive producer (as Chris J. Ball) • Drew Barrymore – executive producer • Adam Fields – producer • Thomas Hayslip – line producer (as Tom Hayslip) • Nancy Juvonen – producer • Casey La Scala – executive producer • Hunt Lowry – executive producer • Sean McKittrick – producer • Aaron Ryder – executive producer • William Tyrer – executive producer • **Production Companies** • Pandora Cinema (in association with) (as Pandora) • Flower Films (II) (as A Flower Films Production) • Adam Fields Productions • Gaylord Films

8. 50 FIRST DATES (2004)

Peter Segal – director • Scott Bankston – co-producer • Michael Ewing – executive producer • Jack Giarraputo – producer •
Steve Golin – producer • Kevin Grady – associate producer • Nancy Juvonen – producer • Larry Kennar – co-producer • Daniel Lupi – executive producer • Jay Roach – executive producer • **Production Companies** • Columbia Pictures Corporation (presents) (as Columbia Pictures) • Happy Madison Productions • Anonymous Content • Flower Films (II)

9. MUSIC AND LYRICS (2007)

Marc Lawrence – director • Bruce Berman – executive producer • Scott Elias – co-producer • Hal Gaba – executive producer • Liz Glotzer – producer • Nancy Juvonen – executive producer • Martin Shafer – producer • Melissa Wells – co-producer • **Production Companies** • Castle Rock Entertainment (presents) • Village Roadshow Pictures (in association with) • Reserve Room • Flower Films (II)

10. GOING THE DISTANCE (2010)

Nanette Burstein – director • Richard Brener – executive producer • Michael Disco – executive producer • Jennifer Gibgot – producer • Garrett Grant – producer • Dave Neustadter – executive producer • Adam Shankman – producer • **Production Companies** • New Line Cinema • Offspring Entertainment

Unsuitable Men

PIPPA WRIGHT

Finding it hard to meet Mr Right?

Perhaps you should try looking for Mr Wrong instead . . .

After eleven years of coupled-up domesticity, Rory Carmichael is single for the first time in her adult life. Even she would admit that her ex-boyfriend Martin wasn't the most exciting man in the world – let's face it, his idea of a rocking night was one spent updating his Excel spreadsheets – but Rory could rely on him and, having watched her mother rack up four turbulent marriages, that's what matters. But when she discovers that her supposedly reliable Mr Right is a distinctly unreliable cheater, she's forced to consider the possibility that everything she knows about relationships is wrong.

In an effort to reinvigorate both her love life and her lacklustre career at posh magazine *Country House*, she sets herself a mission to date as many unsuitable men as possible. Toyboys. Sugar daddies. Fauxmosexuals. Maybe the bad boys she's never dated can show her what she's been missing in life. But if Mr Right can turn out to be so wrong, maybe one of her Mr Wrongs will turn out to be just right . . .